Was the spine- the shadows still up there somewhere, or had he far enough away when I crashed? I shook my head. It made little difference since I had no choice but to take my chances on the road.

I began the ascent, trudging back up the incline. Rain pelted my face like tiny needles. Darkness surrounded me. No moon, no stars, only the deep of night. Heart pounding from exertion and emotions still raw, I slogged upward through mud, brush, and Lord knows what else. Finally, a dim light flickered on the road above. Praying it was a house, a phone, an end to this nightmare, I strained my aching legs to push forward.

"Thank you, God," I whispered, glancing over my shoulder at my wrecked car below.

That's when my foot slipped. I slid backward, spiraled off the rocky ledge. Twisting to grab ahold of anything to keep me from plummeting downward, I lurched, my wet hands and battered body ripping against jagged rocks and brush.

Out of nowhere, a dark figure grabbed my arm. Frozen in fear, I screamed as loud as I could, but the shriek came out a hoarse, low whisper. I lunged against him, yanked to pull free, but I had no leverage, nothing to cling to. Fear choked the air from my lungs. A sharp pain slashed my ankle. Consumed with terror, I flung the entire weight of my body against his grasp. In answer to my prayers, he abruptly let go, but the sudden release hurled me backward, plunging...rolling endlessly...until I splashed into an icy, black abyss.

Praise for Casi McLean

"I love, love, love *BENEATH THE LAKE*. It is at the top of the list of my all time favorite books. I was captured by the first paragraph. Your descriptions were wonderful, the plot was so elaborate, and I'm in love with all of your characters. Superb!"

~Hilary Johnson, PC. Attorney at Law

~*~

"*BENEATH THE LAKE* captivated me. As soon as the storyline developed the heroine and other characters in the town destined to drown, I was hooked. Very creative and suspense filled, as I believed the machinations going on in the present time were with some evil or nefarious intent. Good suspense writing!! Keep it up!"

~Sterling Williams, SVP, The Brand Banking Company

~*~

"I thoroughly enjoyed *BENEATH THE LAKE* by Casi McLean. The story grabbed my attention from the very beginning and kept me hooked as it traveled back in time. The nostalgia was well-researched, with many interesting facts about that time period added. The characters, especially Lacey Montgomery, were multi-dimensional, so I kept wanting to know more about them. Everything came together in an exciting climax; it left me curious and waiting for the sequel!"

~Roma Dubac, English teacher

~*~

"Tears omg. *BENEATH THE LAKE* is crazy good. I felt I was there. When I finished, I felt completely drained. Fantastic."

~Rick Hughett, Retired Division Chief,
Dekalb Dept. of Public Safety

Beneath the Lake

by

Casi McLean

Beneath the Lake Series

Beneath the Lake

Cover Art by *Rae Monet, Inc. Design*

The Wild Rose Press, Inc.
PO Box 708
Adams Basin, NY 14410-0708
Visit us at www.thewildrosepress.com

Publishing History
First Mainstream Historical Edition, 2015
Print ISBN 978-1-5092-0283-6
Digital ISBN 978-1-5092-0284-3

Beneath the Lake Series
Published in the United States of America

Dedication

To all who believe destiny evolves
from the breadth of dreams.

Lake Lanier, Georgia—June 2011

A final thud hurled him backward, flailing through brush and thickets like a rag doll. Grasping at anything to break momentum, Rob's hand clung to a branch wedged into the face of the precipice. Spiny splinters sliced his skin. Blood oozed and trickled into his palms, and one by one, his fingers slowly slipped.

A sharp crack echoed through the silence of the ravine as the bough succumbed to his weight. He plummeted into free-fall. Clenching his eyes, he drew in a deep breath, terrified of the pain, the mauling that waited on the jagged rocks below.

When icy water broke his fall, the chill kept him from losing consciousness. He spun, straining to see, but darkness enveloped him. Soggy clothing pulled him deeper—deeper into the murky, fathomless depths. He wrestled to squirm free from the waterlogged jacket dragging him down to a watery grave, watched the coat disappear into black obscurity. Panic gripped his stomach, or was it death that snaked around his chest, squeezing, squeezing, squeezing the air, the life from his body? Lack of oxygen burned his lungs, beckoning surrender, and a shard of rage pierced his gut as reality set in. He lunged upward with one last thrust and burst from the water's deadly grip, gasping for air. A gurgling howl spewed from the depths of his soul and echoed into silence.

Sunlight shimmered across a smooth, indigo lake, but aside from the slight ripples of his own paddling, nothing but stillness surrounded him. He floated toward the shore, sucking deep breaths into his lungs until the pummeling in his chest subsided. When he reached the water's edge, he hoisted his body onto the soft red clay and collapsed while the sun's warmth drained the tension from his body.

No one knew he had survived. The rules had shifted. Now he could reinvent himself, become a stealth predator. His target: Lacey Madison Montgomery.

Chapter 1

June 2012, one year later at an extravagant clubhouse in Lake Lanier, Georgia

June 9th began like any ordinary day, but for me, nothing would ever be ordinary again. In hindsight, I could see that the rainy night wasn't the catalyst for my twist of fate. The storm was more like a vortex with currents reaching out beyond imagination. Within twenty-four hours I would lose my ability to distinguish dreams from reality. But I digress. The chain of events really started before the storm. As I left Buckhead Plaza on Thursday evening, my cell phone rang.

"You'll come, Lace, won't you? Please. You have to see my new lake house." My best friend, Piper refused to take no for an answer. Of course, she forgot to mention the extravagant charity party she had planned. So, here I was, Lacey Montgomery, introverted attorney, caught in the midst of a crowd of wealthy people I abhorred.

"So this must be Lacey."

The voice wrapped around me like a warm blanket, familiar—and yet not. Perhaps I'd heard it long ago or conjured him in a forgotten dream. I'm not sure what I expected when I turned around, but one glimpse of the incredibly hot man standing behind me, and my legs went weak while a warm tingle slithered into my most sensual spot.

Piper cocked her head and beamed a familiar I-told-you-so smile. "Lace, this is Rob, the neighbor I bragged about last night."

Leaning down to kiss her cheek, his gaze anchored to mine. "I'm glad you could make it to our little soirée, Miss Montgomery."

"Rob is an architectural genius." Piper gushed. "I never could've pulled off the design of my deck without him."

An eerie sense of *déjà vu* washed over me. Strange. I'd never seen him before, but something about this man made my heart race.

"You flatter me, Piper. I'm sure you would've devised a plan of your own."

As Rob's gaze deepened, his conversation with Piper waned to a muted echo. Was I the only one who noticed him staring directly at me? The party faded into the background, and for several heartbeats, time stood still. No one else existed except the man standing in front of me. A surreal heat surged between us. An energy so intense, I wasn't sure if I felt passion, or panic.

Before last night I'd never heard of Rob. He was a perfect stranger. And now...perfect...strange.... *Snap out of it, Lace.* The man was married and, according to Piper, blissfully happy. *And what about Cole?* A wave of guilt flashed through me. I wasn't a free agent despite my boyfriend's abrupt departure, bailing on our weekend getaway, again, for yet another "client emergency." Still, for some odd reason Rob stirred something inside of me that—

"He does have a knack for getting things done."

Piper's friend, Travis, chuckled.

Geezzz. Did I say that out loud? Rob enchanted me, drew me into a mesmeric daze. But, surely I hadn't uttered my curious attraction, or dissed Cole aloud. Had I?

Travis patted Rob on the back. "This guy is the most inspired man I've ever known." He arched an eyebrow. "And speaking about inspiration." Eyeing a voluptuous young woman strutting by, he trolled after her.

Thank you, God. I hadn't said a word. No one had an inkling of the visceral responses Rob's gaze evoked in me, or my momentarily zone-out into La-la-land. I'd never felt a rush like that before.

Piper pursed her lips. "See Rob, even Travis thinks you're amazing." Tucking a strand of golden hair behind her ear, she glanced around to check out the crowd.

Rob didn't respond to her comment. His eyes, twinkling like pools of cobalt fire, burned into mine melting my inhibitions.

Finally managing to speak, I extended my hand, anticipating an intense reaction to his touch. "It's so nice to…meet you."

He reached out in slow motion. I'd have stood there for hours staring into those gorgeous blue eyes totally spellbound if Piper hadn't ripped me away.

"Oh Lace, there's Riley." She tugged on my arm. "Come on, you have to meet her."

Piper dragged me in tow just as Rob's fingers touched mine, and I could swear a flux of electricity rushed between us.

"Riley is a defense lawyer, too, but she

represents…" My friend kept talking as she led me toward the ballroom, but I didn't hear a word she said. Still captivated by Rob, I glanced back over my shoulder at him and shrugged, offering an apologetic smile.

"I guess I'll see you later?" I intended my comment to be a statement, not a question. But I couldn't help myself and wondered why this man was having such a profound effect on me.

"I'll catch up to you," Rob said with an odd grin. "You can count on that." Then, he turned toward Travis and the lady he'd managed to charm.

Despite my disdain for swanky parties, not to mention being tricked into attending this one, I actually was enjoying myself. Something about Piper's friends made me feel relaxed, like I'd known them for years. I felt comfortable around them. Well, not all of them. No matter whom I spoke to the entire evening, I found myself constantly searching for Rob. Part of me felt guilty about the physical reaction I had felt when we met. The attraction could never evolve into anything. Still, I couldn't wait to get Piper alone to ask her more about her intriguing neighbor—and his wife. Unfortunately, I never had the chance.

Between the music and voices, no one noticed the storm approaching until a strong gust of wind blew the main entry door open. I slipped outside to check my car windows then scooted upstairs to the parlor for my purse so I could comb my disheveled hair and dry the mist off my arms.

When I opened the door, I inadvertently walked in on a man and woman stretched across the chaise lounge in a lustful embrace, passionately fondling each other.

Her dress was hiked up around her waist, while his hands roved across her thighs. His face burrowed between her bulging breasts.

"Oh my gosh, I'm so sorry." Turning to leave, I glanced at the reflection in the mirror and froze.

"Cole?" I spun around, trying to make sense of what I saw. A gut-wrenching wound wrought with adrenalin throbbed in the pit of my stomach. Taking a deep breath, I forced the familiar ache into a closet in the back of my mind then slammed the door shut. The ice queen took over.

Cole looked up and his eyes met mine.

"Lacey? What the hell are you doing here?" He twisted around, pushing the woman aside, his confused glare fixed on me.

"I was invited." Controlled anger seethed inside of me. "But I thought you were in New York with your *big client*."

My cold reply must have caught him off guard. "Right, well he… Wait a minute." Cole sat up straight, brushed his rumpled hair off his face. "How did you know where I—Were you following me?"

"Following you?" I sneered. "Don't flatter yourself." I clenched my fists so hard my nails cut into my palms. If I'd been fueled with testosterone, I'm sure my knuckles would have shot directly into his jaw. Forcing my fingers to relax, I rested my hands on my hips and waited for his lame response.

"No, you'd never think to, I mean…. Never mind. Just let me explain." He stood, tucked in the back of his shirt.

The woman pulled down her dress. Straightening her hair, she spoke in a voice laced with annoyance, "I

7

can't wait to hear this explanation."

Did Cole actually say *I'd never think to?* Was I that easy to manipulate? "Don't bother, Cole." I walked around the chaise to gather my belongings, having every intention of storming out the door without uttering another word. Instead, on impulse, I picked up a large crystal globe filled with fresh-cut narcissus from the table beside the sofa, calmly turned, and tossed the entire contents over both of them.

"Fitting flowers for a narcissistic jerk, wouldn't you say?" I grabbed my shawl and purse, turned on my heel, and marched out of the room.

Maybe it had something to do with my discussion with Piper the night before, but seeing Cole's reflection stunned and drenched in daffodils, I felt a sense of satisfaction that tempered my anger. He tore after me, his messy hair and half-buttoned tux shirt dripping and a sprinkling of white and yellow petals lingering on his neck.

"Lacey, wait. You don't understand."

I paused at the top of the staircase and coolly replied. "I understand perfectly. Too bad a flower vase full of water was the only thing handy." Raising my voice a notch, I yelled toward the parlor, "He's all yours." My gaze bored into his. "Go back to your *client*, Cole."

The emotion behind my icy comments must have resounded a lot louder than I'd intended as the crowd below hushed. I turned in a huff, glancing over the banister, and realized I wasn't alone. All eyes gazed up as if some starlet had spilled fine Bordeaux on her snow-white Valentino dress. Dropped jaws and blank stares fell over the entire room and followed me step-by-step down the lavish, never-ending staircase. To make things worse, soft background music amplified through the silence *"...when you find your true love...fly to her side...or you'll dream all alone..."* Perfect: a romantic ballad confirming my loveless life.

I had to say something to break the tension. "Lawyers," I announced, wishing I could just fade into the woodwork and disappear altogether.

Halfway down the steps, I felt a rush of emotion explode inside. My head swirled. *Dear Lord, please don't let me collapse right here in front of everyone.* I held the handrail tightly to keep from losing my balance. That's when a single pair of hands in the middle of the crowd began to clap, slowly at first, inviting others to join. When Rob's cobalt eyes met mine a flood of tranquility flowed through me like warm honey, calming me as if he had willed my composure.

One by one the guests followed suit, clapping until the entire room boomed with a boisterous ovation. I marched down the rest of the stairs with head held high, strutted through the ornate foyer, then sailed out the front entrance to my Lexus. Surely Piper would understand why I had to leave. I'd call her when I got back to the house, but after the whole ordeal with Cole, there was no way I could go back into that party.

I pulled off my heels and darted through the pouring rain. The deluge pelted my arms, and the wind whipped my gown around me. Totally drenched by the time I reached my car, I fumbled with my keys, pressing the remote over and over before the lock finally released. Once inside, I turned the ignition then sped away leaving a trail of rubber despite the rain. Still furious with myself as well as Cole, I tightened my grip on the steering wheel to keep my hands from trembling.

The rain peppered my convertible top like the thrum of a rolling train, beating in unison with the swish-swish of the wipers. The headlights reflected off sheets of rain instead of lighting the way ahead, and the curvy road that had been tricky in broad daylight now twisted hypnotically, daring, luring me forward. The downpour distorted my view. I could barely see the secluded mountain road, and nothing looked familiar.

Tears trickled down my cheeks as the emotion behind my confrontation with Cole sank in. When I brushed the moisture away with the back of my hand, my eyes blurred for an instant. The car hydroplaned, slid sideways, and skidded across the flooded highway as if it were sheer ice, smooth and deadly. Water spewed upward spraying everywhere. I battled the steering wheel, turned into the slide, and managed to regain control. Trembling, I slowed to a crawl and stopped on the narrow shoulder of the road.

"Relax, Lacey," I whispered. "Just breathe." I filled my lungs, held the breath for a few moments, then blew tension out with the air. How could Cole bail on our weekend and blatantly lie to me to hook up with that pretentious, plastic skank?

That's when it hit me. If Cole broke our date to go to Piper's party, he must've known about the event before I did. But that made no sense. Piper's only knowledge of Cole was what she'd heard from me, and from all indications she had little interest in meeting him.

Thunder boomed and I jerked in response, pressing harder on my brakes. The wind whirled around my

Lexus, pushing it against the night while rain interspersed with tiny nuggets of hail bounced off the hood. Fiddling with my phone GPS proved useless: no bars confirmed the nonexistent service. My instincts told me I had to be close to Piper's lake house, but I could barely see the road through the downpour. The defrost fan turned up full blast did little to clear the condensation fogging the windshield. I grabbed my shawl to wipe the moisture-ridden glass.

A flash of lightning burst through the darkness. Glancing in the rearview mirror, I caught a glimpse of a shadow skulking in the distance behind my car. The image quickly faded as inky darkness swallowed the light. A chill ran down my neck to the middle of my back.

"It's just the storm, Lace," I said to reassure myself. "Get a grip." Another burst of lightning streaked through the night followed by a roll of thunder. Lurching around, I saw a ghostly figure hovering a few yards behind me. It darted forward. With my foot pressed to the floor, I threw the car into gear and peeled off down the road spitting gravel behind me. A single thought flooded my mind—escape.

Chapter 2

Lake Lanier, Georgia—June 2011

Climbing the rocky steps carved into the steep ridge, Rob glanced back at the lake now far below him. It was a miracle he had survived. The view from the summit stretched for miles. He took in the panorama for a moment before refocusing on his mission. The chain of events had altered his plans, but not his resolve. Caution took the foreground.

Running his fingers along the aged fence that lined the property, he crept toward the cabin, his eyes fixed on the entrance. He slunk through bushes, edging closer, examining every detail. The solid wooden door, scarred by the years, had been recently stained and smelled of turpentine. Reaching for the knob, he hesitated before slowly twisting the handle. Heart pounding, he slid inside. There was no turning back. Obsession drove him forward. His future teetered on the brink with only one viable outcome. And Lacey was at the pinnacle.

****

The night of the party

My gaze flicked to the rearview mirror, and I felt a rush of relief as the figure faded into the driving rain. I slowed to a safe speed, drew in a deep breath. Who would prowl along a remote highway through a downpour in the middle of the night? Shivering at the possibilities, I glanced into the mirror again just in time to see two dim lights blink on in the distance, like eyes of a panther stalking its prey. They glowed through the darkness, drew closer, closer, mimicking each swerve of my car.

Desperate to put distance between us, I picked up speed. Maneuvering the treacherous road by easing into curves, I pressed the accelerator on straightaways, praying my tires would cling to the wet asphalt. My clammy hands slid on the steering wheel. I squeezed my fingers, gripping with a tension that crawled up my arms and clenched the base of my neck. What was I thinking leaving the party in the throes of a torrential storm? Now, lost in the middle of nowhere on a pitch-black night, some freak had decided to zero in on me, stalk me like a victim in a low-budget horror movie. Really?

Finally, I could see a long stretch of road ahead. I pressed my foot into the floorboard and watched the panther eyes vanish into a hazy mist. "Thank you, God," I whispered. After driving another mile or so, I noticed a small gravel road, a good place to pull off, wait for the storm to pass. With any luck, I'd evade the radar of the creep tailing me. I pulled in far enough from the main road to hide my car, turned off the headlights, locked the doors, and reached for my cell phone to call Piper. Still no service.

My arms and legs prickled like thousands of ants crawling over my rain-drenched skin. Folding my arms across the steering wheel, I rested my forehead on them and closed my eyes. The dank air, so humid I could scarcely breathe, deepened the pounding in my chest.

My mind reeled through the past twenty-four hours, stalling on the one thought that intensified my anxiety: the spine-chilling lake lore Piper had divulged last night about the haunting of Lake Lanier. Images of zombies roaming the shoreline flashed across my mind's eye, adding to my angst as I recounted our conversation.

"Lanier?" I had leaned against the deck railing next to her. "What's so fascinating about the lake?"

"It's man-made, you know."

"Yeah, I heard something about that."

"Well, I bet you didn't know it was haunted." She gazed across the water, as if mesmerized by the full moon's glimmering reflection.

"Right, and the Easter Bunny lives in your woods, too."

After a long pause, she spoke in an eerie whisper. "No Lace, I'm dead serious. The locals swear the lake is haunted. There used to be a town out there." She pointed her chin toward the water. "There still is actually. The skeleton of a ghost town still lingers, decaying at the bottom of the lake. A town completely submerged in 1956 by the Army Corps of Engineers after they appropriated the land to develop Buford Dam. There are houses, churches, schools, even a racetrack under that water."

I'd been to Lake Lanier on numerous occasions, but no one had ever mentioned a town that slept beneath the surface.

"The lake is filled with secrets, too," Piper said with a ghostly tone. "And it never gives up its dead."

"Honestly, Piper?" I shivered, envisioning dead bodies entombed below the cove. "That's totally creepy."

"I know, but it's true. There's even a *Lady of the Lake*. A woman named Susie Roberts. Her car slid off a ridge in 1958, got tangled in the deadfall of sheered-off trees and town remains." She took a sip of wine then continued, "Her car and body were lost, trapped underwater for thirty-two years until 1990, when construction crews expanded the Lanier Bridge, and now—"

A piercing crack of thunder jolted me back to the present. Part of me was sure I'd see a blood-splattered hockey mask or the waterlogged face of Lanier's phantom ghost pressed against my window. My head shot up, hands clutching the steering wheel. My vivid imagination soared, compliments of too many horror flicks and deepened by Piper's creepy anecdotes. But the guy tailing me wasn't an apparition roused from the depths of the lake, not that I believed in supernatural spirits anyway. He was real, definitely following me, and I had no interest in finding out why.

The rain slowed to a drizzling mist, and I knew I should find my way back to Piper's house. But despite the eerie night, this hidden hollow calmed me. Obviously, the cove hid me from my mysterious stalker and separated me from Cole, but it was more than that. I felt a sense of utter serenity nestled here along this ridge beneath the sycamores and pines, secure, like an infant cocooned in swaddling clothes. But Piper's concern had to be escalating. If she wasn't home from the party when I got there, at least I could call her on the landline.

Reluctantly leaving my safe haven, I maneuvered the car onto the highway again. The downpour had probably obscured the entrance to Piper's property, so I headed back toward the party. Winding and dipping through desolate darkness, I stared at the mountainous road before me, noting each clearing, watchful of any unexpected movement in the Cimmerian shade. My anxiety deepened with the reemerging strength of the storm. *Just focus on finding Piper's house, Lace.*

As hard as I tried to concentrate, unwelcome thoughts of my compromises with Cole kept popping up to distract me. Why was true love so hard for me to find? My character judgment proved spot on determining a client's guilt or innocence. But apparently, my expert analytical skills blindly collapsed when it came to telling the difference between a sincere man and a total jerk.

"I wish," I mumbled. "I wish somehow, some way, I could fall in love with a man who truly loved me."

A blazing bolt of lightning streaked across the velvet sky casting a burst of eerie light. Thunder boomed its crescendo to the violent symphony of the pouring rain and buffeting wind. Startled by the sheer intensity of the storm, I glanced into the rearview mirror again, envisioning the ghostly figure hovering behind me. That moment's distraction was all it took for me to veer off the road.

Damn. I jerked the wheel hard to the right. The tires hit a flooded dip. Water surged over the hood, dousing the windshield. Time slowed. My car spun, slid off the road, ripped over rough terrain, crashed through underbrush, and rolled down a muddy hill. I squeezed my eyes shut in response to the brush flying in front of me and slammed into an embankment.

The airbag exploded, hurling the cover into my face with a force that pinned me against the seat. I choked on a spray of white dust that burned my skin, my throat. The caustic powder seeped into my clenched eyes. When I wiped at them, the sting only deepened. Moving on pure adrenalin, I wrestled to push the bag out of the way and peered into the empty back seat as if expecting to see my strange stalker sitting there.

My entire body ached; my head throbbed. Tugging against the airbag, I tried to free myself from the seatbelt and fumbled for my cell phone. *Note to self, find a carrier with a better service range.* I stuffed the phone back into my purse. The driver's side door was jammed. Wedging my left leg upward, I hoisted myself over the console into the passenger seat, kicked the door open, grabbed my purse, and crawled out.

Slogging through underbrush, I scaled the embankment to get my bearings, but the night sky laden with rain made it impossible to navigate. The brush behind me crunched. I whirled around, slid on damp rocks, spinning stones down the bank. They toppled over the ledge and, after a few moments, splashed into water. A chill fisted in the pit of my stomach as I realized the knoll my car had hit was simply a peak in the ridge, the other side of which dropped off into the lake far below. Thank God my car hadn't skidded over the cliff. As I eased back down the hill, a wave of vertigo swept over me, and I collapsed against my Lexus. *Breathe Lacey.* Closing my eyes, I mentally weighed my options.

My car was wedged into the embankment and would have to be towed. I definitely needed help, but no one could even see me down here. Hiking through the woods along the ridge would be perilous. The utter darkness and unrelenting rain was dangerous, but combined with dense brushwood and the lake below? No, I had to take the road. Was the spine-chilling figure that had lurked in the shadows still up there somewhere, or had he been far enough away when I crashed? I shook my head. It made little difference since I had no choice but to take my chances on the road.

I began the ascent, trudging back up the incline. Rain pelted my face like tiny needles. Darkness surrounded me. No moon, no stars, only the deep of night. Heart pounding from exertion and emotions still raw, I slogged upward through mud, brush, and Lord knows what else. Finally, a dim light flickered on the road above. Praying it was a house, a phone, an end to this nightmare, I strained my aching legs to push forward.

"Thank you, God," I whispered, glancing over my shoulder at my wrecked car below.

That's when my foot slipped. I slid backward, spiraled off the rocky ledge. Twisting to grab ahold of anything to keep me from plummeting downward, I lurched, my wet hands and battered body ripping against jagged rocks and brush.

Out of nowhere, a dark figure grabbed my arm. Frozen in fear, I screamed as loud as I could, but the shriek came out a hoarse, low whisper. I lunged against him, yanked to pull free, but I had no leverage, nothing to cling to. Fear choked the air from my lungs. A sharp pain slashed my ankle. Consumed with terror, I flung the entire weight of my body against his grasp. In answer to my prayers, he abruptly let go, but the sudden release hurled me backward, plunging…rolling endlessly…until I splashed into an icy, black abyss.

Chapter 3

Lake Lanier, Georgia—July 2011

Weeks passed, but Rob's fixation only strengthened. It hadn't been difficult to track Lacey to Atlanta, but he had to find a way to—Hearing the latch turn, he shuffled papers to cover the diagrams and notes he had scattered across the table. The front door flew open.

"Okay, you've been hovering over maps for weeks," Drew scolded. "What we need is a plan."

"I have one." Rob shoved the papers aside to reveal the map he'd been studying. "I just need to work out a few details. Lacey will never see us coming."

Gazing down, Drew noticed the bags under the younger man's eyes. "Maybe you should take a break. Why don't you get some rest, eat something."

"I'm fine." Rob scowled, unwilling to divert his attention to something as trivial as food. "I had coffee earlier."

"Then at least let me help."

"All right, old man, maybe there is something you could do." He pulled one of the maps from beneath the paper pile, drew a big red circle. Moments later, both men hovered over the diagrams engrossed in their scheme. Whatever plan they came up with had to work. Everything depended on it.

****

The morning after the party

A muffled voice brought me back to consciousness. My entire body racked with pain. I tried to respond to the voice—what was he saying?

"Ma'am. Can you hear me?"

I managed to open my eyes a slit but saw only his silhouette.

"Are you okay?"

Was I? The sun radiated around his darkened image. I struggled to focus. He looked like an angel— An angel dressed in jeans and a tight, white T-shirt. Was I dreaming, or had I died and gone to heaven?

"Don't worry," he said. "I'll get you to a doctor." He bent over, pulled a strand of hair from my eyes. "How did you end up out here with that dress around your waist?"

Dress around my waist? Still confused, I gazed down, my hands floundering to cover myself.

"It's okay. Here." He pulled off his shirt, slipped it over my limp body, then easily scooped me up. "Can you tell me your name?"

"Lac…Maadi…" I tried to answer, to ask him who he was, where he was taking me, but when I opened my mouth nothing but a low, wistful sigh came out.

"Maddie. That will do for now."

"Wh…"

"Hush now, Maddie," he soothed. "You'll be all right."

He carried me tenderly, and I melted against his warm, muscular chest, snuggled into his scent as it lured me even closer. In and out of consciousness, I tried to piece together what had happened, how I came to be in this man's arms, but I wasn't scared. He was strong, yet gentle at the same time. I felt safe. I strained again to open my eyes, but finally surrendered and drifted off, holding tightly to my sweet angelic dream.

****

I awakened to the sun caressing my face and angled my head back to bask in its warmth. Stretching my arms high above my head, I shifted my achy body before opening my eyes. The sun peeked between branches of towering hardwoods, gleaming as the rays reflected off the morning dew. Sinking into a soft cushion of grass beneath my blanket, I watched a cloud-kitten drift across the azure sky then hide behind lush leaves of a giant oak. A chorus of cicadas whirred and—*Wait a minute.* I sat up abruptly, looked around. *Where am I?*

"Ahhh, Sleeping Beauty awakens."

Turning, I saw an amazingly attractive man grinning down at me. His arms and legs crossed as he leaned against an old jalopy. Glints of light danced across his tousled, sun-bleached hair, and the corners of his lips curled into a sensuous smile.

"I'm glad you woke up." His deep sapphire eyes sparkled when he spoke. "You had me worried for a while there. I was afraid you'd die on me before I got this heap running again. I'll have her fixed in a jiffy."

"Where are we?" I asked, trying to remember. "And how did you get me here?"

"Hold on, Maddie. I'm just trying to help you." Picking up a wrench from the fender, he leaned into the open hood of his car and started banging on something. "Just give me a few more minutes. When I get ole' Bessie running, I'll get you to the doctor. We can pick up some clothes for you along the way. "

"Clothes?" I looked down, horrified, and pulled my knees up under the T-shirt I was wearing. Just my luck, a hot guy swoops into my life, and I'm sitting here half naked. What had happened?

"I take it you don't remember my gallant rescue." He spoke without looking up, continuing his task. "I had planned to take you straight to Doc Meyerson, but Bessie decided to be stubborn. Just like a woman." He chuckled. "Now that you're awake though, we could stop by my house first and grab some clothes from Sandy."

"Sandy?"

"My sister." He pounded on the engine again. "I'm sure she has something you can wear. Your dress is in pretty rough shape."

"Dress?" My head was a little fuzzy, but I was sure of one thing, I wasn't going to let some strange guy whisk me off to his place and take advantage of my condition. For all I knew, he didn't even have a sister. Men weren't to be trusted—*Whoa, where did that come from?*

"You don't say much, do you Maddie? Only a word or two at a time. Are you okay?"

"Sorry. I'm a little confused." Who was this guy? He looked vaguely familiar. I racked my brain to remember. I was at a ball…a ball? Who even says that nowadays? If I'd muttered that aloud, the guy would've thought I was a freak. There was a party, though. Maybe I saw him there.

"Did we meet at the party last night?" Even if we had, how did we end up out here? By all evidence, I was wearing nothing but *his* shirt. Looking down, I scowled. Where in the world were my clothes? "I hope you didn't slip one of those date-rape pills into my drink."

Snapping around, he frowned at me, wiped his greasy hands on a towel. "Is that any way to talk to the man who's trying to save your life? I don't know anything about a party. And I'd never slip a Mickey Finn into anyone's drink, if that's what you're inferring." Grabbing the wrench again, he turned back to the engine. "I do just fine with the ladies on my own."

"Save my life?" What was he talking about? It was hard to believe he didn't know about the party, but then maybe he didn't live close by. I glanced at his convertible. The fender read: Hudson. The car looked new, foreign perhaps, but more likely a restored antique. He wasn't one of the *beautiful people* with a car like that. But he was beautiful. His broad back muscles rippled as he exerted himself, while tiny beads of sweat glistened over his suntanned skin.

A wave of pain throbbed through my head as I sifted through hazy memories. I had no idea how I came to be here, sitting half naked in the middle of Lord knows where with this strange man. Should I be scared? Probably, but for some reason I wasn't. According to him, he was trying to help me, and he seemed harmless enough. Definitely attractive and charming—But so was Ted Bundy. I knew nothing about this guy. Not even his name.

"Pardon me, but what did you say your name was?"

"I didn't say," he answered, granting me a smile as he looked at me underneath his arm. "You never asked.

He turned to me. "I figured you would eventually, considering I carried you here, gave you the shirt off my back so you wouldn't have to walk around indecent."

"Well, I'm hardly myself at the moment." What in the world had happened? There were huge gaps in my memory. "Please excuse my poor manners and thank you for coming to my rescue, mister…"

"Reynolds," he replied, turning back to the engine. "Bobby Reynolds."

"It's nice to meet you, Bobby." The name didn't sound familiar, but at the moment, nothing did. I tucked my stringy hair behind my ears, brushed a clump of caked mud from my left leg. No clothes, no shoes, and no idea how any of this made sense.

"So, Maddie, what's your full name?"

"Lacey Madison Montgomery. But, why are you calling me Maddie?" My father was the only one who ever called me Maddie and only when Mother was alive.

He glanced back at me, lifted his head, and shot me an I-have-my-ways smile. "It's a pleasure to make your acquaintance, Miss Montgomery." Turning back to his work, he kept talking. "When I found you this morning, you told me your name was 'Maddie,' I take it that's short for Madison."

"I'm sure you're mistaken. I wouldn't have said that." I never told anyone about that name. Not even Piper…Piper. Oh my gosh. She was probably sick with worry.

"Well, it was just a whisper. You were in and out of consciousness, but I could've sworn that's what you said."

"My dad called me 'Maddie' when I was little. I suppose I might have mumbled that in my confused state." Running my fingers through my hair, I cringed when they passed over a huge lump on my forehead. Where had that come from? No wonder my head throbbed.

"So, what were you doing out in the woods all alone on such a stormy night?"

That was the six million dollar question. Events of the evening began to coalesce. Piper's party… Cole…the rain. "The storm broke just before I left the party. It poured so hard…my car hydroplaned." I sifted through more disjointed memories. "I crashed…and I had to kick the door to get out."

"Well," he said without looking up from his work, "if your car slid off the road, it can't be too far away. We'll find it, but first things first. When I get Bessie started, we really need to get you to a doctor. You were unconscious for quite a while."

As Bobby spoke, I couldn't keep my eyes off his biceps. They bulged with each effort, stirring embers of desire into burning flames.

"If I could get this hose clamp tight enough…there." Standing, he gazed down at me. "I think she's almost fixed. How's your forehead? I stopped the bleeding, but we need to get some ice on that bump."

"Thanks, but it doesn't hurt much." That wasn't true. Aside from my throbbing head, every muscle in my body ached, and I had a three-inch gash in my right ankle. But I didn't want him to think I was some sniveling baby who needed a man to take care of her. Okay, that was a little harsh. Maybe I did need a doctor.

If I'd been unconscious, I probably had a concussion. The thought of being practically naked and oblivious around a perfect stranger made my skin crawl.

"My memory is still a bit fuzzy. Where is my dress? And how did I end up wearing your T-shirt? I hope you didn't—"

"Miss Montgomery." He looked at me with a crumpled brow. "I'm a gentleman. When I found you this morning, you were out cold, bedraggled, and your dress was...how shall I say this? Your dress was soaking wet and draped around your waist. For modesty's sake," he arched one eyebrow, "yours and mine, I took the shirt off my back and slipped it on you." Turning back to the engine, he tightened something then peered over his shoulder at me. "Your dress and pocketbook are in the car."

Great, now I'd insulted him. He seemed like a nice enough guy. And, all things considered, I really had no choice but to trust him, at least for the moment. Leaning my elbows on my knees, I rested my chin on my fists, enjoying the view. If I had to be stuck with someone, I could have done a lot worse than Bobby Reynolds. That first glimpse of him standing there, staring down at me with those rippling abs, he totally took my breath away. Even Piper would approve...Piper. Oh gosh, I had to call her.

"Bobby, could I please use your cell?"

He looked at me with a scowl. "What interest do you have in the county jail?"

"Funny." I rolled my eyes, and a sharp pain pounded through my head. "I'm serious. I need to make a phone call."

"Well, Miss Montgomery, I can't help you there.

I'm afraid you won't find a phone working anywhere for a good while." He picked up a screwdriver, leaned over the fender again. "The storm last night knocked out all service from here to Atlanta."

Palms flat on the ground behind me, I propped myself up, crossed my outstretched legs. "Perfect." The cell towers must have been damaged. "And it's Lacey. You don't have to be so formal."

"What's perfect?"

"I was being sarcastic. You know, like *oh, perfect*?" I rolled my eyes again, shook my head, which stirred my throbbing headache even more. "Never mind. At least I can get some clothes from my trunk when we find my car."

"You're one strange woman, Miss Montgomery."

First Maddie, now Miss Montgomery. Why was it so difficult for him to call me Lacey? *Whatever.* He did save my life, or at least that's what he said. I flashed on my swerving car rolling down a hill into the mud. That's right. I crawled out...and saw a light. *Oh dear Lord.* The last thing I remembered was going toward the light. Could I be dead? I shot upright, reached over, and pinched my own arm then realized Bobby Reynolds was standing beside me watching my every move.

"Yup, one strange woman." He gazed down at me with a look of consternation. "Bessie is working now, and Doc Meyerson isn't too far from here." Offering his hand to help me up, he continued, "We should stop by, let him take a look at your head."

"Actually, I'm feeling a lot better. Could we please go look for my car first?" I needed to find my Lexus. I'd have to get a tow, but I had a workout bag in the trunk. Yoga pants, a jog bra, and a tank top that actually fit would feel a lot better than wearing nothing but Bobby's T-shirt.

"Are you sure you're okay?"

I smiled and gave him a small nod in deference to my aching head.

"I suppose we could take a quick spin around the area to look for your car. But it's against my better judgment."

"I'm really fine, and I need to find my car."

He offered his hand again to pull me up. This time I grabbed it, popping to my feet, but the quick shift made my head swim. When I wobbled, Bobby caught me.

"Whoa, take it easy, Miss Montgomery." He swept me into his arms and carried me toward his car. "That's exactly why you need to see a doctor. I'm not sure what happened to you, but you're bruised from head to foot with some nasty cuts, especially on that ankle."

"Please put me down. I'm perfectly capable of walking." My plea was totally ignored. "I just got up too fast and lost my balance." I squirmed to free myself. Instead of complying, Bobby gently slung me over his shoulder and continued walking. "Put me down." I demanded, smacking his back. "Do you hear me? Put me down this instant." He didn't.

My head throbbed with every heartbeat. "If you don't put me down this second, I'll—"

"My pleasure." He obliged, promptly lowering me into the back seat of his convertible. After jumping over the driver's side door, he started the engine.

Furious, I pulled myself up, crawled over the seat, and took shotgun. "Thanks a lot," I snapped. "Now, where did you say my purse was? I'd like to at least comb my hair. I can't imagine what I look like, especially after your little antic."

He stared at me, eyed me from head to toe, grinning the infectious smile he kept flashing. "From my side, you look quite beguiling," he paused a moment, "considering." Placing his arm on the seat back, he looked over his shoulder and edged onto the gravel road. "Your pocketbook is in the glove compartment, but there's nothing in it." He put the car in neutral, gazed directly into my eyes. "I didn't even notice it at first. It was caught on your dress. I only looked inside to see if you had some kind of identification."

"My purse was empty?" Opening the glove compartment, I peered inside, grabbed Piper's beautiful beaded bag. "My cell." I whimpered frantically, searching the tiny bag. "Where's my cell? And my cards?"

"Your dress and pocketbook were the only things I saw when I found you. But frankly, I was more concerned with making sure you were still alive." He adjusted the rearview mirror then gripped the huge steering wheel with both hands. Clearly annoyed that I didn't trust him, he stared straight ahead. "If you're so concerned about your cards, Miss Montgomery, you can have a deck of mine."

"What are you babbling about?" The day just kept getting better. So far, I had no clothes, no cell phone, no money, no car, and no credit cards. Not only that, the way he kept calling me Miss Montgomery was getting on my last nerve. "Could you just stop calling me 'Miss Montgomery'? Please?"

"Yes, ma'am." He complied, but his furrowed

expression showed honest concern. "Try not to get so upset, Maddie. Whatever you're worried about, I'll make sure it's okay. I promise."

Breathing deeply to calm myself, I watched Bobby. "I'm not upset, just frustrated. Look, I didn't mean to sound ungrateful or accuse you of taking my things." He stared straight forward and I cocked my head, peeking around to look at him in the eyes. "I'm genuinely grateful you rescued me, but I need to find my car. I think I have some emergency cash in the trunk, and I know there are some workout clothes there, too."

"Hold on, Maddie, you don't need any work clothes. If your car needs repair, I'll fix it. And your money is no good around me either."

"What?" Was he kidding me? I'd tried to be sincere, but I was too stressed to deal with his teasing. "Whatever. Can we just look for my car?" At least he'd called me 'Maddie' this time.

"I'll take you wherever you want to go." He grabbed the gearshift. "Which way?"

"I'm not from around here. In fact, I'm not even sure where *here* is." I looked around again, utterly lost. "I got so disoriented last night I have no idea where I ended up. But my car can't be far from where you found me. Let's just drive around. It shouldn't be that difficult to find."

"You bet, whatever suits your copperosity." He pulled onto the gravel road. "You just tell me when to turn."

We drove for what seemed like miles before finally pulling onto a narrow, paved street. Why was he taking so many back roads?

"If you can get us to the highway, I might recognize something." I didn't mean to snap at him or sound irritated, but the whole ordeal was totally getting to me.

Bobby scratched his head. "How many miles do you think you could have walked after you wrecked your car?"

I shrugged. There had to be a landmark, something that looked familiar. Where in the world were we? Nothing resonated, and my Lexus seemed to have vanished into thin air. Then it hit me.

"The lake," I blurted out. "The party overlooked the north shore. My car has to be close to the shoreline."

"Look Maddie, you must have been really knocked around in that accident, and you obviously hit your head pretty hard. Why don't you let me take you to my house? You can clean up, change clothes, and I still think Doc Meyerson should take a look at that lump on your forehead." He gazed at me with a frown and scratched at his scruffy, unshaven chin. "Maybe you'll recognize something when we get closer to town."

"Town?" Did he mean Gainesville… Dahlonega…New York? Where in the world were we? "What town?"

"Sidney, of course. That's where I live—Lived there most of my life."

I frowned, my head still aching. "Sidney? I've never heard of it."

"Look there's a signpost ahead." He pointed a few yards down the road.

I squinted to read the sign: *Sidney, Georgia 10 miles*. I threw my hands up. We could have been in

Timbuktu for all I knew. "Fine. Just go to Sidney." There had to be a gas station there with a map of the lake. Maybe I could figure out where I went off the road and send a tow truck after my car. I could call Piper, too, on a landline. She was probably frantic by now.

As much as I hated to admit it, Bobby Reynolds had a point. His laidback, matter-of-fact attitude, and quirky sense of humor got my dander up, though. I was exhausted, felt like a Mack truck had hit me, backed up over me then hit me again. And I was in no mood for games. Still, Bobby had rescued me and acted like a gentleman, which in my experience wasn't very common anymore.

I glanced over at him. Maybe he was a little cocky and a bit strange, but he sure was hot. I resolved to soften my tough-girl attitude. What choice did I have? Without Bobby's help, I'd be alone, broke, and stranded in the middle of God only knows where.

"A shower and clean clothes would be nice, but honestly, I don't need a doctor. I'm a little hungry, though."

"Well, that's a good sign." He took a deep breath, and I could see his whole body relax validating honest concern.

"Is there a nice restaurant in Sidney?" I asked, trying to de-stress myself. "My treat of course."

"Of course." He winked at me and chuckled. "Millie's diner, the best grub in town, but unless you plan on washing dishes for food you'd better let me pay. Besides, a woman should never have to pay for a meal with a man."

"That's a little old-fashioned, don't you think?" I

hoped he wasn't some kind of redneck chauvinist.

"Not old-fashioned. I simply was raised properly."

"Right." I smirked. "Well, until I can call Piper and find my car, I guess my life is in your hands."

"I don't mind having you in my hands a bit." He grinned and turned his focus back to the road.

Typical male response, but if Bobby had wanted to take advantage of me, he'd have done so by now. My mind drifted to Sidney. I couldn't remember seeing the town anywhere on my GPS, and I'd lived in Atlanta forever. But for some reason I couldn't explain, I was curious about the town that Bobby Reynolds called home.

Chapter 4

Atlanta, Georgia—August 2011

The Realm sat at the corner of Peachtree and Piedmont in the heart of Buckhead, surrounded by classy bars, sidewalk cafes, and elegant hotels. The high-paced lifestyle distracted Rob, but crowds made it easier to watch Lacey come and go without being seen. No one noticed him there, shadowing her day after day, keeping an accurate schedule of her every move. His detached behavior blended easily into a city of preoccupied people. And if, by chance, someone noticed him loitering, he'd pull the front page of his pad over his notes and begin sketching one of the marble fountains that accented the entry to the building.

The location proved an ideal arena to keep track of her, but getting past her condo security system would be much more challenging. So he watched, followed her, staying just far enough back to keep his unsuspecting target oblivious. He had to be careful. There was far too much preparation ahead of him to be reckless now, and too much at stake.

****

Sidney, Georgia, the day after the party

My entire body ached, but sinking into the comfy passenger seat of Bobby's Hudson eased my agony. Exhausted, I rested my head against the back of the seat and closed my eyes, trying to recall the details of my accident. How did I end up at that nouveau riche gala in the first place? I detested extravagant parties. *Think, Lacey. Think.*

"It will be a night to remember." Piper's promise echoed through my pounding head while the memorable evening eluded me. I breathed in deeply, relishing the aftermath of the violent storm. The air smelled so fresh. The soft scent of damp earth, lush foliage, and pine needles soothed me into an illusory slumber as my thoughts drifted to Piper.

She had kept life interesting from the first day I met her in seventh grade. I had transferred to Pine State Academy a few weeks earlier, and the mean girls had been tormenting me non-stop. When we returned to the locker room after running the track one morning, the prissy princesses found rotted shrimp heads stuffed into the vents of their lockers.

"That'll teach them to mess with us," Piper whispered.

Those perfect, anorexic snobs smelled like dead fish all day. Piper and I became instant friends and were totally inseparable all the way through college. We'd planned to share a condo in Atlanta when we graduated until her Aunt Alice died, leaving her a fortune that included a huge tract of property on the north shore of Lake Lanier.

When Piper invited me up to the lake under the guise of seeing her new house, of course I agreed. It had been ages since we had gotten together. The moment I arrived, she blindsided me. I was to be her guest the following evening at a philanthropic gala which she had organized, but the party sounded more like an elegant ball for the residents of the highly exclusive, gilded community, and I totally loathed high-society parties.

"But Piper, I didn't bring anything to wear that wouldn't tarnish your reputation. Besides, what I really need is to relax and unwind." I knew there was no way my lame excuse would change her mind, so I tried to distract her by gushing over her incredible home. "Your keeping room is fabulous. I love the deep brown walls with white furniture and the vaulted ceiling. You really outdid yourself."

"Not a chance, Lace." Lips pursed and leaning against a column, she crossed her arms and stared at me. "You're so predictable. Don't try to change the subject. I've got a closet full of gowns, and you can have your pick."

Okay, so distracting her didn't work very well, then how about honesty. "Piper, really? You know how I feel about ritzy parties. I'd be happy to donate, though." I reached in my purse for my checkbook. "How much do you want? I'll give you a check right now." Her narrowed gaze shot darts in my direction. Aware the battle was already lost, I rolled my eyes like a fifteen-year-old and collapsed into the overstuffed, white leather sofa.

Her face softened. "I know exactly how you feel about parties. That's why I didn't mention the event on the phone yesterday." She walked over, sat down beside me. "I knew you wouldn't have come. Lacey, are you ever going to get over your past? Having money didn't turn *me* or your dad evil. And my friends aren't money-hungry vultures either. They're great people who happen to be financially secure and want to share their good fortune with some very sick kids."

Piper nailed me. And she was right. My irrational disdain for the filthy rich began when my mom died. I lost both parents that day. Daddy coped by immersing himself in work, leaving me to deal on my own. Oh, he made sure I attended the best schools, had everything a daughter could possibly want—Everything except him. I'd felt rejected, abandoned, as if the only reason he tolerated me had been for Mother.

My ten-year-old viewpoint began to associate wealth with apathy and greed. And the Pine State girls validated my theory. But discovering Piper was filthy rich blew a hole in my philosophy. She was never pretentious and convinced me that my warped ideas were rooted in prepubescent baggage. Piper completely changed my perspective—Well, almost. I still detested the idea that money, when placed strategically, overshadowed truth. Lavish parties brought the good, bad, and beautifully ugly all together.

"You're right." I twirled a strand of my hair between my thumb and forefinger. "It's just that being submerged in a group of—" Her glare stopped me cold mid-sentence. "You're not going to take 'no' for an answer, are you?"

"Please, Lace." She took my hand in hers. "It will be a night to remember. I promise."

****

"Okay, sleepy head. We're almost home."

Bobby's voice stirred me from my semiconscious dream. I wriggled slightly, triggering a sharp pain that shot down my neck. Struggling to open my eyes, I looked up at a canopy of giant oak branches arched high over the road.

"Time to open those baby blues." Bobby reached over and softly nudged my shoulder. "You are still alive, aren't you?"

"Yes," I grumbled. "Barely. And FYI, my eyes are green." I gazed over at him without moving my head.

"More emerald, I'd say." He revealed a slight grin. "It's just an expression you know, baby blues, I mean."

"Right." I stretched my arms, yawned. "Sorry. I must have drifted off for a few minutes."

"That's okay. You needed the rest."

Sitting up, I looked around at the sprinkling of houses dotting the landscape on both sides of the rural road. Well-kept, older homes surrounded by large manicured lots were saturated with tall trees and lush shrubbery.

"So this is Sidney?"

"Not really." Bobby pulled the car into the driveway of a beautiful, Victorian-style home. "I live on the outskirts. Sidney proper is a few miles up the road."

The two-story home, painted a rich moss green, had a stately, white wraparound porch that stretched along three sides. An asymmetrical gable accented the steep-pitched roof.

"Your home is beautiful," I said, admiring the vista. "But I thought we were going to get something to eat."

Raising an eyebrow, he gazed at my bare legs. "We can go eat now if you'd like, but I didn't think you'd want to go anywhere in your present attire."

I looked down at his baggy shirt hanging loosely over my filthy body and pulled it over my knees. "Right. A shower and clean clothes is definitely a good idea."

"You'll feel a lot better after you clean up." Bobby jumped out of the car. "Then we'll get something to eat." He sprang around to the passenger side, opened my door, and swept his hand toward the front entry, bowing deeply. "Madam."

"Thank you, kind sir," I replied, stepping out of the car.

Bobby took my hand, closed the door behind me. "Your bath awaits." He led me up the steps toward the entry. "Shall I draw the water for you, princess?"

If anybody else had said that to me I'd have probably slapped his face, but not Bobby. I don't know why, but there was something about this man. Aside from his quirky attitude, his hot, sexy body, and dashingly handsome face, he made me feel safe.

"That won't be necessary." I followed him up the steps. The porch, with its quaint décor, felt homey. "I've always loved Victorian homes." Where did that comment come from? Now that I thought about it, I did. And I hated modern. Bit by bit, I was getting myself back.

Scanning the entrance to his home, I noticed details not typical of a single man's home. The décor could have been plucked from a picture book. Ferns suspended neatly at equal intervals around the soffit of the porch. A wooden swing hung at the far end surrounded by wicker chairs and a rag rug. Walking across to the front entrance, I imagined Bobby relaxing there on a summer evening. Why did I assume he was single? He'd never said one way or the other, had he?

"Welcome to my home." Bobby opened the inlaid-glass door and motioned for me to enter.

"Thank you." Stepping into the large foyer, I briefly glanced at his left hand. No ring, or tan line where one had been. It wasn't a confirmation, but chances were he wasn't married. I wasn't sure why that mattered, but it felt significant.

Content, for the moment, I checked out my surroundings. On the right, a parlor stretched the full depth of the home. An intricate etched-glass transom adorned the entryway. The adjacent dining room mirrored the same transom with a hallway next to it that led back to where the kitchen must be. The stairs were in front of me to the right, and a powder room peeked from behind them down the hallway.

"The bathroom is directly above us," Bobby said, pointing upstairs. "The towels are clean, and you can use the guestroom at the top of the stairway to dress." He closed the front door. "Sandy keeps some clothes in that closet, so help yourself. I'm sure she won't mind."

Sandy was his sister. That's why this place seemed so homey, a woman's touch. But why would a man, undoubtedly in his late twenties or early thirties, live with his sister? Maybe he was—*Oh please Lord, don't let him be gay.* No. He'd said he does just fine with the women. That comment was definitely delivered by a manly man.

"Thanks, Bobby." Gazing at him through my eyelashes, I flaunted my most helpless look. "I really appreciate all you've done, and I promise I'll get out of your hair as soon as I can get ahold of Piper."

"You're not in my hair, Maddie. Relax, make yourself at home." He sat down at his roll top desk in the parlor and began to leaf through some papers. "If you need anything, let me know," he added without looking up.

Dragging myself upstairs, I felt every bruise and strained muscle ache from the accident. The gash in my ankle throbbed, too. Something had sliced my leg when that creepy stalker grabbed me. A stalker grabbed me? That's right. Thank God that awful man didn't find me first. Bobby really *had* saved me. And he'd brought me here to the safety of his home. No wonder he called me princess. I should have been more gracious.

At the second floor landing, the right-hand door led to the guestroom. I could see another bedroom directly across from it and two more up front with a bathroom between them. Four bedrooms and only one bath, the place could definitely use a renovation.

Hobbling into the bathroom, I closed the door, clicked the small deadbolt. I took two towels and washcloths from the closet then reached behind the shower curtain to turn on the water. Draping my linens across the sink, I glanced into the medicine cabinet mirror and gasped at my reflection. My hair was a scraggly mess, and my filthy face had mascara smudges under raccoon eyes. My accident had been more serious than I'd realized. Dirt and muck partially covered the bruises on my cheek and chin. A blood-crusted lump bulged on the right side of my forehead. I'd flirted with Bobby, like this? I looked absolutely dreadful. No wonder he insisted on taking me to a doctor. He'd called me *Sleeping Beauty*? I looked more like the *Wicked Witch of the West*. Rubbing the caked mud from my face, I cringed. A hot shower would help, but it wouldn't erase the contusions, cuts, and scrapes covering my arms and legs.

Bobby's baggy T-shirt, hanging halfway down my

thighs, completely swallowed me. I undressed, draped the shirt over a hook on the back of the door, and examined my battered body more closely. My entire left side, ankle to shoulder, was one long, blue bruise, and a swollen black image of my seatbelt had left an imprint from shoulder to waist and across my hips. Damn, I looked as if I had been at ground zero during an explosion. Why couldn't I remember what had happened?

Pulling back the shower curtain, I stepped into the flowing water. Shaky, but unwilling to sit in a strange tub, I pulled both washcloths from atop my towels, lay one on the bathmat then painstakingly lowered myself to sit. Hot streams cascaded down, soothing my injuries. The soap dish held a bar of Ivory soap. At home, I used a moisturizing liquid, but not having the luxury of my own toiletries, I grabbed the soap and worked up a lather. On instinct, I rubbed my face with the soapy cloth and cringed at the sharp pain that shot through my head and down my neck. After that, I simply let the suds flow over my shoulders and lightly ran the cloth over my skin. My filthy hair desperately needed attention. I glanced around for shampoo and spotted a bottle of Prell in the corner. Dampening my hair, I squeezed a blob into my hand then cleaned the muck.

After thoroughly washing from head to foot, I leaned against the back of the tub and closed my eyes. Visions of Bobby Reynolds standing by his Hudson crept into my thoughts, coaxing the woman in me to awaken. The warm tingle merged with the soft streams of water enhancing my heated desire. He had rescued me, taken the shirt off his strong, muscular back, and carried me to safety. I hoped he wasn't just another Prince Charming illusion. Either way, the stir of passion trickling through my veins distracted me from my wounds. My memories swirled in a non-cohesive blur to Piper's party, and the mystery that spiraled me into this mess.

****

"I'll see you in a few hours."

"Wait Piper. Are you going to the party already?"

Dashing out of the house, a dress bag in one hand, cosmetic case in the other, she yelled back to me. "I told you last night, Lace. I have to be there early to check on the caterers and instruct the help. Directions are on the dining room table, seven o'clock sharp. Don't be late."

I glanced at my smartphone, four-thirty, close enough to the five o'clock cocktail hour. I poured a glass of pinot noir to calm the unsettling knot in my stomach then strolled out to the wrap-around deck. The sun glistened over the lake casting the same magenta glow as the day before, and the water shimmered, reflecting little glints of orange light.

Leaning against the rail sipping my wine and staring at that breathtaking view, I succumbed to the serenity, nature, and alcohol. The combination had a deeply sedative effect on me. Time paused, and for a while, I slipped into an almost transcendental, spiritual state of mind. Lotus blossoms and Zen music were all I needed to be lifted to an alternate plane. But Piper had been adamant, *"Seven o'clock sharp. Don't be late."* So I closed my eyes, breathed in one more calming lungful, then headed upstairs.

After trying on most of her wardrobe, I finally

found the perfect dress. I felt like Cinderella readying herself for the royal ball. When my cell alarm chimed six-thirty, I slipped into the sleek black gown, applied Poisonberry lipstick, my latest online purchase from Nasty Gal, then pooched my lips and admired my reflection in the full-length mirror.

My long, dark hair curled around shoestring straps, caressing my shoulders. The front of the dress definitely accentuated my more meager qualities with a soft swathed midriff that hid the belly I'd relentlessly tried to flatten since puberty. The back plunged below my waist in a tastefully sexy drape while the length perfectly touched the bottom of my black, strappy heels. The dress fit as if it were tailor-made. I giggled at my witty homophone. Since the dress belonged to Piper Taylor, I guess it was Taylor-made. I picked up the matching shawl, stuffed my cell phone, credit cards, driver's license, and comb into a beautiful beaded purse, grabbed the directions then flew out the front door.

The road led directly to the clubhouse despite the many curves along the way. When I pulled up to the gate and mentioned Ms. Piper Taylor, the guard directed me toward an elaborate circular entryway. Elegant marble columns supporting a two-story ceiling greeted me. Guests were clad in extravagant apparel, probably Gucci, Prada, Armani, Valentino, attire that screamed 'Look at how opulent I am.' Feeling a bit intimidated, I pulled my shawl around me a little closer until Daddy's expectations slid into place, *"Remember Lacey, you're a Montgomery."* When Warren Montgomery spoke everyone took notes, so I gathered my wits and swept forward, smiling as if I fit right in with the beautiful people.

"Lacey." Piper's voice echoed from above. Turning, I saw her rush down a majestic spiral staircase. "You're here." She stood back, inspected my outfit from head to foot before hugging me. "You look amazing."

"Luckily, I happened to stumble upon the perfect boutique." I smirked then admired her dress. I don't think I'd ever seen her look so gorgeous. Glints of dim light bounced off the chandeliers and shimmered through her long, golden hair. "Piper, you look fabulous."

The front of her royal blue, floor-length gown plunged elegantly, slightly separating her breasts. The color deepened her violet eyes. White organdy three-inch-wide straps studded with Australian crystals kissed her bare shoulders, accenting a dress that cinched her waist and emphasized her tall, slender figure. She absolutely sparkled.

"Thanks Lace. I know you're gonna have a fantastic time tonight." She grabbed my arm, pulled me toward the ballroom. "Rob and Travis are already here somewhere, and Drew is right over there."

"Wait. Can I at least put my purse and shawl someplace?"

"Oh, sorry. Here, give them to me." Piper took my things, turned to a valet. "James, would you please take these up to the parlor?" She handed them to the butler. "There. Now, let's go. I think Drew just walked out to the terrace."

I glanced at James as he strode up the stairs with my things. "Are you sure about handing over my purse to a complete stranger?"

She scrunched her brow and her lips flattened highlighting her icy stare. "He's not a stranger, Lace. He's my pastor's son, and these are good people, remember?"

"I—"

"Piper." Whew, saved by the tall, attractive man with strawberry-blond hair. He walked across the vestibule toward us. "Where have you been hiding this vision of beauty?"

Stepping on her tiptoes, Piper hugged him. "Travis, this is Lacey Montgomery, my best friend in the whole world. Lacey, this is Travis Sullivan." She placed her hand on my arm, slightly squeezing her fingers. "Don't let the sweet talk fool you, Lace. He's a great friend, but I'm sure he knew exactly who you were. I've talked about you enough."

"It's a pleasure, Lacey." Travis brushed a piece of lint from his lapel then reached out and clasped my hand in his. "I've been looking forward to meeting you."

Travis certainly fit the image of a lady's man, but it was Piper's mysterious neighbor, Rob, who'd caught me off guard. The connection between us was like nothing I'd ever felt before, and his mere presence aroused...

****

A surge of passion thrust an unexpected flash of pleasure between my thighs counteracting the cooling shower stream. I reluctantly stepped out of the tub. Grabbing my towels, I wrapped my hair in one then draped the other around me. I peeked out from behind the bathroom door to make sure there was no one in sight before padding down the hallway to the guestroom. Opening the bedroom door a crack, I half-expected to see Bobby stretched out on the bed waiting for me. He wasn't.

Instead, he'd carefully placed a white chenille robe on the bed. A comb, a new toothbrush, and a squeeze-flattened tube of Pepsodent lay beside it. Pulling the robe over my sore shoulders, I ran my tongue across my front teeth, grabbed the toothbrush and toothpaste, and crept back to the bathroom. I smiled at the promise scrolled across the tube: *You'll wonder where the yellow went when you brush your teeth with Pepsodent.* Bobby's love for retro sure was consistent: his car, his home, even his toothpaste.

A few minutes later, I rummaged through Sandy's clothes in the bedroom closet, hoping to find a pair of jeans and a T-shirt, preferably one that fit. There were several dresses, skirts, a pair of blue capris, but no jeans or shorts. A few sweaters and a white halter-top were folded on the floor. I considered my options. There was no way I'd borrow anyone's panties, so I'd have to go commando. In light of that, I settled for the capris and halter-top then hunted through a pile of shoes and found a pair of sandals that fit pretty well.

Pulling the towel from my hair, I searched for a dryer and some makeup to cover the bruises on my face, but there was no trace of any girly stuff to be found. With only one bathroom, Sandy probably kept her personal things in her own room. So, I combed my wet hair then hobbled back down the stairs to find Bobby. Glancing in the parlor first, I halted when the aroma of fresh coffee enticed me toward the kitchen. I followed the heavenly scent.

Bobby looked up from his place at the table. "Say,

you clean up right nicely, Maddie." He folded the corner of the page he'd been reading and closed his book. "Are you hungry?" He took a sip of coffee.

"Absolutely famished." I pulled out a chair and started to sit down. But the motion sent a sharp pain through my left side. I gasped and leaned against the back of the chair. "I think the accident bruised every inch of my body."

He jumped up to help me. "I was afraid of that." Wrapping his arm around my waist, he eased me into the seat. "I think we'll spin past Doc Meyerson's after we eat. I'd feel better knowing he checked you out, if that's all right with you?"

"Maybe." It was hard to focus. Between the rush I felt from his mere touch and the throbbing surge of pain, I wasn't sure which one caused my racing heart. "Before we leave, I'd really like to dry my hair. Would it be all right if I borrowed a hairdryer? Oh, and some makeup would be great. Something to cover these awful bruises."

He rubbed the stubbles on his chin then snapped his fingers. "I know just the thing. Sandy has some pancake makeup on her dresser. I'll get it for you." He scooted out the door, up the stairs.

The kitchen was typical of Bobby Reynolds, retro with a black-and-white tiled pattern on the floor and walls. The appliances looked as if he'd pulled them right out of the 1940s or '50s. Piper would love the detailed design. I'd make sure to show her the house when she came to rescue me from Sidney.

When Bobby returned, he had a round compact in his hand. "Will this do?" he asked, handing the makeup to me.

I unscrewed the top and stared at a hard beige-colored surface that looked like some kind of stage makeup.

"My sister adds water to it then dabs it on her face," he said, taking a seat at the table again.

Impressed that he chose a concealer rather than ordinary makeup, I glanced up to thank him. "I'm sure this will work just fine." His sapphire eyes, so deep and close, mesmerized me. I froze for a moment to drink them in.

"There's a mirror in the lavatory right there." He pointed to the door opposite the kitchen.

I took a deep breath to clear my head. "The lavatory?" I assumed he meant the powder room? Talk about old fashioned. I mean I knew the word. I'd just never heard anyone actually use it. "Thanks. I'll be right back."

Bobby stood again and helped me from my chair. Thanking him, I shuffled to the powder room. He certainly was quirky, but that man's touch sparked something inside of me that made me want to jump his bones. Not that I could have in my present condition.

I slathered on the makeup as best I could then patted it with a tissue. The color blended perfectly with my skin tone and worked better than any concealer I had at home. Moments later I was back in the kitchen.

"Say, you can barely see your bruises now, Maddie." He set his coffee cup on the table and closed his book again.

"Thank goodness. I can't believe how awful I look."

He stood up next to me and whispered in my ear. "I don't think you could look awful even if you tried."

"That's nice of you to say." I avoided trying to sit down again, leaning against the kitchen counter instead. "Were you able to find Sandy's hairdryer?"

"I don't think she has one. I'll ask her tonight. But you look fine. Besides, your hair isn't that wet now, and the ride to Sidney will dry it completely. Come on; let's get some food in you." He grabbed my arm to pull me toward the door and I winced.

"Eow. Easy…please."

"Sorry, Maddie. What a lunkhead. I didn't mean to hurt you." Putting his arm around me, he carefully guided me out the door.

The houses began to get closer together as we approached Sidney, typical of a small town. Bobby pulled up, parked in front of a quaint steel diner shaped like an old RV with a red and yellow neon sign that flashed *Eat at Millie's*. Square glass tiles curved around the corners meeting the bright red roof at the top.

"Here we are," Bobby said, getting out of the car. "Millie serves the best eats south of the Mason Dixon. It's no Varsity, but I promise Atlanta's got nothin' better."

When we walked in, I felt like I was sucked into an old-fashioned movie set. The classic jukebox played Ezio Pinza's "Some Enchanted Evening". Really? That song was way older than I was. Mother had loved *South Pacific* and after she died, Daddy had played the old vinyl incessantly on his antique record player. It was a perfect accent to Millie's retro ambiance, though. Formica topped counters surrounded a soda fountain bar lined with red-leather cushioned stools on steel bases. The entire restaurant oozed with authenticity.

"Say Millie, how's the special today?" Bobby

asked the woman behind the counter.

"Bobby Reynolds, do you need to ask? Now, sit yourself down. Fried chicken just came out fresh and hot, so you and your lady friend relax in your booth, and I'll bring out a couple of plates."

"What a gal." Bobby grabbed a newspaper from the bar. "And what do ya know? Today's paper, too." He walked over to one of the booths and sat down. "It's pretty hard to eat standin' up, Maddie. Come on over here and take a load off. I promise I won't bite."

Carefully sliding across the red cushioned seat, I looked around for a menu but couldn't see one anywhere. I crossed my hands on the Formica tabletop. "This place must have cost a fortune to reproduce. Everything is so realistic."

"I'm not sure, but wait till you taste Millie's fried chicken. It'll melt in your mouth, and her mashed potatoes are the cat's pajamas."

"The cat's pajamas, huh?" I smiled, playing along with his slang. "It smells delicious, but honestly, I don't eat fried foods very often. The cholesterol is over the roof, and mashed potatoes destroy my waistline. Do you think I could see a menu?"

He looked at me with a perplexed stare. "Sorry, Maddie. Today's menu *is* fried chicken. But I'm sure Millie would rustle up a hamburger and fries or a hotdog if you prefer."

Before I could answer, Millie stood at the table holding two large plates filled with fried chicken and okra, mashed potatoes with gravy and hot biscuits smothered in butter. She had two huge slices of cherry pie balanced on her forearm. The aroma was amazing, but I could almost feel my arteries harden and the pounds roll onto my hips.

"You dig in. I'm gonna jazz this place up." Bobby bounced out of the booth toward the jukebox. "Any tune you'd like to hear?"

"How about some Doris Day or Ella Fitzgerald?" I replied, keeping in the retro spirit. "Oh, why not be adventurous and throw in some Lady Gaga or Taylor Swift."

He shrugged, turned, and began sifting through songs on the jukebox.

Biting into Millie's chicken took me back to my childhood, sitting in Grandma's kitchen, my feet swinging back and forth beneath the seat, chicken leg grasped in one hand, biscuit slathered with butter in the other. Grandma called it comfort food, when the aroma and flavor brought back wonderful memories. And the fried okra and mashed potatoes only added to the mood.

I practically inhaled the first few bites promising myself that when my body healed, I'd work out extra hard to make up for my splurge. I'd just taken a big gulp of Coke when I glanced down at the newspaper Bobby had brought to the table. I read, choked, and spewed soda across the booth. He'd said *today's* paper, but the date at the top of the Sidney Gazette read: *Sunday, November 6, 1949.*

Chapter 5

Lake Lanier, Georgia—September 2011

The evening sun reflected a crimson glow as it sank into the lake. Rob twirled and swallowed the last drops of his ruby wine, then stacked his notes into a pile. Grabbing the papers, he turned briefly to catch the fiery sphere disappear beneath the horizon before walking across the deck into the house.

He knew Lacey's routine well now. What time she woke up, where and when she exercised, ate, and prayed. He noted her friends and acquaintances, the coffee shop she stopped by every morning before work. He'd even memorized the protein plate and skinny vanilla latte she always ordered.

She was so predictable, but cautious. Her exposure to criminals and violent crime had taught her well. She rarely went out alone at night, lived in a secure building, and always locked her doors. But the safeguards she'd created gave her a false sense of security. His unsuspecting mark had no idea he watched her every move or that he had documented the few people she trusted.

Like the components of a fine timepiece, each sliver of his plan had to fit together perfectly. This week, he would confront his first real challenge, Nick Cramer. Rob had to make sure that Lacey would not simply meet him; over time she'd have to trust him.

****

Sidney, Georgia—November 6, 1949

"Is this some kind of a joke?" Grabbing some napkins, I began to wipe the table to clean the mess I'd made.

"I'll get that, sweetie." Millie rushed toward me with a dishrag in hand. "Are you all right? I hope it wasn't my supper that made you choke like that."

"No, I didn't choke on the food, it was the paper." I picked up the journal, held it up to her. "Where did you get this?"

"The newspaper? Why, Tommy Johnson dropped by a stack this mornin', just like he does every mornin'. Is there some news that upset you?"

"No. It's just that…" Millie stood there staring into my eyes with a dumbfounded look sprawled across her face as if I'd lost my mind. I glanced back at the paper to check the date again. There it was in black and white, *1949* I couldn't explain it, but my reaction had clearly caused Millie to be alarmed. Scratching my head, I made up a lame excuse to buy some time. Something completely weird was going on, but I wasn't going to be the brunt of the joke. There was no way it was 1949, unless I'd hit my head a lot harder than I'd imagined. I needed time to figure this out.

"I'm sorry, Millie. I guess I must have swallowed the wrong way."

"Well, those bubbles can do that to ya."

"Yes." I forced a smile and sat back down.

The jukebox, now playing "Don't Sit Under The Apple Tree," blared from across the room, and Bobby snapped his fingers to the music, gliding back and forth as he pranced back to the booth.

"Say, what's all the commotion over here?" he asked slipping into the seat across from me.

"Nothing, Bobby. But maybe I hit my head a little harder than I thought." I looked at his reaction closely. As a lawyer, I'd become pretty good at identifying a scam. I could almost always spot a liar, too, except when it came to my intimate relationships.

Clearly concerned, he reached for my hand. "I can get you an aspirin."

"No, thanks." I hesitated. "What day is today?"

"It's Sunday, Maddie, all day long." He sat back in his seat.

"No, I mean the date."

Raising one eyebrow, he gazed at me with a disconcerting expression. "Okay, now you're beginning to worry me. November 6th. Are you feeling all right?"

"And the year, Bobby." I examined every line of his stunned face, but there wasn't a glimmer of insincerity. "What year is it?"

He leaned forward. "Maddie, you've—"

"Just humor me, Bobby." I reached across the table, touched his hand. "Please."

"It's 1949, of course."

I nodded my head. He didn't blink, twitch, or change positions. No micro expressions, distress signals, musculature changes, hand to face gestures. There was no body language at all that would indicate he was lying.

Yesterday had been Saturday, June 9th, 2012, a beautiful summery day, until the storm moved in.

"It's pretty warm for November, isn't it?" I asked. If it was truly late fall, how could he explain the warm weather?

"Yup, nothin' like a good ole Indian summer. Looks like we'll have a warm winter this year." His tone softened, but his sapphire eyes burned with concern. "Are you sure you're feeling all right, Maddie?"

"I'm good." I lied again. At that moment, I was anything but good.

"Well, I'm sure of that." He chuckled. "Still, if you feel poorly, I can take you back to my house to rest."

"I'm fine. Really. I just felt a little disoriented for a moment, but I'm okay now. Please, stop worrying about me." I motioned to his plate. "You should eat before your food gets cold."

Another lie, I was far from okay. At first I thought it was all an elaborate joke. But that made no sense. I didn't even know Bobby or Millie, or Sidney for that matter. No, it wasn't a joke. Somehow, some way, today was November 6, 1949. But how? Was I dreaming? No one could go backward through time. I mean, I'd seen several movies and read books about time travel. But that didn't mean I thought for one moment that spinning through time was feasible. Time travel was science fiction, a theory maybe, but not possible. And yet, here I was in 1949 thirty-four years before I was born. The pain of my injury, the smell and taste of old-fashioned fried chicken, all my senses confirmed that reality.

My mind swirled as I tried to wrap my head around the idea. There was no other logical explanation, unless I was drifting through some insane dream. It's torturous not being able to trust your own mind. If this truly was 1949, how could I find my way back home? I couldn't tell Bobby that yesterday was a beautiful June afternoon in 2012. He would think I was a complete nut case. How could he believe me, when I couldn't even believe me? He'd have me in a psych ward before I could tap my ruby slippers together.

No, the truth was out of the question, at least for now. Bobby was the only person I knew here, and I needed him. I would keep my thoughts to myself, determine how I got here, and figure out a way to get back to my life and time. Meanwhile, I would heighten my senses and observe every detail. Perhaps I'd discover some flaw or inconsistency somewhere in the midst of this absurdity.

After lunch, Bobby gave me the grand tour of his hometown. I felt like I was wandering through a scene from *Back To The Future*. At any moment I'd see Michael J. Fox pull up in his DeLorean and warn me about breaking the space-time continuum. But no one could have designed a Hollywood set as perfect as Sidney.

The streets were lined with classic storefronts. Metal signs advertised: *More Doctors Smoke Camel Cigarettes* and *The Smoothest Men Use Barbasol*. When we pulled into the service station, attendants rushed out to the car to fill the gas tank and clean the windshield. People dressed in clothing like I'd seen on *American Movie Classics*. Every detail reeked of an era tucked into the pages of history.

Prices appeared in sync as well. Gas for seventeen cents a gallon, milk for thirty-four cents. And a loaf of bread cost only eight cents. Offhand, I couldn't think of a single item in the twenty-first century that sold for under a dollar. The local theater featured Cary Grant and Ann Sheridan in *I Was A Male War Bride.* Tickets for the show cost forty-six cents. It would have been impossible to create such an elaborate hoax.

The drive around Sidney felt surreal. Was I drifting through a dream, or lost in time? "Moonlight in Vermont" a scratchy, romantic melody, streamed from the AM radio, deepening the uncanny ambiance. Phone booths dotted every street corner and the local A&W drive-in buzzed with activity as carhops roller-skated back and forth serving root beer and burgers curbside.

My senses battled a tug of war with my intellect. Visible reality convinced me I had been swept into the past, while logic screamed impossible. So I focused on what I knew for sure. Bobby had found me after my accident. Instinct was all I had to rely on, and my gut said he was a good man, a little cocky at times, but decent. My mind raced trying to make sense of the vintage town rolling past me. Nothing resonated, until I noticed a road sign that read: Looper Speedway. Looper. I'd heard that name somewhere before.

"Bobby, can we go to Looper Speedway?"

"Sure." His tone revealed a tinge of excitement. "You like the races?"

I nodded, offering an agreeable smile.

"Max Looper and his nephew Edwin are friends of mine. We can take a drive down the Gainesville-Cleveland Highway to see the track if you'd like." He frowned. "Unless downed trees from the storm have blocked the way."

Why did Looper Speedway sound so familiar to me? I'd never been to a racetrack in my life. Had I? No. Why would I want to watch grown men chase each other around in a circle at ridiculously dangerous speeds?"

"Say, if you really want to see the cars race, how about going with me next Saturday? That is, unless you're sweet on someone else."

"I was, but not anymore." My thoughts spun to Cole, drenched, with daffodil petals stuck to his face. The sorry, lying jerk. "The truth is I tore out of the party into that storm, because I walked in on my boyfriend kissing someone else."

A low whistle escaped Bobby's lips. He reached over, touched my shoulder. "He didn't deserve you, Maddie."

"I was so naïve. How did I not see him for who he really was?"

"I know the type. He sounds like a poor excuse for a man. Don't blame yourself, though. You just gave the fella a chance, trusted him. There's no shame in that."

I wanted to say, *Yeah well, I won't do that again*, but I decided on a more gracious reply. "Thanks for saying that, but I should have better instincts." I gazed out the window to keep him from seeing tears well in my eyes. "Saturday would be fine, Bobby. I'd enjoy going to Looper with you."

"Good, then it's a date."

Watching the scenery roll by, I remembered Piper's most recent Cole rant...

****

"Seriously, Lace. What do you see in him?"

A valid question. Especially since she listened to me complain every time Cole blew me off to take care of some business that had "suddenly come up." But he did have his attributes.

"He's attractive, funny, a successful, driven—"

"Right. I've heard his credentials."

"He loves me, Piper." Turning, I draped one of her stunning silver dresses over the back of a chair and quietly continued, "And it feels good to be loved."

I knew that was the wrong door to open before the words left my lips.

"It's not Cole's love you want, Lace. It's your dad's." She stared at me, quietly waiting for my response, but I said nothing. "It's easy to say 'I love you.' Showing love is something else. And honestly, the important question is, do you love him?"

"Yes…sort of. Okay, maybe he's not my knight in shining armor, but…"

Piper's protective instincts went into overdrive. "What happened to the Lacey who was set on finding her soul mate?" Her expression burned with disapproval. "Waiting for the guy who curls your toes with his first kiss?"

"I guess…I grew up. Or maybe I'm just tired of sitting at home alone, waiting for *the one*. I don't believe in fairy tales anymore."

She fell back on the bed, staring at the ceiling. "I'm worried about you, Lace. Did you ever consider Cole might have an agenda? I mean, you're a great lawyer and not bad arm candy with those green eyes and long legs."

I'd never considered Cole might be using me. I simply deduced that if I dated someone I wasn't quite so crazy about, I wouldn't fall apart when things ended. And it was nice to have someone who would simply say the words 'I love you.'

"Face it Piper, the best thing I can say about my track record with men is that it's consistent." I stopped looking through her closet for a suitable dress, sat down on the bed, and crossed my legs Indian style. "All my relationships play out the same way rhyme and verse, just a different time, place, and cast of characters."

She rolled over and glared at me, leaning on her elbows. "Look, I admit your love life is littered with different versions of the same man. But that doesn't mean you should give up, or settle, especially for Cole. He never puts you first, Lace. Ever. I'm just sayin'." She pulled her knees up, wrapped her arms around them. "Besides, he's already in love…with his career. From where I sit, Cole loves Cole. And what he does is for *him*, not you."

****

Bobby gave my shoulder a soft squeeze. "Maddie, the fella you trusted was a fool. A real man won't treat a woman like that."

I wiped my eyes before looking at him. "A real man? I guess I've been looking for love in all the wrong places." I chuckled before realizing he had no knowledge of my movie reference.

"I don't think love is something you look for. It just finds you." He glanced over at me. "But you have to recognize it."

His philosophical comment caught me off guard. It was something Piper would have said, not a man. "You're right. Cole doesn't deserve any more of my energy." I forced a smile before changing the subject. "So, tell me more about your racetrack."

"You bet. We'll take a spin in that direction. If the road is clear, we might catch some of the guys practicing."

"I'd like that." Maybe I would recognize

something along the way." I couldn't shake the feeling I had heard of Looper Speedway.

He turned the car, headed down the main highway leaving Sidney. "They run mostly Ford coupes at the track. One guy drives his Plymouth though. Gober Sosebee races there a lot. He's got the keenest, souped-up Ford I've ever seen. Eddie Samples and Chester Barron race at Looper, too, and a woman. Have you ever heard of Sara Christian from Dahlonega?"

"No, the name doesn't sound familiar." The oversized seat and lack of a seatbelt made turning toward him comfortable, I leaned against the car door and listened while Bobby told me about the drivers.

"Well, Sara may be a looker, but she's nobody's chump. She's gonna be driving Max's car next Saturday, should be an interesting race. The guys have been prodding her for weeks. They just want to gloat when they beat her."

There it was, the familiar chauvinism I was so used to hearing. "Oh, so you think just because she's a woman, she couldn't possibly win?"

Bobby laughed. "Hey, not me. I'm rootin' for Sara. I think she can beat all of 'em." He looked over at me obviously checking my reaction. "But a lot of guys don't think she has a chance. Should be a fun race to watch. Those men won't know what hit 'em. I think she'll leave them all in the dust."

That's when it hit me, Looper Speedway. I remembered where I'd heard it before. It was the old dirt racetrack that Piper had mentioned Friday night. As I dug through my thoughts to recall what else she'd said, it occurred to me I might find her property if we drove the shoreline of the lake.

"Hey, Bobby. I changed my mind."

"I suppose that's a woman's prerogative," he teased.

"Would you mind if we drove to the lake instead? We could hang out there for a while, unless you have plans."

"Well, I was thinking about taking a nap in the hammock this afternoon, but I guess I could spare a few hours." His grin turned to a perplexed scowl. "Maddie, what lake are you talking about?"

"The lake, Bobby. You know, Lanier?"

"I don't think I've ever heard of a lake named Lanier. Not north of Atlanta anyway."

"Seriously, don't tease me." I tucked my hair behind my ears, cocked my head, and looked at him with a demure smile.

"I'm not teasing," he replied. "There are a few lakes in the area." He ran his fingers through his thick, sandy hair, scratched his head. "Burton is fairly close and there's Raburn. There are a lot of waterfalls around here, too, with the mountains so close. I've run across several of them hiking through the foothills."

He'd never heard of Lanier? What rock had he been sleeping under—geez, that's right. The track, stands, and everything were a casualty of progress, all submerged when they created Lake Lanier. If this was truly 1949, the lake didn't exist. Not yet, anyway. I needed to get my bearings, and some historical facts wouldn't hurt either. It would take time to figure out details of this era. But for now, I needed to cover my blatant faux pas.

"Oh, I…" My mind went blank. How could I possibly explain looking for a lake that didn't exist?

"Say, you mentioned a lake earlier this morning, too. Are you thinking about looking for your car again?"

"No, no. My car can wait. There's really nothing I can do about it, at least until the phones are back in service."

"I've got an idea." Bobby slowed the car, pulled into a gas station. "I don't know why I didn't think about this earlier. I'll buy a Georgia map so we can figure out where you ran off the road. We'll find your lake and your car."

"Never mind, Bobby. I thought I remembered Piper mentioning Lake Lanier, but now that I think about it, she may have been talking about South Carolina." Another lie, but it was the only way to avoid sounding completely insane.

He parked, hopped over the driver side door. "A map could still help us find your car. I'll be back in a jiffy." He hurried into the station.

When Bobby returned, he handed me a map of Georgia, started the ignition, and pulled out. "The map should help you get your bearings. If not, it's smart to keep a map in the car anyway. Ya never know when it will come in handy."

I put his gift in the glove compartment. "Thanks. I'll look at it later, but for now let's just hang." Before he replied, I knew I'd done it again.

"Hang? Hang what, Maddie?"

I never realized how much twenty-first century jargon had crept into my English. *Focus Lacey.* "I mean we can go wherever you'd like. I'd enjoy seeing your hometown."

"Swell, then sit back and relax. I'll cruise around

Sidney and show you the major attractions. And, if you play your cards right, maybe I'll even treat you to an ice cream cone at the park later."

He spun the car around, heading back toward Sidney, beaming with details of his childhood home. I heard stories about everyone from Sidney's mayor and chief of police, John Baxter, to Mary Jenkins, his sixth-grade teacher. And I listened, but my mind kept drifting back to Lake Lanier and the blaring fact it didn't exist yet. This whole area must have been in the construction zone. Looper Speedway, the roads and—no, not Sidney. Piper said a whole town had been submerged when they built the lake.

I sat up rigid and gasped, interrupting Bobby's guided tour. "They couldn't have…"

"What's wrong, Maddie?" He leaned forward, alarm flushing his face. "Are you okay?"

Not Bobby's town. That had to be why I'd never heard of Sidney. I scrambled for something to keep him from thinking I was a complete mental case.

"They couldn't have what? You okay, Maddie?"

I racked my brain then spit out the first thing that came to mind. "My purse. I think I left it at the diner. You don't think someone could have stolen it, do you?"

"Thank goodness." He leaned back in his seat again. "I'm sure your pocketbook is back at the house, but we can swing by Millie's and check if you want to. Don't worry, though." He touched my arm to comfort me. "If you left your pocketbook at Millie's, she'll set it under the counter. It'll be safe there. Sidney's not like Atlanta. Nobody even locks their doors around here."

"I'm sure you're right. There's nothing in it anyway. It's just that my purse is the only thing I have

65

right now that's actually mine." *Well, Piper's, anyway.* "It's pretty unsettling to wake up in a place you've never seen before. My purse is my only tie to home."

"I can't imagine. You've got to be feeling pretty stranded." His sincere expression convinced me further that, as bizarre as it seemed, I was not in Kansas anymore. He slowed the car, pulled over. "Say, how 'bout getting that ice cream I promised you earlier? Maybe that will make you feel a little better."

I nodded. "That sounds good."

He made a U-turn, back toward the center of town. Leaning back in my seat, I watched the scenery, reflecting on what could have happened if he hadn't found me. "Thanks for everything, Bobby. You have no idea how much I appreciate all you've done for me today."

Glancing over at me he smiled. "I didn't do anything special. Besides, you're an interesting woman, Maddie Montgomery."

As Bobby parked the car, I thought about the lake, the construction, and desolation of his town. The puzzle pieces fell into place. Bobby's home, the town he grew up in and loved so much, was about to be swallowed by Lake Lanier. And he seemed to have no idea. Could that have something to do with why I was here?

When we reached Sullivan's Drug and Soda Shop, we bought home-made ice cream scooped onto crisp cake cones, then walked across the street to the square and wandered along a worn path lined with lush greenery dotted with toad lily blooms. Strolling through the park with Bobby, licking an ice cream cone, did make me feel better. It felt odd to stop and smell the roses so to speak. My fast-paced lifestyle had been drenched in constant chaos. Now, a relaxing walk stopping now and then to watch children play Kick the Can or Red Rover, seemed so surreal. And then there was Bobby. What was it about this man that enticed desire deep inside of me?

When we reached the pond, Bobby tossed the last pieces of our cake cones to the ducks then we sat on a bench and talked, watching as the sun descended into the horizon. By the time we finally pulled into his driveway, I felt amazingly calm, considering that only a few hours earlier I had been ripped through time to another era.

Bobby took my hand as we walked up the steps to the front door. "Sandy is home now. You ready to meet my little sister?"

"Should I be nervous?" I joked.

He grinned. "I would be." He reached for the doorknob.

Chapter 6

Lake Lanier, Georgia—October 2011

Rob looked through the glass door at the elderly woman sitting on his deck. A brilliant researcher in her time, she was still sharper than most individuals half her age. Even the lines in her face implied a much younger woman. Her confidence and skill would have enticed him regardless of who she was, but Drew's knowledge regarding her expertise had sealed the deal.

He smiled pondering the irony. Lacey had no idea of the hoops he was jumping through. The stakes were inconceivable. He'd put everything he owned at risk, including his life, and Lacey's.

****

Sidney, Georgia—November 1949

Sandy threw the front door open before Bobby had a chance to turn the knob. Her rich brown hair combed back from her forehead draped her shoulders with soft curls, and flawless porcelain skin deepened her emerald eyes. She was about my height, five foot seven or so. A white blouse tied just above the waistband of her black pants accentuated her long, slender legs.

"So this is the mystery woman Millie told me about."

Bobby laughed. "Sandy, this is Maddie," he said with a glint in his eye. "She's going to be our houseguest for a few days until the roads are cleared."

"It's nice to meet you, Maddie." Her smile beamed sincerity. "Come in. Please, come in."

The moment we walked through the door, the aroma of roast beef enveloped me. The familiar smell summoned memories of my mother. I felt instantly relaxed.

"You two mind if I run upstairs and take a quick shower?" Bobby asked.

"Go ahead," Sandy said. "That'll give us time to get to know each other." She hooked her arm through mine as if we were best friends.

Bobby sprang up the steps, leaving Sandy and me to get acquainted. Something about his sister drew me in from that very first moment I laid eyes on her, as if we were oddly connected. We strolled into the parlor arm in arm, her curiosity bubbling over.

"So, Maddie, what brings you to Sidney?" She settled into a large cushioned chair.

I carefully sat on the edge of the sofa, trying to think of a creative way to avoid explaining a shift in time that even I didn't understand. "I guess you could say I blew in with the storm. Last night it rained so hard I couldn't see the road in front of me. I lost control of my car, slid off the highway, and slammed into an embankment."

"Oh Maddie. That must have been awful. You do look a bit bruised." She fluffed the back cushion and turned sideways in the chair, leaning partially against the arm so she could face me. "But, how did you meet my brother? Did he give you a lift?"

"Actually, he found me. I remember kicking my way out of my car and trying to find the road. After that

I'm not really sure what happened until this morning when I woke up to see your brother standing over me."

"Jeepers." She giggled. "That would've scared me to death."

I laughed and scooched back into my seat. "Well, he surprised me for sure, but I'm thankful he discovered me lying there unconscious in the middle of nowhere. Who knows what would have become me if he hadn't."

"Bobby's good at taking care of damsels in distress," she said.

And there it was, the description of Bobby I'd been afraid of hearing. "So he has a knight-in-shining-armor complex, huh?"

She looked at me with a scrunched forehead as if I were speaking Greek. "What do you mean, complex?"

She had no idea what I was talking about. I scrambled to cover my jargon. "Oh, I was just wondering if he'd rescued other women before?"

"Well, when Becky Stewart fell into the pond at the square last summer, he jumped in after her." She pulled her knees up and brushed some lint from her pants. "Not that she needed saving. Everyone knew she fell in on purpose just to get Bobby's attention. She's been sweet on him since high school. Even Bobby knows it."

"So, Becky is Bobby's girlfriend?"

"Noooo. She's too kooky," Sandy replied emphatically. "My brother could have his pick of just about any girl in Sidney. He's nice to all of 'em, goes out with a whole bunch of girls, but…"

She left her sentence hanging, a blatant tease.

"But what?" I acted nonchalant. I knew the type, love them then leave them. Damn. It figured. Hot as hell, but Bobby was just another smooth-talking player. From the sound of it, he got off on manipulating women, had dozens trolling after him. Typical. Mr. Reynolds could have his itch scratched whenever he desired.

"I guess what I'm trying to say is: I don't think my brother has ever been in love." Sandy paused for moment before continuing. "He's never even dated anyone seriously. You know, with plans of marriage."

Like I figured, pump her then dump her. Clearly, jerks were alive and thriving in 1949. "So he's a serial dater?" I asked.

"I'm not sure what you mean." She looked at me clearly perplexed. "He says he wants the brass ring."

The brass ring, what did that mean? I couldn't ask her without raising suspicion as to why I didn't know, so my expert deductive skills sprang into action. I'd seen some brass rings at a bullfight once, when I was in Mexico. The matadors said the rings helped control dangerous animals. Bull's noses were sensitive, and when someone grabbed a hold of a nose ring, the bull became compliant and could be led anywhere.

I simply put two and two together. Bobby never got serious with a girl. He just led them around by the nose. Men. The stereotype probably dated back to the Ice Age where males hit their women over the head and dragged them to their cave.

"So your brother is a classic player." I guess all men were the same. Even slipping through time, I couldn't escape their narcissistic egos. *Whoa,* I scratched my head stunned at the depth of my pent up animosity toward the opposite sex.

"I guess so," she said. "He played sports in high

school."

Releasing a brief chuckle, it occurred to me that Sandy had no idea what I'd been talking about, which was probably a good thing. I'd clearly have to watch my slang more carefully in the future, or should I say in the past? Regardless, a subject change was in order.

"What in the world are you cooking? It smells wonderful." A chef always loves to be complimented. In this case though, it was the truth.

"It's only pot roast," she replied. "Say, do you need any help bringing your things in from the car, Maddie?"

And now we were back to square one. How could I tell her my Lexus had simply disappeared?

"Unfortunately, I don't have any things. I must have wandered pretty far from my car before Bobby found me, because we couldn't find it." Looking down, I realized with a jolt that I was wearing her clothes. "Oh my gosh, I'm sorry. That's why I had to borrow your pants and top. Bobby said it would be okay with you. I hope you don't mind."

"Maddie please. I don't mind at all. You can use whatever you need while you're here." She shifted in her chair and offered a convincing smile. "It'll be fun to have another woman around the house for a few days."

"Thanks so much, Sandy. And I insist on doing my share while I'm visiting, so please let me help with whatever needs to be done."

"Well then, in that case let's go get supper on the table." Standing, she looked down at me and extended her hand to help me up. "Come on. Bobby will be finished with his shower soon." She walked toward the kitchen and I followed. "So, what happened after my brother found you?"

Maybe it was the enticing aromas or Sandy's innocent sincerity, but I felt strangely at home. By rights, I should have been panicked at my circumstances, or worried that I was quite insane, but instead, a surreal calmness washed over me. Like Bobby, Sandy Reynolds had charmed me. I continued my account of the day's events making sure to leave out the few minor details that involved slipping through time.

Walking into the dining room, Sandy laughed. "He actually picked you up, slung you over his shoulder, and dropped you into the back seat?"

"Pretty much. He was careful not to hurt my bruised body, but there was no way he was going to put me down until he was good and ready."

"That's my brother all right." She took three white porcelain dinner plates from the hutch and handed them to me. The scalloped edges set off clusters of red roses blooming around swirling green stems. The antiques were flawless, but then I guess they weren't antique, yet. I set them on the table and continued my story.

"I was so angry at him," I said, placing the pitcher of iced tea on a coaster. "I smacked him on the back demanding he put me down that instant. But he totally ignored me."

"I'm not surprised. Bobby is a great brother, but he never lets me get away with a thing." She folded linen napkins, added flatware to the place settings, sterling silver edged with a rosebud design.

Opening the hutch, I reached for some crystal goblets with pine needles etched into the glass, placed them next to the vintage china. The table setting was a far cry from the paper napkins and dishes I typically used. It was elegant, yet comfortable and homey at the same time.

Sandy placed a platter filled with sliced roast beef, carrots, onions, and gravy directly in front of the head of the table. I filled the serving bowls with lima beans and mashed potatoes. Eating habits sure had evolved over the last sixty-three years. If I didn't find my way home soon, the cholesterol and excess calories would wreak havoc on my diet, and my hips.

"So, how long have you and Bobby lived here?" I asked.

"Forever, I guess. It's the only home I've ever known." She picked up a pitcher of water, filled a glass then handed it to me. "Mother died when I was five, and Daddy worked to pay the bills, so Bobby practically raised me."

I could identify. At least she had a brother to look out for her. "My mom died when I was a child, too. It's hard for a little girl to grow up without a mother." I placed the glass on the table. "You were lucky to have Bobby."

"I know. He's a great brother and a really good guy, Maddie. He's always had a soft heart, taking in stray dogs, defending the little guys. He'd take the shirt off his back for you—" Realizing the irony of what she'd just said, we both broke out laughing.

When Bobby returned from his shower, we sat down to dinner, chatting as if we'd all known each other for years. We had barely finished eating when he stood.

"Well, ladies, that was a fine dinner. Now if you two will excuse me, I have some paperwork to attend to."

"Thank you both for your hospitality," I said. "I don't know what I would have done if Bobby hadn't rescued me and brought me here."

"You're welcome to stay as long as you need to, Maddie." Bobby walked into the parlor. Sifting through mail, he sat down at his desk.

Sandy went into the kitchen, filled the sink with sudsy water, and started washing the dishes while I began to clear the table as if we'd gone through the same routine for years. Carrying plates and bowls from the dining room, I couldn't help but glance across the foyer at Bobby. What did he do for a living? We had spent the whole day together, and he never once mentioned his work. Why hadn't I asked him?

Bobby opened envelopes, read them, then filed each one into built-in pigeonholes in his desk. I had almost cleared the dining room table when I noticed a distinct change in his demeanor. As he read through a letter, the color drained from his face. Dropping his hands to the desk, he looked up and stared blankly out the window at the dusky sky. I pushed back through the swinging door to drop off the rest of the dirty dishes, but quickly returned ostensibly to wipe the crumbs from the table, my eyes focused on Bobby. He searched frantically through his desk drawer, pulled out a map, measured, and scribbled some notes.

I had to say something. "Is everything okay, Bobby?"

Startled, he looked up at me. "Oh…" He shoved his paperwork to the back of the desk. "Yes, of course," he replied with a strained smile. He pulled down the roll top, hiding the work that had him so concerned. "Say, why don't we go sit out on the porch for a while?"

Sandy peered around the door from the kitchen. "You go ahead, Maddie. I'll finish up, fix something for us to drink, and be out in a jiffy."

"Come on Maddie, you've had a long day." Bobby opened the screen door and stood back, waiting for me to walk through to the porch.

"Well, since you're twisting my arm..." I strolled outside, eased myself onto the swing, and began gliding back and forth. The lifestyle in Sidney with its laid back, tranquil ambiance seduced me, a generation torn from the pages of history where family took precedence over what would one day become the hustle-bustle of a high-tech society. Here, people took time to enjoy their lives and each other. I basked in the utter serenity of an era lost to the passage of time and progress. At any moment, I expected Sandy to burst through the screen door with a batch of mint juleps and an elaborate dessert she'd just whipped up in the kitchen.

"Penny for your thoughts," Bobby said.

Suddenly aware of the smile on my face, I leaned back into the swing. "I was thinking how peaceful it is here. Atlanta is so different."

"Yup, it's hard to imagine living anywhere but Sidney," he replied. "I just hope..."

I looked over at him and watched as the fire in his sapphire eyes dimmed. Something in the mail had him deeply troubled. "You hope what, Bobby?"

Seeing my concern, he lightened the conversation. "Awe, nothin'. So you like our little town?" He sat back in the rocker and began to push to-and-fro.

Smiling, I followed his lead. I'd let his distress slide, for now. "Yes. I really enjoyed the day. Thanks for taking the time to show me around."

"Believe me, Maddie, the pleasure was all mine."

A full moon peeked through the curling leaves of a big oak tree highlighting his grin, and my mind spun with amorous thoughts, until Sandy kicked the screen door open. She walked outside carrying a tray with three glasses and a pitcher of lemonade. We sat there for hours on that porch, talking, laughing, and enjoying the evening like—like a family.

Fireflies, long past their time, twinkled beneath tree branches like tiny earthbound stars dusting the evening. And crickets chirped their song beckoning the night as darkness crept toward the dim horizon, slowly swallowing the twilight sky. It seemed odd to feel so peaceful, absorbing the seductive ambiance after awakening that very same morning in a foreign world.

"Well, ladies, it's time for me to hit the hay." Bobby stood, stretched his arms, and yawned. "I have to get to the plant early tomorrow morning. And Maddie, you must be exhausted after everything you've been through."

The plant? I'd still never asked him what he did for a living. But that could wait until tomorrow. It was clear I wasn't going anywhere for a while, at least until I could figure out how I got here in the first place, and I was exhausted.

"Now that you mention it, I am pretty tired."

"Me, too." Sandy looked at her watch. "My goodness, it's almost ten o'clock."

****

As I turned out the lights and slipped my bruised body between smooth cool cotton sheets, I reflected on the events of the day. I had no idea how I managed to awaken in 1949, but it wasn't so bad. I could see what Bobby loved about Sidney. The slower-paced lifestyle captivated my heart, a time when strolling through the park eating an ice cream cone on a Sunday afternoon was a way of life. And the people were so laidback and friendly. Still, I needed to find my way home and had no idea how to even begin that task.

In the meantime, Bobby and Sandy were about to be blindsided by the Army Corps of Engineers. There had to be a way to help them, help all of the residents of Sidney, or at least ease their transition. I could make sure the displaced families would be fairly compensated for their homes. It wouldn't make up for the loss they faced, but it would certainly benefit their descendants.

There was something about this place, this time and Sidney, that made me feel like I belonged here. My life in 2012 had been good, but I had always felt something was missing, an inner contentment and a sense of being needed. I'd only been in Sidney for one day, but somehow it felt like home.

The moon glistened through the leaves of the old oak outside my window. Beyond, a velvet night sky sparkled with more stars than I had ever seen. Was it only the night before that I'd stood on Piper's deck gazing at the reflection of the same moon as it shimmered across the lake? So much had happened in the past twenty-four hours.

I wondered how Piper had taken the news of my disappearance. She must have been beside herself with worry. And Cole. My relationship with him seemed like a lifetime ago, and I guess it was. Piper and Cole no longer existed. No, they hadn't been born yet. The only connection I had in this world was Sandy and Bobby

Reynolds.

The vision of his rippling abs, his hot, sensuous body leaning against that old car sprang to my mind again, sparking a stab of desire. Cole had never made me feel that way, how I felt simply looking at Bobby. No one had. When he brushed against me or touched my hand, he ignited a longing deep inside of me, but the last thing I needed in my life was another Romeo. I wouldn't be just another notch on Bobby Reynolds' bedpost. I needed his help and friendship but, for once in my life, I was determined not to act like a starry-eyed adolescent. Both Piper and Nick had warned me about Cole from the beginning, and I should have lis—*oh my gosh, Nick.*

Memories of my last encounter with Nick Cramer flooded back into my mind. When I saw him Thursday evening, something he said gave me the heebie-jeebies. I had left my office intending to go straight to the garage, but the elevator opened to the lobby where I mindlessly stepped forward.

"Hey Montgomery, thanks again for scoring those tickets. You rock." Nick's deep brown eyes, tousled sun-blond hair, and dimpled smile could charm Medusa before he even opened his mouth. The moment we bumped heads reaching for the same book at the law library last year, I knew we'd become friends. He just had an air about him.

"Braves tickets are the least I could do after all you've done to help me."

"I guess Harrison & Forbes has its perks after all." He smiled a toothy grin that barked you-should-listen-to-me-more-often.

I forced a curt smile back at him, and he looked at

me with his sympathetic eyes. Everyone deserves his day in court, but it was hard to feel good about winning cases that put pedophiles, rapists, and murderers back on the streets.

"The law is a whore, Nick. And working my butt off so lowlife criminals can roam the streets scot-free isn't what I signed up for."

Nick helped me see the bigger picture. Harrison & Forbes was a prestigious firm, and it looked great on my resume. I simply had to get over my naïve dreams. The stark reality of the legal system hit me like a Mack truck when I realized that a defense attorney's profession was a far cry from my superhero dreams as a law student. I hated the feeling I was selling my soul to the devil. I might've walked away from my career altogether if it hadn't been for Nick. He had a unique ability to envision the future. Not like a crystal ball, although I often wondered about that, too, he'd simply dusted off the dreams my passion could accomplish once I paid my dues. Nick totally got me, and it was hard to sulk around him.

"Something else is bothering you, Lace." He touched my arm to coax me. "Spit it out."

I placed my briefcase on the front desk. "It's nothing, really," I replied, checking my cell phone for messages to avoid his gaze.

"Nothing?" He raised an eyebrow. "Your glum mood must involve Cole."

"Funny." I rolled my eyes as my boyfriend's defense spewed from my mouth. "Okay, so Cole canceled our weekend plans at Hilton Head, again, but it wasn't his fault. He landed a huge client and had to fly to New York." And there it was.

Nick was right, though. Cole had more last minute business matters to handle than anyone I knew. But if there's one thing becoming a defense attorney had taught me, it was 'be ready for the curveball.'

"Sorry, Lace." He nudged me with boyish empathy.

"It's really not a big deal." I dug through my purse for a hair clip to pull my long, brown mane into a ponytail. Then, slinging the strap over my shoulder, I turned back toward the elevator. Nick picked up my briefcase and walked alongside of me.

In truth, I was getting used to Cole canceling our plans. He always had a good reason for bailing on me. But my last case had been a grueling nightmare. I was so ready to spend an intimate weekend feeling sand between my toes, breathing in cool, salt air, and watching the sunset from a beachfront cafe. A frou-frou cocktail and the soothing sound of rolling surf were hard to shrug off. To make things worse, Cole had a way of twisting things so I felt guilty for feeling disappointed.

"I'm just sayin', Lace." Nick shook his head. "Cole just gives me bad vibes."

I didn't take his sentiment lightly. Nick was one of the few men I actually trusted and lately, his vibes freaked me out, like he had a sixth-sense or something. He seemed to know things, like premonitions of events before they actually happened.

I glanced at my watch. Almost eight o'clock. "I don't know how you juggle this job with law school, help research my cases, and still find time for a life."

"It's simple. Vampires don't sleep." Laughing, he scooted in front of me before pushing the down button.

"Seriously Lace, I've wanted to be a lawyer since I was a kid. And I'm so close. Sometimes my energy is so intense, I feel like I could take off and fly."

I nodded like I knew the feeling. I didn't. At least, I hadn't felt like that in a long time. "Speaking of being a lawyer, I have depositions in the morning. Afterward, I'm taking off for a few days. I'll see you Monday, okay?"

He grabbed my shoulder, drew in a deep breath. "Wait. I thought Cole canceled on you."

"He did." I wrinkled my forehead, gazing at him curiously. "But Piper called a few minutes later and asked me to come to the lake for the weekend."

"Sweet." He grinned a wry smile, and I couldn't help but wonder what devilish thoughts about my best friend lurked in his mind.

"Serendipity." I smiled. "Or maybe Piper can read my mind. I think both my best friends have mystical powers."

Too bad the enchantment hadn't rubbed off on me. When the elevator opened I stepped inside, but Nick leaned against the door to keep it from closing.

"Do you believe in destiny, Lace?" His gaze bore into me with a probing glare.

"Not really. But Piper's call was strangely coincidental." Taking my briefcase from him, I had to push further. "Why? Do you?"

He grabbed my other hand into his and squeezed. "I do now." Staring deep into my eyes he whispered, "Lacey…just…be careful this weekend. Please." Then he stepped back releasing the elevator.

On instinct I responded, "Of course," but stared at him, bewildered, as the doors closed while a chill slithered down my spine. It wasn't that his parting comment had been particularly odd. But the way he said *be careful* raised the hair on the back of my neck.

I yawned, fluffed my pillow, and gazed out the window at the starry night. Nick had tried to warn me. He must have known I'd be in danger. Was his vision about Cole, that I'd see him at the party, fly out into a storm? Maybe he'd foreseen my accident, my plunge into the lake or perhaps my slip through time.

Drifting into sleep, I pondered how absurd the whole idea sounded. Could I have actually spiraled through time to 1949? Perhaps I was really in a coma lying in a hospital somewhere. I'd wake up tomorrow and find this was all a dream, a sweet, lovely dream. But if this was sleep, I wasn't sure I wanted to wake up. Ever.

Chapter 7

Midtown—November 2011

Nick Cramer sat at the counter of the Comfort Diner in Midtown. When a strange man sat next to him, he looked up from his newspaper.

"Sorry," he said, folding the paper to make more room for the new customer.

"Not a problem," Rob replied. "Do they serve anything here that's edible besides coffee?"

"I've been coming here for years. It's not the cheapest diner in town, but the food's pretty good. Great Eggs Benedict." He took a sip of coffee. "You from out of town?"

Smiling, Rob thought of the irony of Nick's suggestion, Eggs Benedict. He introduced himself, led the conversation exactly as he'd planned, while Nick, vulnerable, unsuspecting, reacted like the pawn that he was.

Rob left nothing to chance. Before long, he'd have Nick placed precisely where they wanted him. Lacey needed a man to trust, and Nick was the obvious choice. Rob would arrange for them to meet in the Emory law library where he and Drew could observe and orchestrate the entire event.

****

Sidney, Georgia—November 1949

It had been a week since I arrived in Sidney. Odd way of putting it, but how does one describe being ripped through a time warp into another era? I woke up early, slipped into the chenille robe Bobby had given me, and headed downstairs for coffee. Sunlight refracted through the cut-glass doors casting rainbow prisms that danced across the foyer wall. A paperboy tossed the morning edition onto the porch, as he peddled by on his bicycle. The whole scene left me feeling like an extra in a Technicolor version of *Leave it to Beaver*.

Opening the door, I took a deep breath of fresh air, picked up the Saturday paper, strolled toward the kitchen. Instinctively, I filled the old percolator with water, scooped Maxwell House coffee into the strainer, and turned on the burner. Not quite the morning Starbucks latte I longed for, but the aroma of brewing coffee did have a soothing effect.

The headlines reported that phone service had yet to be restored in Sidney, but Southern Bell had the problem well under control, expecting all lines to be operational by Sunday evening. That presented a major problem for me. By tomorrow night I had to concoct some elaborate ruse to rationalize why I couldn't call Piper or return home. Either that or come clean and tell Bobby about my inexplicable journey through time.

The more I thought about it, the more I realized I had to level with him. As bizarre as the truth sounded, a time slip was the only explanation that made any sense at all. Besides, I needed Bobby's help to find my way home. How could I make him believe the truth? I was living proof and wasn't sure I even believed my situation.

He'd surely think I needed professional help, unless…unless I could somehow prove I knew the future. Unfortunately, I didn't have an almanac like Marty McFly. My history expertise was limited to facts memorized for exams, not retainable knowledge. Until a few days ago, I hadn't even been sure who was president in 1949.

I'd determined that Bobby and Sandy worked at a nearby Coca-Cola bottling plant. They spent most of their time there during the week while I explored Sidney. When I stumbled upon the local library, my attention turned to familiarizing myself with *current* events and researching preliminary plans for the construction of Lake Lanier. I read magazines, examined old newspapers, and searched through microfiche probing for facts that would tell me exactly how far the Corps of Engineers had gotten with their plans to eradicate the town.

Harry S. Truman was president. Scanning a few newspapers had revealed that tidbit of information. But material about Lake Lanier proved far more elusive. After researching the whole week, I'd learned less than what I could have uncovered in two minutes on the Internet. The allure of 1949 may have enchanted my heart, but advanced technology of the twenty-first century had spoiled me, and the lack of available info at the touch of a finger constantly challenged my creativity.

Old newsprint articles confirmed that Buford Dam had been recommended for construction November 20, 1945. The project, initiated to protect Atlanta from flooding, would also supply power and water for industrial and residential growth. I guess they figured those benefits were more significant than the families and businesses the construction would displace. Still, the residents had been aware of the proposed plans for several years. So why had Bobby, and the whole town for that matter, seemed so oblivious to what was about to happen?

"M-m-m, that coffee sure smells good."

My hand flew to my chest, and I looked up to see Bobby standing over my shoulder. "Oh my gosh, I didn't hear you come in." The soft scent of English Leather mingled with the clean smell of Ivory soap, swirling a tingle down to my toes. I buried my nose deeper into the paper trying my best not to stare at his tight jeans and bare chest. "I'm sorry I woke you," I said, keeping my focus on the news.

"Nah, you didn't. I'm usually up by now, but why did *you* wake up so early on a Saturday?"

"I thought I'd make some breakfast for you and Sandy this morning since you've done so much for me."

"Well, don't let me stop you." He grinned that smile, that made my arms and legs go limp and swirled butterflies in and out of my stomach. He pulled out a chair and took a seat at the table. "Anything interesting in the news this morning?"

"Nothing much." My stomach pitching somersaults, I wanted to hurl myself into his lap but, instead, I folded the paper and handed it to him. "Here, you read and relax while I start breakfast." I stood, poured a cup of hot coffee, set it in front of him. "Now, what's your pleasure, eggs and bacon, pancakes, French toast?"

"Surprise me," he said, glancing down at the

headlines. "I guess you'll be heading home soon. It looks like you'll be able to get a hold of Piper by tomorrow night."

A lump tightened in my throat. "Yes, it does, doesn't it?"

I wanted to spill everything right then and there, but I knew blurting out the truth wouldn't be in my best interest. All week I'd run numerous scenarios though my mind and each explanation had ended in disaster. Despite my creativity, there was really no easy way to break that kind of news to Bobby, and my time was running out.

"So, I guess you'll be heading back to Atlanta soon?" Bobby asked.

Avoiding his question, I placed the frying pan on the burner, adjusted the flame, and popped several strips of bacon into the pan, then began whipping eggs in a small bowl. Dead silence.

Bobby put the paper down, poured milk into his coffee before taking a sip.

"Say, we're still on for our date to Looper today, aren't we?"

"Of course. I'm looking forward to it."

If I kept my attention on breakfast, maybe Bobby would go back to reading his paper. When the bacon crisped, I set the strips aside, poured the hot grease into an old can leaving only a glaze on the pan, then I cut veggies into small squares, dumped them onto the grease-coated skillet, and sautéed them.

"I have to run up to the plant this morning for a delivery." He flipped the paper over and sipped his coffee again. "I don't suppose you'd like to ride with me? I could show you around before we spin over to

Looper for the races."

"Sure. That sounds like fun," I replied without looking at him.

The ride would give me a chance to talk to Bobby about the lake and maybe about *future woman,* too. Besides, the old Co-cola bottling facility would be interesting. My mind drifted back to a Saturday I'd spent with my father when I was a little girl. Before Mother died, Daddy would take me to lunch almost every weekend. More than likely to give Mom a Lacey break, but to me, those days were heaven, our special times. He'd treat me like a princess. I could order anything I wanted on the menu, even if my choice was ice cream with a milkshake dessert. That particular Saturday, I'd had trouble deciding my drink de jour, and Daddy offered an old slogan to coax my verdict.

"Things go better with Coke," I announced without thinking.

"Things go better with Coke?" Bobby echoed. "That's right catchy. It might make a good jingle. Do you mind if I mention your idea at the next bottler's convention?"

Clearly the slogan postdated 1949. And I couldn't take credit for someone else's catchphrase, could I? What if the aftermath somehow changed history? The responsibility of being a visitor in the past suddenly became more significant.

"Bobby, it's really kind of dumb, don't you think?" I asked, trying to dissuade him.

Regardless of my best intentions, I continually slipped, using phrases that were obviously not typical 1949 vernacular. So far my lame excuse of city-girl slang had kept the Sidney residents from questioning my jargon. That combined with my ever-improving ability to change the subject had become my first lines of defense in concealing the mystery of my inimitable arrival to their ill-fated town.

"Breakfast is almost ready." I wiped my hands on a dishcloth then turned toward Bobby. "I hope you're hungry."

"It sure smells good," he replied, his nose buried in the paper.

I folded eggs over the veggies before melting thin grated pieces of cheese over the omelet and garnished the top with some fresh herbs from the garden.

"Can I pour some orange juice for you?"

"No thank you. Coffee is fine." He folded the paper, looked up at me. "What do you say we leave after breakfast?"

"That sounds lovely." Lovely was a good 1949 word, wasn't' it? Better than "sweet" which was what I almost said.

I looked forward to hanging out with Bobby…to sit next to him and drink in his intoxicating aura …*no, stop it Lacey. Don't get sucked in by a sweet-talking, self-absorbed…mmm, hot…absolutely dreamy…*Okay, maybe the '40s were starting to seep into my psyche. But I had to keep my mind clear and my body far enough away from Bobby that the chemistry, lust, or whatever was wreaking havoc with my common sense, wouldn't entice me. What was it about this man that stirred my deepest desire? Whatever it was, I had to block it out.

Despite my determination to thwart any infatuation, I found it difficult to resist flirting with Bobby Reynolds. This time I'd tempted him with a gourmet omelet stuffed with cheese, tomatoes, and peppers fresh from the garden. Bacon strips and grits on the side added the piece-de-resistance to my epicurean presentation. Why was I playing cat and mouse with someone I couldn't...or at least shouldn't get involved with?

The last thing I needed was to complicate my life, especially here. Sandy had confirmed that Bobby was a Casanova. And I'd totally had my fill of men like that. Still, whenever he got close my desire burned. Every inch of my body craved his touch.

"Here you go." I reached around his tanned, bare chest to place an over-filled plate in front of him.

"Ahhh, you sure know the way to a man's heart." He breathed in the aroma then looked at me. "Where's yours?"

"Oh, I never eat much in the morning." I set the pan and spatula in the sink, wiped the counters.

"I guess that's how you keep that swell figure."

Without looking around, I could feel him eyeing me. He wanted me, and the feeling was mutual.

"That, among other things." I cocked my head and smiled over my shoulder. "Enjoy your breakfast. I'll just go upstairs, slip out of this robe, and get dressed." That's right. Put a visual into his mind. *What am I doing?*

"Well then, I'll be waiting by the car with bells on." His fork sliced into his omelet, but his gaze followed my every step.

I reached for a strip of bacon, tore it in half, popped a piece into my mouth then slowly licked the grease from my lips as I left the room. Once out of sight, I shook my head in disgust, for my flagrant flirting. I just couldn't help myself. Bobby was addictive. How in the world would I be able to confess my absurd predicament, solicit his help, and still keep him at arm's length?

By the time I returned to the kitchen, he had finished eating, cleaned most of the dishes, and was outside leaning against the hood of his car reading the newspaper again.

"Sorry I took so long." I walked down the porch steps toward him.

"I'm happy to wait for you, princess, especially after you made such a delectable breakfast. You're a right good cook, Miss Montgomery."

I smiled knowing I had succeeded in impressing him, and the battle raged on inside of me.

"It'll take us about twenty minutes to get to the plant," Bobby said, pulling out of the driveway. "I'm glad you agreed to come with me this morning. Seems like we haven't really had a chance to talk much this week. You know, with Sandy around most of the time."

"I guess." *Oh, Lord. Please don't start asking questions I can't answer.*

"I've never met anyone like you before, Maddie. You say the strangest things, but you're smart, interesting, a real doll. It's been nice having you around the house." He fidgeted with the radio dials until a station came in clearly. "The phone lines will be up soon and you'll be going home, but I was hoping you'd let me come see you in Atlanta, take you out sometime."

"Yes, about that, Bobby." I had a week to think about this moment and still had no idea what to say.

"Before you say anything, I know Atlanta's not

right around the corner, but I don't mind the drive."

"No, you don't understand."

"Look Maddie, I know that Cole treated you badly. But most fellas aren't like that." He actually sounded a little nervous. "I'm not a bad sort once you get to know me. So, before you put the kibosh on the idea, can I tell you a little about my past?"

Maybe this was the break I needed. If Bobby opened up to me, it might make it easier to tell to him about my space-time continuum ordeal.

"Okay, go for it." I pulled my knees up on the seat and shifted toward him.

"Gofer it?" He scratched his head. "Right. Well, I know it may seem odd that my sister and I live together, but it hasn't always been easy for Sandy and me." He explained how he'd taken care of his sister after his mother's death, some of the details I'd already heard from Sandy. "It was the height of the depression. Dad had just started a new business and worked constantly. I'm sure the demands of the company were time consuming, but…I think he stayed at the factory to keep from thinking about Mother." Bobby glanced in my direction, and I nodded my head. I could tell it was hard for him to talk about his mother's death. I could identify.

"I know what you mean. My mom died when I was young, too. Dad had trouble coping so he threw himself into his work."

"Then you understand how Sandy and I ended up so close. I made breakfast, packed her lunch before school, and when I got home, I'd clean up, make dinner, help her with homework, and got her to bed if Dad wasn't home from the plant by her bedtime."

"That must have been hard for you."

He adjusted the rearview mirror, casually glanced at my reaction to his *Mr. Mom* scenario before continuing. "Nah, Sandy was a good kid. As she got older, we shared the household duties and took care of Dad together. When I graduated high school, she took over completely so I could attend the University."

"You mean the University of Georgia in Athens?"

"Yeah. I'd always dreamed of moving to New York someday, becoming a famous architect. I'm pretty good at drawing. Sketching plans and configuring angles came easily to me. I spent three and a half years at Georgia before the war broke out." He glanced at me again. "You remember how it was in 1941. All the fellas enlisted in the army, and I was no exception."

"Of course." I responded as if I'd been around then. "Pearl Harbor, 'a date that will live in infamy.' How could I forget?" One of the few quotes I recalled from that war.

"Yeah. So, when I returned to Sidney in '45, Dad was sick. Sandy and I took turns working at the plant and taking care of him while we both attended school. I still had my heart set on becoming an architect, but New York was no longer an option."

"Reminds me of Nick Cramer, a good friend of mine." I could tell his past was hard for Bobby to talk about, and I wanted him to know I understood. "Nick was the security guard at my office building, but he used to live in New York. He worked so hard to become a lawyer, but life threw boulders in his path."

"Boulders? What do you mean?" Bobby's interest clearly heightened.

"For starters, both his parents died before he was

ten. His grandmother raised him, but he had to work his way through school. Carly, his fiancée, convinced him to go to Columbia Law, assuring him that she could handle their bills. He had just started his first year classes a week before Al Qaeda flew into the World Trade Center. I'm not sure if Carly was in one of the towers or not. Nick never said, but I know she died in the—"

"Wait a minute. When the who flew into to the what?" He looked at me with a completely baffled gaze.

That was the worst screw up I had made since I arrived in Sidney. The World Trade Center, Al Qaeda, what was I thinking? "Oh my gosh, I'm so sorry. I didn't mean to go off on a tangent. You were talking about wanting to become an architect, but a lot of things happened to keep you from your dream. Your story just reminded me of Nick's. It's awful to have your dreams ripped away like that."

"That's life, I guess. Things happen when you least expect them." He slowed the car, turned right. "I'm not complaining though. Sandy is a peach. And Dad was going through a lot of heartache."

"I've been lucky in that respect. My dad pretty much planned out my entire life and made sure it happened…. So, you had to forget about your dream?"

"No. I just had to change my plans a little. I applied to Southern Tech, you know, that new school in Marietta. There were one hundred sixteen of us in that first graduating class, most of us Vets. My dream was within my grasp, but…" His voice trailed off.

"So what happened?"

"The day after graduation, Dad had a massive heart attack and passed away. Sandy and I were left to run the bottling plant."

"I'm so sorry, Bobby." I touched his arm, squeezed it. "Wait a second. So you two *own* the plant? I thought you both just worked there."

"Nope. You're looking at the head honcho." He grinned that smile, that damn irresistible smile. "But owning the plant isn't what I wanted to do with my life." He turned and nailed me with that sweltering sapphire gaze, and I felt as if he could see straight into my soul. "Don't get me wrong. I love Sidney, hoped to settle here one day, but I've always had the feeling I was meant to—"

"Do something significant." I completed his sentence. "I know exactly what you mean. It's like something is missing from your life."

"Right." He nodded. "Say, you're an independent woman, Maddie. And you seem to get along swell with Sandy. Don't you think she could handle the plant by herself?" He slowed the car down, turned onto another side road.

I adjusted my visor to block the sunlight. "Your sister may be trusting, but she's clever and perceptive. I think she could do anything she sets her mind to."

"Then you don't think she'd feel abandoned if I left things in her hands?"

"Not at all. Talk to her, Bobby," I encouraged. "Let her know how you feel and that you believe in her." It was hard to give him that kind of advice knowing full well his plan would never happen.

"That's what I thought, too. What we've been through has made us both stronger. And I wouldn't go to New York." He looked over at me. "The past few days, Atlanta looks pretty darn good to me." He purposely cleared his throat. "It's just that there are a few events happening here right now that I didn't expect. I need to stick around until things get straightened out."

Of course, the dam construction, he *did* know. "What things, Bobby?" The letter that had upset him that night must have been about the lake project. There was no way plans of that magnitude had escaped Mr. Reynolds.

"Hey, I didn't mean to get sidetracked." He quickly pulled the subject back to the original conversation. "I just didn't want you to think I was some ole country bumpkin with no future. I'm a proper suitor."

I tried to lead the conversation back to the lake project. "Bobby, I sensed something was bothering when you opened the mail last weekend. What's going on? Maybe I can help."

"Nah, I don't think there's anything you or anyone can do. Heck, you probably don't have any idea about what's happening up here in the boondocks."

"You'd be surprised at what I might know." This was my opportunity, the chance to gain his confidence and maybe help him, too. "You'll never know unless you trust me enough to tell me what's up."

"Oh, it's not that I don't trust you, Maddie. I guess we've all hoped the problem would simply go away. They've been jabbering about the plans for years and nothing has happened so far. But now..." His voice trailed off again.

"Go on." I prodded. "What's happening now?"

"They're trying to destroy—no, they're trying to erase Sidney from the map. And from the contents of the letter I received last week, they just might succeed."

I knew it. That's what put him in a tailspin, and rightly so. "Bobby, I'm so sorry." I put my hand on his shoulder, rubbed his arm.

"Hey now, I didn't mean to carry on about my problems. I just wanted you to know that I really like you, Maddie, and that I'm an okay fella. I'd like to keep seeing you. That is if you think you might be interested."

How could I dodge such a direct admission? I stammered. "Uh, you're a really great guy, Bobby, but—"

"But, I never like a response that includes a 'but'. I don't think I even like that word. Listen Maddie, the folks around here think I'm a pretty good catch."

"I'm sure you are. From what I've seen and heard you have plenty of interested women sniffing around." I turned my head away from him, sinking into my seat.

"Ah ha, so you've been checkin' up on me, huh?" He chuckled.

"Not at all, Mr. Reynolds. But it's a small town and people talk." There it was again, my obvious sassy flirting.

"And just what do 'people' say?"

"Never mind." *Concentrate on the lake project, Lace.* "Let's talk about your problem. What do you mean someone's going to erase Sidney? How could that even happen?"

"That's the worst part. The country I fought for, risked my life for, plans to eradicate my home, business, everything my family has built for decades." He made a left hand turn, drove toward a big red and white Coca Cola sign in the distance. "The Army Corps of Engineers want to tear down Sidney. Heck, they plan to take over most of the land between here and Gainesville to construct a dam and basin. Can you believe that?"

Scrambling for the right words to say, I shifted in my seat. "But maybe the dam will be really important to this area."

"Yeah, a reservoir could benefit the area, but do they have to destroy Sidney in the process? They want to help the public, but we *are* the public." Bobby's passion took over, his voice laced with rage. "Some of the families around these parts have owned their land for generations. And they have businesses, too, like Sandy and me."

It was hard to play devil's advocate. "Bobby, if the government has made plans like that, there isn't much you can do to stop them."

"We have to do something. Mayor Baxter scheduled a town meeting for next Friday night. Folks from all over the area will be coming here to Sidney to join forces. They can't fight us all." He pulled into the plant, parked the car, then turned to me and continued to plead his case. "Besides, we don't want to stop their plans completely, just move the dam further north or west, anywhere except smack dab in the middle of Sidney. We're going to fight it. The Corps of Engineers will have to carry us out one-by-one before they dig one shovel full from our land."

We both sat there for a moment in the aftermath of his fury before I spoke. "And they will, too." My tone was way too direct. Bobby reacted.

"What? Say, I'd never take you to be the enemy. You know about their plans?"

Oh, God. Where do I go from here? I had to tell

him the truth. "Yes, I know, but not the way you think." I bit my lip, twirled a strand of hair, pulling on it as if it would somehow spark an ingenious idea. How in the world was I going to break this to him?

"Maddie, if you know something that will help, you have to tell me." He twisted, looked straight into my eyes. "Please. What have you heard?"

I fumbled for the right words, but drew a complete blank. "Hey, why don't we go inside for now, talk about this later. I can't wait to see the plant. And we don't want to miss the first race either." I couldn't hold off the inevitable for long, but with any luck I could put it off until tonight.

"Wait a minute. You can't announce something like that then brush it off as nothing. Why do you think they'll succeed in destroying Sidney?"

"Believe me, Bobby, I'm not the enemy. I don't want you to lose your home, but I do have some insight about what will happen. I'll tell you everything I know. I promise, just not now." I opened the passenger door, paused, then spun back to look into his eyes. "Can we please go see the plant and enjoy the afternoon first?"

Realizing my exasperation, he drew a deep breath. "Yes, of course. I'm sorry I got worked up. I've been trying so hard to keep my feelings about this whole thing under control so I don't upset Sandy." He stepped out of the car, walked to the passenger side. "I have to find a way to make things okay for my sister, but not today." He offered his hand to help me out, and I obliged.

Strolling inside, Bobby began another of his illustrious guided tours explaining every inch of the factory, including how the assembly line worked. The process was antiquated, but fascinating. Still, I couldn't take my mind off of our imminent discussion.

I wasn't sure how to explain a crack in time to Bobby. He had opened the door to the truth, but walking through it wouldn't be easy. I couldn't simply blurt out the details. There had to be some way I could soften the blow and convince him I wasn't crazy at the same time.

Every single person he knew would be uprooted, forced to leave the land and homes they'd built, loved for generations. How could I explain there was nothing he could do to hold back destiny? But I had to warn him, tell him that in my world his future was etched in history books.

Chapter 8

Lake Lanier, Georgia—December 2011

Reeling in Nick had been a formidable challenge. It took months to lay out a plan, make arrangements, and set in motion a strategy to *secure* the security guard. Rob smiled at his ingenuity, how fate had played into his hands. Every element was crucial, cogs moving in unison to create the precision of a delicate timepiece. Each day he fine-tuned details, watched the puzzle pieces fall into place one by one. He would lead Lacey to the depths of the lake and spiral her into the grasp of death, to hell with collateral damage.

****

Sidney, Georgia—November 1949

The drive from the plant to Looper Speedway took about ten minutes, not nearly enough time to get into a heated conversation, thank goodness. With no idea of how to tell Bobby that his efforts to thwart the construction of Buford Dam would fail, or that the woman he found unconscious in the woods was a time-traveler, I needed every precious moment to brainstorm. Fortunately our racetrack date appropriated a few additional hours to sift through my options and come up with a feasible solution.

Though I really had no interest in seeing a bunch of car enthusiasts strut their stuff to prove who had the most testosterone, the races at Looper turned out to be a pleasant surprise. The drivers took such pride in their cars and hit curves at speeds well beyond the capacity of typical cars of this era.

The highlight of the evening was watching the men eat crow when Sara Christian raced old Max's car and left them in the dust. When she won that race, every one of those guys had their manhood knocked down a notch. The mere notion of a woman winning must have been a travesty. She deflated their chauvinism. Sara took home the checkered flag that afternoon, a giant leap for woman's lib, and much to my surprise I had a lot of fun.

On the drive home, we talked and laughed about the day's events.

"Sara really shut down those guys this afternoon." Bobby reached up, adjusted his rearview mirror. "She's a real spitfire."

"Yeah, she totally blew them away," I replied.

"Totally blew them away? That's an interesting description. I like it. Where in the world—"

"Isn't the evening beautiful?" I interrupted, derailing his train of thought.

"It has been nice today," he replied. "The weather has been unusually warm for weeks. Most years, morning frosts shrivel our garden by mid-October. I sure hope we don't end up paying for this warm streak next year."

"I had a lovely time, Bobby. Thank you for bringing me to Looper."

"The night's still young. Sandy has a date with Richie Thompson, so she's not making dinner. What do you say we take a spin around the square, then grab a burger and shake at Millie's?"

"I'd say that sounds delightful." Smiling, I leaned back in the passenger seat and gazed at the crimson colors flooding the sun-drenched horizon. A lone star shone brightly, winking at the dawn of the evening sky.

"Star light, star bright, first star I see tonight. Wish I may, wish I might, have the wish I wish tonight. Bobby, if you could have one wish, any wish at all, what would you ask for?"

"I don't know." He parked, hopped over the side of the car and opened my door before I had a chance to sit up straight. "When I was a boy, I'd wish that all the wishes I could ever make would come true. But, in point of fact, sometimes the things I thought I wanted most didn't turn out to be such great ideas after all." He held out his hand to assist me out of the car onto the gravel parking lot. "I guess I'd wish that I could make things right for my sister and for you, too, Maddie." He slipped his hand around mine, gently led me toward the path. "How about you? What would you wish for?"

"I'd wish for happiness, love, and the ability to make the right decisions."

"That's an odd wish," he said, putting his arm around my shoulder.

"Not really. It's not so different from your wish. What if you knew the future, what was best for your sister, but she thought she wanted something far different. Would you wish her to be happy now, or later?"

"Good question." He scratched the stubbly nubs on his chin.

"I'd wish the choice that would benefit her life the most." I looked at him, hoping he'd agree with my analysis.

"That's one thing I love about you, Maddie. You look at life differently than anyone I know." He pulled me closer in an affectionate hug.

We strolled to the pond then sat on a wooden bench just in time to see the sun's crimson farewell. Twilight welcomed a burst of starlight to the evening sky, and the full moon reflected off the water casting a romantic glow that shimmered over an audience of two.

"It's so beautiful, Bobby." I rested my head on his strong shoulder.

He angled my head to align our eyes, tucked a strand of hair behind my ear. "Yes, beautiful." He stared at me with a hypnotic gaze while the back of his forefinger grazed my cheek. "Emerald eyes, soft skin, smooth luscious lips...You're bewitching, Maddie Montgomery." He pulled me closer. "I've never felt like this with anyone before." Running his fingers through my hair, he gently tightened his grip, his breath soft against my cheek. "You're so different from the girls I've known. I burn inside when you're close to me."

When he opened his mouth over mine, I melted into his soft, warm kiss. My sub-conscious echoed a pale warning, a feeble attempt to keep me from getting hurt, but the muffled whispers drowned into a sea of desire.

****

Shoal Creek Baptist Church stood at the crest of the Chattahoochee River. Most Sundays, like this one, Bobby and Sandy sat in their family pew at the right front side of the sanctuary. It had been years since I'd attended a traditional church, but the hymns struck a familiar chord somewhere in the dusty corners of my mind. I felt a bit irreverent sitting there while my thoughts drifted back to the enchanting, sensual evening Bobby and I had shared the night before. I berated myself for getting sucked into the romance of the moment, succumbing to classic player tactics, but I could still feel the embers of desire smoldering deep inside of me.

After we got home from church, Sandy disappeared inside the house to get ready for her picnic with Richie, leaving Bobby and me alone for the first time since our romantic encounter.

"You want to go for a walk before we head inside?" Bobby asked.

"Sure." I was a bit nervous about what might happen should we find ourselves alone again.

He grabbed my hand, walked toward the sidewalk. "Say, about yesterday morning. I'm sorry I got so riled about the dam." He laced his fingers between mine, squeezed my hand. "I'm sure we'll get the Corps of Engineers to change the site, but I'd really appreciate any information you may know. The more ammunition I have going into the meeting Friday night, the better chance we'll have of saving Sidney."

"Well, I..." Scrambling for something to say to further put off the inevitable, I could think of nothing.

"I understand your hesitance Maddie, and I'm not asking you to take sides. But this is the United States. I fought to defend this country, our rights, and freedom." He stopped walking, grabbed my other hand, his eyes searching mine. "The Declaration of Independence defends our right to life, liberty, and the pursuit of happiness. That's what we're fighting for. And it isn't a trivial pursuit. Our land and homes are at stake. A lot of us have lived in Sidney for generations. Mothers gave birth here, and our ancestors are buried in the cemetery."

"Wait, Bobby, that's it," I jabbered.

His soapbox speech shattered, he looked at me completely muddled. "What are you talking about?"

"Oh, it's nothing. You just reminded me of something. Sorry, please go on."

Bobby's voice faded into the background as my own thoughts ruminated on the key to my dilemma: Trivial Pursuit. Piper and I had won tons of trivia tournaments in college. No one had a better repertoire of random information than we had. I may not be a history buff, but my mind brimmed with trivial facts and arbitrary data. I simply had to conjure up a match.

"Bobby." I interrupted again. "When is the town meeting?"

"It's this Friday evening, November 18th. Why?" he asked, clearly annoyed that I wasn't taking his explanation seriously.

A shiver trickled down my spine when he said November 18th. "My dad's birthday," I whispered. And exactly what I needed, a sure-fire way to convince Bobby I was undeniably from the future. This Friday, November 18th, 1949, I knew precisely what would happen. Not at the town meeting of course, but thanks to Daddy and Trivial Pursuit, that date had been etched into my memory. The perfect event, significant, unexpected, and irrefutable evidence to confirm I knew the future.

"Maddie, are you okay?"

Smiling, I reached for his hand. "I'm more than

okay. I'm fabulous."

"Well, I'm not gonna argue with that, but where did you go? You drifted off in a daze."

I squeezed his hand and threw out a lame excuse to cover my musing. "Sorry, I guess it's been a long day." Glancing around, I noticed we were approaching the elementary school playground. "Hey, let's walk over to the swing set. It's been ages since I sat on a swing." A bomb was about to drop on Bobby's life, and he might need to sit down when he heard what I had to say.

"All right. I could push you if you'd like."

It was a sweet gesture, but hardly what I had in mind. "Maybe, but let's sit and talk for a while, first."

I sat on a swing, began pressing my feet against the ground just enough to glide back and forth. *Here goes.* I drew in a long breath then slowly exhaled.

"I told you yesterday I knew some things about the dam, but I didn't tell you why."

Bobby sat in the swing next to me. "It doesn't really matter why. I just need as much information as possible to convince the Army Corps of Engineers that Sidney—"

"Bobby, this is important," I cut him off. "Maybe the most important thing you've ever heard in your life. So please, just listen." Grabbing the chain on his swing, I held him still. "You said yesterday that you trusted me, right?"

"Sure I do, but what does that have to do with Sidney?"

"It has everything to do with the dam project." Letting go of his chain, I pushed the dirt beneath my feet with the toe of my shoe, setting my swing in motion again then gazed over at the passionate man sitting next to me. My heart broke for him. What he was about to hear would devastate his life, change it forever. "What I have to tell you is going to be beyond difficult for you to believe, but I swear it's true, every word of it. So, please promise me you'll keep an open mind and hear me out." This was harder than I thought. I stopped swinging, clasped my hands, and stared at the ground. How could I explain my trip through time to Bobby without sounding absolutely certifiable? But I had to try.

"I promise, Maddie. Please, tell me everything you know. I'll believe you."

Turning, I searched deep into his eyes. "You say that now, but in a few minutes you may change your mind."

"I didn't mean to sound cavalier. I trust you." He reached over, grabbed my hand. "But trust is a two-way street. Can you believe in me enough to tell me what's troubling you so?"

"Okay, here goes. You remember when you found me in the middle of the woods, and we couldn't find my car anywhere?" Bobby nodded. I continued. "Well, there was a reason for that." I pulled my hand from his, ran my thumb over my bottom lip trying desperately to choose the right words. "And you've also said many times that I confuse you or say strange things, like we're not communicating very well."

"Yes. Go on." Clearly grasping how difficult this was for me, he squeezed my hand with reassurance. "You can tell me anything."

I looked at him with pleading eyes, praying he'd believe me. "Last Saturday night I was visiting my friend Piper at her lake house. We went to a party at a club on the north shore of Lake Lanier."

"I remember you talking about a party, but there is no Lake Lanier anywhere around here. You must have traveled a lot further than you thought."

"That, Bobby, is the understatement of the century." I closed my eyes, took another deep breath, held it, and then slowly released the air. *Just spit it out Maddie.* "I did travel a long way, but not by car."

"Okay, now you're confusing me." He rested his elbows on his knees, clasped his hands.

"I know. It doesn't make sense. But it's true." I squeezed my eyes shut tightly for a moment; softly bit the end of my fingernail. "Bobby, when I saw Cole fooling around with that woman at Piper's party, when I flew out into the storm, it was Saturday night."

"Right, I found you the next morning. We already talked about all of this." He reached for my hand again. "What's eating at you, Maddie? Tell me. You can trust me."

"I do. This is just so hard to explain. You see, I wrecked my car on Saturday night. But you didn't find me the next morning. You found me…sixty-three years earlier." I bit the corner of my lower lip, looked into Bobby's eyes and added, "Piper's party was Saturday night"—I paused—"May 26, 2012."

"What?" He dropped my hand, wrinkled his brow, and glared at me. "Judas Priest, Maddie. This is not the time to joke around."

"I wish I was joking. The reason we couldn't find my car is because it wasn't there. Not in 1949 anyway. My car, Piper, and my life is, was, or will be in 2012. When I fell backward, rolled down the ridge into the lake, I somehow passed through a crack in time, or a worm hole, some strange anomaly that brought me here to 1949."

"What in the world are you talking about? Do you even hear what you're saying?" He stood, gazed down at me as if I was completely insane. The compassion drained from his face.

"I know how crazy this sounds. I didn't believe it myself at first. I thought it was some kind of a joke, too." Grabbing the chains of my swing, I pulled myself up. "I'm trying to tell you that I can't call Piper or go home."

I shoved the seat out of my way, walked a few steps then leaned on a tetherball pole, and stared at Bobby, waiting for some kind of a reaction. There was none. He simply glared at me. I didn't know what I was expecting, but I figured he'd at least have some kind of physical reaction. "Bobby, do you have any idea how hard this is to tell you? I don't know how I got here. I don't know why. I don't know how to get back to 2012. I don't know if going home is even possible. I don't know how to explain any of this. All I know for sure is that I'm here, and I was born in 1984."

Finally, I saw his tension drain. He walked toward me. Did he believe me? Was he coming over to console me?

"Maddie, come on. You hit your head really hard the other day and were out cold for hours. You're probably still confused. You need to see a doctor."

Absolute denial. He really thinks I'm completely certifiable.

"You said you trusted me. So believe me when I say I'm not confused." I paused my explanation for a moment to let the news sink in before continuing. "I

111

know exactly where I am, where I came from, but more importantly, I know about the dam, what will happen to Sidney, because in my world your future is past history."

He placed his hands on his hips. "That's impossible. Surely you don't expect me to believe—"

"I expect you to keep your promise. I'm telling you the truth, and I can prove it."

"Sure you can." He reached out his hand to me. "But for now, come with me. We'll go back to the house, and you can lie down for a while."

Jerking away, I felt my body stiffen. "Stop patronizing me. I can prove that your future is my past." I shot the tetherball out of my way with a burst of temper, but it swirled back around the pole and hit me in the knees.

"This should be good. Okay, exactly how do you intend to prove to me that you flew here from the future, landed 1949, thirty-some years before you were born?"

"First of all I didn't fly. I fell, or was sucked here, or materialized by some strange anomaly. I don't know. How I arrived is moot." Every muscle in my body tensed. Bobby had to believe me, and how I delivered this news would determine what would happen next, for both of us. "This coming Friday, November 18th, 1949, I know something that will happen that day. Something that I would never know for sure unless the event was written in history."

"And just what would that be?" His sarcastic tone would have infuriated me if the circumstances had been different. My fists clenched as I swallowed my anger.

"The National Baseball League is going to

announce its Most Valuable Player. Who do you think will win?"

He kicked at the dirt, bent over to pick up a small stone. "Probably Stan Musial, Ralph Kiner, or maybe Pee Wee Reese. What difference does that make?"

"What if I told you none of those guys will win? What if I said Jackie Robinson was going to win the National League? And the American League MVP, I know that winner, too." I never thought I'd be thankful for the hours I spent memorizing baseball facts. The date stuck in my mind because of Daddy's birthday. He loved baseball. Memorizing little tidbits of baseball trivia was one more attempt I'd made to win his love. Obviously that had failed miserably, but at least the information might convince Bobby that I knew the future.

"Maddie, it's unlikely Jackie Robinson will win. He's a great player, but face it, people are prejudiced." He fiddled with the stone in his hand then inspected it closely. "Robinson may deserve to be recognized, but no one expects him to win."

"Well, believe me when I say that Jackie Robinson will win. And Ted Williams will win the American League."

He stared at me in silence, with an odd glower.

"Say something, Bobby. I'm not crazy. I swear I'm not."

"I promised I'd keep an open mind," he said, "but I'm not a chump. Even if you manage to guess the MVPs—"

"It's not a guess. I know how insane this sounds. Believe me. I've been trying to unravel this paradox all week. God, I wanted to tell you. But I was afraid you'd lock me up in some loony-bin."

Disappointment flushed his face and grew into a contorted frown. "I'd never do that. I don't think you're crazy, just confused." Clenching his left fist around the stone, he ran the fingers on his right hand through his hair.

"I'm not confused, Bobby. Please, just defer your judgment until Friday. If the events I've cited don't happen, then you can take me to a doctor or walk away, whatever you want. But if I'm right, will you believe me then?"

Rolling the stone between his fingers again, he paced back and forth in a small rectangle before speaking. "What do you think you know about the dam and Sidney?" he asked.

"I know that no matter how hard you try, you can't save your hometown."

He shot a fiery glare my way. "Why?"

I walked over to his side, touched his shoulder. "Because in my world, Sidney no longer exists. They built that dam and a lake, too, a huge lake with seven hundred miles of shoreline. In the process, they displaced a lot of people and submerged a town, your town, Bobby. In my world Sidney lies at the bottom of Lake Sidney Lanier."

"Lake *Sidney* Lanier? How appropriate." His eyes exposed the internal wound he must have felt. "No." He bellowed, flung the stone from his hand then slammed the tetherball with his clenched fist, spinning the ball until the rope wrapped completely around the pole. "We're going to fight the dam. And we'll—"

"You'll lose, Bobby." My emphatic tone melted into empathy. "Please trust me about this. I know it's not what you want to hear, but nothing you do will save Sidney. The lake will swallow this entire area."

Pushing the unwinding tetherball aside, he kicked at the dirt again. "Why are you saying this?" He sneered. "Did the Corps of Engineers put you up to it?"

I let out a long deep sigh and dropped my chin. "You know that's not true."

He ambled to the edge of the dirt playground, bent over, picked up a worn baseball half hidden amongst blades of grass and weeds, and began tossing the sphere upward, then catching it. His glare bore into me. "I *will* save Sidney. They can't just sweep in here and destroy our homes, our lives."

Tucking my hair behind my ears, I edged closer to him. "If you don't believe what I've told you, wait until Friday. See who wins the MVPs. I wouldn't lie to you, Bobby. I just want to help you."

Snapping around, he scowled with the rage of a thousand betrayals. "Help me?" He tossed the ball higher, rolled it in his hand. "According to you there's not a damn thing anyone can do."

"I can't save Sidney, but maybe I can do something to help you and your friends. In my time, I am a lawyer. I know the laws are probably different here, or rather now, but I might be able to help you and the people who live here negotiate with the Corps of Engineers."

Still tossing the ball, he grimaced. "You don't get it, do you? This is not about money. It's about our homes, our lives. Our grandfathers built this town with their bare hands, built homes, schools, and stores. This community is our birthright, our heritage. For God sakes, Maddie, don't you see? We all built our dreams around this town. And now you say they're going to obliterate everything that took generations to build? They want to demolish the entire town as if it were some old, worn-out building."

"I get that, Bobby. I'm not heartless. God, you have no idea how much I wish Sidney would be spared, that you could change the future. But in 2012, Sidney no longer exists. It's nothing more than a ghost town submerged beneath the lake."

I walked across the grass, stood next him, silently staring into the lush, green woods. My thoughts swirled, envisioning a sea of water engulfing the trees, swallowing the land, schools, and churches. "It will all disappear, Bobby, the square, shops, homes…and the racetrack, too. That's why Looper sounded so familiar to me. Piper had just told me about Looper resurfacing during a drought."

"Maddie," his eyes burned a deep cobalt blue. "This is our home, the only home most of us have ever known. They can't do this. I won't let them." He pulled back and threw the baseball as hard as he could, projecting his rage through the ball. The tiny sphere ricocheted off a telephone pole, shattered a streetlight, and skidded down Main Street.

"If you did that in my time—"

"I'd be arrested?" he hissed, snapping at me.

"No, you'd be skipping that ball like a rock across the lake." My heart broke for him. I wanted to hug him, pull him close, and let him know that everything would be okay. But it wouldn't be okay. I wasn't sure if his life would ever be okay. "You can't change history, Bobby," I whispered, taking his hand in mine.

He yanked away from me. "I can try," he said and started back toward the house.

"Not if you really want to help your friends." I caught up to him, grabbed his arm trying to comfort him, but he jerked away and continued walking, still glaring at me, his eyes burning with fury. "I can't talk about this anymore. I need time to think." Picking up his pace, he kicked at everything in his path.

"Bobby, please, let me help you." I jogged, trying to keep up with his pace. "Where are you going?"

He shrugged, said nothing. We walked back to the house in separate silence like strangers. Nausea rolled through my stomach. My heart ached. I couldn't bear to see him like that, broken, defeated. I wasn't sure if he believed me or hated me for playing such a cruel joke on him. Either way, he would see the truth, in time. Jackie Robinson would be named the National League MVP, Ted Williams would win the American League…and Bobby's beloved Sidney would sink into the bowels of Lake Lanier.

Chapter 9

Lake Lanier, Georgia—January 2012

The construction site for Piper's new home was just across the ridge, visible from the far corner of Rob's deck. He'd watched the crew struggle for weeks, knowing exactly how to solve their problem. If he'd planned the whole incident, he couldn't have devised a more perfect scenario to befriend Piper. The solution was simple mathematics and an ideal opportunity to win her trust.

Sweet-talking the opposite sex had always come easily for him. His charm and dashing good looks left women defenseless. Predictably, Piper played into his hands. He would have enjoyed Piper had he not been so preoccupied. His obsession drove him. He woke up thinking of Lacey, spent his days plotting a foolproof strategy to rip her from the life she knew and spiral her into the gates of hell. His end would justify the means.

****

Sidney, Georgia—November 1949

As I suspected, my crystal ball fortune telling hit Bobby in the head like a baseball bat. After our talk Sunday evening, he buried his nose in paper work, retired early without saying goodnight to me, or his sister. The entire week he stayed at work late into the evening, missed dinner, and I heard him leave at the crack of dawn each morning as he headed back to the plant. Sandy said he had the holiday rush to contend with, but I knew he was avoiding me, which only deepened my attraction to him.

All week I slaved over maps at the Sidney library, searching for familiar roads, trying to calculate the future shoreline of Lake Lanier. When I walked into the house on Friday evening, Bobby was sitting on the edge of a parlor chair. His hands clasped, arms resting on his knees, he stared intently at the radio as if it were a TV, listening to John Cameron Swayze's *Camel News Caravan*.

"Let's go hop scotching around the world for headlines," Swayze said, beginning his fifteen-minute report. Most of his words drifted silently on the air, but just before he spoke his famous "That's the story, folks..." he announced the highlight of the day: the National League MVP winner, Jackie Robinson.

"God made him to last," Bobby whispered, then put his hand over his mouth and fell back into his chair. A few moments later, he turned the radio off, walked outside, leaned on the porch railing, and lit up a cigarette.

"Those things will kill you," I said, walking through the front door.

"Another one of your predictions?" he asked.

"No, another fact from the future." I leaned against the rail next to him. "Besides, I've never seen you smoke before, why now?"

"Yeah, well I never really enjoyed cigarettes like everyone else seems to. I just keep a pack in the desk, smoke from time to time, you know, when the guys get together." He flicked the ashes off into the bushes below. "I don't really know why I lit up. But I guess if there was ever a good time to smoke, this would be the moment."

"So, does that mean you might at least entertain the idea I could be from the future?"

Turning, his eyes locked on mine. "Maddie—"

"Never mind, you don't have to say anything, Bobby." I looked down the street at the setting sun. "I know how bizarre this whole story sounds. But I'm not certifiable." Leaning against a post, I looked down at my shoes.

"Certifiable?" he asked.

"Another expression from my time. It means crazy. I'm not insane, so don't even think about signing me up for a padded room."

He took a short drag from his cigarette, blew out the smoke. "That's what I was about to say."

"That you think I should be locked up in a loony bin after all?"

"No, Maddie." He flicked his ashes again, stared at the red tip as the smoke swirled into the air and disappeared. "I was about to say that I didn't think you were crazy, even last week. I can't explain why. But as whacky as your story was, I was terrified you were telling the truth."

"Really?" My jaw dropped open, and I stared at him, speechless.

"Yeah. Maybe I'm the one who is certifiable. But all last week I went over and over every detail I could recall about you, everything that had happened since the moment I found you. Odd things you said, not finding your car, the lake you kept asking about…" He ran his fingers through his hair, a habit I'd noticed he performed repeatedly whenever he was troubled. "I thought about your wish on the star," he continued. "And the question you asked me earlier that evening. The truth is your explanation pulled everything together."

"Oh Bobby, you do believe me." I let out a deep sigh of relief, moved closer to him. "I have no idea how this happened, or why. It was a freak event—I mean an absolute anomaly."

"That would be an understatement." He raised an eyebrow, and for the first time in over a week, his lips softened into a smile.

"But things happen for a reason. Maybe that's why I'm here, to warn you or help you somehow. You have no idea how difficult it's been for me to wrap my head around—sorry, I mean to accept that I'm actually here in 1949."

"I'm sure your ordeal must have been terrifying. The hardest part for me, though, was trusting my own instincts." His eyes searched mine. "When I thought about that night at the pond, how we'd grown so close in such a short time, I knew *you* believed every word you told me. And I was so torn, confident you wouldn't lie to me, but half praying you would."

"Half-praying I lied?" I asked, a bit confused.

"Yeah." He pushed a stray strand of hair from my cheek, tucked it behind my ear. "Don't you see? If you were telling the truth…" He drifted off in thought for a few seconds before continuing. "I knew what I felt, what *we* felt, was real, but that also meant that Sidney would disappear from the face of the Earth." He grabbed my hand. "And if by some outside chance you were lying, I might save Sidney, but I'd lose the only woman in my life that I've ever l—"

"Bobby." I cut him off abruptly as a march of tiny ants nibbled at my spine sending a shiver down to my toes. I couldn't bear to hear him say the hollow words I'd heard so many times before: that he loved me, wanted me, or that I was somehow significant to his life. Pulling my hand back, I turned away, unable to look him in the eyes. "Please, don't go there. We had a few moments, but that was all."

Sandy had confirmed her brother was a womanizer. Facts were facts and I had to keep them ever-present in my mind. He had tempted me, but I wouldn't, no, I couldn't fall for him.

He flicked his cigarette into the grass, watched the last embers on the butt flicker and die. Then, placing his hands on my shoulders, he turned me to face him. "You can't say you felt nothing that night at the pond, or when we—"

"We kissed, that's all." It was hard enough to be played by a jerk like Cole, but Bobby had touched my heart like no one ever had before. If we got much more involved, I'm not sure I'd survive him walking out of my life. Besides, sooner or later I'd have to return to my own time. Bobby Reynolds and the entire town of Sidney would simply vanish; fade into nothing more than a distant, foggy dream.

"Maddie." He crooked his finger, placed it under my chin, and searched my eyes. "I know what I felt, and you were right there with me."

Trembling, I pulled away. "Yes, I felt something, compassion for the man who found me after my accident and opened his home to me."

"Compassion?" His brow wrinkled, the light in his

eyes dimmed. "Maybe, but you couldn't have kissed me that passionately fueled simply by compassion. Something happened between us that night and you felt it, too. Why are you trying to shrug those feelings off as a meaningless kiss?"

"Listen Bobby, once I do what I can to help you and your friends, I'll need to find a way to get back to my own time."

Despite every effort I'd made to dissuade him, he was right. We had connected, and I wanted him more than any man I'd ever known. But his own sister had warned me that love was simply a game to Bobby. He took pride in conquering women to add to his mental trophy case, led them around by the nose with his imaginary *brass ring* and boy was he good at it. I wanted to believe him, let myself love him, run into his arms, not simply his bed. No, I had to stop myself from falling in love with Bobby Reynolds before it was too late.

The cobalt fire in his eyes turned cold, filtered by an icy blue haze. "Right. Of course you want to go back to your own time. You've built a life there." He turned away from me, walked to the other side of the porch. "Well then, let's get to work. Baxter's town meeting is at seven thirty. We have a little over an hour to figure out how we'll explain why the leader of this crusade against the Army Corps of Engineers has changed his tune. Obviously, we can't tell them about your journey from the future. But we have to come up with a feasible story to justify why I'm switching camps, and be ready to convince hundreds of families that they have no choice but to give up their homes."

****

The meeting, held at the local theater, drew scores of men and women. Most lived within a hundred-mile radius of Sidney, and all were filled with anger, apprehension, resentment, bewilderment, and a host of other emotions. Over seven hundred families on the displacement list would be uprooted, relocated to other areas to allow the construction of Buford Dam and the yet unnamed Lake Lanier.

Mayor Baxter called the meeting to order, thanked the crowd for attending, and went over the basic issues they all faced before yielding the floor to the keynote speaker. When Bobby Reynolds took the stage, the audience roared and clapped. Some whistled and everyone cheered. But once he began to speak, a hush fell over the entire room.

"It's wonderful to see this big turnout," he began. "I see so many friends out there and a few unfamiliar faces, but we're all in the same boat here and there's a lot at stake. Like me, some of you live in family homes that were built by your great grandparents. It's hard to imagine living anywhere else."

A lanky man in the middle of the crowd stood up and yelled, "That's right. And we're not gonna let anyone take our homes away." Everyone clapped in approval, nodding and yelling out short quips.

"You tell him, Mac," an elderly man added.

"Yeah, they can't take our land," said a tall blond man standing in the back of the room.

"It's a hard pill to swallow when your own country tries to take your home," Bobby agreed. "And it's not just our homes. Churches, businesses, cemeteries, schools, our whole lives are rooted in this land."

A loud whistle came from the back of the room and

more cheers followed.

"Most of you know me," Bobby continued. "You know I've opposed this dam's location since the Army Corps of Engineers first announced their plans."

"You've been fighting for us from the beginning, Reynolds." Tom Richards shot up and yelled from the far back right. "But the question is, how can we stop 'em?"

Bobby held up his hand motioning Tom to sit back down. "Yes, I've been at the battle front of this fight from the start. We all know that Congress authorized the Dam in '46. And most of us agreed and understood that a dam could really benefit the area."

Bobby ran his fingers through his hair, and I knew he was searching, struggling to come up with just the right words to strengthen his case. "Joining the Chattahoochee and Chestatee Rivers will improve downstream navigation, flood control, and provide a great power supply to our area. And most of you know that they even plan to build a huge reservoir." He glanced over at me, then back to the crowd. "Actually a lake. All those things will make the land around here more valuable and improve our lives."

"You're right, Reynolds, but not if our land is under water. When they decided to destroy our homes, the picture changed," Sidney's resident doctor, Gary Meyerson, said.

"Exactly. It's not the dam we're fighting, it's the location."

"Yeah," came a voice from the middle of the crowd.

"Why can't they build the dam out in the state forest somewhere so it don't make none of us move?"

A leather-faced man to the left added.

"Good question," Bobby broke in. "And that's exactly what I've been working on, especially this past week. I met with every official that I could corner who was involved in the dam project. We've gone over maps, driven up and down the countryside and calculated every inch of territory from Atlanta west to Alabama and north to the Carolinas looking for possible alternative locations."

"Fweeeit," Laurence Johnson whistled. "I knew it was a good idea to have an architect on our side. If anyone can find a way to save Sidney, you can, Bobby."

"Thanks Larry. And I've looked at every piece of land remotely feasible. I calculated and discussed each option...but the problem is...the Sidney area is the obvious logical choice. It's a perfect natural basin and the most efficient, no, the only place the dam makes any sense."

The crowd hushed, every eye glared at Bobby.

"So they finally got to you." A voice from the crowd yelled. "How much did it cost 'em?"

"Yeah, what's the going price to put the screws to your friends these days?" A bald man jeered.

Bobby ignored the heckling. "I understand your feelings. And...we can fight it, but in the end it won't make a difference. The government has the legal right to take our land. It's called Imminent Domain. And they're determined to do just that."

Soft murmurs rumbled through the theater. The shock at Bobby's apparent turncoat position rolled like a tidal wave through the rows of people. It quite possibly could have created a riot had it not been so evident that their spearhead representative had as much or more at stake as the rest of them.

"Now calm down, everyone." Mayor Baxter stood near the stage. "You all know Bobby. Give him a little respect."

"Thanks, Mayor," Bobby said. "Look, everyone just settle down and hear me out. I don't want to lose my home any more than you do. My plant is in Sidney, too. We're all in this together and you know me."

A man dressed in overalls from the back row stood up and yelled, "We thought we did."

Jeers and boos roared through the room as people nodded in agreement to the hecklers.

"Any government man comes on my land, he'll be lookin' into the barrel of my shotgun," Bill Jones, a local farmer threatened.

"Then you'll be my guest in a jail cell at the station," advised Baxter.

"We have a right to protect our property," George Milton demanded.

"Come on Bill, and you, too, George; give Reynolds a chance to speak his mind," Michael Bailey, the preacher from Shoal Creek, said.

"That's right," Jim Butler added. "He's been with us all the way. Let's hear him out."

"All right, everyone take a seat," Bobby insisted. "Listen, you all know I've been the ring leader of this whole movement. I was the first one to challenge congress and the ACOE when they suggested that the dam be built here. Sidney is the only home I've ever known, and it kills me to think of losing it." He walked to the front of the stage. "But there comes a time when we have to face the facts. And the reality is we can't stop the dam construction. The Corps of Engineers have made up their minds. Our energy is better served now thinking of how we're going to adjust. We need to prepare ourselves, take steps to come out of this as whole as we can."

"A lot of us are going to lose acreage." Bobby announced. "And if you don't know whether your property is in the construction zone or not, I have maps with me here to show you exactly where the lines are drawn, but we don't have to lose our homes."

"What do you mean, Reynolds?"

"I mean the government will pay for our parcels, compensate us for the structures built on them. Or, arrangements can be made to move existing homes to new sites."

"What good will that do, Bobby? And what about Sidney?"

"We can negotiate our compensation and some of you may even end up with better land or homes than you have now." He pointed to an older man in the front row. "You, Harvey. Your land hasn't produced a good crop in years. And your barn, Earl, is about to collapse. You'll be able to build a brand new one." He paused, looked toward the back of the room. "And Frank, you've been talking about moving your family away from that flood plain, up to the foothills for the past five years. This doesn't have to be a disaster if we stop fighting the inevitable and start thinking about our options."

"And Sidney?" A soft voice from the far end of the first row questioned. "What about Sidney."

Bobby gazed down at the tearful face of his sister. "We can't save Sidney, Sandy. But we can rebuild the town around the shores of a great new lake, instead of that old pond." He glanced over at me, then back to his sister. "Say, maybe we can even convince them to name the reservoir Lake *Sidney*. As God is my witness, Sandy, I promise you that as long as I am able, I'll find a way to rebuild our home."

It was hard to put a price tag on years of hard work, countless memories, childbirths, and deaths. And it would take a long time to soothe their souls, but most of them listened intently as Bobby explained his reasoning, one he wasn't completely convinced of himself. When he introduced Miss Madison Montgomery, the lump in my throat burst into a full-fledged anxiety attack.

"Maddie is a very close friend of mine from Atlanta, and she knows a lot about the law. She's offered to help us in any way she can. You can trust her." Bobby paused, looking straight into my eyes. "I'd trust her with my life," he added and motioned for me to join him on the stage.

I stood, walked slowly up the steps to the platform. When I got to center stage I looked at Bobby.

"Go ahead," he whispered. "You can do this."

Turning, I gazed out at the impassioned crowd. "I can't even imagine what you all must be going through," I said. "But if anyone needs help negotiating compensation or has questions about the best relocation options, please let me know. I'll be staying with the Reynolds for a while to make myself available, free of charge, to anyone who might need assistance. And I promise I'll do my best to make sure your family will come out of this smelling like a rose."

Bobby and I answered questions for the next hour

or so. We stayed until every last query had been satisfied, sitting down with individual families to provide as much support as we could. I pointed out where I believed the most valuable land would be and suggested they look into procuring those areas. A 2012 map of Lake Lanier would have been a Godsend, but my memory would have to suffice.

We planted seeds of their destiny, but it would take years for them to take root and grow. Their lives were etched into the heart of the land. Most of the people in that theater respected Bobby, knew whatever he said was in their best interest, but many still swore they would greet the government with loaded rifles in order to protect their homes.

****

After the meeting, when Bobby and I were finally alone, I realized his aloof behavior during the previous week hadn't been what I assumed.

"So that's why you were out early and home late all last week," I said as we drove home. "You weren't at the plant at all. You were driving the countryside, talking to all the right people."

"Yeah, well I really was hoping to come up with an alternative site. But when I got down to the nitty-gritty with the Corps of Engineers, I knew we didn't have a chance of beating them."

"So even before you heard that Jackie Robinson was the MVP, you knew I was telling you the truth."

He glanced over at me, chuckled. "Hey, your story is the craziest thing I've ever heard. It defies all common sense, but sometimes if a leap of faith is all you have, you've got to take it."

"Your faith must be pretty strong." I touched his

shoulder. "Thanks for believing in me."

"You did a fine job back there, Maddie. I'm thankful you backed me up."

"Backed you up? I feel as if I destroyed your dreams. The least I could do was try to help your friends."

"You didn't destroy anything. But I understand your wish now," he replied as we pulled into the driveway. "You knew what would be best for me, for everyone. And you chose to help us instead of letting us work for God only knows how long on a futile delusion. Thank you for that."

We got out of the car, walked inside.

"It's been a long day. I guess I'll turn in for the night." I started up the steps.

"I'll walk up with you." He put his arm around my shoulder.

"I truly hope in time you'll see that—"

"Shhh," he said, stopping at the top of the staircase. "Not another word of apology. It took a lot of guts to do what you did, especially after what you'd been through." He moved his body closer to mine, backed me into the open door of my bedroom. "Tell me about the future, Maddie. What's it like living in a world sixty-three years from now. Do we finally find a way to end wars? What wonderful inventions does the world discover?"

We sat down next to one another on the edge of my bed, and I told him about my world.

"We still fight wars, just differently." I explained the cold war, Vietnam, and the Al Qaeda attack on the World Trade Center that killed almost three thousand innocent people, including my friend Nick's fiancée,

Carly.

"It doesn't sound like we learned anything from WWII after all."

"The future isn't as different as you might think. We've walked on the moon and can see someone on the other side of the earth as we talk to them on the phone. We can hold computers in our hands, and everyone has a mobile telephone they carry with them called a cell phone." I continued explaining some of the major changes that would evolve over the next sixty-plus years.

"Convenience and speed prompted new inventions. Things are a lot faster, like transportation, cooking, and ways to communicate. There are passenger airplanes that travel at one point five times the speed of sound, and the Internet, a communication system wired into machines that look like flat television screens, can give us almost any information at the touch of a finger." I went on and on, explaining everything from microwaves to jet skis. "You'd love them." I instinctively placed my hand on his knee and he caressed it in response. "It's like riding a motorcycle, speeding across the lake surface with a watery wake spraying behind you." He smiled in approval. "People are mostly the same, though. We found a cure for a lot of diseases. Polio and smallpox no longer exist, but others have taken their place." I'd never really thought about the magnitude of inventions and innovations society had made over the last sixty years, or reflected on the tragedies we'd endured.

"Overall, the future sounds pretty keen," Bobby said. "I wish you could show me your world, Maddie." His voice softened. "How do you plan on getting back?"

"I don't have a clue." That was something I hadn't thought about since the first day I arrived here. Was there some kind of door I passed through? And if I whooshed through time for a purpose, would I be pulled back to the future when I completed the task? There were no answers.

"Well, perhaps we can figure out that clue together," Bobby said. "We'll go back to the place I found you. Of course, if I help you." He paused. "I'll be cutting off my nose to spite my face." Then, raising an eyebrow, he offered a wry grin.

"What do you mean?"

"I'm getting used to having you around, Miss Montgomery. Maybe it's selfish, but part of me doesn't want you to find your way home."

He moved closer to me. "Don't fight it, Maddie. I don't know why or how you're here, but something strong and good has brought us together. And I know you feel it, too."

He touched his lips to mine, lightly at first, then deeper, harder as our desire burst into an impassioned flame. Warm honey flooded my veins. We fell back on the bed, clinging to each other as if our life force fed upon that kiss. I melted into him, yearned to crawl deep inside of him and never come out. What was it about this man? His kiss erased my memory of the past and of every other man I'd ever known. We held each other entwined in an insatiable embrace and drifted into forbidden fantasy.

Hours later, I awoke, still wrapped in Bobby's arms with a soft contentment radiating over me. But I knew it was only temporary. Soon, we would find the time portal, and I would be sailing back to my own world. I had always believed everything happened for a reason. I wasn't sure why, but deep in my soul I knew I was meant to be here with Bobby, perhaps to come to terms with his future, his destiny. But when I fulfilled that purpose, would I have to return home, alone, to find my own?

As much as I had fought our connection, when Bobby simply held me in his arms, I felt as if our very souls merged. I'd never experienced emotion like that before. Even though I knew full well he was a *cad*, I also knew I'd never love anyone like I loved Bobby Reynolds.

Chapter 10

Lake Lanier, Georgia—February 2012

"Tell me more." Piper said, giggling like a schoolgirl.

Rob almost felt guilty that manipulating her had been so easy. She fell right into his hands. He spent hours each week massaging their friendship. Piper had to trust him implicitly. She would be the key to his success, or failure. No element held more importance.

As Lacey's best friend, Piper had become the perfect pawn to lure his unsuspecting mark to the lake where he would implement the final stages of his intricate plot. There were still many details to set in place, but he had Piper right where he wanted her. And Lacey would have no idea that an innocent visit with her best friend would change her life forever.

****

Sidney, Georgia—November 1949

When Bobby returned home from work early Monday afternoon, he found me sitting on the front porch swing, engrossed in *The Diary of Anne Frank*, a recent release Sandy had loaned to me. I'd always thought about taking the time to read the classics and, as they say, *there's no time like the present*, or in my case, the past.

"So, are you ready to go find your crack in time?"

he asked, leaping up the steps.

"Already?" Placing the book beside me, I gazed up at him.

"Now is as good a time as any. Besides, I thought you wanted to get back to your life. I don't expect it'll be as easy as putting on some ruby slippers and clicking your shoes together saying 'there's no place like home,' Dorothy," he teased.

"True, but there's still so much I promised to do here. A lot of people are depending on me."

"Well, I don't think we'll trip over a time warp the first time out. But I thought we could take a gander around the area." He offered his hand.

"I guess we could start searching for clues." Taking his hand, I stood, walked down the front steps toward the car.

In truth, I wasn't at all ready to return to my own time. If I found my way back to my world, I'd never see Bobby again. Despite my internal alarms screaming 'beware', I was drawn to him on some cosmic level. I couldn't bear the thought of never again looking into those intoxicating sapphire eyes. And even if he was a cad, that didn't mean I couldn't enjoy myself temporarily. If I only had a few weeks left to be with Bobby then maybe I should make the best of that time. Carpe Diem, right? Surely I could protect my heart for a few weeks and enjoy what little time I had left with the man of my dreams.

****

"This is it," Bobby said, pointing to a fifteen-foot wide clearing at the base of a steep ridge in the middle of nowhere. "This is where I found you. It was doggone hard to get you back up that hillside, too." He smirked and raised his eyebrows.

"Wow, what in the world were you doing out here?" I asked. "It's pretty far from Sidney, and there's nothing but forest in all directions."

"From down here, there isn't much to see, but when you're up there"—he pointed to the peak of a steep precipice—"it's like standing at the edge of heaven. That ridge is my favorite place in the world. I come here to gather my thoughts. You can see forever. When I'm up there, I see life in perspective. Come on, I'll show you."

Grabbing my hand, he pulled me up a winding trail to the top of the ridge. We could see for miles, all the way to the mountain range that lined the horizon beyond the basin. The view was breathtaking.

"See. What did I tell you?" Placing his fists on his hips, he gazed across the panorama, marveling at the landscape before him.

"It's beautiful, Bobby. How in the world did you ever find this place?" The ridge was far from the beaten path. Dunes of lush foliage hid the narrow mountain road beyond.

"Hiking with friends. We were searching for the falls. Look over there, through those trees." He pointed to a clearing where a picturesque waterfall splashed over a rocky ledge into a pool and creek below. "The first time I saw this view, I was hooked. I've been coming back here for years. Lucky for you, huh."

"No kidding." I shuddered at the thought. "If you'd never found this place, I might have died down there." Gazing across the ridge again, I felt a chill trickle down my back. "Have you ever experienced *déjà vu*? You know, when you feel like you've been somewhere before? Some people say déjà vu is sensing an experience from a past life."

"Sounds like science fiction to me, but then your time-jump sure opened my mind to consider the realm of the impossible." He paused a beat. "You have been here, though. I found you right down there." He pointed to the clearing below.

"I know. But standing right here feels distinctly familiar, like I've seen this view, that mountain range before."

"Is that possible?"

"I don't know. The view feels comforting somehow." Maybe I had been here before, but when?

"Say, you said you were at a party that overlooked the lake, right? Maybe you didn't drive that far from Piper's home after all."

"That's it, Bobby." I threw my arms around his neck, hugged him.

"Glad to be of service." He chuckled, pulling me closer. "So what did I say to get that kind of reaction from you? I'll be sure to implement a repeat performance."

I kissed him on the cheek, hugged his arm. "It was what you said about Piper's house. I remember the details as if it were yesterday. When I drove to the lake to spend the weekend with her, you know, the day before the party?" Bobby nodded, narrowing his eyebrows in interest. "The moment I arrived, a sense of awe washed over me. Her property was so beautiful." My memories kicked in as I recounted the details of that afternoon.

When I turned into her driveway, the gate opened to a half-mile jaunt through a secluded forest glen. Her elegant stone and timber frame home snuggled into the mountainside and was surrounded on three sides by the sparkling lake. Piper rushed from the front door, arms out to hug me before my car came to a complete stop.

"How did you know I was here?" I asked, stepping out to greet her.

"I'm not psychic." She laughed and hugged me. "The front gate triggers an alarm."

"Good idea." I glanced around at her complete seclusion. "You're pretty isolated out here."

Mountain laurels surrounded by the last blooms of wild flame azaleas painted the landscape. Beyond, a cliff lined with lush greenery abruptly plunged into the shimmering lake. Her home had an open porch nestled between two half-round, outdoor stone rooms; one led to the front entrance, the other a covered porch. The tone accented the background with unpretentious elegance.

She gave me the grand tour then glanced at her watch, "Let's go relax with a glass of wine, sit on the deck for a while. You have to see the view over the lake while there's still enough sunlight to see the mountains."

She tugged at my T-shirt, and I followed her into the kitchen where she poured two glasses of pinot noir before heading outside. I'll never forget that amazing view. The deck, nestled into a natural ridge, stood high above a silent, glimmering cove lined by slender sand-beaches cocooned in hardwoods. The sun reflected off tiny ripples that glittered over the water.

I gazed across the panorama. "This is amazing, Piper." Hidden behind the gentle curve of the shoreline, I felt a sense of secret seclusion.

"I never get tired of it." She motioned for me to sit down in the wicker chair next to her. "I've got steaks ready for the grill. We can watch the sunset while we cook, then sit in the hot tub later."

"So, dressed in T-shirts, old worn cut-offs, and barefoot we sipped fine wine and grilled filets, relishing in Piper's paradise. The sunset was breathtaking. The glowing sphere cast a magenta flame as it sank into the glistening lake. I leaned against the deck rail, mesmerized, watching the last spark fade into the evening sky.

A squirrel scampered up a tree close by, bringing me back to the moment.

"Bobby, this is the same view. I'm sure of it. Those mountains. I watched jet skiers dart in and out of that cove the next afternoon, too." I mused. "I think her home was over to the right a bit, maybe a few hundred yards, and the trees were much larger, but there's no doubt in my mind. This is the view from Piper's house. Of course the lake was down there below the ridge." I pointed to the area where Bobby had found me.

"So this is the shoreline of the new lake?" he asked.

"I'm absolutely certain it is."

"Then this is the site for my new home. I've thought about buying this property for the last few years. And now that I'm forced to move from Sidney, I can't think of anywhere I'd rather live." He gazed across the panorama as if envisioning the future view. "Sandy will love it, too. I could buy enough land to build a place for her over there"—he pointed to the right—"so she can live right next door."

"No, Bobby." I looked at him with an air of

concern. "Not over there. Piper is going to inherit that land from her Aunt Alice. You can't buy that land or you'll change the future. And if you build a house for Sandy there, I might never come back to 1949."

"Okay then, I'll buy all the land off to the left. When you help people relocate, you better be sure to steer them away from all of this property. Say, did you ever mention Piper's last name?"

"Taylor, why?"

He belted out a deep belly laugh. "Piper's aunt is Alice Taylor?"

"Yes. Do you know her?"

"Know her? I guess you could say that. Sandy babysits for the Taylors now and then. She loves to watch their five-year-old daughter, Alice."

"Well then, I guess I need to make sure that the Taylor family buys the property next to yours." I laughed.

"Okay, well now that we have that solved, let's go down and search for your time portal."

"I wish I knew what to look for."

We made our way down the steep hill, looking through bushes, stomping on the ground, anything we could think of that might help us uncover a crack in the earth's surface or a warp in time. After hours of roaming the area, we were still mystified at how I'd transported from 2012 to 1949. We were about to leave when Bobby saw something glittering in the brush.

"Say, what's that shining in the thicket over there?"

"Where? I don't see anything." Squinting, I perused the area.

"Right over here." He walked into some tall grass, bent over, picked something up, and inspected the object. "Aww, I guess it's nothing." He rolled it over in his hands. "It's just some broken piece of something or other. The sun reflected off the metal. Whatever this thing was, it has seen better days."

"Let me see that." I strolled toward him. He reached out, dropped the fragmented object into my hand. "Dear Lord," I said, inspecting the piece.

"You know what that thing is?" he asked, wrinkling his brow.

"It's pretty mangled, but yes. This is my cell phone, or at least what's left of it."

"Your what?"

"Remember when I talked about the future? I told you how everyone had telephones they carried with them. This is my phone, Bobby, and solid proof I was transported through time."

"Let me see that thing." He grabbed the phone from me. "You mean this little thingamajig is a telephone?"

"Yes. You've never seen anything like this before, have you? Of course you haven't. Don't you see what this means?" I didn't wait for answers. "This proves with absolute certainty that I'm not crazy."

"I never thought you were. Well, maybe at one time I may have questioned the idea, but I believed you, Maddie. Really I did." He inspected my phone more closely.

Looking around, I scavenged the area again for anything else that may have traveled through the portal with me.

"To be honest, there were times I even thought I might have lost it. But this proves I came from the future. There really is a portal. And it's got to be around here somewhere."

"I wouldn't go showing this contraption to anyone else, Maddie. You could open a real can of worms." He handed my phone back to me.

"No worries, I won't show this to a single soul, except maybe Sandy, when the time is right." I wasn't about to have anyone else think I was a nut case.

"Yeah, we'll have to tell her the truth pretty soon. But for now, let's focus on the issue at hand."

"The portal is close, Bobby. It has to be. We may not see it, but it's here." I kicked at the underbrush, pushing bushes aside, searching for something that looked different or odd. Bobby walked a few yards away, spread his feet apart and crossed his arms.

"This is where I found you, stretched out here." He pointed to the ground directly in front of him. "So, if you can't see a crack or a door of some kind, how will you get back to your own time?"

"I don't know. I can't help but think I was transported back to your time to do something. Maybe I'm not finished yet."

"Let's say you're right. Does that mean that when you do whatever it is you're supposed to do, you'll get pulled back to the future?"

"I have no earthly idea. I'm new at this time slip thing, too, remember? I guess we just have to wait and see."

****

Sidney, Georgia—December 1949

For the next few weeks, I spent most of my time working with Sidney area residents. I wasn't surprised when Ben Taylor phoned and asked me to sit down with him and his pregnant wife Margaret to discuss their property options. I met Alice Taylor that day. Piper's father was about to be her brand new baby brother. When she looked up at me with innocent eyes, a flash of the last time I ate dinner with Piper conjured a memory.

"Aunt Alice always dreamed of living here on the lake." Piper picked up the spatula and flipped the filets while I gazed across the deep blue water beyond her deck. "She really liked you, Lace. Aunt Alice said that from the moment she met you, she'd felt comfortable, as if she'd known you all her life."

"Alice treated me as if I were her own niece, and I loved her." Twilight dusting the horizon across Lake Lanier drained every ounce of tension from my muscles. I turned my attention back to my friend and the enticing aroma of sizzling steak. "She was the only mother figure I had. You're a lot like her you know?"

I smiled at the thought of Piper's comment. Alice had known me all of her life, at least she had met me as a child. How odd. Before I slipped back in time, I had already met Alice. The memory of me must have slept deep in the corners of her mind for years before she met me as a ten year old.

Alice talked nonstop about her mommy's new baby. She hoped it was a girl, so she could dress her up and play dollies with her. But, knowing what I did, that her younger brother would be Piper's father, I took the opportunity to tell her how wonderful it would be to have a little brother. Her little ringlets bounced with every word. She looked so adorable. It was hard to believe that cute little girl would grow up to be Piper's aunt.

Bobby proved serious about the property up on the

ridge. He purchased the acreage, spent hours walking the lot, measuring, and making calculations to determine exactly where to build his new home.

A few days before Christmas, on a Saturday morning, Sandy and I had just started to clear the breakfast dishes when Bobby hopped up and announced he had a surprise for me.

"Come on, Sandy can finish the dishes this time." He glanced up at her and winked, took my hand, and led me toward the front door.

"He's right. You go on, Maddie. My brother has been working all week on his secret project."

"Oh, so this is a conspiracy. How long have you two been plotting against me?" I teased.

"No plot, now get out of here. I'll see you this afternoon," she said.

"This afternoon? Where *is* this surprise?"

"You'll see." Bobby squeezed my hand, pulling me out the door. "Let's go."

He refused to tell me anything about his big surprise, but it didn't take long for me to figure out he was headed up to his new "lake" property. He had forged a dirt road through the woods allowing the Hudson to pull right up to the ridge instead of parking below and hiking up the steep incline like a few weeks earlier.

"You've really been working hard on this land. It's only been a couple of weeks since you bought the property. How did you do this so fast?"

"When I set my sights on something, I don't dilly-dally," he said, granting a toothy grin. "I just called in a few favors. A couple of tractors cleared the brush out. We worked around most of the trees."

"What a nice surprise." I smiled.

"Oh, this isn't your surprise." His mouth bowed into a boyish smile. "I'm laying the foundation for the house next week, but there's something I wanted to build first. Come on, I'll show you. It's this way."

He hopped out of the car, opened my door then paused. "I hope you like it."

"I'm sure I'll love whatever it is."

Hiking through the excavation to the little trail that led down the hillside, we made our way to the clearing where Bobby had found me.

"Now close your eyes," he said, taking my hand to guide me. "Over here just a few more feet. There." He put his hands on my shoulders. "Okay, open your eyes."

"Oh my gosh." Bobby had constructed a wooden bench on the exact spot he had found me. On the back of the seat he'd carved a heart and etched the words, *Bobby & Maddie, November 6, 1949.* "The day we met. Bobby, it's…it's wonderful."

"I don't ever want us to forget this place, *our* place, where you came into my life, Maddie Montgomery. Come sit down."

"This is so amazing." I ran my fingers over the outline of the heart. "I love it."

"I was hoping you'd say that. That heart means something, you know."

Raising my eyebrows, I gazed at him through my lashes. "It does?"

"Don't tell me that love becomes obsolete in the future." He smirked, took my hand and whispered, "I'm crazy about you, Miss Montgomery."

A lump formed in the middle of my throat. "I…I don't know what to say."

"You don't have to say anything. I know you want to return to your own world. But if you, I mean when you do, I want you to know you'll be leaving behind someone who loves you very much."

"Thank you, Bobby."

I really didn't know what else to say. I knew what I felt, but I couldn't...wouldn't...or at least shouldn't. So, I gave him a big hug and kissed his cheek. "Thank you so much for this," I whispered in his ear then rested my head on his shoulder and stared across the clearing. My emotions were in overdrive. There was no denying I loved Bobby, too, but what difference did that make? Any way I looked at my situation, I ended up hurt, again.

We'd determined that the portal had to be where he'd found me, right in front of Bobby's new bench. But if that was the location of the door, apparently the opening had a mind of its own, like a game master, and I didn't have a copy of the rules. I had no idea when, or if, the time fairy would yank me to another era. Maybe some great force triggered the whole process, or perhaps my time-slip was a one-time event and I'd be stuck in the past forever.

The truth is, that scenario wasn't so bad, not if I would be near Bobby. I wouldn't mind being stuck with him. But then again, his affections, as amazing as they made me feel, were fleeting at best. I didn't want to be simply one of his conquests.

"Bobby, I feel like I'm in some kind of limbo here. I could be sucked back to my own time at any moment, or maybe never. I don't know what to feel."

"I guess doing all this was a little presumptuous of me." He ran his crooked finger across my cheek.

"No, not at all. The bench is a very sweet gesture and means a lot to me. I just need time to figure out this whole ordeal."

"I understand," he said, but his face said something else entirely.

"I love the bench. Really I do." I paused for a moment, unsure of whether I should say my thoughts or not, then decided to continue. "You do know this beautiful bench will end up at the bottom of the lake though, don't you?"

He chuckled. "I know, but that doesn't matter. We'll know it's here. Besides, I built another one just like it at the top of the ridge." He pointed up and slightly over to the right. An identical bench built into a natural ledge stood at the top of the ridge, facing what would one day be Lake Lanier. "I'm hoping someday we'll sit on that one and look out over the water together."

"That's a lovely dream," I replied. "It's funny; I've gone on and on about what *your* future holds. I wish I knew what the future held for me."

"It will be what you make of it, Maddie," he said, stroking my hair.

"I don't think it's that easy." I ran my fingers over the back of his hand. Just touching this man stirred desire deep inside of me.

"Life is like a box—"

Instantly I sat up straight, grabbed his arm, and burst out laughing. "You're not really going to say that are you?"

"Say what?"

"A box of chocolates?" I asked.

"No, but that's not a bad analogy."

"Sorry, go on," I said, still giggling to myself.

"Life is like a box of Cracker Jacks. You won't see your prize until you reach in and pull it out. What I mean is, you can't be too afraid to go after what you want in life, Maddie. But first, I guess you need to figure out what that is."

A knot coiled in the pit of my stomach when he said those words, and I knew he was right.

"You're shivering. Here, take this." He took off his jacket and draped it around my shoulders. "Let's get you back to the house."

The whole drive home I thought about what Bobby had said and done. He really stuck his neck out trying to convince me that he cared, that he was falling in love with me, and it was getting harder and harder to resist his charismatic charm.

****

We'd put off Sandy countless times, evading the truth about my unique arrival in Sidney. Her curiosity about why I'd chosen to stay here instead of going home to Atlanta mounted with the passage of time and living in the same house made avoiding the inevitable increasingly difficult. Though Bobby had purchased some clothes and personal items for me, nothing got past Sandy. She sensed a mystery. From day one she had opened her home to me, offering whatever I needed without question. More than anyone else, Sandy deserved to be told the truth.

I'd always planned on revealing to her the details of my time-slip, but after enlightening Bobby, I knew the incident wasn't easily explained despite my knowledge of the future. How could I even broach the subject with Sandy? *Hey Sandy, lovely weather isn't it?*

Oh by the way... No, the truth about my bizarre arrival in Sidney had to be delivered with finesse. Bobby would help ease the blow of course but try as we might, we couldn't figure out an easy way to break the news to her.

On Christmas Eve, the whole ordeal erupted when Sandy cornered me. Where was Bobby when I needed him?

"Hey, Maddie. Can I ask you a personal question?"

I looked up from my book and gazed at Sandy sprawled across the oversized chair she adored. "Sure," I said, closing the hardback.

"Now, don't take this the wrong way. I really like having you around. It's like having a sister, but..." She drifted into thought for a moment.

I knew exactly what was coming. And this time there would be no evading her questions. Sandy knew Bobby was at work and pouncing during my downtime provided an inescapable scenario. In short, I was trapped.

"What's up?" Taking a deep breath, I crossed my fingers and braced for the inevitable.

"I was wondering why you never talk to your family or friends. That just strikes me as odd. Are you hiding from the Mafia or something?"

I laughed. "No, nothing like that." Fidgeting with the fringe on the pillow next to me, I tried to think of an appropriate answer. "It's hard to explain."

"I'm all ears, and I'm good at keeping secrets, too. Just ask my brother." She eked out an I-got-you grin, pulled her legs up, and wrapped her arms around them.

"I'm sure you are." Placing my book on the side table, I repositioned myself to look straight at her.

"So what's cookin'?" She raised an eyebrow, waiting for my response.

"I'd like to explain. I'm just not sure where to start." I paused; bit the corner of my lip. "Let me ask you a question first. It may sound a little strange, but humor me, okay?"

"Sure, ask away." Relaxing, she put her elbow on the arm of the chair and leaned her chin into the palm of her hand.

"Do you like science fiction?" *Good ice breaker, Lace.*

"Jeepers. That's an odd question. Like *The Invisible Man*, or *Flash Gordon Conquers the Universe*?"

I laughed. "Maybe both."

"Sure I do." Her forehead crinkled and eyes narrowed. "Hey, you're not really an alien from another planet, are you?" She spoke in jest with no idea how close she really was, but at least she had an open mind.

"Not exactly." Crossing my legs, I sank into my chair, preparing for the explanation of the century.

"Okay, now you've got me worried. Should I call the men in the white suits?"

"Not yet. But before I'm finished with my story, you just might want to."

Sandy glared at me in utter silence, confusion filtering across her face. A soft thump on the front door broke the quiet. Simultaneously, our heads snapped to see the doorknob slowly turn. The front door creaked, opened a few inches, spraying a brilliant beam of late afternoon sunlight into the foyer. Our eyes glued to the entryway with aliens percolating through our minds; I think we both half-expected some extra-terrestrial to make a timely entrance. Sandy edged toward the fireplace, grabbed the poker. The opening door blocked our view of the entrance prolonging the eerie stillness.

A moment later, Bobby strolled inside, one hand carrying his briefcase, a donut in his mouth, and his nose buried in the newspaper.

"Jeepers-creepers, you scared us to death," Sandy scolded. "Don't sneak around like that."

"Didn't you say you'd be home late this evening?" I added.

"Say, can't a fella walk into his own house without getting smacked with the third degree?" Chuckling, he put his briefcase down. "I finished inventory sooner than I expected, but I'll go back to work if I'm not wanted."

"Absolutely not, Bobby, you're just in time." I opened my eyes wide suggesting a heads up. "Sandy was just asking me why I haven't talked to my friends or gone home."

"Well, it's about time you spoke up, Sis." He laughed. "This will be a lot more interesting than an old newspaper." He threw the paper on the ottoman, plopped down in his favorite chair, crossed his legs, and rested them upon the hassock. "Don't let me stop you, Maddie. Go right ahead. Gopher it," he said and winked at me.

"Okay, what's the big secret here?" Sandy asked. "Did I miss something?"

"No. But sit." Arms crossed, I pointed my chin toward her chair. "I think you need to be sitting when you hear what I have to say."

For the next hour, I revealed the entire recondite story, leaving out the sordid details about Cole, of course, as well as some intimate moments with her brother. I described Piper's party and all of the lore about Lake Lanier, my car accident, hurling into the black lake, and spiraling through a time warp. Bobby chimed in now and then, explaining my MVP prediction, and the information he'd discovered about the dam construction. Sandy sat beside us completely absorbed in every word.

By the time we finished the story, her mouth hung open, and she gaped at us, wide-eyed and blown away. She asked a few questions, but her overall reaction flabbergasted me. I expected skepticism, some smart remarks, and tons of questions, but I never expected her to sit back in her chair and accept everything she heard as God's truth.

"I know your story sounds really kooky, but ever since you showed up here, Maddie, I knew there was something extraordinary about you. The way you talked, reacted to certain things. But holy mackerel, you're from the future, this is killer-diller."

"Are you serious?" I asked. "So, does that mean you believe me?"

"Of course I believe you? Bobby does, and I trust him. Besides, as cock-eyed as it sounds, your story makes sense, in a wacky sort of way."

"Oh my gosh, I was so afraid you'd think I was nuts. But I'm not, Sandy, and I can prove it." Dashing up the stairs, I tore into my bedroom to retrieve my proof. Moments later, I stood in front of Sandy, holding the mangled smartphone in my palm.

"Jeepers, what is that thingamajig."

"It *was* my cell phone." I handed my mangled phone to her.

"And that means what?" she asked, inspecting the object.

I sat back down and went through another litany of the many advances the future held. I told her how computers had changed the world of communication, explained the Internet, cloud computing, and how everyone in the future carries their cell phones with them everywhere.

"You mean everyone has one of these, and they can talk to anyone in the world whenever they want to?" she asked, examining the phone more closely. "How'd they ever come up with a doohickey like this?"

"You got me." I laughed. "But if you ever hear of a company called Apple or Google for that matter, invest everything you've got in them."

She gawked at me, smiled as if I'd given her a key to the future. "I'll remember that."

"Sandy, I'm so relieved you don't think I'm crazy."

"I know you're not a weirdo or anything. Really and truly Maddie, you're story is about the keenest thing I've ever heard. I've always thought it would be so boss to go back in time, especially if I could change things and make them better." She gazed upward, smiled as if imagining the possibilities.

"That's what scares me. I don't think it's a good idea to mess with time. What if I change some little thing, say or do something that could have a domino effect? I might slightly alter a seemingly insignificant detail that could cause me to never be born. Or what if I saved some child who was supposed to die, but instead grows up to be someone like Hitler. The thought scares me."

"I don't look at it that way," she said, leaning back in her chair again. "Maybe you're here because it's your destiny. What if everything you do here in 1949 is supposed to happen?" she asked. "Still, just the idea of time travel, it's fantabulous."

Bobby's sister couldn't hear enough about the future. She plied me with questions and said fate had brought me to the past, to them. She agreed I might have been sent here to do something important, but was convinced the entire process was my destiny.

The odd thing was, unlike Bobby, Sandy never questioned my sanity or doubted my word. She listened to the most bizarre story she'd ever heard and trusted me enough to believe me. Trust had never been my strong suit, and I felt compelled to protect her blind faith. In hindsight, I think maybe, just maybe, Sandy Reynolds had niggled at a festering wound within me, a defensive pattern that had haunted me since childhood.

Chapter 11

Lake Lanier, Georgia—February 2012

"I can't tell you how much this means to me, Nick." Rob shook his hand, patted him on the back.

"Hey, I'm the one who owes you," he replied. "It's the least I could do. Cole is a freakin' opportunist. It's high time he tasted some of his own medicine."

It had taken Nick several weeks to befriend Cole. The man wasn't easily dissuaded from his self-gratifying agenda unless something gave him reason to believe it was in his own best interest. But Nick's aspiring attorney prowess would prove far more effective than a sleazy silver tongue. Rob had warned him of Cole's Achilles' heel, and Nick exacted the perfect plan. An offer to play wingman fed into an already inflated ego to forge a dangerous liaison that would snare Cole in his own deceptive web.

****

Sidney, Georgia—April 1950

The clipping sound of a rotary lawn mower floated through my open window, stirring me from slumber. I awoke enveloped in soft scents of cut grass, honeysuckle, and jasmine. Rubbing sleep from my eyes, I squinted to see the Little Ben on my nightstand. It was almost noon. I yawned, stretched my arms high above my head. Then, dragging myself from bed, I plodded toward the bathroom.

The last three and a half months had been a whirlwind of activity centered on the plans for the new Buford Dam. I felt like Erin Brockovich crusading for the rights of the locals. For the first time in my life, I was touching lives in a truly significant way and my passion soared. Meeting with scores of individual families, I walked countless lots and read tons of legal contracts. But despite the mountain of work, I was totally energized. This was the reason I'd studied law, not to defend low-life criminals.

But changing the world was exhausting. I'd been waking at the break of dawn and working most nights into the wee hours. This morning had been a real treat. I hadn't slept till noon since I was a teenager. After showering, I brushed my teeth and hair, threw on some capris and a T-shirt, then ambled downstairs to join the rest of the world. The most scrumptious aroma of fresh peaches, cinnamon, and coffee lured me toward the kitchen. Filling my cup, I called out to Bobby and Sandy then searched for the yummy baked goods that had been prepared.

The house was still. Where could they be? "Hey, is anybody home?" No answer. "Bobby…Sandy…anyone here?" Grabbing my coffee and the morning paper, I wandered into the parlor, sat on the sofa.

The Sidney Gazette continually amazed me with its uplifting highlights and positive news, a far cry from the murder and mayhem that splashed across the pages of the newspapers back home. Today's feature boasted the upcoming Georgia State Fair, opening the first week of May at the Central City Park in Macon.

A flash of movement on the front porch drew my

attention. Placing my cup and paper on the coffee table, I moved closer to the window, pulled the sheers aside with one finger just enough to see without being seen. There, with his back to me, Bobby knelt on the porch floor; his muscular back rippling with a rhythmic motion, thrust and pull, thrust and pull, thrust and pull. My heart raced. I glared hypnotically, breathing heavier with each movement.

"You must really like peach ice cream," Sandy whispered from behind me.

Snapping around, I held my hand over my heart. "Geez, don't do that," I screeched. "My gosh, you scared the bejesus out of me."

"Sorry. I didn't mean to frighten you. I wasn't sneaking around though. You were just really preoccupied when I walked in."

"Oh that, well, I was just…"

She laughed, placed a glass of iced tea on the coffee table, and sat on the sofa. "I know exactly what you were doing. You were watching my brother again."

"No I wasn't." My emphatic reply was lame at best.

"Were, too. Golly Maddie, I'm not blind. I've seen the way you look at each other. You can't keep your eyes off of him, and you'd have to be oblivious not to see how crazy he is about you."

"You're imagining things, Sandy." I pranced away from the window, leaned against the back of the overstuffed chair.

"Did you have a steady fella back in Atlanta?" She sank into the soft pillows, sipping her tea.

"Actually I do…did…will…" Visions of Cole flashed through my mind. What did I ever see in him?

He had been a classic image of the perfect catch on paper. But my criteria for relationships had truly shifted since I arrived in Sidney.

Sandy raised an eyebrow. "It sounds like you're not very sure."

"Well, I'm sure about one thing. I have absolutely no romantic interest in your brother. We're just friends." That was the biggest lie so far. I couldn't stop thinking about Bobby, but there were so many reasons not to get involved with him.

"Are you trying to convince me, or yourself?" She licked her finger then ran it around the top of her glass, creating a high-pitched whirring sound. "It's so obvious you both are crazy about each other. What I don't understand is why you try so hard to fight the attraction."

"It's...complicated." What could I say? *I love him with all my heart, but I refuse to date a player again.* And then there was the whole ripped through time thing. I had no idea when or if I'd simply wake up one morning back in 2012. This was a prime time to change the subject again. "So, what did you mean when you said I must really like peach ice cream?"

"Come on, I'll show you." She popped up from the sofa and grabbed my hand, pulling me toward the front porch.

When I saw Bobby laboring on his knees my heart ka-thunked so hard I felt sure he could hear the pounding. Braced between his thighs was an old wooden bucket that had been hidden from my window view. The pail overflowed with rock salt and water and had an inner container locked into the center attached to a crank and handle. When we approached, he paused from his task, sat back on his heels. He wiped his arm across beads of sweat on his forehead then looked up at us with that dreamy smile.

"Say, where's that iced tea you were going to bring me, Sis?"

"Oh, sorry, Bobby. Maddie distracted me. It's in the parlor, but I drank most of it. I'll go pour you a new glass." Stepping back inside, she quickly disappeared.

Bobby's sweaty chest glistened as sparks of sunlight danced across his muscular abs. Tiny streams rolled over hills and valleys before vanishing below the waistband of his jeans. My eyes fixated on the vision before me, I breathed deep silent breaths trying desperately to contain my burning desire.

"Good morning, Maddie," he said, breaking my daze.

"Good morning." My eyes drifted up to his face. "It's a beautiful…morning."

"It's close to lunchtime, isn't it?" He glanced down at his watch.

"It sure is," Sandy answered, pushing the screen door open with her foot. She walked across the porch, offering a glass of iced tea to her brother. "But it's high time Maddie slept in for a change, so don't you tease her."

"Yes, ma'am." Standing, he took the glass from Sandy, downed the entire contents, and handed it back to her. "Thanks, Sis, and you're right. Maddie deserves a little pampering. That's why I decided to make ice cream." He wiped his brow with the back of his arm again. "So which one of you ladies is ready to relieve me for a few minutes?"

"I will." Sandy bent down, began churning,

cranking the handle round-and-round. "Millie's peach ice cream recipe is the best I've ever tasted. And half the fun is making it."

"I thought you two might enjoy it." Bobby added, "I hope you like peach, Maddie."

"I just love peaches." The thick, southern drawl loomed from behind me.

Turning, I saw an attractive young woman strutting up the front walkway toward the porch. In her hands, she held a platter covered with aluminum foil.

"Ugh. Sharon Howard," Sandy whispered.

The woman sauntered up the steps. "Bobby Reynolds, I do believe you've been ignoring me lately." She offered her package to me. "Be a dear won't you, and take these scrumptious, chocolate brownies into the kitchen."

Stunned, I held out my hands on instinct, took the plate. Who was this brash excuse for a woman? Her bright pink shirtwaist dress, flared with far too many petticoats, clashed with the short, bright red hair she had curled in a Liz Taylor want-to-be style.

"You promised you'd call me weeks ago, Bobby, but I haven't heard a peep from you." She batted her eyelashes, practically drooling over him. "I know how busy you are with the dam business, so I thought I'd drop by and bring you some of my blue-ribbon brownies. I'm entering them in the state fair again this year. I know how you adore chocolate, and I just couldn't resist bringing a batch to you."

"Sharon." Bobby's eyes widened. He glanced over at me, then back at her. "How nice of you to think of me."

A self-centered smile splashing over her face,

Sharon reached for the plate I was still holding, pulled a brownie from underneath the foil, then walked over, and began feeding it to Bobby.

"There now, aren't they delicious? So, what is all of this talk about peaches? I love them so."

"I don't know many Georgians that aren't partial to them. It must be an unwritten law." Bobby leaned against the column and crossed his arms, enjoying every second of Sharon's overbearing attention. "My favorite dessert is peach cobbler with homemade ice cream on top." He licked his lips, and my heart did flip-flops. But I wasn't sure if it was Bobby's sensual smile or Sharon's insufferable seduction that sent my blood boiling.

"There's one cooling in the pie safe on the back porch," Sandy said. "I saw you pull out that old freezer this morning, so I baked a cobbler to go with the ice cream."

"So that was the amazing aroma that lured me into the kitchen," I chimed in. "Sandy, you are such a wonderful cook." Even though I spoke the truth, I felt compelled to make Sharon well aware that Bobby was doing just fine without her pretentious pampering.

Sandy looked at me and smiled as if she read my mind. "I think this is about done. It's getting hard to crank." She stood. "I'm gonna pull out the container and take the ice cream inside to the icebox."

"Let me do that for you, Sis," Bobby immediately offered.

"No. You stay here with your friend. I can handle it." She bent over, drained the salt water before picking up the bucket, then walked toward the door. "I'll throw some sandwiches together and bring them out for the *three* of us. In the meantime, Bobby, I don't believe Maddie has had the pleasure of meeting Sharon." Raising an eyebrow, she glanced at me and cocked her head. Bobby sprung over to hold the door for Sandy until she disappeared inside.

Focusing his attention back on Sharon, he apologized. "I'm sorry. I thought you two met at the town meeting last November. Sharon, this is Maddie Montgomery, my...uh...he stumbled for the right word and found...'houseguest'." Turning, he introduced Ms. Howard to me. "Maddie, this is Sharon Howard, a family friend."

"Why Bobby Reynolds, you know we are way more than friends. Your daddy practically had us married years ago," she gushed. "And I did see Miss Montgomery in November, but she was surrounded by all those needy little people." She glanced over at me. "Bobby told me you were a lawyer from Atlanta here to help the residents relocate. How benevolent of you."

Her comment somehow felt like a slap in the face. And the way she cooed over Bobby was the most blatant, disgusting display of flirtatious nausea I'd ever witnessed. How dare she act as if she owned him? I'd been living with the Reynolds for five months and had never seen her before. But the worst part, Bobby was thoroughly enjoying every second of her obnoxious display.

He looked at me then back at Sharon before walking across the porch to the sitting area. She rushed up beside him, threaded her arm in his, and pulled him into the swing to sit next to her, leaving me by the steps holding her brownies.

"It's nice to meet you, Sharon," I offered, still

stunned by the whole scene.

"Yes, I suppose it is, Miss Montgomery. You'll take Bobby's brownies inside to the icebox now, won't you?" she asked, without taking her eyes off of him.

"Of course." Walking inside, I shook my head trying to unravel what had just transpired. I strode straight into the kitchen then deposited Sharon's baked goods directly into the garbage can, plate and all.

Sandy promptly burst out laughing. "Someone moving in on your territory?"

"The unmitigated gall of that woman." After wiping my hands over the trashcan, I pulled a chair from the table and plopped down. "What rock did she slither out from under?"

"I thought Sidney was well rid of Sharon Howard when she took a job with IBM in Charlotte, but it would appear we've all been blessed with her return." Sandy handed me a glass of iced tea, then pulled up a chair beside me. "I'm telling you, Maddie, that woman has been trying to get her hooks into Bobby for fifteen years." A cynical smile washed across her face. "Of course, that wouldn't be of any concern to you since you and my brother are nothing more than friends, right?"

Shifting in my chair, I hesitated before answering. "Oh, right. We're just friends. I mean I could be pulled back to 2012 at any moment. It wouldn't make sense to—"

"Fall in love?" she completed my sentence. "Maddie, you can deny all you want, but you're flat out in love with my brother. And who knows, you may be stuck here in the past forever. Like I said before, 1949, and Bobby more specifically, is your destiny. But regardless of what I think, real love is too hard to find for you to just brush it off. Whatever is keeping you and Bobby apart, you'd better work it out. And with Sharon back in town, I wouldn't waste any time."

****

And so my internal battle raged on. For three days I felt sick to my stomach, ever since Ms. Howard decided to insinuate herself into Bobby's life again. I couldn't bear to see any woman pawing over him, least of all her. Ever since he confessed his feelings for me on the ridge that December afternoon, the nagging tug-of-war had sparred inside of me, and Sharon had only added ammunition to the conflict. Drawn to Bobby, I'd flirted relentlessly, but whenever he responded, an internal alarm screeched in my head, warning me to keep my distance. My erratic yo-yo behavior must have confused him into frustration. A man can only take so much disappointment before looking in another direction.

The last thing I wanted to do was play games, especially with Bobby. I'd never met anyone like him. I trusted him with my life, but for some reason, I still couldn't trust him with my heart. When he stood close to me, I felt a burning desire to crawl inside his arms, lose myself in his deep well of passion. Sheer primitive lust intoxicated me; our chemistry soared off the charts into space. But the attraction wasn't simply physical. The mystical connection between Bobby and me defied explanation. What if destiny had thrust me through time simply to find true love?

On the flip side, Sandy had made it clear that Bobby enjoyed a classic playboy lifestyle. He'd never been in love and had scores of women constantly sniffing after him, with Ms. Howard apparently topping the list. That woman evoked odium inside of me I didn't like harboring, and I felt compelled to shield Bobby from her vicious, predatory claws. So, I sharpened mine.

Tuesday evening after dinner, Bobby and I were sitting on the front porch. Sharon, who'd "just happened to be in the neighborhood," was thankfully saying her goodbyes.

"You *will* come to the State Fair this weekend to see me win the blue ribbon, won't you Bobby dear? I'll be manning the kissing booth, too." Fluttering her eyelashes, she raised a shoulder and granted him a smile overflowing with flirtatious vomit. "You simply must come, Bobby." She kissed the tips of her fingers, blew the imaginary sentiment toward him then flittered her fingers waving goodbye. "See you soon, Sweetie."

Watching Sharon step into her big black Packard, pull out and drive away, I bit my tongue to keep from heaving. The syrup that drooled from that woman's lips made me absolutely nauseous. She epitomized the most pretentious, sickening-sweet mega-skank I'd ever met. When her car disappeared around the corner, I sank into the swing.

Bobby smiled. "What do you say we all take a spin down to Macon for the fair on Saturday, have some fun for a change?"

I offered the first thing that popped into my head to dissuade him from going anywhere near that woman. "Macon is a bit of a drive from here don't you think?"

"It's only a few hours away. I'll ask Richie if he'd like to escort Sandy, and we can make it a foursome."

It would be nice to go to the fair with Bobby, and Sharon couldn't swoop in on him with me standing right by his side. "That sounds like fun," I conceded.

"I think Saturday is"—he scratched his head—"the opening day, so there will be a lot of extra festivities going on." Eyeing me he paused before adding salt to my wound, "I'm sure Sharon will appreciate our support."

I twirled a strand of hair around my finger. "And we wouldn't want to let her down, would we?" My sarcastic remark followed a rolling of my eyes. Reconsidering the reality of the event, I added, "You know, I don't think I've ever been to a State Fair."

"Really? Don't they have them in the future?" Bobby asked in earnest.

"Possibly. I've just never thought about going to one."

"Well then, Miss Montgomery. You're in for a big treat. Say, my best army buddy owns an old Civil War Mansion on College Street in Macon. I have an open invitation to stay there whenever I'm in the area. What do you say I give him a ring, see if we can make arrangements for the weekend?"

"You're sure we wouldn't be imposing?"

"No sir-ree, Frank loves to show off the grand ole place. It's a piece of history, authentic to the hilt." He started rocking his chair. "When he bought the place the bedrooms even had names, so he kept them that way. When I saw the old homestead, I felt like I was taking a walk in the past. Can you imagine that, Maddie?" He laughed at his own wit.

"It's right up my alley." I agreed. "Lately I've developed quite a passion for history."

Chapter 12

Lake Lanier, Georgia—March 2012

"See this Piper? I've added beams here and over there, so your two-story ceiling will be easily supported." Rob stretched the plans out further across the cement foundation, placing stones on the corners to hold them down. "And if you extend these supports and add rafters, you can elaborate on your deck design and wrap the porch around both sides."

"You're a genius, Rob." Piper knelt on the edge of the blueprints. "So, now I can bring the deck out here so it overlooks the entire cove?"

"That's right."

"It's perfect. Thanks so much for your help. I love your ideas. Won't you reconsider and let me pay you something."

"We're neighbors, Piper, and friends I hope." He sat back on his heels.

"Yes, friends. If I can ever do anything to help you, please let me know."

"I'll keep that in mind."

He would, too. Piper didn't know it yet, but she stood at the core of his entire game plan. Helping with her deck established an obligatory gesture to which the young woman would feel a need to reciprocate. Rob had strategically set up a chess play. A few more moves and the queen would be captured, then, checkmate.

****

Atlanta, Georgia—May 1950

The skyline evoked an eerie sense of twisted reality. It was the first time I'd seen Atlanta since my slip through time, and I wasn't prepared for the cityscape's alternate reality. The bustling six-lane Interstate-85 of my world had mystically transformed into a quiet two-lane boulevard lined by streetlights. Black metal lamps arched over the road at equidistant intervals, sporting large globes that lit the thoroughfare at night. The florescent illuminated superhighway no longer whooshed between familiar high-rise buildings, signifying Atlanta's skyline. They had yet to be constructed, and my condo was but a dream in an architect's mind.

But when Bobby, Richie, Sandy, and I stopped at the Varsity for lunch, the Art-Deco style building looked roughly the same. Square blocked-glass windows replaced the see-through clarity of those in 2012, but aside from that, the exterior differed only by the lack of skyscrapers surrounding it. As we pulled in, a familiar aroma filled my senses.

"What'll ya have?"

I almost burst out laughing at the memorable hail that had greeted me in the past, or rather the future. The carhops didn't exist in my time, but staff behind the long counter welcomed customers with the same three words, and the chilidogs, hamburgers, fries, and onion rings hadn't changed in sixty-plus years. Though I usually stuck to a more healthy diet, I had to admit I welcomed the familiarity.

Richie grinned as he grabbed his food from the tray

attached to the car window. His deep red hair, cut in a flat top, glistened in the sunlight from the abundant blob of Butch-wax he used to keep the strands standing straight up. The light sprinkling of freckles on his pudgy nose reminded me of a cartoon character, not that he wasn't attractive in a cute, boyish sort of way. He just looked mischievous. I giggled watching him stuff mounds of junk food into his mouth as if he hadn't eaten in days.

My order consisted of a hotdog smothered in sauerkraut and topped with mustard. Rationalizing one hotdog with no fries, I could justify drinking a large chocolate milkshake. Bobby and Sandy ate hamburgers with onion rings and sipped on *Co-cola*.

A few hours later, we pulled into Macon, turned off 2nd Street onto College. There was no mistaking Frank Adam's beautiful antebellum home. With exquisite Greek-Revival design straight out of *Gone With The Wind*, romantic southern charm radiated from its seventeen-columned wrap-around veranda.

Frank, a handsome young man with dark brown hair and mustache, greeted us as we drove up. He looked so much like Clark Gable I chuckled.

"Welcome, Bob," he said, holding out his hand for a customary shake. "It's been a while. Good to see you." He turned to me. "And this beautiful woman must be Maddie."

"It's a pleasure to meet you, Frank," I said. "Bobby has told me a lot about you."

"I'm looking forward to getting to know the mystery woman he's been hiding from me in those north Georgia foothills." He turned to Sandy. "So nice to see you again, Sandy. I'm glad you could make it this time."

"Hey Frank. Thank you for letting us stay with you," she replied, then introduced Richie.

Frank extended his hand, patting the younger man on the back.

"Yes, thank you for having us, Sir," Richie said.

"Now, stop all the sir business. You make me feel like an old man. Please, call me Frank."

"Well then, thank you, Frank. Richie gazed at the mansion in awe. "You've got a beautiful home here."

"Come in, come in. I'll show you all around."

Inside, majestic fireplaces and authentic period furniture transported us to the Civil War era. I felt like Scarlett O'Hara waltzing through Tara as we strolled from room to room. After a grand tour, Frank showed us to our respective bedchambers so we could freshen up. Sandy and I shared the Magnolia room, and ironically, Bobby and Richie were shown to the Sidney Lanier. When we returned to the parlor, I had to comment.

"So, you two are staying in the Sidney Lanier bedroom," I said. "Y'all know who he was, right?" I lowered myself into an antique armchair.

"A poet," Bobby replied, walking over to inspect the huge fireplace.

"And a lawyer," I added.

"I never cared much about poetry." Richie shrugged.

"I love Lanier's poetry, it's so lyrical." Sandy sat down on an 18th century settee, ran her hand over the soft, blue brocade.

Bobby walked across the room toward us. "Quite a coincidence." His eyes met mine. "I've recently read about Lanier. He was a soldier, too, born right here in Macon."

"I think you're right," I replied, happy they were familiar with Sidney Lanier since the new lake would be named after the poet. The name would be a fitting tribute to their hometown as well.

"Frank said to come and go as we please." Bobby placed his hands on his hips. "He has plans this afternoon, but requested we join him for dinner."

"So, what shall we do in the meantime," I asked.

"We'll spend the day at the fair tomorrow." Bobby looked at his watch. "Why don't we walk around town a bit before dinner? What do you say, Richie?"

"I promised Sandy we'd go see some historic sites this afternoon. You and Maddie go ahead. We'll meet you back here in a few hours."

"Suit yourselves. Are you ready to stretch your legs a bit, Miss Montgomery?" He crooked his elbow.

What kind of enchantment did this man hold over me? Simply wrapping my hand around the bulge in his bicep sent goose bumps down to my toes. As hard as I tried to convince myself to keep my distance, nothing had worked to douse the heat pulsating between us. And Sharon's unexpected arrival had me more invested in Bobby than ever.

Strolling around an antiquated Macon felt as dreamlike as touring Frank's Civil War estate. Sandy may have been looking at historical sites, but I was living them. We headed down College Street, turned left on Georgia Avenue, and up Coleman Hill where we could see the entire city. The Insurance Company of North America stood at the top of the hill, the focal point of what I knew as Coleman Park. The three-story building, which looked like a replica of Independence Hall in Philadelphia, would one day be the home of Mercer University's Walter F. George School of Law, the one place in Macon I actually knew well.

Adjacent to the insurance building, Overlook Mansion adorned by moss-draped trees and bursting blooms of white dogwoods interspersed with blush pink azaleas, stood guard over downtown Macon. The manor I knew as Woodruff House, the Law School's events venue. I'd visited the campus on numerous occasions to network and hear big-time lawyers speak to law students. Now, the scenery radiated a strange time-warped authenticity.

It was almost five o'clock when we returned to Frank's home, still an hour before dinner, so Bobby and I wandered around the grounds. Discovering a swing nestled into a lovely garden hidden at the back of the property, we sat down to relax amidst the seclusion.

"So, has Macon changed much since the last time you saw it?" Putting his arm around me, Bobby pushed the swing slightly to set it in motion. "I was watching your reaction as we walked. The town must have made some big changes in sixty years."

"I did notice a few things, but nothing major." I sat down beside him, nestling into his warm chest. "I don't know Macon that well, only the law school. But Atlanta definitely looked different." Pulling my knees up, I rested them on his muscular thighs. "My I-85 is six lanes in both directions. And you'd flip over the skyscrapers that line Atlanta's future cityscape."

"Maddie, I...I'm glad we found this place." He pulled me closer, and I rested my head on his shoulder.

"Macon?"

"No." He chuckled. "This little garden. I've wanted to get you alone for weeks, but we've both been so busy with the dam project. It's been hard to find time. I think we need to talk, about us."

"Us?" I acted surprised by his comment.

"Don't be coy. You know how I feel about you, and I can tell you are drawn to me, too. But I don't understand why you fight the connection between us."

My behavior must have been driving him crazy. I'd practically thrown myself at him time and again, only to turn cold and distant a few minutes later. "You're right. I'm sorry I keep giving you mixed signals."

"Mixed signals?" By this time he expected strange slang to spew from my mouth, and though it occasionally threw him off guard, he eventually figured out the intended sentiment through context clues.

"Yes, I'm obviously attracted to you. I mean, who wouldn't be? You're handsome, smart, and definitely hot."

"Hot? Am I sweating?" When he pulled up his arm to check his pits, I burst out laughing.

"No, calling you hot is like saying you're a hunk, you know, handsome. Anyway, I don't have to tell you those things. You could have any girl you want. Especially Sharon."

"If I'd wanted Miss Howard's attentions, I'd have had her years ago. She means nothing to me, Maddie. Don't you know by now that I want you?" He pulled me closer, kissed my forehead.

At that moment I could have crawled inside of him. I wanted to yank him off the swing, push him down on the grass, and take him right there. But the fortress forged around my heart pulsated a persistent protective mantra: *don't hurt, don't trust, don't love.* If only he wanted me, only me, for his future instead of his toy. But I knew that wasn't Bobby's M.O.

"You say that and sometimes…" Pulling away, I looked into his sapphire eyes while the ache in my chest intensified. "It doesn't matter. We've talked about this before." I twirled a strand of my hair between my thumb and forefinger. "There can't be an *us*. Any day now I'll be sucked back to my own time, and you'll never see me again."

"We don't know that. It's been months, and you're still here. What if you never get pulled back? Did you ever consider that maybe you were meant to come here to be with me?" He placed his hand on my hair, smoothing it with his fingers. "Would that be so bad?"

His touch ignited desire in the deepest depths of my soul, a burning, bubbling molten lava flowing through my veins. There was no denying we were two parts of one heart. Deep inside a flame exploded, seething wildly, melting walls that had kept passion neatly contained, walls that suppressed the tears of a little girl. The real battle raged within, where burning desire collided with a liquescent stream of latent fear.

"I love you, Maddie. I don't want you to go back to the future. Not ever."

Those words, I'd longed to hear them my entire life. The emptiness had crippled the little girl's spirit, sweltered in her soul for nineteen years, paralyzing any image of love that dared to venture into my life. I wanted to fall into his arms. No one had ever touched me, body and soul, like Bobby, but when I heard him say I love you, visions of Cole flashed through my mind followed by the deceitful similes of every man who'd professed undying love to me, including the most important one, Daddy. A cold dagger stabbed through my chest. The ice queen took over.

The raging internal battle exhausted me. Love shouldn't be difficult. As much as I wanted him, craved him, I wouldn't be hurt again, especially by Bobby. It had to stop here, tonight...now.

I sat forward on the edge of the swing. "You just don't get it."

"Get what. I know you're afraid to trust love. But I promise you, I—"

He stopped mid-sentence. Leaning forward, he looked deep into my eyes, softly touched my cheek then tucked a strand of hair behind my ear. Sunlight danced across his face. His warm breath tickled my ear, sending effervescent bubbles rippling down my neck. He gently pressed his lips over mine, and I melted into him, swimming in a stream of deep passion. Fisting his hand around my hair, he pulled me closer. The pounding of our hearts beat in harmony, and a warm tingle radiated down to my toes. I kissed him deep, hard, long, clinging to the last kiss we would share...then pulled back and turned away.

"Stop. Don't you see? I've tried to make this obvious, but..."

"Make what obvious?" He was totally confused.

So was I. "That I don't feel that way. Why can't you see that?" I wiped a conspicuous tear from my cheek, then turned and stared at him. "I want to go back to my life, Bobby. And I...I don't love you, not like that anyway."

The pain sweltering in his eyes ripped through my heart. Running his fingers through his hair, he fell against the back of the swing.

"I…then all this time, you—"

"I've been trying to help you, that's all." I stood, ambled over to the edge of the garden. A deafening silence screamed between us until he finally spoke in a cold voice I'd never heard before.

"Well then. I guess people from the future really are different." He got up and began to walk toward the house. "We better get back. It's almost dinnertime." He looked at me with vacant eyes. "You don't have to worry, Maddie. I finally *get it*. I won't bother you again."

****

Richie, Sandy, and Frank sat in rocking chairs enjoying a glass of deep ruby wine as Bobby and I approached.

"Pull up a chair," Frank said. "I have a nice bottle of Chateau Lafite Rothschild. It's only a 1948 vintage, but it's quite good."

"Thanks Frankie," Bobby replied. "I don't mind if I do."

Frank poured a glass of wine, handed it to Bobby then began filling another to offer me. "And you, Maddie?"

Reaching for the glass, I smiled. "I'd love some wine. Thank you, Frank."

Then, choosing the single rocker next to Sandy, I turned away from the crowd and looked down the street instead of joining the conversation. Bobby chose a rocker at the other end of the porch, the far side of Frank's.

They talked and sipped wine until dinner was served, a superb meal that would challenge the cuisine of any five-star restaurant. Pushing most of the food around on my plate, I ate very little. Afterward, the men moved into the parlor to chat over a glass of cognac. Excusing myself, I opted to retire early, ostensibly to get a good night's sleep before attending the fair the next day. My roommate followed suit.

"Don't stay up too late," Sandy said to the men as she pranced up the spiral staircase. "Tomorrow will be a long day."

"Sweet dreams, you two. We'll see you in the morning," Richie replied.

Bobby was already deep in conversation with his friend, which I'm sure was his way of handling my rejection. I, on the other hand, had no way of dealing with the empty hole I'd shot through my own heart.

"What's cookin', Maddie?" Sandy's radar was right on, but I tried to derail it.

"Not a thing." I slid out of my dress, slipped between the sheets, intentionally lying on my side facing the wall instead of Sandy.

"If you say so." She turned off the light. "Good night, Maddie. We'll talk about it in the morning. Sleep well."

"You, too," I sniffled. "And there's nothing to talk about."

"We'll see."

I tried my best to hold back silent tears, but they welled in my eyes, flowed down my cheeks, and drained into the down pillow. I loved Bobby with my entire heart and soul. And I somehow knew I always would. Breaking things off with him had done nothing but bring the pain to both of us sooner. I prayed our lives would work out better this way, that this moment my pain was the worst I'd ever have to feel. It would get easier now. I repeated that phrase over and over until sleep numbed the ache in my heart and soothed my swollen eyes.

****

"Get up, Maddie," Sandy shook me. "Come on. We're going to be late for the grand opening of the fair."

"Okay, okay. I'm up." Dragging my body to sit up, I rubbed my sore, puffy eyes.

"Let's get going. The men have already eaten and are off on the grounds with Frank. Our breakfast is getting cold." She looked in the mirror and pinched her cheeks.

Leaning on my elbows, I stared at her. "You do that all the time. Why do you pinch yourself in the face?"

"For color. Rosy cheeks makes a woman look healthy, more alluring."

I shook my head. "Right. I've always relied on makeup. It doesn't hurt." I hoisted my legs over the side of the four-poster bed. "You go ahead. I'll be down in a few minutes."

"Speaking of appearing alluring, Maddie, you look just awful." Sandy stood beside the bed gawking at me in amazement. "Are you feeling okay?"

"I feel fine." Another lie. Dear God, why did I always have to hide my true feelings? I felt terrible. My head hurt, and my eyes were so swollen I could barely see. "I must have had some kind of an allergic reaction. I'll be fine as soon as I splash some water on my face."

"Well, Miss Allergy, my makeup is in my cosmetic suitcase. If you need to borrow anything, just help yourself."

"Thanks, now go. I'll be right behind you." I glanced at my reflection. Sandy was right. It would take a major makeup miracle to hide the swelling. I drank down three glasses of water and held cold washcloths on my eyes, hoping to rehydrate and minimize the puffiness. After a quick shower, I drenched my face in cold cream, patted it dry, then covered the dark circles with pancake makeup. As a last-ditch effort, I pinched my cheeks over and over to add some color. Within fifteen minutes I had performed magic on my face, dressed, and met Sandy downstairs, ready to eat breakfast.

"Wow, remind me to get you to teach me how to put on makeup when we get back home, Maddie."

"Not a bad job, if I do say so myself." I smiled.

"Yeah, how'd you get rid of the swelling?"

"Trade secret. But I'll show you if you ever need it."

"Good. The next time I cry myself to sleep, I'll come find you." She jumped up and took her dishes to the kitchen before I could swallow and reply.

Chapter 13

Lake Lanier, Georgia—March 2012

Rob swallowed the rest of his bottled water, rolled up the plans, then handed them to Piper.

"Thank you so much." She walked across the plywood subfloor and gazed out over the glistening lake. "Your wife must be beside herself waiting for your renovations to be done. I can't wait to meet her."

"I'm sure you two will be great friends."

"So has she at least come by to see your progress?"

"No. I've planned a lot of surprises for her, but I wanted to wait until everything was perfect. It won't be long though. I think my masterpiece will be in place by June." Rob glanced at his watch. "Time to get back to work. I'll stop by in a few days to see how the house is progressing. See you later."

"Okay, thanks again." Piper waved and watched him stroll back across the ridge. "Whew, if you weren't married, I'd jump you myself," she whispered softly.

But Rob had his own agenda.

****

Macon, Georgia—May 1950

It was drudgery walking the few blocks to the Georgia State Fair held in Macon's Central City Park. The brief hike on such a crisp, beautiful morning should have invigorated us, but the obvious distance between

Bobby and me faded festive anticipation. His conversation focused on Richie and Sandy with polite acknowledgements to anything I happened to add.

When we arrived, the menagerie of tents, antique rides, and assorted food stands bustled with activity. Myriad aromas lured children of all ages to lick ice-cream cones, slurp sodas, and stuff themselves with hotdogs and cotton candy. Brightly dressed vendors enticed passersby to participate in games of chance or watch once-in-a-lifetime shows. And pavilions exhibited blue ribbon winners like Sharon Howard's brownies, for everything from the best apple pies to the fattest pigs.

"Let's ride the Ferris wheel first," Sandy said. "That way we can see the whole fair from the top and decide where we want to go."

"Good idea, Sis." Bobby looked at a flyer to get general directions and motioned for us to follow him.

The closer we moved toward the ride, the more apprehensive I got. I'd never been fond of heights to begin with, and the apparatus creaked and rattled as it turned as if it could take off and roll across the park at any moment.

"You three go ahead. I'll just wait for you here." My trepidation prompted Richie to tease me.

"You're not afraid to go on a Ferris wheel are you, Maddie?" he asked. "It's a child's ride."

"No, it's not that." It may have been a kiddie ride, but that rickety framework scared me more than the most elaborate thrill ride I'd experienced. I didn't have a death wish.

"I know you're not going to make my brother ride alone are you?" Sandy asked.

"Come on Maddie, I won't bite," Bobby said. "You'll enjoy it."

"Okay, I'm coming." I reluctantly followed them.

After waiting a few moments in a short line, Bobby and I stepped up to the platform and sat down in a flimsy swaying seat. The Ferris wheel started and stopped in short spurts until each seat filled. When we reached the top the whole apparatus jerked, released a sharp grinding noise then started to spin. My stomach did, too. As if on instinct, Bobby grabbed my hand.

"It's okay. Just sit back and take in the panorama." He stretched his arm around the back of the seat lightly touching my shoulder, avoiding the complete contact of having his arm around me. "Look, over there on the right. Do you see the carousel? And that corral over there, the crowd is waiting to see which animal will be this year's prize cow." As he pointed out the highlights of the fair, my nervousness dissolved. "That big tent is filled with the best pies and cakes you'll ever taste."

"Like Sharon's brownies?" He raised an eyebrow at my sarcasm and smiled, but said nothing.

Even after last night's performance, my claws were still sharp when it came to Ms. Howard.

"So, are you glad you came?" Bobby asked.

"It's pretty amazing." Despite the rickety old wheel, I felt safe with Bobby so close beside me.

A flurry of rides, games of chance, and carnival fare consumed our entire day. Hiking the fairgrounds numerous times, we delighted in every sideshow, booth, and amusement save one, the carousel. When the sun dipped into the horizon, the festive atmosphere heightened. Multicolor lights burst through the dusk, each twinkling a pirouette to the amplified calliope music. Exhausted, we finally sat down at a picnic table to catch our breath.

"So, what do you think, Maddie?" Bobby asked.

"I—"

"About the fair, I mean."

"Oh, it's awesome."

"Awesome, huh. I guess that means you enjoyed yourself. I'm glad." He turned to Sandy. "It's late Sis, and we have a long ride ahead of us tonight. Are you two ready to hit the road?"

"Bobby, no. We haven't ridden the merry-go-round yet." Sandy pleaded. "We can't leave without riding at least once."

"Aren't we a little old for that?" Bobby asked.

"No, come on. I'll never be too old to ride the carousel. Please?" She stuck her lower lip out so far I had to laugh.

"What do you think, Richie? Should we indulge my baby sister?"

"Unless you want her pouting all the way home. Besides, I've always enjoyed that ride. Come on, Bobby. I'll challenge you."

"Challenge me? Do you want to wager something on that cocky attitude?"

"Sure, let's go." Richie nudged Bobby.

"We'll meet you girls over there, okay?" They yelled back in unison, sprinting across the park leaving Sandy and me in their dust.

"Well Maddie, I guess we better catch up to the guys."

"What was that all about?" I asked, as we strolled toward the ride.

"Richie's good, but Bobby is the best. I've never

seen anyone beat him."

"Beat him at what? Aren't we going to ride the carousel?" I looked at her with complete confusion. "Unless things have changed incredibly in sixty years, I'm pretty sure the horses can't best the mounts in front of them." I laughed.

"Golly Maddie, haven't you ever ridden a carousel before?"

"Sure, when I was a little girl, but you can't compete on a stationary horse."

"You mean they don't have rings in the future?" She gazed at me with her another-time-gap glare.

"Rings? What are you babbling about?"

"Come on. I'll show you."

Sandy tugged at my blouse and began running across the grounds. Not to be outpaced, I caught up and jogged alongside of her. We got to the ride just in time to see Bobby and Richie mount two beautifully carved steeds, both situated on the outside of the carousel. They secured their left hands tightly gripping their respective poles, leaned out of the saddle to the right as far as they could, and clinging to their horses with sheer leg strength.

"What in the world are they doing?" The ride began and I was baffled at the determination that flooded Bobby's face. "They're going to fall off."

"No they won't." Sandy assured me. "You see the attendant over to the right?" She pointed at the young man operating the ride. "He's going to throw out that mechanical arm…See? It holds the rings."

"What rings? What are you talking about?"

"Little silver rings, about this big." She put the tips of her thumb and forefinger together to form a circle.

"They're small and hard to catch ahold of with the horses moving up and down as they speed past. But each time someone hooks their finger in a ring, another one slides down to replace it."

"Okay, I see what they're doing, but what's the point?" I stared as each outside rider strained to reach for the little rings.

"The person who captures the most rings gets a free ride."

"So they're risking their lives to see who can get the most rings?" I shook my head.

"Yes, but that's only part of it. The big prize is the brass ring. There's only one of those, and if you catch the brass ring you get the grand prize, free rides the whole year." Sandy grabbed my arm, pulling me close to the balustrade that encircled the carousel.

A little boy stood next to me holding his mother's hand, but his lower lip hung out in a little pout, and unlike the rest of the crowd, he wasn't watching the entertainment. He seemed so sad I couldn't help but react. I reached over, grabbed a balloon tied to the rail, then stooped down to hand it to him.

"Don't you like to watch the carousel?" I asked him.

"Mommy says I'm too little to catch the rings."

"How old are you?" I asked.

He held up three fingers.

"Wow, three years old. You'll be able to ride those big horses soon, but that sign over there says you have to be five to ride." I pointed to the notice a few feet away.

"I know." He dropped his head and continued to pout, protruding his lower lip even further. "I can read a lot of words, and I know my numbers, too." He looked back up at me. "When I get big I'm going to make the rules."

"I'm sure you'll make important rules so everyone can have fun and stay safe, too."

He grinned, took the balloon from my hand. "I will," he replied.

"Maddie, what are you doing?" Sandy asked. "Stand up. You have to watch this."

I patted the child on the head and turned back toward the carousel. "Watch what?"

"The thing is the brass ring doesn't appear every ride. It only comes around a few times each day. No one has caught it today or their name would be posted over there." She pointed to a sign next to the attendant.

"So why is the brass ring so important?"

"If you're lucky enough to be on the big ride and catch the brass ring—let's go, the ride stopped so we can get on now. Come on, Maddie. Ride an outside horse, and you can try for the rings yourself."

We jumped aboard, and I hopped up on the first available outside horse. When the carousel started again, I held my pole and leaned slightly out to reach for the rings, but I couldn't come close to touching them. Sitting back up securely on my animal, I watched Bobby, Richie and Sandy play the game with expertise. A few moments later the crowd roared.

"Look Maddie, it's the brass ring," Sandy yelled from behind me.

Turning, I saw a gleaming brass colored ring sparkling on the end of the mechanical arm. Every eye watched to see who would catch the treasure. Richie leaned out as far as he could. He touched the ring but his fingers fumbled. Bobby approached the mechanical arm, leaning in with ease. He crooked his finger, caught the ring then, raising his hand high above his head, displayed his prize to the crowd. Everyone cheered. When the carousel stopped, the crowd gathered around Bobby to congratulate him.

"That was terrific, Bobby." Sandy gave him a big hug. "You can bring it back next year and get free rides the whole time you're here."

"Good job, Bob," Richie held out his hand for a congratulatory shake. "You're a right good competitor."

We left the fair filled with wonderful memories and one shining brass ring, then strolled back to Frank's house, laughing and reliving the highlights of the day. The state fair had been a delightful experience despite the tension between Bobby and me. No matter where "or when" I ended up, I knew we'd always be connected.

Back at the house, I packed my things, said my goodbyes to Frank thanking him for his hospitality then walked out to the car.

Bobby, already leaning against his Hudson, jumped forward to take my bag as I approached.

"What a marvelous day. Thanks for bringing me here," I said. "And the carousel ride. I never realized. They don't have those mechanical arms in my time. Too dangerous I expect. But it was so cool to watch you grab the brass ring. Can I see it?"

"Here, I want you to have it." He put the ring in my hand, closed my fingers over it. "I caught this for you."

"No Bobby, I couldn't." I inspected the little brass ring then gave it back to him. "You keep it. I probably won't be around next year for the fair anyway."

He reluctantly put the ring back in his pocket. "I wanted to be angry with you about last night. But try as I might, I just couldn't fault you for not feeling the same way as I do. I can't make you love me." He shuffled his feet, kicking a pebble out of the way. When he ran his finger through his hair, I knew it was difficult for him to find the right words to say to me. "But that doesn't mean I'll ever stop loving you. I don't know what the future holds for you Maddie, but I always want you to be happy."

"That's a sweet sentiment. And I want the best for you, too." I turned my head to wipe away the tear rolling down my cheek.

"I thought you might want to keep the brass ring for good luck," he said. "And maybe to remind you of me when you return home. But I guess that's silly. You really can't pack your things for the kind of trip you'll be taking." He crooked his finger, lifted my chin, forcing me to look into his eyes. "I hope you find your brass ring, Maddie. You deserve to have your dreams come true."

His words hit me like a bolt of lightning. "Find the brass ring...holy crap." I stared at him, dumbfounded.

"What's wrong?" he asked.

"That's what Sandy meant when she said you were waiting for the brass ring."

"What? Did my sister say something to you?"

"Yes, when we first met. She was talking about you. How you had never been in love...that you were waiting to catch the brass ring...and I thought...Oh my Lord."

"Maddie, what's wrong. What are you talking about?"

"I have to go find Sandy." I threw my arms around his neck, hugged him with energy from months of pent up tension, then leaned back to drink in his sensuous eyes. "I love you, Bobby Reynolds." Arms still draped around his neck, I kissed him hard, smack dab on the lips then pulled away. "I've loved you from the moment I met you, and I'll love you forever," I said, then tore off toward the house.

"What just happened, Maddie?" he called out as I flew toward the porch. "And why the hell are you running away from me after a statement like that?"

"I'll be right back. I promise. I just have to find Sandy, first." I sprinted up the steps into the house, then briefly turned back to look at him.

Bobby shook his head. "Maddie Montgomery, you're the most confusing woman I've ever known."

I smiled then tore through the front door in search of his sister.

****

"For heaven's sake, Maddie. Why didn't you ask me what I meant? I had no idea you didn't know about carousel rings when we met. They've been around my whole life."

"Yes, well, you didn't know about Future Woman then either, or anything about me. At that point Bobby didn't even know. I just assumed from my own frame of reference…it doesn't matter. What matters is I know now." I hugged her then sat on the bedside while she finished packing.

"I've been telling you for months that my brother is crazy about you. He loves you, Maddie. Can't you see that?" She folded her nightgown, placed it into her bag. "He's never said, 'I love you' to anyone before. There's no doubt in my mind that *you* are his brass ring. The question is…" She paused, looked me dead in the eyes. "Is he yours? Do you love him that much?"

"Yes. Yes, I love him with all my heart. I think I have from the first moment I saw him."

"Then my advice is you might want to tell him."

"I think I just did. But I'll have to wait until we get back home to explain why."

"Well, don't take too long." She fastened the latches on her suitcases, walked toward the door. "Remember, Ms. Howard is ready to pounce on her prey."

"Let me help you with one of those." I jumped up, hugged her again, then grabbed the cosmetic case from her hand. "Don't worry, Ms. Thing won't get a single claw into your brother. I'm staking my claim."

"It's about time." She laughed.

The whole drive home, I couldn't take my eyes off of Bobby. I went over-and-over the details in my mind, how naïve I'd been and impetuous. I thought about how I'd explain what had happened, why I'd mistrusted him, and prayed I could make it up to him. It was almost three o'clock in the morning when we pulled into the Reynolds' driveway, far too late to begin any discussion. Richie crashed on the sofa, and the rest of us dragged ourselves up to bed.

As I fell asleep, I imagined having a real future with Bobby. The only obstacle now was time. I simply had no way of knowing how much time I had left in the past. But one thing was certain, no matter how much or little time we had together, I wanted to spend every moment loving and being loved by Bobby Reynolds.

Chapter 14

Lake Lanier, Georgia—March 2012

Rob spent weeks on the Internet researching, gathering every tidbit of information he could find. Determined not to leave one pebble unturned, he spared no expense in doing whatever necessary to insure his plan's success.

Piper doted on him. Forced to mention his *wife* to keep Miss Taylor at arm's length, Rob rationalized his decision. Any problem that reared its ugly head would be handled later, like casualties of war. And this was a war. He waged a battle against all odds. It was a gamble, but one he had to take. Everything would come down to one crucial moment. And Piper held the key.

****

Sidney, Georgia—May 1950

"I love you, Bobby Reynolds. I think I always have."

"It's too late, Maddie." Bobby turned and pulled Sharon closer then gently kissed her. "I love Sharon."

"No, it can't be too late," I cried, jolting up in bed. Brushing the scraggly, damp hair from my face, I looked around my bedroom. *Thank God.* I got up and ambled downstairs to an empty house. Of course, Monday morning, they were already at work. I'd talk to Bobby and confess my foolishness as soon as he got home, before Ms. Howard could get her slimy fangs into him.

I made a fresh pot of strong coffee, spread my dam files across the kitchen table, and dove into my own work. The phone rang about two o'clock, breaking the silence and my concentration.

"May I speak with Miss Montgomery, please?" The voice on the other end of the line was laced with desperation.

"This is she," I replied.

"Miss Montgomery. I hope you remember me, Robert Sullivan's the name, you know, from Sullivan's Drugstore?"

"Oh yes, the soda shop. Absolutely, Mr. Sullivan. I remember you."

"Say, I've heard talk that you're the fine lady who is helping folks relocate."

"Not in a legal capacity, but yes, I'm helping in any way I can." Picking up a pen and paper, I began jotting down notes about Robert Sullivan.

"If you're not too busy Miss Montgomery, could you drop by the drugstore sometime? I could really use your help."

"I'd be happy to, Mr. Sullivan. I'm free this afternoon. Would that work for you?"

"Any time that suits you, Miss. I'll be here till we close."

"Actually, I'm just finishing some paperwork." I glanced at the clock. "I could drop by in about an hour or so."

"Thank you, ma'am."

"Please, call me Maddie."

"Well then Maddie, you call me Sully. I'll be

seeing you."

I hung up the phone, gathered my files, then ran upstairs to shower and get ready for my meeting. When I arrived at the drugstore, the soda jerk pointed toward the back room. I tapped lightly on the door, waited a moment, then peeked inside. Robert Sullivan sat hunched over his desk studying mounds of paperwork.

"Sully, it's Maddie." I stepped inside the office.

Startled, he looked up. "I'm sorry. I didn't hear you come in. Please, come sit down."

We chatted for a few minutes before Sully began to relax.

"This shop has been in my family for as long as I can remember. I'd planned on passing it down to my son, Robbie, and eventually to his children someday. But now I'm not sure what to do." He pulled out a map of north Georgia; spread it out on his desk. "They've made me a fair enough offer, but without Sidney, I'm not sure where I'd go. The drugstore and soda shop is the only business I've ever known."

"How about Gainesville? It's growing quickly and will only get bigger," I said. "Developments will be popping up all around the new lake." I indicated the area I had in mind. "This looks like a great location to start a new pharmacy, and a soda shop, too." I pointed to the general area along what would be the northeast shore of Lake Lanier.

"Maybe. I wish I knew that for sure." A crumpled brow showed his apprehension.

"Trust me on this one, Sully. I'm sure of it."

"Folks say you have a good sense 'bout where to look for property. My wife Betty and I built our home with our own hands, and she loves that ole house. We live down by Shoal Creek." He glanced up at me. "You know that area?"

I nodded.

"Betty sits out and watches the water nearly every day." He leaned back in his chair. "I promised her we'd try to rebuild a nice home on the banks of the new lake. But truth be told, I don't have an inkling where that'll be."

"It's hard when those maps and drawings are the only source you have." I pointed to the rest of the plans stacked on his desk.

"I've talked with the Corps of Engineers, but so far it seems like a crap shoot, too many variables that can alter the shoreline."

"Perhaps, but I can advise you based on my own research." I knew Bobby and Sandy thought the world of Sully and would love to have him for a neighbor. "Bobby bought some property on this summit." I indicated the ridgeline. "And you know the Taylors, don't you, Ben and Margaret?"

He stood to get a closer look at the map. "Sure, Ben and I have been friends since we were knee high to a grasshopper."

"Well, they're buying property on the ridge, too, near Bobby and Sandy. There's a lot of land in that area that no one has laid claim to yet. It's a bit north of where some Sidney residents are settling, but there's a great view of the Blue Ridge foothills, and it's closer to Gainesville, too."

"It sounds nice, but how do you know it will be on the shoreline."

"That's a good question, Sully. And the answer is simple. The ridge is too steep there to build anything in front of it." I'd said the same thing to the Taylors. It sounded logical, a lot better than saying, *because I'm from the future and I've seen it.* "If you don't mind living at the base of the Blue Ridge, the location could be perfect. I can show you the land I'm talking about if you'd like."

"That would be terrific. We can take a spin up there this afternoon if you have the time. Tommy there can watch the store while I'm gone."

"Sweet—I mean, that will work out well for me."

"I just have to finish a few things first. Why don't you have a seat in the shop? Order anything you like and tell Tommy I said it's on the house." He sat back down at his desk and began organizing his papers.

"That's so nice of you, Sully. But a simple glass of Co-cola would be fine. Take your time though. I'm in no hurry." I slipped out the office door, walked over to a table, sat down.

Tommy brought me Co-cola from the soda fountain while my thoughts drifted to the night before. I felt awful about toying with Bobby for the last seven months. But now, a veil had been lifted, and I could finally see everything with crystal clarity. I couldn't wait until he got home from work tonight. There was so much I needed to tell him, confess to him. Finally, I could give in to my deepest desires and—

"Hey, what were you doin' in there? Can't you even read, Boy?" The angry voice faded the jukebox, hushed the room.

I looked up to see a heavyset teenager with fire in his eyes, his light brown, flattop thick with Butch-wax. He stood, fists on hips, with an air of rage flushed across his chubby face.

"You hear me, Boy? There's a bathroom in the back for *Coloreds*. I shouldn't have to relieve myself with your Negro germs all over everything."

The man cowered, apologizing to the brash teen.

"I was just cleaning in there, Sir." His bronze skin and dark eyes almost gleamed in contrast to the crisp white shirt, pants, and apron he wore. "Mr. Sullivan said the room needed a good scrubbing, asked me to take care of it." Bowing out of his predicament, he scuffled away.

The teenager yelled after him. "Well, don't be spreading any of your sweaty, black germs around our facilities." He walked into the men's room, slammed the door behind him.

I watched the poor abused man in dismay. He began sweeping near the counter as if nothing had happened. I approached him completely appalled by the behavior of the insolent punk.

"Are you all right?" I asked. "I'm so sorry he treated you like that. There is no excuse for his actions. That boy's father needs to teach him some decent manners."

"Thank you, Ma'am, but I'm just fine. I'm pretty used to that kind of talk. It's likely his daddy is the one who taught him to hate coloreds in the first place." He set the broom aside, picked up a stack of books from under the counter, then rested them on his hip. "You're Miss Montgomery, aren't you?"

"Why yes. How did you know that?"

"Most everyone in Sidney knows who you are, Ma'am. You've helped a lot of people 'round these parts. I don't suppose you'd waste your time with the coloreds though."

"Nonsense. I'd be happy to work with you and your family. People are people. Skin color makes absolutely no difference, and one day in the not too distant future, racist jerks like that insecure punk will be put in their place. What's your name?"

"Elijah, Ma'am. Elijah Parks at your service." He wiped his hand on his apron then extended it to me. "You're quite a woman, Miss Montgomery."

Shaking with my right hand, I clasped our grip with my left. "It's a pleasure to meet you, Elijah. How can I help?"

"It wouldn't be in your best interest for us to converse more here, Ma'am, right now I mean. But if you could spare time this evening, I'd really appreciate your help with relocating my family."

"I'd be honored, Elijah. And please, call me Maddie. I'm showing Sully some property on the ridge north of town this afternoon, but when we get back you and I can sit down and chat."

"Thank you, Ma'am. I mean Maddie." He smiled. "I'll be here." Turning, he disappeared into the kitchen carrying his books on his hip.

****

Sully and I spent the rest of the afternoon on the ridge. Thrilled with the site I showed him, he felt sure Betty and his son, Robbie, would love the property. When we returned to the soda shop, we crunched numbers and looked over plans. I showed him some sample contracts, too. By the time we finished, it was almost seven o'clock.

"Done." I pulled the papers into a file." I'm sure you can handle the rest from here."

"Maddie, you've been a great help. What do I owe

you?"

"How about a free milkshake now and then?" I smiled and turned toward the door.

"At least let me drive you home."

"Thanks for the offer, but it's such a beautiful evening, Sully, and I've only got a few blocks to walk. I could use the exercise. Besides, I want to talk to Elijah before I leave."

"All right then. Thanks again, Maddie. You're a real gem."

I waved goodbye leaving Sully's office then looked around for Elijah. As anxious as I was to get home to Bobby, I felt even more compelled to help the young man I'd met earlier. My empathy for what Elijah had to endure took precedence, and I resolved to do whatever I could to make his life easier. Prejudice reared its ugly head even in paradise.

I found Elijah studying at a table in the back of the kitchen then worked with him for almost two hours, weighing out his options. He'd managed to save a good bit of money, enough to purchase a small piece of prime property on the north shore of the ridge near Bobby's land. Knowing the future value of his purchase delighted me. Elijah was such an articulate, hard-working, lovely man with the patience of Job. I had taken one small step toward a much-needed civil rights movement.

It had been a gratifying afternoon. I loved handpicking Piper's potential neighbors. Bobby, Sandy, the Sullivans, and Elijah would live close to the Taylor property, which somehow would end up being Alice's, and ultimately Piper's. It felt good to know my friend would have respectable families around her.

No wonder I'd enjoyed Piper's neighbors at the party that fateful night. I had handpicked each of them. Bobby knew most everyone in and around Sidney. And by choosing the nicest people he knew and planting them strategically throughout the ridge, I felt like I had enriched Piper's life somehow. I may never see her again, but at least I could do something to positively affect her future. Of course, some families might sell their property over the course of the next sixty-two years, but chances were, they'd understand the value of hanging onto their land.

Walking down Peachtree Road, I fantasized running into Bobby's arms, kissing him, a hot passionate kiss filled with seven months of pent up desire. He and Sandy might already be asleep after our late evening the previous night, but waking him might be fun. I accelerated my pace, my heart beating faster in anticipation. Yes, I could see the lights on, hear them talking on the front porch.

Moving toward the veranda, I suddenly realized the female talking with Bobby had a thick southern drawl, definitely not Sandy's, but thankfully not Sharon's either. Her tone was drenched with anxiety. I thought about using the rear entrance to avoid interrupting what sounded like an intimate conversation, but my innate curiosity got the best of me. I paused behind the bushes next to the front porch.

"Bobby, I don't know what I'd do without you." Her soft voice, filled with adoration, caused a knot to fist in the pit of my stomach. "I love you. You're the most caring man I've ever known."

I strained to peek through the thick azaleas, trying desperately to see her face, and his, without stirring the bushes. Leaning in further, I pressed against the shrubs, eased myself closer, mindful of avoiding any obtrusive sound. The last thing I wanted to do was draw attention to my espionage. *Okay, say it like it is, Lace*, I didn't want them to catch me spying on them, but espionage sounded so much more civilized and made me feel a little better about snooping.

There they sat, cuddled together in the swing, practically on top of each other. Bobby's arm stretched around her, her head nuzzled close to his chest. Long blonde hair curled around her bare shoulders, spilling onto his arm. Her bent knees nestled under her sundress, rested on Bobby's lap as she snuggled into him. A sudden wave of nausea rolled from my stomach into my throat. I silently choked down the bile.

How could he? Not twenty-four hours after I professed my undying love. There he was, blatantly wooing some strange woman right there on the front porch. What if I had walked up? I wanted to confront them, to validate that I had been right about his playboy antics all along. He was a cad, no different from Cole or the laundry list of other jerks that had played me.

Shrinking away from the bushes, I noticed the back of her white car on the driveway, pulled up close to the shrubbery. I didn't recognize the vehicle or the woman, but I had never noticed Sharon before either. Both of them just appeared on Bobby's front porch out of the blue and groped him as if they owned him. The whole scenario was too much for me to deal with. I snuck around back, slunk in through the rear door. Tiptoeing through the silent house, then up the stairs, I slid into my room. I eased the door closed, collapsed onto my bed. But I didn't cry. Instead, I felt broken inside, defeated, hollow and cold. I lay in the dark room blankly watching moon shadows dance across the walls, wishing I could vanish or wake up from the nightmare that had ripped through my soul.

Eventually, I heard them creep up the stairs.

"Shhh, Sandy is asleep. We don't want to wake her," Bobby whispered.

"Okay," she replied softly, passing by my room.

I heard the bedroom door softly creak, shut. Water ran in the bathroom. The commode flushed, footsteps padded across the floor, then a door squeaked to a close again. My imagination spun out of control visualizing the torrid affair frolicking behind Bobby's closed door. How many times had he bedded some sleazy skank while Sandy and I slept? The lump in my stomach squeezed tighter.

I couldn't face him, not now, after everything I'd seen. I wanted to disappear, but—wait a minute. I actually *could* disappear. Bobby and Sandy would worry at first, but at some point, they'd believe I'd been sucked back to my own time. No confrontation, no explanation, no tears. I'd simply vanish. Perhaps I could hitch a ride somewhere, maybe Atlanta, and forget Bobby Reynolds even existed. Plans wove through my thoughts, numbing the pain until slumber soothed the rip in my heart.

****

When I awoke Tuesday morning, the house was silent. Bobby and Sandy had left for work. Convinced that fleeing Sidney altogether was my obvious choice, I started packing my few belongings, then realized that if I were sucked back to my own time, the exit wouldn't have been planned. That meant I wouldn't have time to pack. To make sure Sandy and Bobby believed my untimely departure, I'd have to leave everything behind except the clothes on my back. The things I called my own since my arrival in Sidney weren't really mine anyway. Most were hand-me-downs from Sandy and the rest were gifts from Bobby.

I'd managed to earn a little cash, but for the most part, I'd simply bartered with my clients. A few, like Elijah, gave me gifts far greater than money. Helping people come to terms with the hand they'd been dealt gave me a sense of fulfillment I had never experienced. Significance had been missing from my life, like why I'd attended law school in the first place. I wanted to help innocent people fight for justice. But now that would be gone, too. As hard as I'd tried to protect myself, I had self-destructed again.

Reaching into my top drawer, I grabbed my small roll of money, stuffed it into my pocket. I took one last look at the bedroom that had been my home for the past seven months before wandering downstairs. It would be hard to walk away from Sidney and all of the people I'd grown to love. Strolling into the kitchen, I felt the ache inside deepen. Bobby had, as usual, meticulously placed my favorite coffee cup next to a freshly brewed pot, and Sandy had left a plate of food wrapped in aluminum foil sitting on the stove.

I took one of her leftover biscuits, stuffed a bite into my mouth, then emptied the coffeepot into my cup. Like a real family, or at least what I'd always envisioned one to be, Bobby, Sandy, and I had cared about one another. We had an omnipresent bond instinctively doing things for each other. I loved both of them but, no matter how much it hurt, I had to leave. I couldn't face Bobby. I didn't know if I ever could again.

Ambling out to the front porch, I reminisced about the wonderful life I had to leave behind. For the first time, I'd felt like I belonged. Sidney, so peaceful and beautiful, had become a real home surrounded by family and friends who treated me like someone worth knowing, worth caring about. I didn't have to earn acceptance here. I'd had respect and trust from the beginning, thanks to Bobby and his sister.

Sitting down on the porch swing, I sipped my coffee thinking about them. Sandy was like a sister to me, and I couldn't bear the thought of never seeing Bobby again, never smelling the English Leather scent that always soothed my inner turmoil. I'd never look into those burning sapphire eyes again or feel the passion he evoked with a simple kiss. He was my soul mate, but I had to accept that I wasn't his.

I stood, placed my empty coffee cup on the side table, and walked to the porch steps. Pausing for a moment, I took a deep breath and began the descent. The ache in my stomach clenched tighter with each stride forward, but I had to leave, and I loved Bobby too much to ever return.

Chapter 15

Lake Lanier, Georgia—March 2012

Rob waffled for months before finally deciding to approach Warren Montgomery. It would be a bold move, and risky. From all indications the man was calculating, intimidating, and cold. His authority over his self-made dynasty appeared impenetrable. No one questioned, manipulated or even tried to influence the man, including his daughter, Lacey.

If Rob could sway Montgomery...yes, Warren Montgomery could be an asset, an incongruous ally. Rob felt sure he had the resources to entice the man. He'd had no problem convincing Drew of the benefits at stake, even when he divulged the truth and his bizarre intentions. In the end, there was only one variable Rob couldn't completely control, the timing. The domino effect had to be triggered precisely. A few seconds either way would have devastating consequences.

****

Sidney, Georgia—May 1950

"Maddie, is that you? What are you doing out here so early?" Sully sat down on the park bench beside me. "The sun hasn't even broken the horizon yet. Are you all right?"

"Yes, I'm fine," I lied. "I just woke up early and

decided to take a walk." The truth was I hadn't slept at all. I'd wandered around Sidney all day yesterday taking mental pictures of everything. I traced each street, wandered through every shop, and sat in the library for hours. There wasn't an inch of town I hadn't covered.

"I've been coming here every morning for months, now." Sully marveled as a crest of the fiery sphere broke the horizon. "The sunrise is really somethin' here, isn't it?"

A bluebird winged past us, perched on a tree limb to warble her enchanting trill. I babbled a rote response that had nothing to do with his comment. "It's strange how the birds flit around chirping every morning. The world wakes up, starts fresh as if yesterday never happened." My mind churned, mesmerized by the scene before me, the wildlife flourishing amidst rich foliage, and glints of sunlight dancing across the pond. It would be so much easier to forget about yesterdays and greet every morning happy and renewed. *Why do I cling to painful, haunting memories?*

"I suppose it does. Not a bad attitude though." Sully's voice floated through my musing. "It's peaceful this time of day."

"Yes, peaceful," I replied blankly.

"Ever since the dam business commenced I've had trouble sleeping. But coming out here to watch the sunrise helps me put things in perspective."

His remark ignited my passion, and I turned toward him in earnest. "Things will work out fine for you now. I promise. The north shore of the lake will be beautiful and besides, Sully, it's the people that make up a town, not the land."

"I'd never thought of it that way, Maddie. But I reckon you're right."

I turned to him and continued my discourse. "If your house burned down you could rebuild, right?"

"Yes, as long as my family was safe, I could start over."

"Exactly. And if Sidney sinks into the lake, the town will still live on as long as family and friends stay together. People matter in life, not things." Thoughts of Bobby, Sandy, and the whole town spun through my mind. "As long as you have people who love you, everything else is icing on a cake."

"You're something else Maddie Montgomery. I don't know what brought you here, but Sidney sure is lucky you arrived. You're really making a difference to a lot of people." He stood and stretched. "I'd better get home. Betty will have my hide if I'm not back before breakfast. I have to open shop soon, too. I'll be seeing you."

"Tell Betty I said 'hi'." I smiled. "See you later." Would I? Twenty-four hours ago, my world made sense. I had a future, a life filled with promise, love, and happiness. But now...my thoughts drifted back to yesterday.

By three o'clock, I'd wandered robotically through Sidney reliving most of the past seven months. Convinced I had to leave, I'd simply taken off, but my impulsive departure had me mindlessly meandering through memories with no direction or destination. When I found myself at Millie's for the umpteenth time, I finally went inside, instinctively sat down in Bobby's booth. I needed to think, to create a plan for my future.

Millie brought me a hamburger, french-fries, and a chocolate shake. Hoping the comfort food would prompt some semblance of a game plan, I pulled out a pad of paper and a pencil to jot down my ideas. I'd just taken a few bites and doodled a broken heart when Ben Taylor slipped into the seat across from me.

"What's cookin', Maddie?"

"Nothing much." I flipped the pad over, pushed it to the side. "How's Margaret feeling?"

"She's getting bigger every day. I tell you, that baby's gonna be a handful the way it's kickin' inside her belly." He chuckled.

"And Alice?" I picked up a fry, swiped it through a dollop of ketchup then bit off the end.

"It's the strangest thing about Alice. She had her heart set on a baby sister. Then out of nowhere, she's singing praise about a brother." He laughed. "Like Art Linkletter said the other day on his radio show, 'Kid's say the darndest things.' You never know what they're thinking."

"You're right, Ben. You never know." I smiled remembering my talk with little Alice. "So, what brings you to Millie's this afternoon?"

"I wanted to grab a quick bite before I head to Gainesville. I've got some business there and will likely miss dinner tonight."

I nodded. That's it, Gainesville. I'd been there plenty of times in the past or rather the future. At least the town would be remotely familiar, and it wasn't far from Sidney. I could keep tabs on everyone here and maybe get a job with a lawyer. It could work.

"Hey Ben, do you think I could hitch a ride to Gainesville with you?" I asked. "I have some things I'd like to check into there as well." I took a big bite of hamburger, and the grease dribbled down the corners of my mouth.

"Sure, Maddie. I'd be happy to give you a lift."

"Thanks." I wiped my lips.

Millie strolled over to fill my water glass. "The special today Ben, or has Maddie's burger tempted you?"

"It smells too good to pass up," he replied. "But bring a Co-cola with it, please."

She nodded, ambled back to the kitchen.

"By the way," Ben said. "Margaret is really excited about building a home on the lake. She's even started drawing some amateur blueprints." His enthusiasm distracted me from my problems.

"She'll enjoy living so close to Bobby and Sandy, and your property will be right on the shore of the new lake, too. Margret will love that."

All through lunch and most of the drive to Gainesville, we chatted about Ben's new lot, house plans, Betty, the new baby, Alice, and how excited the family was. I knew the Taylor's would buy that property but couldn't help wondering why they never built the house Margret was so thrilled about. Alice inherited the land and passed it on to Piper. Something happened to change Ben's mind about building and whatever transpired happened soon. I hoped it wasn't a tragedy.

It was a little after five when Ben and I finally reached the center of Gainesville.

"I'm heading to Jenkins and Smith on Athens Highway. It's about a mile down the road. Can I drop you off somewhere first?" Ben asked.

"No, no. Don't bother. That's actually close to where I need to go. I'll just get out there."

"It's no trouble, but if you're sure." A few moments later, he pulled into the parking lot. "I expect to be here for a few hours, until about nine o'clock give or take a few minutes. Meet me here by nine, and we'll drive back, okay?"

"Thanks, Ben, but I won't be needing a ride back to Sidney. I appreciate the offer though. It was so nice of you to let me come with you."

"Are you sure, Maddie? I'd hate for you to be stranded here."

"I'll be fine." I scrambled for a reason to explain my decision. "I have friends here." It wasn't a complete lie. I did have friends in Gainesville. Of course they hadn't been born yet, but that was just a little detail he didn't need to know.

"Well, if you change your mind, this bus will leave at nine o'clock sharp. I'll look around for you then, just in case."

"I don't expect to change my mind, but thanks." I opened the car door, stepped out.

"See you later, Maddie." Ben hustled toward the building. "I enjoyed the company."

"Bye." I waved then took off down the sidewalk. Once out of sight, I strolled through the center of town with no idea where to go. Gainesville had an old-fashioned ambiance not unlike Sidney. Hopefully I'd find the same sense of serenity here. I wandered the streets in search of something that felt...right. The people were friendly enough, nodding as they passed, men tipped their hats and women smiled. But it wasn't Sidney and I felt so utterly alone.

As I walked past a boarding house, I pulled the small wad of money out of my pocket to see if I could afford to spend a few nights there. It was possible, providing I didn't eat. I began to realize I hadn't thought through my brilliant idea very well. At least in Sidney I had established a basis for a job. The community was more than willing to pay me for helping them transition. But here in Gainesville there was little need for my expertise. My law degree was of absolutely no use in 1950 either, and though I might find work assisting a lawyer, they weren't quite as plentiful as I'd imagined. Perhaps I could get a job serving food somewhere.

My mind reeled trying to figure out a plan that made sense. I looked for window signs advertising help wanted, inquired about jobs in various shops, and queried in flophouses for a suitable room. The area was lovely, quaint, friendly, but I had an inexplicable sense of the surreal, like I was drifting through a movie set. I couldn't shake the feeling that I didn't belong here.

It was getting late. The sun slipped below the horizon casting an eerie twilight glow, and I shivered trying to rid myself of the uneasy feeling. Most of the shops had closed, and a sprinkling of lights began to dot the streets. Drawn to the window of a small clock shop, I thought it odd the store stayed open so late. I stepped inside.

The place looked deserted, silent except for the tick-tick-tick of countless clocks, all chanting the time, in unison—eight forty-five. Time reverberated all around me. I strolled toward the back of the store, but saw no one.

"Hello. Is anyone here?" No answer.

Gazing around the shop, I perused the clocks, hundreds of them, all sizes and shapes, chanting the passage of each second with their own metronomic hum. The incessant sound consumed me. My head spun, swirling to the monotonous pulsating whir as it amplified louder, louder, louder.

A surge of nausea rolled from my stomach into my throat, biting, stinging along its path until I couldn't breathe. Throwing my hands over my ears, I tried to mute the relentless clatter. But the ticking persisted, echoing in my head as if time itself was chanting the frenetic warning. I squeezed my eyes and let out a bloodcurdling scream, "Stooooopppppppp!"

The assiduous racket abruptly dissolved into a soft whir. Finally unshackled by the incessant sound, I fled from the little shop, sprinted down the road, scanning every street sign, searching for Athens Highway.

When I saw the signpost, I sped toward the Jenkins and Smith building, my lungs pleading for oxygen. An inexplicable force pushed me forward. I couldn't miss my ride home. It was my only connection to Sidney, and Bobby. As I approached the parking lot, I saw Ben Taylor get into his car and back out. I frantically waved, yelled to him. But he turned the opposite direction, drove off down the road then abruptly stopped. Backing up, he pulled next to me.

"You sure cut things close, Maddie Montgomery. You're lucky I saw you running this way in my rearview mirror."

He reached over, opened the passenger side door. I jumped inside, pulled the door closed, then collapsed into the seat.

Breathing heavily, I looked over at him. "Thanks

for waiting, Ben."

"I'm happy for the company." He put the car in gear and headed home. "Say, what made you change your mind about staying in Gainesville?"

"I guess I finished quicker than I thought."

"Right. Well things don't always work out like we plan them. But, as a wise young woman recently brought to my attention," he cleared his throat and gave me a side glance, "sometimes the things you think are the worst that can happen turn out to be the best. If your plans didn't work out here, Maddie, maybe it's for the better in the long run."

"I hope you're right, Ben."

I settled into my seat for the drive home. Ben flipped on the radio, and we drove away from Gainesville listening to Judy Garland crooning, *Somewhere Over The Rainbow*. Closing my eyes, I began to relax as her words painted a somewhat familiar vision on the canvas of my mind.

I softly hummed while anguish drained from my body. I was going home, and at that moment I knew that regardless of the reason, I was meant to go back in time to Sidney. Sandy was right. No matter what happened between Bobby and me, my dreams wouldn't come true unless I stopped fighting against them.

We got back to Sidney around eleven o'clock. Ben dropped me off in front of the Reynolds' house. I thanked him again, waving goodbye until his car turned the corner. But I couldn't go inside. Instead, I walked to the park and spent the rest of the night sitting on the bench listening to katydids chirp endlessly and frogs croaking as they peeked above the rippling pond. I watched the moon chase the stars across the indigo sky to greet the first glimpse of morning. That's where Sully had found me, quietly praying that God would help me make the right decisions.

I'd been independent my entire life so why not now? After all, I'd come into this town with nothing but a little beaded purse and—oh no, Piper's purse. My only real possession, and I'd left it in my bureau. I shot up, scurried back toward the house. I'd purposely closed my bedroom door. Perhaps Bobby and Sandy had assumed I'd gotten in late last night. Glancing at the sun, I estimated the time to be close to eight o'clock. They would have left for work by now. I could slip in, get my purse and maybe grab a cup of coffee and something to eat. I'd have to face them of course, but not before I had figured out what I was going to say.

Bobby's car was gone and so was his friend's. I tiptoed up the front steps, slid inside just in case someone had overslept, then crept up the stairs into my room. Finding Piper's purse in the top drawer of the dresser, I held it close to my chest in relief.

The rich aroma of fresh brewed coffee filled the house. I could almost taste a fresh cup of Joe. I peeked out of my room, noticing Bobby's open bedroom door. He had definitely gone to work and had most likely taken Sandy with him. Her door was closed though, so I tried my best to creep down the stairs as quietly as possible.

Two empty coffee cups sat on the kitchen counter and two plates had been placed in the sink, each with remnants of pancake and syrup. The coffee pot was still warm, so I reached for an empty cup, filled it, and wrapped my hands around the steaming mug. The rich aroma of the strong, nutty brew filled my senses as the hot liquid slipped down my throat.

As usual, a plate of food had been set-aside for me. Sandy and Bobby had no idea I'd been gone for the past thirty-six hours, let alone that I'd passed through the *Twilight* Zone in the process. They trusted I'd simply worked late and was fast asleep in my room.

I pulled the foil back and popped a piece of bacon into my mouth. I hadn't eaten a bite since Millie's hamburger yesterday afternoon, so I scarfed four pancakes down without bothering to use a plate, or syrup. Then, taking my coffee and another piece of bacon out to the front porch, I sat in my favorite place, the swing. It was time to get down to business, where to go from here. Deep in thought, I hadn't heard the soft footsteps padding down the stairs, but the creaking of the front door as it opened startled me. My eyes shot toward the entrance.

"You must be Maddie. It's so nice to finally meet you."

Spinning around, I saw an attractive blonde woman dressed in nothing but a baggy white T-shirt. A sense of *déjà vu* washed over me as I thought of myself dressed identically only a few months earlier.

"Yes," was all I could muster out. I stared in disbelief, watching her prance toward me nonchalantly peeling a tangerine.

"Bobby told me all about you." She popped a wedge into her mouth. "How you're helping his friends and…"

Bobby told her about me? And she had the unmitigated gall to strut downstairs, half-naked and flaunt her tryst? This was way too much to take in.

"…I was hoping to meet you yesterday," she continued. "But you are one busy woman."

"Meet me?" I muttered through my stunned stupor.

"Yup. I tried to stay awake to catch you. Sandy's spare bed isn't very comfortable, but don't tell her I said so. I've tossed and turned for two nights now. I must have drifted off though, cuz I never did hear you come home."

"I…" Did she say *Sandy's* bed?

"It's okay though. I can't look a gift horse in the mouth now can I?"

"But, your car?" I questioned.

"Oh, Sandy took it to work this mornin'. Bobby left real early, and I wasn't gonna use it." She sat down in the rocking chair beside me. "She said you were always workin' late, but was sure I'd catch up to you this mornin'."

"Catch up to me?" My brow wrinkled as I surrendered utter confusion.

"Yeah, Bobby said we had a lot in common. That's why I ended up staying over for a few days."

"He did?"

"You don't talk much first thing in the mornin' do you, Maddie? Yeah, he insisted I meet you. Truth be told, I could use a few days away from home though. Hey, any more coffee?"

"No, I'm afraid this was the last cup. Who—"

"That's okay." She leaned back and slowly rocked her chair. "I'll make more in a few minutes. Have you eaten yet? I'm pretty good at making scrambled eggs if I do say so myself."

"Yes, Sandy left some pancakes on the stove. Who did you say you were?"

"Oh, heavens to Betsy," she said in her thick southern drawl. "You must not have seen Bobby or Sandy this morning either." She wiped her hand on her shirt then extended it to me. "I'm Carrie Ann Williams...Bobby and Sandy's cousin...from Asheville?"

"I'm sorry, but I—"

"I de-clare, I would have thought they'd at least have mentioned me." She pulled her legs up under her T-shirt. "Not that they'd have much reason to. I might not have seen them for another year or two if it hadn't been for that scoundrel husband of mine taking up with his secretary."

"Husband?"

"Yes." Her perky attitude faded, and she continued with a more solemn tone. "That's how I ended up here. I went to Billy's office to surprise him, and there he was with his arms around her."

Tension drained as the puzzle pieces fell into place. Bobby had been comforting Carrie Ann, not wooing her. She was his cousin, and she'd slept in one of Sandy's twin beds, not in Bobby's arms. Relief drained the stir of emotions welled inside, and I suddenly felt like a complete idiot.

"What was his explanation?" I asked.

"I don't know. I got in my car and the next thing I knew, I was at Bobby and Sandy's front door. When we were little, Bobby was like a big brother to me. Whenever I needed anything, he was always there for me."

"I can totally identify with how you felt, taking off like that, I mean." As Carrie Ann explained, I realized what a complete fool I had been for assuming she and

Bobby were involved. What if I hadn't come back to Sidney or to the house in search of Piper's purse? My impulsive reaction could have destroyed everything.

"Bobby convinced me to stay to meet you. He said you know a lot about men, and I'd be wise to get an experienced woman's point of view."

"Experienced?" I wasn't quite sure how to take that comment. "Well, I've had my share of relationships, but I'm not sure I'm the right person to give any advice."

"My cousin has never steered me wrong. I trust him, so what would you do, Maddie?"

"I have to admit my first instinct would be to take off like you did." I couldn't very well tell her otherwise in light of my reaction to seeing Bobby with her.

"See, that's what I told Bobby. He seems to think I—"

"But," I interrupted her. "Instincts aren't always right. It depends on how they developed."

"What do you mean?"

"In my case, I think I've always associated love with abandonment. My mother died when I was young, and Daddy shut himself off from everyone including me. My instincts told me that love caused pain."

"So you think my instincts made me run instead of confronting Billy?"

I shifted in the swing, pushed it slightly. "Only you can answer that. But something made you doubt him."

"I saw him with my own eyes."

"You saw him with his arms around another woman. That's circumstantial evidence."

"Maddie, you sound just like a lawyer."

"Guilty, as charged. I have studied law, but that's

not the point. Listen Carrie Ann, I grew up so afraid of getting hurt that I couldn't trust love. The vague image of it sent me running in the opposite direction, and every boy I chose to date validated my fears." Pulling my feet up, I rested them on the chain, pushing the swing in a sideways motion. "I chose men destined to fit into my warped image of love. You know the type, so full of themselves there's no room for anyone else." I wasn't sure where all of that was coming from, but somehow the thoughts came together like a crystal ball glimpse into my past.

"Yeah. I've known a lot of guys like that," she replied.

"Maybe you jumped to the conclusion that Billy was having an affair because of something in your past. Could he have simply been consoling her?"

"I suppose." She finished her tangerine, wiped her fingers on her T-shirt.

"You'll never know unless you ask. You married him, so I'm assuming that you love him, right?"

"Yes, but I never thought he could—"

"Maybe he didn't. You can't love without trust, Carrie Ann." Did I say that? The words fell from my lips into a pool of revelation.

"Before I took off, I left Billy a note telling him Sandy needed me, and I'd be back in a few days. He doesn't even know what happened. I'm not sure why my first instinct was to doubt him. He's never lied to me or anything."

"Maybe pride or fear. Who knows? One thing I know for sure though, things aren't always as they appear to be." I twirled a strand of my hair between my thumb and forefinger. "Whatever you do, don't let your thoughts or fears grip your soul so strongly that it strangles your future."

"I didn't even tell Bobby or Sandy this, but the truth is I'm pregnant. That's what I was gonna tell Billy when I went to his office, but when I saw him I got scared."

"Oh my gosh, your hormones must be all over the place. No wonder you reacted that way." At least she had an excuse. I, on the other hand, had taken off because I refused to trust the most wonderful man I'd ever known. I stood, bent over Carrie Ann, and gave her a huge hug. "Congratulations. And don't worry about Billy. Just talk to him."

"Thanks, Maddie." She pulled herself up, gave me a proper hug back.

"Let's go get you and that little one some breakfast. There's still a stack of pancakes and some bacon on the stove." I offered my hand to pull her from the rocker.

Carrie Ann and I talked away the afternoon until Sandy got home with her car. Then, she hugged us goodbye and headed back to Ashville to talk to Billy and break the news about the baby.

Bobby and Sandy never knew what I did, but I'm so glad it happened. That morning, sipping coffee with Carrie Ann, I finally realized I could trust love and even more importantly, I could trust Bobby. I vowed to never doubt him again. It was a conscious decision that lifted an albatross of fear from my life. When Bobby pulled up in the driveway that evening, I rushed to his car and greeted him with a bear hug.

"Wow, what a nice surprise."

"I've missed seeing you, and I owe you a huge

explanation." I kissed his cheek.

"Explanation about what?" He put his arm around my shoulder, and we walked up the front steps together.

"About the most confusing woman you've ever known."

Bobby laughed. "I take it you finally met my cousin."

"Yes, and I loved spending the afternoon with her." I stopped short of the door to look into his beautiful eyes. "But Carrie Ann isn't the woman I was talking about."

"Well then, Miss Montgomery, this will be one talk with a female that I'm looking forward to." He grinned, put his arms around my waist, and lifted me up, pressing his soft, warm lips against mine.

When my feet finally touched the ground again, I took his hand and led him inside.

Chapter 16

Lake Lanier, Georgia—April 2012

"Piper, with your sense of design, you're perfect for the job." Rob touched her shoulder. "I'd consider it a personal favor if you'd coordinate the party for me."

"After all you've done for me, I could hardly say no. I'd be happy to help."

"I hoped you'd say that. The clubhouse is already reserved for June 9th. Let's make it a Black-Tie event. Don't spare any expense. I'll take care of the invitations, but feel free to include your friends, especially the single women. The most eligible bachelors in the country will be at this party."

"Oh? Then I definitely know some women who would love to attend." She smiled. "This will be fun."

"I thought you might enjoy planning the event. Let me know if you run into any problems. I've got to get to work now, but you have my phone number." Rob waved, walking away with an ear-to-ear grin. "Done," he whispered to himself. Soon, very soon, he would have Lacey. "Game, set, and match."

****

Sidney, Georgia—July 1950

"You're shivering. Come here." Bobby pulled me closer.

"I never get tired of this." Snuggling into him, I

drank in the panorama from our bench on the ridge. The soft scent of honeysuckle floated on the crisp morning air. "Look." I nudged Bobby, pointing at two squirrels chasing each other around the tree, flying from branch to branch.

"The epitome of our relationship, princess." He chuckled, stroked my hair. "In a few years, I expect this view will be even better. I try to imagine a lake out there, but for you it's a memory."

"Yes, but the memories we're making now are far better than any lake view."

It had been almost two months since our trip to Macon, two glorious months with Bobby. I'd never known that kind of happiness before. Trust is a magical element. And living a life free from the baggage I'd lugged around since childhood had transformed something inside of me.

"I don't ever want to stop making memories with you, Maddie. Say, since we're on the subject"—he tucked a curl behind my ear—"you know I love you. And I can't imagine my life without you."

"I love you, too, but what does that have to do with making memories?"

"You mean you weren't the least bit curious why I insisted on bringing you up here so early this morning, especially on the Fourth of July?"

"I thought it was kind of romantic." Nudging him again, I fluttered my eyelashes like a schoolgirl.

"My thoughts exactly." He slid around, kneeled on one knee, then held out a small black velvet box. "Lacey Madison Montgomery," he said with a slight crack in his voice. "Will you marry me?"

Goose bumps effervesced across my entire body, a

cool stream of champagne exploding from my stomach, bubbling, tickling my senses from head to toes. "Oh my gosh." I took the box from his hand, slowly opened it…then burst out laughing. There, displayed against the deep velvet background, was Bobby's brass carousel ring gleaming in the sunlight.

"This is perfect." I threw my arms around his neck, and we laughed until our sides hurt.

"So, do you like your Independence Day gift?" He sat back on his heels.

"I love it, but…"

"But what?" His eyes pierced through my unruffled exterior, probing into my soul. "Were you expecting something else?"

"No, this is perfect. Really."

"Oh?" He reached deep into his pocket. "Then I guess you wouldn't be interested in something more like this?" He held out his fist, pried opened his fingers one by one.

In his palm, he held the most beautiful diamond ring I'd ever seen. A brilliant solitaire sparkled atop a blazing background of smaller, close-set, full-cut diamonds. The setting was breathtaking.

"No matter what happens in our future, I'll love you forever, Maddie."

Tears exploded over my eyes. "Me, too," was all I could manage to squeak out.

"So, I'll take that as a yes?" He raised both eyebrows.

"Yes, Bobby. Oh yes." He slid the diamond on my finger, kissed me, a long, deep, passionate kiss. Then, pulling himself up, he sat beside me, draped his arm around my shoulder, and squeezed me close.

"Good, I'm glad we finally have that settled. You really made me chase after you before you caught me." He let out a belly laugh. "Just like your squirrels this morning."

Admiring my beautiful new ring, I nuzzled my head against his chest. "It wasn't easy, what with the language barrier and all."

"Right, well when we met I wasn't aware that you didn't speak the King's English."

I gazed up at him through my eyelashes. "You're never going to let me forget that, are you?"

"No ma'am. It's too much fun teasing you about it. Whatever possessed you to believe I wanted to or, for that matter could, lead you around by the nose?"

"It was rather an absurd assumption." I poked my elbow at him, giggled.

"I have an idea." Bobby stood, grabbed my hand, and pulled me up from the bench.

"Where are we going?" I asked, ducking the branches and bushes behind him.

"You'll see." He led me through the brush and trees until they opened to the base of his picturesque waterfall.

Flowing over smooth rock, the water splashed from the peak of the ridge and plummeted down the summit where streams fell into a sparkling natural pool.

"Are you up for a morning swim?" he asked, slowly unbuttoning my blouse.

"But the water is so cold this early," I whined, proffering my best childlike pout.

He slid the sleeves off my shoulders. "I promise I'll keep you warm."

My shirt dropped to the ground. His strong hands

roved across my bare back sending ripples of desire down my neck that swirled around my body until they found refuge in my most sensual areas.

I fumbled with the buttons on his shirt, slowly undressing him, kissing around his neck and shoulders, then down his chest. When I reached his pants, I nibbled at his waistband, unhooked the button, then pulled the zipper down with my teeth before pushing the fabric to the ground.

Kicking his pants aside, he pulled me close and eased my denims down my legs. Then he carried me, wading into the water, kissing and nibbling with each step, until we reached the falls. The water cascaded over us caressing our bodies, but it couldn't cool the heat of burning desire. We clung to each other in a blissful embrace. Feeling nothing but the warmth of his skin on mine, I completely surrendered in an explosion of unbridled passion.

Smoothing soggy hair away from my face, he leaned down and kissed my nose. "I'm so glad we finally unraveled your issues."

"Me, too," I said, pushing into him. "I never realized how traumatic my mother's death had been. When she died I lost both my parents, and the abandonment haunted me."

"You couldn't trust anyone?" He picked me up, carried me to the shore of the pond.

"Not until you." Resting my head on his chest, I listened to the ka-thunk, ka-thunk of his heartbeat.

"Well, when we have a little girl, we'll be sure she knows love."

I pulled away to look into his eyes. "A little girl, huh. We're going to have a little girl?" I brushed the water off my bare skin, rubbing my hands together, hoping friction would warm me from the chill in the air.

"I thought at least one of each. You do want kids don't you?"

"I never used to, but I've changed my mind about a lot of things lately. I think I'd like to have children with you, someday."

Shaking the water from his hair, Bobby gathered our clothes then began dressing.

"What do you think about a November 5th wedding?" he asked, buttoning his shirt.

"Whoa, hold on. That's only four months away." I bent over and squeezed the excess water from my hair, gazed over at Bobby then down at the sparkling rock on my left hand.

His smile brimmed with pride and satisfaction. "So, you're one of those ladies who likes long engagements?" Leaning against a bolder, he put on his shoes.

"Not at all. November 5th?" I smiled. "You remembered."

I would marry the man of my dreams in November. It *was* fast. How could I ever plan a wedding in only four months? But he remembered November 5th, the day I fell through the portal and landed in 1949. His sweet gesture was so romantic. And Sandy would jump at the chance to help us with the plans.

"I know we didn't officially meet until the 6th, but the 5th is when you arrived in Sidney and it falls on a Sunday this year. Sunday is a better day for a wedding than Monday, don't you agree?"

"I think November 5th is perfect. But let's keep the wedding simple, okay?"

"That sounds good to me." He grinned the wonderful smile I had grown to love. "But with a helluva honeymoon."

"Oh? Do you already have plans for that?" I grabbed his hand lacing my fingers between his.

"I wouldn't be much of a fella if I didn't." He squeezed my hand. "I was thinking we might go somewhere exotic."

We hiked back up to the ridge discussing the plans for our future. *Our future.* The idea sounded so surreal, so wonderful. Finally I could look at a future, a life with the man I loved.

Bobby glanced down at his watch. "We need to get back. Sandy must be about to explode."

"So she knew you were going to ask me to marry you?" I asked, heading toward the car.

"Do you think I could keep something like that a secret from her? You are familiar with my sister, aren't you? Nothing gets past her."

"Good point." I laughed. "Maybe we should just walk in nonchalantly as if nothing happened."

"Oh that would drive her bananas." He opened the car door for me, sprang around to the other side, hopped into the driver's seat.

"Exactly," I said smugly. "Just once I'd like to be one step ahead of Sandy Reynolds, even if it's only for a few hours. Besides tonight would be the perfect time to announce our engagement, at the 4th of July Festival."

"Yeah, but if Sandy finds out we're toying with her, there may be a lot more fireworks than the rockets they're launching at the square tonight."

By the time we returned home, Sandy had

breakfast waiting. I slipped my engagement ring into my pocket before we sat down to eat, acting as if the morning had been no different from any other. Bobby and I exchanged numerous looks through breakfast. We even tried to prod Sandy into inquiries with less than subtle hints. But her demeanor remained steadfast with not even a hint of curiosity. By mid-afternoon my excitement had been held back long enough. I was about to burst.

"Richie will be by in a few minutes to pick me up for the festival," Sandy announced. "You two are going, right?"

"We planned to pack a picnic dinner and bop over about four o'clock or so," Bobby replied.

"It's gonna get pretty hot at the square today. I think I'll pin my hair up. Be a doll and let Richie in when he gets here, Maddie. I'll be down in a few minutes." She giggled and started up the stairs, then paused. "I can't wait for the fireworks. They make the celebration perfect, don't you think so?"

I looked at Bobby and he looked back.

"She knows," he whispered.

"She does. And she knows we know she knows." I laughed softly.

"That's my sister."

I slipped the ring from my pocket and put it back on my finger. Not two seconds later Sandy bounced down the stairs.

"Finally," she said. "You two have spent way too much time fighting destiny." She hugged both of us, grabbed my hand to admire the ring. "It's beautiful. I'm impressed Bobby, and on the Fourth of July, too. I never realized how romantic my brother was under that

229

cool exterior."

By the time we got to the festival, Sandy had told the whole town about our news. The flurry of congratulations and good wishes overwhelmed us before we even got to the square, which added to the excitement. The Independence Day celebration, already in progress, was different from any I'd seen before. An atmosphere of patriotism and pride coupled with down home cooking, family and friends. The square was decked out in red, white and blue, with balloons, ribbons and streamers everywhere and a festively dressed band stood in the gazebo playing patriotic tunes like *Yankee Doodle Dandy* and *God Bless America*.

The parade began at precisely six o'clock while the whole town stood by, clapping as they watched the pageantry. Majorettes twirled batons, mimes ran in and out of the procession, and the Sidney High Marching Band wowed the crowd. Decorated motorcades carried celebrities from Mayor/Police Chief Baxter to the recently crowned Peach Princess, Betty Miller. All strutted down Peachtree to Main Street and past the bandstand, celebrating the birthday of America's Freedom.

Bobby spread out a blanket by the pond, a perfect location to view the fireworks. When I unpacked the fried chicken, potato salad, baked beans, and peach cobbler from the picnic basket, I found a bottle of champagne and two glasses he'd slipped into the cooler. He popped the cork just before the fireworks began, poured the bubbly into the glasses, handed one to me.

"To us," he said, clinking his glass to mine.

"Always," I replied.

Rockets soared, shimmering through a star-studded sky as we sipped our champagne. Children swirled sparklers, twisting them back and forth and watching in wonderment. When a balloon burst just above our heads, the red ribbon drifted down onto our blanket, jogging a memory. I reached in the picnic basket for a knife, cut off two small strands of ribbon.

"What are you doing?" Bobby asked.

"There's an ancient Japanese legend," I began, "that the god of destiny ties an invisible red string around the little finger of destined souls." I tied a small red ribbon on Bobby's little finger. "The red thread connects those two people through eternity. And regardless of time, place, or circumstances they're drawn together. The magical cord may stretch or tangle, but it will never break."

"Destiny brought you through time to be with me, Maddie." He took the other piece of ribbon and tied it on my little finger. "And nothing will ever separate us."

We gazed up again, watching skyrockets burst into a glittering display, and I couldn't help but feel that somewhere beyond the velvet sky, ancient Japanese gods were smiling.

****

Lightning streaked across the night sky casting an eerie glow that shimmered through the mist, a dense haze so thick the droplets choked the oxygen from the air, and my lungs. The smothering sensation consumed me. I squinted to see through the gloom, my heart racing.

"Bobby?" I screamed, winding my way through the suffocating fog.

"Maddie, where are you?"

I caught a glimpse of his faint image. "Bobby, I'm here." I ran forward reaching for him but grabbed nothing but silvery haze. His figure faded, dissolved into the mist. Tears pooled in my eyes streamed down my face. "Bobby. Bobby."

"Maddie, I'm here. Wake up." He shook me. "Wake up Sweetheart. It's just a dream."

"Oh Bobby." I opened my eyes and sat up abruptly, throwing my arms around him.

"Sweetie, it's all right. I'm right here."

"But you weren't. I could see you, but you kept drifting further and further away, vanishing in murky fog. I lost you."

"You'll never lose me, Maddie. I promise." He pulled me closer, held me until my anguish subsided.

The dream had haunted me for months now. But this time, I felt Bobby drifting away, saw him fade and vanish into the mist. It terrified me to think I could be pulled back to the future. I didn't want to leave. Not now. Not ever. Was my nightmare an omen? Bobby was the love of my life, my destiny. The world I'd left behind held little more than a hollow, empty shell. I couldn't bear the thought of being sucked through time again, torn away from everything and everyone I'd come to love.

Chapter 17

Lake Lanier, Georgia—April 2012

Rob sat on the deck gazing down at the lake below. The dark, shadowy water hypnotized him. His cocky attitude faltered in moments like this. Countless times he had thought about just diving in, sinking into oblivion, deep, beyond the lake's depths. It would be easier, but he didn't want to die. He had to see his plan through.

"I was wondering where you were." Drew walked up behind him.

"It's a good place to think, old man."

"With age comes wisdom," he said. "Besides, I'm not *that* old."

Rob looked at Drew. Silver hair, a few smile lines around his deep blue eyes exhibited signs of his years, but his skin had few wrinkles for a man of his age.

"I'm sorry, you're right. I'll stop calling you that."

"Are you okay?" Drew's twisted expression showed concern.

"I will be," Rob replied. "Thanks to you. You've really come through for me."

"Hey, we both have a lot at stake here. You get what you want. I get what I want. Hang in there. Only a few more months and this whole thing will be a distant memory."

"Right. And our lives will change forever," Rob agreed.

"Good. Now come on inside. I have a few things to go over with you." He patted Rob on the back and they both strolled back into the house.

****

Sidney, Georgia—November 1950

"Are you sure you don't want to wear these?" Sandy dangled her beaded white gloves in front of me. "You still need something borrowed."

"And blue, but yes, sweetie, I'm positive. I may be stuck in 1950, but I don't have to give in to antiquated traditions or frou-frou styles for my own wedding." I sat down at the vanity to put the finishing touches on my makeup. "Sorry Sandy. I'm just nervous. Do you really think Bobby will like my dress?"

"Maddie, you could wear a gunnysack and he'd still have a huge smile on his face when you walked down that aisle."

"No really, Sandy. I hope I made the right choice. I mean it's so different from what most brides wear these days. But I've had a vision of my wedding since I was a little girl, what I'd wear and…I guess that's kinda silly."

"Personally, I would have chosen the white lace with the red sash. You know, the one that had all of the red petticoats under it."

"Really?" I asked in earnest.

She laughed. "No, I'm kidding, Maddie. Most little girls dream of their wedding. Your dress is…*you*, sophisticated and gorgeous. White velvet is perfect. It's so cold this year." She walked up behind me, looked at my reflection in the vanity mirror. "Trust me, Bobby will love it. Every woman out there will think you look like a dream, men, too, for that matter. That is if you ever get dressed. Now let me help you."

"Okay." Standing, I drew in a deep breath. "Thanks, Sandy." My nerves are hanging by their last thread. And I so want everything to be flawless.

"Here, lean on my shoulder and step into the dress so you don't muss your hair."

Sandy slid my white velvet floor-length gown over my hips then pulled the gathered-velvet strap-like sleeves onto my shoulders. The front dipped in a loose drape accenting the top of my breasts and the back plunged low to my waist. It was simple, elegant, and very twenty-first century.

"Okay, now hold still." Sandy clipped a long, antique veil to the back of my flowing hair. "I don't remember her very well, but I know Mother would have loved you wearing her wedding veil."

"It's absolutely beautiful." I admired the vintage lace.

"You're so sweet to say that. Now you, milady, look breathtaking."

"You, too, Miss Reynolds." Sandy's maid-of-honor dress was similar to mine, but instead of white, her velvet dress was a deep, Christmas red and the back fell in a simple scoop.

"Thanks, Maddie. I know you wish Piper was here, but I hope I'll make a good substitute for her."

"Honestly, it would have been a tough choice. I think I would have had two maids of honor."

"Oh, I almost forgot." She flew out of the room then returned a few moments later with a small oblong jewelry case. "Open it, Maddie." She handed the box to me.

"Oh, Sandy." Pulling a necklace from the case, I felt so heartened. "It's beautiful."

"Garnets and diamonds I think. I don't know where Mother got the necklace. Daddy never would say, but on the few occasions I wore the piece, his smile radiated so it had to be special to him."

The choker, primarily diamonds, had garnets interspersed. A single red teardrop fell from the center surrounded by small white diamonds. The necklace complemented my dress beautifully, and knowing the necklace was a family heirloom made my "something borrowed" even more meaningful.

"Now all you need is something blue," Sandy said.

"Well then, I just might be able to help you out with that one," a voice chimed in from behind us. Spinning toward the thick southern drawl, I saw a familiar smile peeking around the door.

"Carrie Ann." I reached out my hand to her, lunging forward.

"Now you just stay right there. Let me come to you. I don't want you tripping over that gorgeous train."

"Look at you; you're about ready to pop." I hugged her then drew back and rubbed her swollen belly. "You must be due any day now, and traveling all this way? You really shouldn't have come, but I'm so glad you're here."

"Nothing would have kept me from this wedding. Seeing Bobby get married is a once-in-a-lifetime event. Besides, I wanted to thank you, again."

"Thank me? For what?"

"For talkin' sense into me, convincin' me to go and

talk to Billy. He may not be perfect, but he's a good man and you were right. A body's mind can make things look a whole lot different from reality."

"That's for sure." I agreed. "I learned that one from you."

"From me? How's that?" She pooched her lips.

"Never mind. I can't go into it now, but someday I'll fill you in."

"Well then, I'm glad we helped each other." She reached deep in her pocketbook and pulled out an antique diamond brooch, a swirling stem bursting with crystal flowers, each one with a tiny sapphire in the center. "Here, we can pull your hair back on one side and fix this in it with bobby pins. Sit down. I'll show you." She swept my hair above my right ear and clipped it in place. "There. What do you think?"

"I love it." I stood and gave her another hug.

"You're welcome." She stepped back and admired me. "You're an absolute vision, Maddie."

A knock on the door preceded Millie's voice, "It's time. You all set, honey?"

"Just about." Turning back to Carrie Ann, I hugged her again. "Thank you for coming to the wedding and for letting me borrow your beautiful sapphire broach."

"It's nothing. Now I better get out there before Bill's eyes wander too much. You're the best thing that ever happened to Bobby, Maddie," she said. "Remember that." Then she disappeared out the door.

"So, are you ready to marry my brother?" Sandy asked.

I pinched my cheeks then smiled at her. "I've never been more ready for anything in my life."

"Now don't dawdle." She hugged me then scooted

down the hallway. A moment later, Sully stood at the parlor door.

"They're playing our song." He crooked his arm, and I slipped my hand around it. We walked into the vestibule of Shoal Creek Church and stood at the back of the sanctuary. Sandy scurried around me adjusting my train and veil, then dashed in front of us and stood next to the flower girl.

When the phonograph started to play Patti Page's "With My Eyes Wide Open", Sandy touched Alice Taylor's arm.

"Now, sweetie," she whispered.

Little Alice, dressed in a red velveteen dress with a white lacey pinafore, strode forward in cadence, her tiny red slippers gliding down the white runway. A basket of crimson rose petals looped over her arm, she dropped a few along the aisle with every step, sprinkling first to the right, then scattering some to the left.

Robbie Sullivan followed close behind her, a small satin pillow with two platinum rings pinned securely to the fabric, filled his chubby little hands. Sandy trailed behind the two children signaling the bride's debut. As the song ended, everyone turned toward the vestibule expecting to hear the traditional "Here Comes the Bride," but nothing had been conventional about Bobby and me and our wedding kept true to form. When Ezio Pinza's "Some Enchanted Evening" began, Sully squeezed my arm.

"Here we go," he said.

"Thanks again for giving me away, Sully," I whispered.

"It's an honor," he replied with a wink.

The sanctuary, drenched in candlelight, was standing room only. Gardenias and crimson roses cascaded across the altar and garlands dotted with the same blossoms draped the pews on both sides stretching the entire length of the aisle. The whole town squeezed into that tiny church. And they weren't just Bobby's friends either. Entire families, most of whom I'd worked with in some capacity, smiled and nodded as they watched me gait past.

I took a deep breath and focused on Bobby standing on the pulpit. Dressed in a sleek black tux, he looked so dreamy. His legs stood slightly apart, hands folded in front of him and that amazing grin stretched across his face. My fairytale wedding and smiling faces faded into the background and, for a moment, Bobby Reynolds was the only person in my world.

"Dearly beloved, we are gathered here in the presence of God to join this man, Robert Michael Reynolds and this woman, Lacey Madison Montgomery in holy matrimony, which is instituted by God, blessed by our Lord Jesus Christ, and to be held in honor among all men..." Reverend Bailey recited the overly familiar words, but it was the first time I ever truly listened to them. Forsaking all others...bear with each other's infirmities and weaknesses...in honesty...provide for each other...to love, honor and cherish...I wondered how many millions of people had taken those same vows. And how many had tossed them aside at the slightest turbulence.

Slipping back in time was still inconceivable to me, but it had happened, and it had changed me. This little town and everyone in it contributed to my new sense of purpose. Sandy, Carrie Ann, Sully, and even Alice

Taylor gave me a glimpse of what it's like to really connect with friends, a rare treasure in the self-centered *me-society* of 2012. Honest relationships and sincere concern for other people can get lost in a fast-paced culture.

Bobby showed me the meaning of love. In the past, I wanted to be loved so badly that I fell victim to romantic gestures and hollow promises, never taking time to learn who a man was on the inside. Looking into Bobby's eyes now, I couldn't imagine any other life than one with him. I trusted him completely and knew he would always have my back. No matter what happened in the future, he was my destiny.

I had written vows, but staring into Bobby's eyes, my memory waned and my pledge flowed from my heart.

"Bobby, I never knew what love was until I met you. You are my best friend, my soul mate and my heart. Today I give my love and life to you. I promise to cherish and respect you, support your dreams, encourage you through life's challenges and comfort you in sorrow. I'll laugh with you, cry with you and stand beside you no matter what our future holds.

"My love will endure in the best of times and never falter in times when love may not seem like enough, because you are a part of me. I cherish each moment we have together and I will never take you for granted. You are my life, my love, my world. From now until forever, I pledge these things to you."

Bobby squeezed my hands as he began his vows.

"Maddie, I love you with all my heart and as the years and decades pass, my devotion and love will only grow deeper. I promise to make decisions with you in mind, to be the first to say I'm sorry when a misunderstanding looms, and I will support your dreams and aspirations. I promise to be compassionate when you hurt, to listen when you need to talk, and provide a strong shoulder when you need to cry.

"I will strive each day to become the man you imagine me to be, solicit your help when the world threatens my strength and be vulnerable with you about my weaknesses. I vow to protect your heart as if it were the finest china or fragile crystal and when the years turn us old, I will hold your hand and see your beauty inside and out as clearly as you stand before me right now. Your love is a gift which I will forever cherish and I give mine freely to you for eternity."

When he slipped the ring on my finger, Bobby took my hand, and we walked to the candelabra in the center of the altar. Each taking a candle, we touched our flames together to light the third then blew out our individual flames. We were one, and the silent sanctuary suddenly roared with whistles, cheers, and a bustle of clapping hands.

****

"I love to feel sand between my toes," I said, scrunching them as the surf stole the beach beneath my feet.

"I wanted to take you to Bali or Tahiti, some exotic place you'd remember your whole life, but for now, Honeymoon Island will have to do."

"It's perfect, Bobby. What more could anyone want? The beach is breathtaking, private, romantic, and I'm with you. I couldn't have dreamed of a more perfect honeymoon."

He smiled, grabbed my hand, and we walked down

the beach. "When I saw a newsreel about this place: undiscovered pleasures for newlyweds with palm-thatched bungalows, tropical climate, balmy breezes and scrumptious cuisine…I couldn't resist."

"Well, they were right." I swung our clasped hands back and forth while we walked. "It certainly is secluded. I've never even heard of Dunedin, Florida." Pulling Bobby closer to the water, I glanced up and down the white sand beach. "Look, there's not another living soul in sight." Kicking at the surf, I splashed water on both of us.

"Oh, so you want to get wet, do you Mrs. Reynolds?" He picked me up, threw me over his shoulder, and rushed into the waves.

"No, stop. I didn't mean to splash so much water. Bobby, don't. "But he didn't listen to my pleas.

"Not a chance, wife." He dove head first into a wave. I gasped for air a split-second before both of us plunged beneath the rolling surf. Our bodies embraced, we spun together swirling with the pull of the ocean surge until Bobby pushed off from the sandy bottom hurling us to the surface.

Bursting through the waves screaming, I gagged on saltwater sliding down my throat. "Oh my gosh, I'm completely soaked."

He carried me to the water's edge where only soft surf splashed across his feet.

"Just look at me," I said.

"Believe me, I am." He loosened his grip just enough for me to slide down his bare chest.

Sapphire eyes deepened by the reflection of the cobalt sea sparkled in the sunlight, and for a moment I stood mesmerized by their hypnotic allure, my arms still draped around his neck.

"You're so beautiful." He wiped a bead of saltwater from my upper lip.

My daze broken, I dropped my arms, grabbed the skirt of my sundress and twisted it, squeezing out the excess water. "Okay, you got me back. Are you satisfied?" I threw my wet hair behind my shoulders.

"Not yet," he whispered. "You have no idea how stunning you are, do you, Maddie?"

"I'm sure I look absolutely beguiling right now." My drenched white cotton sundress clung to my body, and droplets of water rolled down my face dripping onto my neck and chest. Bobby reached over, pulled a strand of salt-water drenched hair away from my mouth, and caressed my face.

"I've never seen you look more lovely." Glints of sunlight sparkled on his damp, sandy hair and his sun-drenched skin glistened.

He pulled me close, kissed my cheek with moist, tender lips. "I never thought I could love anyone like I love you, Maddie." Warm breath tickled my ears sending shots of delight down my back. He nuzzled my neck between strings of sopping hair, his passion intensifying until his mouth finally found refuge on mine. Entwined, we fell to our knees, the subtle ebb and flow of tepid waves lapping at our bodies.

Slipping the straps from my shoulders, he leaned back slightly, his thighs gently pushing against me. He nudged the bodice lower. When his fingers brushed my breast, another wave of desire tingled down my spine, down, down through my thighs, my legs until my toes curled with sheer delight. Strong hands slid beneath my cotton shift, skimmed across my stomach, descended between my legs. I pulled him into me, tugging at his shorts, fumbling with his zipper. A seething fire burned between us.

His soft lips grazed across my skin, nibbling, teasing along their path. Desire burst into urgency, a thirst quenched by deepened sweltering passion, cooled only by the whisper of the gentle ocean breeze. I dropped my head backward, conceded to his sensual seduction.

He tenderly lowered me to the sand, kissing, tasting, devouring me. My heart, fueled by raw unbridled hunger, beat in cadence with Bobby's, urged further by the rhythmic ocean. I gasped for breath, clung to him, pulling him closer, closer in sweet surrender as burning desire exploded into ecstasy.

****

We rinsed off in the surf before walking back to the lodge hand-in-hand, the tide bubbling tiny waves and soft sand across our feet. The sun, now low on the western horizon, glistened on an aquamarine sea like twinkling stars on a midnight sky. Miniature whitecaps coxed by the gentle breeze studded the water.

When we got back to the room, Bobby stripped the wet sundress from my body, lifted me into his arms, and carried me into the shower. The warm stream cascaded over us as he lathered the soap and washed the saltwater from my face and shoulders. Pulling me closer, he ran soapy hands over my body, but the soft spray melted the suds rinsing my suntanned skin. He poured shampoo into his cupped hands, slid his fingers through my hair, tenderly massaging my head to wash away the sand.

I reached my arms around his neck, softly stroking

his head with my fingernails, and he purred with delight, a lion offering his mane craving more attention. Small droplets rolled down his face diluting salty sea spray. I licked a bead of water from the edge of his mouth, ran my tongue around his lips. Then, softly kissing my way to his muscular chest, I slid my hands down his body, enticing his desire. He turned the water off, lifted me and, without a word, wrapped me in a soft, warm towel and carried me to our bed, nuzzling my neck along the way. The soft surf whispered over sand dunes and floated on the gentle breeze through our hidden bungalow, a lulling rhythm enticing submission to passion's yearning.

Chapter 18

Lake Lanier, Georgia—April 2012

Nick had become a valuable ally finding Cole to be precisely the kind of man his friend had suspected.

"You were right, Rob. He's a complete jerk. It's guys like Cole that give men a bad rap." Nick shook his head with contempt. "Lacey deserves so much better."

"Well, this time he's bitten off more than he can chew." Rob set his fork across his plate, pushing back from the table. "I have an idea. I want you to tell him about a party we're having in a few weeks. Tell him the gala will be saturated with filthy rich women and that you might be able to scavenge an invitation for him. His greed and playboy agenda will do the rest."

"He'll bite, but what about Lacey? It would really hurt her if she gets wind of this. She would see the setup as a vicious betrayal." Nick drew in the aroma of his fresh cup of coffee before taking a sip.

"Don't worry about Lacey. I'll take care of that end. She'll be fine, much better off without him, right?"

"I guess. But I feel kinda guilty. Shouldn't we at least warn her first?" Pushing his plate to the side, Nick set his coffee cup in front of him.

"Not a word to Lacey, Nick. She'll simply confront Cole before the party. Then he'll lie his way back into her good graces. Trust me on this one."

"All right, if you think that's the best way to help her get over that sleazy dude."

"It's the only way. She's too stubborn to be told anything. Besides, have I ever steered you wrong?" Rob downed the rest of his coffee, set the cup on the table.

"No. And you're right. She's pretty independent. I just don't want to see her hurt."

"Believe me when I say her future is the only thing I'm concerned about. Just drop that information on Cole." Rob smiled a deep, satisfying grin. Another detail had fallen into place.

****

Sidney, Georgia—November 1950

"Maddie, I'm so glad you're back," Sandy squealed, hugging her new sister-in-law. "Come here. I have to show you something."

"So what am I, chopped liver?" Bobby asked.

"No. I missed you, too, but I'm sure you aren't as interested in wedding pictures as your wife is. Look at these, Maddie. They turned out beautifully."

Pushing my luggage aside, I rushed into the parlor.

"Oh, now I'm left with all the suitcases, too. Ahem." He coughed. "I guess the honeymoon is over."

"Sorry, honey. I'll help you in a few minutes. Come look at the pictures first. Oh, look at Alice and Robbie. And Sandy, you looked stunning."

"I like this picture of Sully walking you down the aisle." Bobby pointed to his favorites making comments on each one. "And this one of all of us standing at the altar."

"You dress up pretty good, Bobby," Sandy teased.

"I have my moments," he snapped back.

"Oh Maddie, look at this picture. It's absolutely the

most beautiful photograph I've ever seen. The candlelight glows in the background around you and Bobby kissing."

"That one is mine." He snatched the picture right out of Sandy's hand, pulled his wallet out of his back pocket. "This one is going in my billfold."

"Can I at least see it first?" I asked. He reluctantly handed the photograph to me. They were right. The picture had captured more than our faces. It radiated the emotion, the love between us.

"You can have that photo for now," I said, handing the picture back to my husband. "But I want a copy."

"Okay. For now though, it stays with me."

We looked at pictures and reminisced about the wedding for nearly an hour. Sandy wanted to know every detail of the honeymoon, which we told her, leaving out some of the more intimate moments.

"The island sounds dreamy." Sandy closed her eyes and smiled. "I can almost see you two out on the beach."

"I hope not," Bobby whispered to me. "We took a lot of pictures on the honeymoon. I'll drop the rolls off with Sully tomorrow on my way to the ridge." He stood and stretched.

"You're starting back to work on the house so soon?" I asked.

"Thanksgiving is next week, honey. If I'm going to have that house ready for us by Christmas, I need to get a move on."

"Bobby, we don't have to move in by Christmas. Can't we just relax, spend time together, and enjoy our first holiday season as a married couple."

"That's why I want to get the house finished." He

raised an eyebrow, leaned over, and kissed me on the cheek.

"While you two get all gushy, I'm going to start dinner." Sandy closed the wedding album and put the loose photos back in a box.

"What's the date today, anyway?" I asked. "It's easy to lose track of time in paradise."

"It's November 15th." Sandy stood up.

"Daddy's birthday is Saturday." The date opened floodgates to memories of another lifetime. I had always tried to do something unexpected on Daddy's birthday. I wondered if he missed that, or me. "I wish he could have been at our wedding."

"Me, too, sweetie," Bobby said. "Say, I wonder if we could find him here. He wouldn't recognize you of course, since he'd be about the same age as Alice Taylor, but you may be able to at least see him."

"I never thought of that, and Mother, too. Oh, Bobby, Mother is alive." I jumped up and hugged him.

"Maybe. When was she born?" he asked.

"April 4th, 1950."

"That would make her about seven months old. Do you know where they lived? Or should I say live?" He scratched his head. "I can see how confusing this is for you."

"Daddy grew up in Decatur. I'm not sure about Mom, but Granddaddy was a doctor. Isn't there some kind of register that lists physicians? Have they created the American Medical Association yet?"

"I'm not sure. Medicine isn't exactly my field of expertise, but we can get John Baxter to search for your grandparents. It may be difficult to come up with a logical motive for contacting them though. I'm assuming you don't want to enlighten them with your stroll through a random crack in time." He smiled. "And, we'll need to consider the ramifications of the space-time continuing thing you told me about."

I chuckled. "You mean space-time *continuum*, which may not even exist. It's only a theory. In reality, I think time travel and anything related enters a realm of uncharted frontier. I guess we would need to be careful not to change history though." I pursed my lips. "Or I might never be born. But, oh Bobby, I'd love to see my parents even if they are little kids."

"Then I'll give Baxter a ring, see what he can come up with."

"Have I ever told you how much I love you, Mr. Reynolds?" I threw my arms around his neck again and kissed his cheek.

"I'm not sure you have, Mrs. Reynolds."

"Okay, now I'm really going to the kitchen." Sandy shook her head and walked down the hallway. "Newlyweds."

"We'll take our things upstairs. I'll be down to help you shortly." I had just picked up my bag and started up the steps when Sandy called back to me.

"Oh, Maddie, by the way, I took the liberty of moving your things into Bobby's bedroom. I didn't think you'd have the energy when you got home." She giggled. "Take your time...unpacking. I'll see you in a while."

"Thanks, Sis." Bobby grinned, grabbed the rest of the luggage and shot up the stairs. "Come on, wife." He leaned over the banister, crooking his finger at me.

"Wife, huh? I'm not sure I like the way you said that."

"Then you better get up here and put me in my place." He smiled and vanished into the bedroom.

****

Before we got married, dam consultations and wedding plans had dominated most of my time. Bobby kept up with the bottling plant, but the construction of our new home had been his top priority. The trip to Florida re-energized both of us, and with Thanksgiving only a few days away, my new husband was more determined than ever to have our house livable by Christmas. November 1949 had been unseasonably warm, but this year made up for the Indian summer in spades. Bobby spent so much time on the ridge in the bitter cold I began to get concerned.

"Honey please, there's really no rush to get the house finished. Lake excavation won't begin until late next year. We have plenty of time."

"I know, but I need to start on Sandy's house, too. Besides, it would be nice to have some privacy with my gorgeous new wife. I love Sandy, but…"

"Me, too, and I know what you mean. Still, it's not worth you catching pneumonia."

"I've got a thermos filled with hot coffee." He held up the container to show me. "And if I wear any more of your 'layers' I'll sweat to death."

"Okay, I don't want to start our marriage as a nagging wife, but please be careful."

It was the same story every day that week, and I consistently lost the battle. The day before Thanksgiving the news reported a major winter storm brewing, but Bobby shrugged off the forecast. He wanted to get the windows installed before the holiday and worked on the ridge until late that evening.

When the wind picked up the next morning, he feared the new widows would be damaged by the storm, so he borrowed Sully's truck to haul a load of plywood up to the ridge to secure them.

I set Bobby's breakfast in front of him. "Honey, the weather is brutally cold and listen to that wind. Please don't go up there today." Draping my arms around his neck, I nestled close, softly nibbling at his ear. "I promise you'll have a lot more fun here."

He turned, kissed my cheek. "As much as I'd love to spend the entire day snuggling with you in bed, I have to go. Those windows won't hold up to this kind of wind. They're barely secured in place."

Frustrated, I sat down in the chair next to him. "Will you at least get someone to help you?"

"It's Thanksgiving, princess. I can't ask anyone to give up their holiday, let alone go out in this weather just to help me hammer a few boards over those windows." He took my hand in his. "Look Sweetheart, I'll be back before you know it."

Biting the corner of my lip, I continued to throw out alternatives. "Then let me come with you. With two of us working, we can finish before the storm hits."

He squeezed my hand. "I like your spunk, but Sandy needs your help with Thanksgiving dinner. Sweetie, you don't need to worry about me. I'm a big boy. I'll be fine. And I won't be long. I promise."

The wind whistled as it swept around the chimney and stole through the open flue into the room. I shivered, feeling the chill of the late autumn morning. I reached for the sweater draped over the back of the desk chair and pulled it over my shoulders.

"Bobby, I just have a bad feeling about this. That

wind—"

"I know, princess, so let me get out of here to secure those windows before the storm hits."

"All right." I reluctantly gave in. "I guess there's nothing I can say to convince you to stay home."

He shot me a grin laced with frustration, and edged toward the door.

"Wait." I impulsively grabbed my purse from the hallway chiffonier, reached inside for the carousel ring Bobby had given to me when he asked me to marry him. "Take this." I handed the ring to him. "For good luck. I know it's silly, but it'll make me feel better."

He conceded, slipped the brass ring into his tight, blue jeans pocket. Then, wrapping his arms around me, he lifted me off of my feet with a big bear hug, twirled me around and kissed me.

"I love you, Maddie Reynolds. And I'll be back in two shakes of a dog's tail." He looked at his watch. "If I'm not home by five at the latest, you can call out the militia." Opening the front door, he stepped outside, looked back at me. "Don't you two start dinner without me, okay?"

I pulled my sweater tightly around my shoulders and ventured out on the porch. "We won't, I promise. And I love you, too. Please be careful and hurry home."

Watching him drive off down the road, I could see the storm looming in the distance. The deepening blue-gray clouds darkened the late-November morning sky to a creepy midnight glow. Trees swayed as the wind whipped across the yard tossing leaves randomly through the frosty air. When Bobby was out of sight, I strolled back into the house and secured the door behind me.

By ten o'clock, soft snowflakes flurried, quiet, beautiful, but the ambiance didn't evoke a familiar cozy comfort snuggled inside. Instead, it conjured a still coldness, eerie, lethal. By late afternoon, the wind had fashioned deep drifts that climbed up the windows creating a silent shroud of snow, an icy tomb eclipsing any glimpse of life, of Sidney.

Sandy and I kept busy, stuffing the turkey, peeling potatoes to mash, snapping green beans and making their customary two pumpkin pies. It was half past five and Bobby still wasn't home.

"Something's wrong. I can feel it." I walked to the window, pulled the sheers back with my finger. The crystalline fantasyland froze the pit of my stomach. "Where is he?"

"Maddie, you're just a worrywart." Sandy placed the huge turkey on the dining room table. "Bobby is fine. Now, come help me get this food on the table. My brother will walk through that door any second, and he'll be hungry as a bear."

"I guess you're right. He has Sully's truck. The snowy roads must have slowed him down, but that four-wheel drive can handle the slick roads." I opened the hutch, pulled out the company china, and began setting the table. We put the beans and mashed potatoes into serving dishes, placed them neatly around Sandy's centerpiece. She had placed crisp autumn leaves beneath a cornucopia overflowing with colorful gourds and accented the piece with tall orange candles at each end. Aromas from roasted turkey and pumpkin pie mingled through the air reminding me of Thanksgivings' past. But as comforting as they were, they couldn't ease the sense of dread lurking inside of me.

By six thirty it was completely dark. The storm snuffed out any moonlight that may have illuminated the evening sky. Instead, a pitch-black darkness deepened an already obscure sky.

"Sandy, something is definitely wrong. I can literally feel it. Lord, I'd do anything to have a cell phone right now."

She glanced at the grandfather clock in the corner. "Maybe you're right. Bobby really should be home by now."

I looked out the window for the umpteenth time. "Just look at this snow. I've never seen snow fall so hard and deep in Georgia."

She walked over to the window and stood next to me. "Oh my gosh; I've been so busy in the kitchen, I hadn't really noticed. It's a blizzard out there."

"That's it." Grabbing my heavy coat from the closet, I shook my head. "I'm not going to sit here and wait any longer."

Sandy took ahold of my arm. "We can't go out there in this storm. Even if you could dig out the car, you wouldn't make it out of the driveway. Besides, it doesn't make sense for all three of us to get stuck in this mess."

Jerking away, I snapped back. "We have to do something. Bobby could be hurt. He's out there in that snow, and we have to find him." I stuck my arm in the coat sleeve, but Sandy grabbed my collar.

"Okay, let's think about this rationally." She pulled my coat away. "Suppose you're right. We can't just go out there halfcocked." Draping my wrap over the back of a chair, she continued. "We need a plan."

"What we need is some help." I picked up the phone receiver, already scanning through Bobby's address book. "That's it, John Baxter." I began dialing his number.

"Wait, hold on, Maddie." She pressed the disconnect button, stopping me from completing the call. "Do you really think we need to call the chief of police right off the bat? I mean it is Thanksgiving."

"I don't care if today is his wedding. Bobby is in trouble. Nothing else matters."

She loosened her grip. "You're starting to scare me now. Do you really think he's in trouble?"

"With every fiber of my being, Sandy." I jerked my arm away, and she reluctantly let go.

"Okay, then go ahead, call Baxter."

The line rang over and over. Finally a giggling voice answered. "Hello."

"This is Maddie Mont—I mean this is Maddie Reynolds. I need to talk to John right away. It's an emergency."

"Daaaaddyyyy. The telephone is for you. It's Maddie Reynolds. She says it's an emergency." A few moments later Baxter came to the phone.

"Hello Maddie, Happy Thanksgiving. What's up?"

"John, I hate to bother you on a holiday. I wouldn't if it wasn't a matter of life or death. Bobby went to the ridge this morning to secure some new windows." My voice trembled. "He promised to be back hours ago. Something has happened to him."

"Now calm down, Maddie. I'm sure he's held up somewhere because of the storm. You just relax. He'll be home when he can."

"No John. He's in trouble. I know he is," I insisted.

"Please, you have to do something."

"What could I possibly do in this blizzard? The roads are impassible. Haven't you been listening to the radio?"

"No. And I don't care about the damn weather. Bobby is in trouble. If you won't help me, I'll go after him myself." I screamed into the receiver, not one of my better moments, but nothing, no one was going to stop me from finding my husband.

"Settle down," Baxter soothed.

"Listen John, if it weren't for Bobby, you would have had a riot last year when the Buford Dam news hit Sidney." I didn't want to pull the "we helped you" card, but I had no choice. "You owe him. Please."

"All right, all right, Maddie. I'll grab a few of the fellas and try to get out there. But promise me you'll stay inside. This weather is treacherous. They're saying it's the worst storm to hit the east coast in recorded history. It's no place for a woman out there."

Drawing in a deep breath of relief, I offered my appreciation. "Thank you so much, John. We'll stay inside, but please call me the moment you find out anything, even if he's hurt. Promise me that."

"I promise you we'll call with any information. Now you relax. I'm sure Bobby is fine."

"I hope you're right. We'll be waiting to hear from you. Thanks." I pressed my finger on the button to disconnect the call, began dialing again."

"Who are you calling now?" Sandy asked.

"Local hospitals. I want to be sure Bobby hasn't been in an accident."

"Good idea." She walked over to the radio, flipped it on. "Maybe we'll hear something on the news." She scanned several stations all broadcasting the same thing, news about the extraordinary snowstorm.

"They're calling this storm a cyclone, Maddie. Come listen."

When I finished my calls, I hung up the phone, and joined Sandy sitting next to the radio. "Bobby's not in the Gainesville hospital or Dahlonega."

"That's good news, but listen to what they're saying." She turned up the broadcast.

"…The large extra-tropical cyclone moving through the Eastern United States is causing significant winds, heavy rains east of the Appalachians, and blizzard conditions along the western slopes of the mountain chain. Power outages are reported to some one million customers across the east coast.

"The cyclone has set up a perfect storm condition formed from a strong upper-level low-pressure system moving south from Minnesota. That low-pressure system spawned an intense surface low across the Carolinas and is pushing inland through the Appalachians. Now sandwiched between two strong high-pressure systems, the cyclone is intensifying and the impact is reaching through twenty-two states. Record low temperatures are recorded throughout the area as far south as Savannah, where a low of three degrees has broken the previous record. The severity and lack of warning of this winter storm is wreaking havoc across the entire east coast and has already been cited as the worst snowstorm in recorded history. The death toll is rising…"

"Whew," the local news reporter broke in. "If you don't have to be outside, stay in. Baby, it's cold out there."

"Maddie, now I'm really scared." Sandy put her head on my shoulder. "Bobby is lost somewhere out in that awful storm, and there's not a thing we can do to help him."

Chapter 19

Lake Lanier, Georgia—May 2012

"Hey, come take a look at the size of this full moon." Drew walked across the deck, his eyes fixed on the evening sky. "They say the moon is so close to the Earth that its pull can influence destiny."

"Hmm, I don't know about that." Rob gazed briefly at the shimmering reflection in the lake then returned his attention to Piper's deck. "She moved in yesterday, you know."

"Thank goodness. She'd still be struggling with those support beams if you hadn't helped her."

Looking upward, Rob mused over the star-filled sky. "Sometimes destiny needs a little help."

"It's May 5th already. We only have a few more weeks before—"

"Don't worry. We're right on schedule."

Drew tapped his fingers on the rail, his body language revealing concern. "You're still sure you can pull this thing off?"

"Absolutely." Rob stared at the glaring moon then peered into Drew's deep, blue eyes. "It's destiny."

****

Sidney, Georgia—November 1950

The grandfather clock pendulum swung back-and-forth with a droning tick-tick-tick while I stared in anxious silence watching minutes melt into hours. Three o'clock in the morning and still no word from Bobby or Baxter. Sandy sat curled up by the fireplace dozing in and out of a restless sleep. A cold Thanksgiving dinner remained on the dining room table signifying our immobilized lives as we prayed for Bobby's return. When the phone finally rang, I jumped to answer it.

"Bobby?"

"No, sorry Maddie. It's John Baxter."

"Oh John, please tell me you found him. Is Bobby okay? Where is he?"

"Slow down, Maddie. We've done as much as we can right now. I've got three trucks stuck out in that storm. We can't even get out of Sidney to look for Bob. It's impossible." He paused a moment waiting for my reaction, but I couldn't speak, my body went numb. "Nothing is moving. The drifts out are as tall as me. We can't do anything more until daylight."

"No." Collapsing against the wall, I slid down until I sat on the floor. "My husband is out there somewhere, freezing, hungry, maybe hurt. You can't just give up."

"We're not giving up. We're simply letting the storm die down a bit. Maddie, we've been trying to get out of Sidney all night. The men are exhausted, frozen to the bone."

"Like my husband?" I wiped a tear from my cheek. Why was this happening? God wouldn't be that cruel to take Bobby away from me after everything we'd been through, not now.

"There's nothing more we can do tonight. The storm seems to be moving toward the ocean. When dawn breaks, the sun should melt some of this mess.

We'll pick up the search then."

Hoping John would do anything to keep us safe at home, I played my last card. "I guess Sandy and I will have to go look for him ourselves."

"Now, don't you girls dare to go out in this squall. I don't want to have two more on the missing list."

"You leave me no choice. I won't sit back and relax while Bobby is out there somewhere." Pulling myself to my knees, I looked up at the ceiling and prayed a silent request.

"Maddie, don't make me put you in lockup to keep you safe. Bobby will have my butt if I let you go out looking for him."

Deflated, broken, I spoke softly. "John, I can't just sit here."

"That's exactly what you're going to do. Try to get some sleep. We'll get out there and find Bobby as soon as we can. He's a smart man. He'll be fine. I'll call you when we find something, tomorrow."

"Right," I whispered. "Goodbye, John."

"Mind what I said now. You two stay put. Good night." He hung up the phone.

I placed the receiver in its cradle, walked over to stoke the fire.

"What are we going to do, Maddie?" Sandy's voice quivered with fear.

"I hate to think of him out there. But if Baxter and his men can't even get out of Sidney...I don't know, Sandy." Placing the poker beside the mantel, I watched the fire spit sparks that fluttered as they whirled up the flue.

"I guess we should put the food away." Sandy dragged her limp body from the sofa.

"No. He said to hold dinner. He made me promise." I fought to hold back tears, but the emotions swirled inside and finally burst. "Leave the food there. He'll be back. He has to be." Sandy fell into me, squeezing with a tight hug. We sobbed, holding on to one another until I finally found the strength to pull myself together. I had to be strong. Bobby would want me to take care of his sister.

"I'm sorry. You're right, sweetie. Bobby won't want all that food to go bad. We should wrap everything up and put it in the icebox. He'll be famished when he gets home. We can warm a plate for him then."

"He will be a bear, won't he?" Her eyes searched for some tiny spark of hope. "You really think he's okay?"

"Your brother is the smartest, most resourceful man I know. And he's not going to let a measly storm keep him from coming back to us. Come on. Let's take care of these dishes. Are you hungry?"

"A little." She wiped the tears from her cheeks.

"Well then, you get a plate and eat something while I clean up."

"What about you, Maddie? You should eat something, too."

"I nibbled on some turkey when you were sleeping." I didn't want to lie to her. But I knew if I ate a single bite the knot in my stomach would erupt. "I'm fine. You get some food. Take what you want, and I'll put the rest away."

"Thanks." She sat down and put a slice of turkey and a scoop of mashed potatoes on her plate.

I stacked the rest of the dishes, put them back in

the hutch, picked up the bowls of beans and potatoes, then shuffled into the kitchen. Robotically, I covered each dish, put them in the fridge, and closed the door. Limp with anguish, I fell back against the wall, slid down to the floor again, then dropped my head into my hands and sobbed.

****

Three days passed before John Baxter's crew dug their way out of Sidney and forged through the snow to the ridge. With no word from or about Bobby, I felt numb. My life on autopilot, I mindlessly went through the motions of daily routine, trying with every ounce of my strength to stay positive to keep Sandy calm. We slept most of the time, if you could call it sleep, trying to pass the hours until Bobby came home to us.

When John Baxter showed up at the door on Monday afternoon, Sandy rushed to greet him anticipating good news. But a sense of dread heaved through my stomach. I couldn't breathe. The scenario felt like one I'd seen in movies over and over. They never called with bad news. The police always came to the door to deliver the news of a death.

"He's okay, right?" Sandy asked a stone-faced John Baxter slouching against the front door jamb.

"Let's go sit in the parlor." He put his arm around Sandy, led her into the room.

"John, don't treat us with kid gloves." Sandy and I sat on the edge of the sofa. "What happened? Where is Bobby? I want every detail."

"Well-sir, there's not a lot to tell you, Maddie." He pulled Bobby's desk chair from its place at the roll top, placed it in front of us and sat down.

"Where's my brother?" Sandy's desperation flew

into rage.

I took her hand. "Let him talk, sweetie." I glared at Baxter. "The whole story, John. What you saw, found, tell us everything."

He rubbed the scruffy stubbles of the budding beard on his chin. "We don't rightly know."

"What do you mean you don't know?" I snapped. "You went to the ridge, right?"

"Yes. When we got to your property we felt relieved to see Sully's truck still in the driveway."

"And?" Sandy nervously bounced her legs up and down.

"And, we went into the house thinking he had held up inside there, kept warm with a fire the whole time."

I closed my eyes, opened them slowly. "But?" There's always a 'but' with things like that. They tell you the good news first, then lay the 'but' on you.

"But when we went inside the house, we saw nothing. No fire, no signs anyone had been there." He paused a beat then added, "And no Bobby. We looked everywhere, hiked up and down the ridge for miles calling out for him, searched the forest for any sign at all. As far as we could see, he just flat-out vanished."

"Vanished?" I squeezed Sandy's hand. "That's a copout, John. And it makes no sense. Bobby has to be somewhere."

"Copout?" He stared at me with a perplexed expression.

I'd obviously used slang he didn't understand, but I didn't care. "You can't just give up."

"We looked everywhere. Best we could come up with was he fell off that old scaffold. There were nails up on the platform and some plywood beneath. If he fell off—"

"No," Sandy shrieked.

I squeezed her hand tighter, placed my other arm around her shoulder. The ice queen within flew to my rescue, spitting out her cold response. "And?"

"That scaffold hangs over the ridge, Maddie. If Bobby managed to survive the fall, bears roam all over those foothills. Wildcats and boars rove north of the ridge, too. They get mighty voracious when snow makes it hard to find food. Blood attracts—"

"That's quite enough, John. What you're inferring isn't possible."

Sandy buried her face in my chest and sobbed.

"There's no way he could have lived through that storm without some kind of shelter."

I rubbed Sandy's back to sooth her, my icy retort spatting a venomous demand at Baxter. "Bobby is resourceful. He's alive, John. Find him."

"Maddie, I know this isn't what you want to hear. Heck, the whole town loved Bobby, but you've got to face facts." Leaning back in his chair, he crossed his arms and shook his head.

"John, you're a friend, so I'll say this politely one time. Please don't talk as if there is no hope of finding Bobby. I won't have it. Giving up is not an option. Unless you can find proof of his death, I won't let this slide."

"If he slipped on that slick scaffold and fell unconscious, a wild animal could have easily carried him to its lair. There wouldn't be a trace left of him."

Sandy stood and let out a bloodcurdling scream. "No, No, Noooooo. That's too awful. How could you suggest that some animal ate my brother?"

I shot up, held Sandy in a tight embrace, stroking her hair. "It's okay, sweetie. That isn't what happened." I scowled daggers at Baxter. "Enough, John."

"Look, you told me not to sugar-coat this just to make you girls feel better. We didn't find a single footprint on the scene. The scenario I described is the only one that makes sense."

"Don't you dare justify not finding my husband with a scenario or turn this into a recovery instead of a search. My husband isn't dead. He's out there somewhere, and your job is to find him."

"Maddie, did you hear anything I said? There are no signs whatsoever to indicate that he's still alive."

"And there's nothing that implies that he's dead either. You go back out there and do your job, find signs." I grimaced. "Sandy and I will help. We'll get the whole damn town out there if we have to. Bobby is out there somewhere. He's alive, John. And we're going to find him."

Chapter 20

Lake Lanier, Georgia—May 2012

"It's nice to finally meet you, sir. You're a hard man to see face to face." Rob reached out, firmly shook the hand of Warren Montgomery. "I'm glad you decided to hear me out."

"I have to admit my initial response had you pegged as a scam artist. But your email was quite compelling." He sat down in his over-stuffed executive chair, leaned back. "Don't think for a moment I haven't investigated your background thoroughly."

"I expected nothing less."

"Have a seat." Adjusting his glasses lower on his nose, he peered at Rob over the rims. "You're a very interesting man, and gutsy, too. I'll give you that."

"I'm glad to see I've piqued your interest." Rob smiled, sat down, and crossed his legs.

"You've gotten my attention. Now give me specifics. I want to hear every detail about this merger."

"It's about risk verses reward. You have nothing to lose by coming on board, sir, but a lot to gain."

After fifteen minutes of explanation and discussion, Rob rested his arms in his lap and silently stared at Montgomery, waiting for his reaction.

"Intriguing." Warren tapped his fingers on the desk.

"So I assume that means I have your support, sir?"

"For now. But if you cross me, let's just say your risk will blow up in your face."

****

Sidney, Georgia—December 1950

For the next two weeks search parties continued to rake the area within a fifty-mile radius of the ridge, hunting from Dawsonville to Dahlonega and Cleveland to Gainesville. But not a single lead materialized. Sandy and I pushed Baxter, who initially called in some favors from authorities out of his jurisdiction, but convinced Bobby was dead, he put only enough effort and manpower into the search to pacify us.

Sandy cried inconsolably through the first week, but as the snow thawed and seeped into the ground, her resolve melted along with it. She finally gave up on her steadfast belief that Bobby had simply wandered away and had gotten lost in the storm. Still, she wouldn't entertain the possibility of his death.

I still felt numb, emotionless. If I allowed any pain to creep in, the magnitude would have consumed me. And so I focused on Sandy and our own search. At first the townspeople were anxious to offer their time, but one by one, the majority gave up hope as well, until eventually we were left with only a core of close friends who faithfully combed the forests on a daily bases. When I wasn't perusing the woods, I pulled everyone's notes together, updating a detailed map, daily marking every mile the volunteers covered.

Neither Sandy nor I had relaxed since Bobby's disappearance. If we weren't scouring the countryside or dealing with factory issues, we threw ourselves into some project to avoid thinking about Bobby. When

Sandy came home, she baked or cleaned until exhaustion forced her into sleep. I sifted through endless notes and maps desperately searching for a lead or some kind of evidence to prove what I felt in my gut, that Bobby was alive. But my own resolve weakened with each passing day. Fear and dread hovered over my shoulder like angels of death. It was Friday evening, December 8th, when we got our first lead. The shrill telephone ring triggered streams of adrenalin, twisting the knot in my stomach tighter.

"Maddie, can you get that?" Sandy yelled from the kitchen. "My hands are a mess."

I stared at the phone before picking up the receiver, praying the call would at least give us a glimmer of hope. "Hello."

"Mrs. Reynolds?" The voice on the other end of the line sounded agitated.

"This is Maddie Reynolds. Can I help you?"

"As a matter of fact, you can." There was a long pause. "Stop your search. You don't know who you're messing with. Stop searching for your husband before you get hurt."

"What?" My life was a nightmare and this jerk was threatening me. Really? "Is this some kind of a cruel joke?"

"I'm dead serious." He spoke in a whisper, but his words were strong and direct. "Stop looking for your husband."

"Who is this?" I couldn't believe what I was hearing. "There's no way we're going to stop looking for Bobby."

"Then you could suffer deadly consequences."

My heart raced, adrenaline fueling my response.

"Who the hell are you?"

"A friend. Mrs. Reynolds. So trust me, you're making dangerous enemies."

A friend? No friend of ours would ever threaten us. "What dangerous enemies?"

"That doesn't matter. I'm trying to help, to warn you. Call off the cops or you and your sister-in-law might disappear, too."

Riddled with anxiety I fought to feed the burst of energy toward anger instead of fear. "How could our search possibly concern anyone?"

"You have no idea what you're getting into."

Rage laced with constant bursts of adrenalin burned inside of me. No one could make us give up on Bobby. "Look, you tell me who the hell you are or I'll call the—"

"Calling the cops will make matters worse. Believe me. I'm not your enemy. The cops are the problem. Just mark my words. Stop the search or you both could end up on a slab in the morgue." He abruptly hung up.

What I wouldn't have done for caller ID. Completely stunned, I placed the receiver back in the cradle and leaned against the bannister. What had just happened? It was terrifying enough to be dealing with my husband's disappearance. But why would anyone want us to stop searching for him...unless they were responsible?

"Sandy," I screamed, "Come in here, quickly."

"Can you wait a minute, I'm—"

"Never mind." I pushed off the railing, flew into the kitchen. "The phone—"

"Was it for me?"

"No, well sort of. It was odd, and creepy." Turning

my back to the cabinets, I lifted myself to sit on the kitchen counter still shaking, fuming at what I'd just heard.

"What do you mean?" Sandy stopped what she was doing and stared at me.

"The phone call was a man warning us to stop searching for Bobby."

"For heaven's sake, why? What did he say?"

"That we're making dangerous enemies."

She opened the oven, placed the coffeecake she'd just made onto the rack, closed the door. "Should we call Baxter?" She wiped her hands on a dishcloth. "Maybe we're getting too close to finding out what really happened to Bobby."

"That's what I thought, too, but I don't think we should call Baxter. The man on the phone warned me not to call the police. He said they were the problem and calling them would only make things worse." I clutched her arm. "He also said he was a 'friend' trying to keep us from danger."

"A friend, huh." Her furrowed brow dissolved giving way to an enlightened expression. Tossing the dishtowel on the counter, she walked out of the kitchen.

"Sandy, don't just walk out." I followed her. "This is scary. That man said we could disappear, too, maybe die."

"Shhh," she said, putting one finger over her lips and the other on the sheers. She moved them slightly to the side, stood behind the drapes and peeked out the window. "You see that black Ford out there?"

"Yes." I reached for the sheers to open them wider but she grabbed my hand.

"Don't touch the curtain. I don't want them to

know we've seen them."

"Who?" A gaggle of spiders scurried down my back and spun a web around the canker clenching my stomach.

"I've seen that car, or one like it, parked across the street from us every day for over a week now. At first I shrugged it off, but each day I've gotten a little more concerned. Someone has been watching us, Maddie." She let the sheer slip from her finger then leaned against the wall beside the drape. "They follow us when we leave and park somewhere along our street whenever we're home. Seeing them out there gives me the willies. But all they do is watch."

"Wait a minute, Sandy. Someone has been watching us for over a week, and you didn't think that was worth mentioning to me?" I scowled at her.

"You have enough on your mind, Maddie. And besides, like I said, all they've done is watch us. I thought it might be Baxter's men, at first. The last day or two though…" She shook her head and drifted into thought.

"Sandy, this is too weird. Baxter would never waste his manpower watching us." The knot in my stomach tightened even more.

"I know. You're right. But after that call I think I have an idea who might. And if I'm right we really could be in danger. The question is why?"

Placing my hand on her shoulder, I squeezed slightly. "Who in the world would want to stalk us?"

"Stalk us?" Her blank look made me acutely aware that she didn't know the term.

"Sorry, I mean watch our every move. Why would anyone do that?"

"Oh. I'm not a hundred percent sure, but that call gave me a pretty good idea." She peeked around the sheers again, trudged into the parlor then collapsed onto the couch.

She sat there, deep in thought for several minutes before speaking again. "Maddie, I've got to run out for a while. I need to talk to a friend of mine. He might be able to shed some light on what's going on. In the meantime, whatever you do, don't talk to Baxter."

I sat down beside her, took her hand. "Sandy, please tell me what you think this is all about before you leave."

Pulling her hand from mine, she stood. "There's no time now. I need to check with him before I can speculate anyway. I've got to go. Now."

"Him who? And why can't you just call him?" I wrung my hands nervously. "What if Bobby was kidnapped? You could be in serious danger going out by yourself."

She grabbed her coat from the closet, pulled it on. "Maybe, but if my suspicions are correct, Baxter really could make things worse, so no matter what happens, don't call him." She grabbed the car keys from the desk and looked back at me. "Stay here and try to relax. Oh, and pull the coffeecake out when it's done. It should be another fifteen minutes or so. I'll be back soon."

"No Sandy. You shouldn't do this alone. At least let me go with you." I got up, grabbed my sweater from the banister. "This sounds way too dangerous."

She put her hand on my arm. "That's not a good idea, Maddie. I'll be fine, I promise."

"Bobby promised he'd be fine, too," I snapped back at her. "I can't lose you."

"This is different. I'm not fighting a storm. And I'm pretty sure I know what's going on, but there's only one way to be sure. I'll be back in a few hours. Trust me." She disappeared out the front door.

Peering through the window, I watched as Sandy backed out of the driveway and drove off. A moment later the black Ford pulled onto the road and followed her.

****

Sandy had been gone for almost three hours, and it took every bit of willpower I had to keep from picking up the phone to call John Baxter. When she finally pulled into the driveway, I ran out the door and threw my arms around her as she stepped out of the car.

"You had me scared to death. Are you all right?" I stood back, examined her from head to foot then hugged her again. "What took you so long?"

"I had a little trouble tracking down my friend." She tucked her hair behind her ears.

"Don't be so mysterious. Who is your friend?" I strolled toward the house, but she didn't budge. "Come on Sandy. What's with the mystery? Fill me in."

"I'll tell you everything, but you should meet him first so you'll understand the situation." Turning, she stepped back into the car. "Hop in, Maddie. We don't have a lot of time."

"Okay, but let me grab a coat first. It's freezing out here."

"Hurry. It's already nine forty-five. Al has to work later tonight."

I rushed up to the porch skipping steps along the way, dashed into the house, grabbed my coat then flew out the door toward the Hudson.

"Who is Al? Wait, first, did you find out anything about Bobby?" I asked, jumping into the car.

She backed out of the driveway. "No. I'm not sure his disappearance has anything to do with that phone call, but we'll find out soon."

"Then where are we going, and who is Al?"

"I'm taking you to Dahlonega to meet him. He's been a friend of mine since grade school, and he's got an interesting vocation."

"An interesting vocation, what does that have to do with Bobby?"

"Just relax, Maddie. This will all make sense soon. I promise."

My questions mounted. I told Sandy the black Ford had followed her when she drove off earlier, but she already knew. She'd danced around the facts, which set my nerves on edge even more.

"Sandy, you're talking in riddles. Just spit it out. What does Al have to do with any of this?"

She glanced over at me. "He's a shiner."

"He's a what?" Turning my entire body to face here, I leaned against the door.

"A shiner." She glared at me as if I should know what that meant. "You've never heard of the shiners? He runs moonshine, Maddie. Bootleg whiskey? White lightning?"

"Okay, I know what that is, but I still don't get what that has to do with Bobby."

"I realize you're from sixty-some years in the future, but I thought surely you would have heard of the shiners. How about stock car racing?" My mind spun in confusion. "The races, Maddie. I know you went to Looper with Bobby."

"Yes, of course, but I still don't understand. What does car racing have to do with bootleg whisky? Sandy, I'm not trying to pester you, but could you please get to the point and tie all of this together?" Slinking back my seat, I crossed my arms and huffed. My entire life had been turned upside down, and I was in no mood for games.

"Oh my gosh, Maddie. The shiners have been running whiskey from the north Georgia backwoods to Atlanta since Prohibition. You have heard of Prohibition, right?"

"Of course I have. So you're saying they still make whiskey around here? Why? It's legal now, isn't it?"

"Yes, it's legal to drink but not to manufacture. They run bootleg because it's big business, pulls in a lot of tax-free money."

I understood that Sandy had made some great cosmic discovery, but her roundabout way of getting to the point tested my last nerve.

"Think about it, Maddie. First of all, whiskey may be legal, but bootlegging isn't. Hidden stills saturate these foothills, and they have to transport most of the whiskey to a big city to sell it." She glanced at me, then back at the road. "The shiners have souped-up cars to make their runs. Guys like Al make deliveries late at night, but the police are always after them, the government, too."

"So Al runs bootleg whiskey. That's not really the kind of friend—"

"Oh Maddie, they're regular guys, not criminals."

Where had I heard that before? My sister-in-law sounded just like Piper.

Adjusting the rearview mirror, Sandy continued her

explanation. "Al's daddy started him running shine when he was only twelve. He had to sit on two telephone books just to see over the steering wheel."

"You don't believe that, do you?" Hopefully Sandy wasn't diving into some crazy drama to get her mind off of Bobby. "He wouldn't have even been old enough to get a driver's license."

She laughed. "Yeah, no joke, Sherlock. The whole business was illegal, so not having a driver's license really didn't matter."

"You're right, lame comment. But if he got caught—"

"He made sure he never did." She slowed, turned right. "Shiners like to keep the business in the family. It's safer that way. The fewer people that know about an illegal activity, the better."

An interesting story, but I couldn't see where it was leading or what it had to do with Bobby. "So how long has Al been doing this?"

"Ask him yourself, Maddie. He's right over there." She pointed to a dark figure hiding in the shadows, and I had a sudden surge of eerie *déjà vu*.

We pulled into the gas station right across the street from the courthouse on the Dahlonega Square and parked. A few moments later, we slipped into the back seat of Al's car. The driver pulled out and headed down Main Street before uttering a word. Then, he looked into the rearview mirror.

"It's nice to meet you, Mrs. Reynolds."

"You," I snapped back. "You're the one who threatened me on the phone this morning. I recognize your voice."

"Yes, ma'am." He turned right onto Route 9 and

peeled off down the road with Sandy and me clinging to each other in the back seat of his souped-up black Ford.

Chapter 21

Lake Lanier, Georgia—May 2012

Rob tapped on the front door of an old frame house.

"Allow me." Drew turned the knob, stuck his head inside. "Anyone here?"

"In the kitchen. Come on back." The voice was one of a mature woman. "It's about time you two got here."

"Any luck?" Rob sat at the small round table.

She raised an eyebrow. "Surely you're not doubting me?" Her confident tone was reassuring.

"Not for a second," Drew replied. "No one knows this stuff better than you."

"It's my life's work." She wiped her hands on a towel then sat at the table next to Rob. "I know exactly where, when and how this has to play out."

Rob smiled. "You are one impressive woman." Leaning back in his chair, he listened while she went over the execution of what others would describe as an elaborate fantasy.

****

Dahlonega, Georgia—December 1950

"Okay Al," Sandy shrieked, "You've made your point. Your car is fast, and we can see you know how to drive it. But you don't have to scare us to death."

Laughing, Al slowed down to a normal speed. "I

thought you wanted me to give her a demonstration."

Sandy leaned forward, resting her arms on the back of his seat. "I did, but I didn't think you'd scare us to death in the process."

"I assure you, Sandy, I'd never risk your lives. I've been driving the 9 for eleven years now and never got so much as a scratch on the finish, not on this road anyway." He pulled off into a vacant gas station in the middle of nowhere, drove to the back, stopped the engine. "Those dirt back-roads are another story, though. Some of 'em aren't much wider than my car. When you hit a pothole at that speed, let's just say you have to be a helluva driver to run shine through these woods."

We got out of Al's car then strolled over to some old chairs behind the shop. The full moon shone high in the night sky, casting a soft glow that illuminated the secret hamlet like the first dusting of twilight. Al bent down, lit a match to some logs in the small pit in front of us. Clearly, he'd used this clandestine meeting place before.

Setting the chairs around the pit, he dusted them off and motioned for us to sit down. "Have a seat."

His handsome face glowed in the firelight. About the same height as Bobby, six feet or so, his athletic physique defined by his tight white T-shirt and jeans drew Sandy's attention. In fact, she couldn't keep her eyes off of him. When he turned back to attend the fire and bent over to stoke the logs, she leaned to the side to admire his attributes and just about fell out of her chair. As attractive as Al was with his thick chestnut hair slicked back in a ducktail and his charming attitude, I remained suspicious about his intentions. Sandy giggled at his impetuous behavior, but still upset by his intimidating phone call, I wasn't equally impressed.

"I get you two are friends Al, but making an anonymous phone call to threaten us?" I glared at him with the most menacing eyes I could muster. "What were you thinking?"

"Sorry about that, Mrs. Reynolds." Al sat down in the chair next to Sandy. "I had your best interest in mind. The search for your husband has caused a lot of ruckus around here. When you run a still, you don't cotton to people snooping around your livelihood."

"People have gotten murdered for less, Maddie," Sandy chimed in.

"Yup, a few years ago, Lightning Lloyd Seay was shot in the head by his own cousin over the cost of sugar," Al added. "Moonshine is still big business around here and if someone discovers a stash or worse, a—"

"So are you insinuating a moonshiner killed Bobby when he stumbled upon a bootleg operation?" I spat.

He leaned forward, rested his elbows on his knees. "Could have, but I think I'd have at least heard some whispers if that had happened."

"So, what does all this have to do with us then?" The heat from the fire burning my face, I shifted my chair.

"Think about it, Mrs. Reynolds. You've got the police and most of Sidney scanning the countryside looking for Bobby. Sooner or later, someone is bound to run across a still or a stash." Leaning down, he picked up a stick, poked at the fire sending sparks flying. "I've heard talk. They'll stop your search no matter the outcome. I just don't want to see anyone hurt. Frankly, I've been really worried about Sandy." He glanced over at her with adoration then turned back to me. "And you, too. But I didn't dare come to your door, not with a tag team of them lurking around you both. They've been keeping tabs on you with a twenty-four hour vigil."

"So why didn't you simply call and tell Sandy what was happening instead of threatening us?"

"Maddie, it's not that simple. Al's livelihood is at risk." Sandy leaned forward. "If anyone found out that he's admitting to running shine or even talking about other shiners, he could wake up with a gun pressed into his stomach."

Trying to wrap my head around the whole situation, my thoughts churned. "Sounds a bit dramatic to me. But if you made the call to us, who was parked in front of our house?"

"That wasn't my car," Al replied. "Most of us have 1939 or '40 Fords though. They're easy to modify. I'm not sure who all is watching you at this point, but it's definitely shiners and confirms what I've been trying to tell you." Leaning close to the fire pit, he stoked the logs again. "You two are in over your head. Sooner or later your search will provoke the wrong person and Bobby won't be the only one missing."

A shiver ran down my back despite the warmth of the fire. "So we're seriously in danger?" I was at the end of my rope already. Now this?

"I wouldn't have taken the chance to meet with you here if you weren't. It's not just talk anymore. They've been watching you for weeks."

"Why in the world are you involved in transporting illegal hooch anyway, Al?" I asked. "You seem like a nice man, smart. It doesn't make sense that you'd put yourself in the middle of such a dangerous business."

"Well, for one thing, the money's damn good. I pay about $2.50 a gallon for good whiskey around here, but when I haul it to Atlanta, I can sell it for $3.50, sometimes more."

"That doesn't sound like much." I shifted in my seat again. "Not enough to risk your life."

He got up, walked to his car, and flung open the doors. He tilted his head, nodded a request to join him. "You take out this back seat and my car will hold two hundred gallons a run. I reinforced the chassis with steel rods to carry that kind of load. And I use cans instead of jugs. They stack better, so I can fill it tight, all the way into the trunk."

"So you make $200.00 a trip?" Sandy's eyes widened. "I think I'm in the wrong business." She laughed.

"Don't even consider that, Sandy." I glared at her. "Bobby will tan both of our hides."

"It's hard to walk away from that kind of cash." Al chuckled. "You do that a few times and see. It adds up."

"But what if you get caught or arrested?" I pursed my lips.

"I won't. We help each other out, like swapping license tags to throw the law off our trail. I've been runnin' white lightnin' since I was a kid and haven't been caught yet, knock on wood." He reached over and thumped on a wooden log.

"There's always a first time." How did my grandma's words find their way out of my mouth?

"That's not gonna happen. The police and IRS retaliate with faster engines, but we always stay one step ahead of them. You see this switch?" Al pointed to a toggle on his dashboard.

"Yes." I nodded.

"It turns out my tail lights. We deliver from about one in the morning till sunrise. The only people out on the roads at that time are shiners and cops. We run the hooch down the 9, but when we see headlights approaching from the back, it can only mean one thing."

"The police," Sandy offered.

"Yeah, I figured that." Peering over her shoulder, I strained to get a good look at the toggle.

"So, I flip my switch and pull off onto the back roads." Al demonstrated with a flip if his finger. "I know those roads like the back of my hand."

I had to admit his story fascinated me. "Don't they follow you?"

"Sure, if they get close enough to see me." He closed the car door. "The most important thing in this business is a fast car, one that will handle sharp turns when you're carrying a load of whiskey." We walked back to the fire while he continued his explanation. "I've installed extra carburetors that jack up the engine's capacity to burn fuel, and there's a Caddy engine under the hood that gives me a lot of extra horsepower. I can hit sixty miles per hour, in low gear."

"That's how NASCAR racing got its start, Maddie," Sandy added.

"Wait, you're losing me with the whole racing thing again." I tucked my hair behind my ears. "What does hauling moonshine have to do with NASCAR?"

"Racing started out through the spirit of competition, a way to compete with our cars and skills legally." Sitting down again, Al leaned back in his chair. "We're always bragging about how our vehicles can go faster than anyone else's and how our driving skill is superior. We started out racing on dirt roads, beaches, anywhere we could show off our talent. I guess it was inevitable that racetracks started popping up."

"And stock car racing evolved from that?" I pulled my chair to the side, sat back down next to Sandy.

"Yup. Then, about three years ago, Bill France founded the National Association for Stock Car Auto Racing, N-A-S-C-A-R."

"NASCAR. Of course, but I never realized it evolved from the moonshine business." I rubbed my hands together, held them close to the fire's warmth. Interesting, but we were getting way off track.

"Maddie, our search has got the moonshiners nervous and we could end up—"

"On the wrong end of a shotgun." I interrupted her. "I get that, but we can't give up the search, Sandy. I won't stop looking for Bobby, not ever."

"Me either, but Al has a plan." She looked over at him with a beaming smile.

"A plan?" I raised an eyebrow. "Great, fill me in. If it will help find my husband, I'm there."

Al shifted in his seat, crossed his legs. "I think you should tell the police to stop their search," he said bluntly.

"Not a chance. I just told you, there's no way we're going to—"

"Hold on, Mrs. Reynolds." He held up his hand in defense. "Hear me out. I figure, instead of the police combing the area and riling up the whole moonshine operation, why not solicit the bootlegger's help instead?"

He got my attention. "I'm listening." My tentative reply begged elaboration.

"Well, I'm pretty sure I can spread the word that you need their help, and Bobby is well liked by just about everyone around here." He rubbed his chin. "There's nobody that knows these woods better than the shiners. They can cover this territory faster and more efficiently than the police or any of your friends ever could. I could set up a meeting between you and some of the biggest operations."

"What do you say, Maddie?" Sandy's eyes lit up with excitement. "I think it's ingenious."

I bit my lip, pondering the idea. "It could work."

"Of course it will. Not only that, Al says if any of them know anything about Bobby's disappearance, it's bound to surface."

"I never thought I'd be saying this to you tonight, but thanks, Al."

"Bobby is a good man, Mrs. Reynolds."

"It's Maddie," I said. "Please call me Maddie. And thank you for saying he *is* a good man instead of he *was*. I'm so tired of hearing condolences. My husband is alive. I feel it with everything I am."

"If anyone can find him, Maddie, we will. But for this to work, you can't let on that we're helping you. Just tell the police to stop the search."

"We will." Sandy smiled like a Cheshire cat.

Al stood. "Okay, I'll be in touch after I set up a meeting." He picked up a bucket, scooped some water from a rain barrel, then doused the fire.

****

Several days later, Al called us with the details of the get-together. We met with a few men who could "hypothetically" discuss a plan to search deep into the North Georgia foothills and the base of the Appalachians. The moonshiners were nothing like I'd imagined. A few may have been poor and some were illiterate down-home boys, but they were all sharp businessmen. Most of the runners were little more than children, fourteen to twenty-something. Many had served in the war and some attended college, but their driving skills challenged any professional. And they could tear apart a car and put it together faster than an assembly plant.

Sandy was right when she said Al Rowland was a good man. His daddy owned a lumber mill north of Dahlonega, hid copper-pot stills and stash somewhere on his mountain. That's where he made mash, fermented and distilled his whiskey. Al had run his daddy's moonshine to Atlanta and neighboring towns since he was big enough to see out the front windshield of a car. It wasn't an option, more like his part of the family business, but clearly the competition gave him a rush.

Roland's white lightning wasn't half-bad either. Al dropped a jug of peach brandy by the house a few days after our first meeting, a gift from his dad. The hooch was so strong it took my breath away, but I could see why his business thrived. By twenty-three, Al had run shine for eleven years, attended North Georgia College, served in the war, and graduated from the University of Georgia. The business had paid for most of his education. He was a well-read shiner, who proved to be a valued friend.

The bootleggers scanned the back hills of North Georgia, searching for any clue that would lead them to Bobby and continued long after the police gave up their investigation. On December 18th, a week before Christmas, the newspapers reported that no trace of Bobby Reynolds had been found. He had simply vanished. They attributed his death to the storm, suggesting wild animals had likely consumed his remains.

Sandy and I never believed their lame assumption, and we didn't want to hold a funeral. It would be accepting the unacceptable. As long as the shiner's kept up their search, we still had hope. But the town insisted on saying their goodbyes. So Sully planned a service, a memorial held at Shoal Creek Church on December 22, 1950. He created a tribute and everyone donated pictures of Bobby laughing and full of life. The display was ironically exhibited on the very same altar where less than a month and a half earlier, Bobby and I had said our wedding vows. As I vacantly stared at the collage, John Baxter walked up and stood beside me.

"I'm truly sorry, Maddie." He reached in his pocket, pulled out an envelope and handed it to me. "This probably isn't the best timing, but I promised Bobby I'd have this to him by Christmas. And I'm a man of my word."

I took the letter from his hand, placed it in my pocketbook, then left the church.

Chapter 22

Lake Lanier, Georgia—June 2012

As the twilight sky burst into a sea of stars, Rob, Drew and Nick sat on the deck contemplating snifters of cognac. Drew gazed at the starry sky remembering his childhood wish. It never changed. Night after night, year after year, the wish had remained the same. And now, looking toward the twilight of his own life, his dream might very well come true.

"Only one more week," he said.

Nick had a wish of his own. And meeting Rob had put life back into the dreams he'd thought had died over ten years earlier. "Yes," he replied. "This whole ordeal will fade into a distant memory."

Rob's obsession had driven him to unfathomable lengths and irrational expense, but for all the riches he'd acquired, he could put no price tag on his ultimate reward. He raised his glass, moved in toward the other two men.

"Our lives will never be the same," he said. "To success."

The three men clinked their glasses before leaning back into their respective chairs.

Drew swirled the last jigger of brandy in his glass then gulped the bronze liquor in a single swig. "My stomach knots tighter each day."

"We never said this would be easy." Rob mused.

"Let's focus on the upshot." Nick turned to Drew, "You think Mrs. R's calculations are accurate?"

"No doubt," Drew said. "There's not a person on the planet that knows the dynamics better, and believe me, she has a vested interest in our success."

Rob stood, wandered toward the rail, glaring at the silvery moon now peeking above hardwoods. "If it's humanly possible to pull off our plan, we've got this." He glanced down at the reflection in the indigo lake. "Failure is not an option. There will be no second chances." He turned, shot conviction toward the other two men. "I'll succeed, or die."

****

Sidney, Georgia—March 1951

"Maddie, pushing your eggs around your plate won't help you feel better. You have to eat something. Bobby would want you to take care of yourself."

Shoving my plate to the side, I tried to swallow the lump that had nested in my throat for weeks. "I can't, Sandy." I placed the fork, prongs down, on the edge of the dish and leaned back in my seat. Every time I ate more than a bite or two, I had to run to the bathroom to hurl.

"Okay, this has gone on long enough." Sandy stood, took my plate and placed it in the sink. "You've been picking at food since Bobby disappeared. No wonder you're sick. He wouldn't want you to shrivel up with worry like this. Either you call Doc Meyerson or I will."

"I don't need a doctor." What I needed was a glimmer of hope that Bobby had survived. "If I don't feel better in a day or two, I'll call and get something to help me relax."

Sandy sat back down, grabbed my hand. "Promise?"

"I promise."

****

It had been four months since Bobby's disappearance. A veil of gloom shrouded Sidney, typical weather from January to March, but for Sandy and me the unremitting, silvery drizzle reflected the desolate mist that loomed in our hearts. In the throes of depression, we walked through life, robotically performing mundane chores. A world once filled with love and laughter held no interest. We were drowning in a sea of despair.

I focused on the one thing Bobby loved, his hometown. Helping his friends shift their lives to areas around the imminent lake kept my mind from dwelling on the unimaginable. Richie tried to console Sandy for weeks, attempting to distract her, but she completely shut down. She felt guilty when she wasn't focused on finding Bobby and couldn't bear to go out, laugh or have fun, as if it would somehow diminish his importance. Eventually Richie gave up, finding refuge in Becky Stewart's sympathetic arms. So, Sandy and I went through the motions of our rote life, relying solely upon each other.

A glimmer of light sparked in our mundane lives though. When Al Rowland intervened with the bootleg operation, he vowed to keep the search for Bobby alive, renewing our hope. One Saturday afternoon, he convinced us to come to Looper Speedway to see the shiners compete. I'm not sure why, but somehow watching those souped-up cars race around that old dirt track soothed the tension that had gripped my soul. And my heart warmed to see Sandy smile again.

Before long, we found ourselves looking forward to Looper Saturdays. We got to know the drivers, rooted for our favorites and the excitement of the races released our pent-up anxiety. But on Saturday, March 24, 1951, my life twisted in an unexpected direction.

"Maddie, are you coming?" Sandy called up the stairs to me. "We need to leave or we'll miss Al's race."

"You go on out to the car. I'll be there in a minute." I wiped my mouth with a washcloth, brushed my teeth, and grabbed the Tums from the medicine cabinet. Hiding my nausea from my sister-in-law challenged my creativity; I tried everything I could to keep her from worrying. Stuffing the antacid into my pocket, I glanced in the mirror, drew in a deep breath then scooted down the stairs to the car.

When we arrived at Looper, Al's '40 Ford with the Caddy engine was already revving at the starting line. Sandy jumped up on the concrete bandstand waving excitedly and Al gunned his motor in acknowledgement. When the checkered flag dropped, the cars tore off leaving a stream of dust and exhaust in their wake.

Gagging, I choked down the remaining contents of my stomach. Sandy, completely absorbed in the race, didn't notice me stand and make my way through the crowd toward the bathroom. Between the rumble of engines, the roar of the mob, and the combination of motor fumes, hotdogs and popcorn, my stomach turned flip-flops. My heart pounded, and my head began to swim. Trying to steady myself, I breathed in deep long breaths, but when the race ended, everyone jumped up from their seats and screamed while my world faded into black nothingness.

I awakened in a fog, lying in the back of Sully's truck with Doc Meyerson hovering over me. Sandy stood close by, peering down at me as Al walked up.

He put his arm around her. "What happened? I saw everyone gather around, but I couldn't see what was going on."

"It's Maddie. She collapsed." Sandy's tearful voice whispered. "Please wake up, Maddie."

My mind in a haze, I strained to answer her. "I'm…fine." I murmured.

Doctor Meyerson tucked his stethoscope into his bag. "She'll be okay, now. Just let her catch her breath."

Sully squeezed through the crowd with a wet dishrag in hand and approached his truck. He handed the cloth to the doctor. "What's wrong with her? Why did she collapse like that?"

"She's been sick for weeks," Sandy said. "I try to get her to eat, but she only pushes the food around on her plate."

"Settle down now." Doc Meyerson wiped the cool cloth across my forehead then slid off the back of the truck. "Maddie will be fine, but I don't hold out too much hope for the rabbit." He smiled and winked at me.

"You mean she's…?" Sandy looked at the doctor and raised her eyebrows.

"Well, we can't be completely sure just yet, but my guess is that this young lady is definitely—"

"Expecting. Oh Maddie, you're pregnant with Bobby's baby." Sandy jumped up on the back of the truck and hugged me.

"I'm pregnant?" Pulling myself up, I stared blankly at the doctor. "But how?"

"Well, my guess is that you and Bobby—"

"Right, I know how. I just mean the thought never crossed my mind."

"Then it's about time you started thinking." He patted my stomach. "Get plenty of rest and eat, young lady. That baby has a lot of growing to do in the next five months."

"Five months?" How could this baby be coming so soon?

"As I see it, you two must have conceived this little one sometime before Thanksgiving. It doesn't take a doctor to figure out that your baby will be born this summer." He grinned, offering a hand to help me out of the truck. "Come by my office on Monday, and I'll examine you further. We'll know a little more later this week."

"Thanks Doc," Sandy said, hugging me again. "Don't worry; I'll take care of her."

"Bobby's baby." I looked down, spread my hand across my belly, and rubbed gently. "Sandy, a part of him, of us, is growing inside of me."

"That's so wonderful, Maddie. I think we should go home and let you rest." She looked over at Al. "You don't mind do you?"

"Of course not," he replied. "Say, I'd like to drop by later this evening to see how Maddie is feeling, if that's okay with you two?"

"Please do." Sandy smiled. "I'd like that."

"Okay Sandy, I'll let you plan my afternoon this once, but I'm not an invalid." I'd never been in the habit of letting anyone make decisions for me and wasn't about to start now. "I'm not fragile either. Babies are born every day, and now that I know I'm pregnant and not sick, I'll take better care of myself."

"You've been through a lot over the past few months, Maddie." Doctor Meyerson put his hand on my shoulder. "And being pregnant on top of that?" He shook his head. "The morning sickness usually eases in the second trimester. You take it easy for a day or two, and you should be fine."

"Thanks." I turned to Al. "And you, Mr. Rowland, are welcome to come by any time you'd like. You've been a Godsend to us."

****

The next few months flew by and my belly grew bigger. Sandy tried to convince me to move into the house on the ridge. It was bigger and had more room to raise a baby, but I couldn't bear the thought of living there without Bobby. He was alive. I could feel his aura like a ubiquitous energy. I couldn't explain it, but our souls had connected, and even though it was against all odds, I knew he couldn't be dead.

Sandy believed me, too, so Al kept the moonshiners searching. The two of them grew closer in the months before the baby was born. Al finished the house Bobby built on the ridge and began excavation on Sandy's lot next door.

Meanwhile, I converted my old room into a nursery, painted the walls yellow, and replaced the bed with a crib, changing table and rocking chair.

"It looks wonderful." Sandy stood behind me, admiring the room.

Straightening the stack of baby blankets, I looked

around at my handy work. "It does, doesn't it?"

"So, have you decided if you're having a girl or a boy?" Sandy cocked her head and smiled.

"I don't think a decision on my part has anything to do with it." I laughed.

"I know, but I just wondered if you had a feeling. Bobby said Momma knew I was going to be a girl." She smoothed the sheets in the crib, placed a tiny teddy bear in the corner.

"I'm not that intuitive, but if it's a girl, I think she's gonna be an athlete."

"Why?" She crinkled her nose.

"Look at this." Pulling up the side of my maternity shirt, I exposed my bulging belly. Directly below my right ribcage was a protrusion with the distinct imprint of a tiny foot.

Sandy burst out laughing. "Just like Bobby."

"I wish he was here." I rubbed my stomach, and the foot relaxed. "He's missing so much."

"Yeah, me, too. We just can't think about that though. We have to focus on the baby." She picked up the paint can, put it on the stool, and replaced the top. "Maddie, the dam excavation has already started. Are you sure you don't want to move to the ridge? It will be a lot harder after the baby comes."

"You're probably right, but the reservoir isn't due to be completed for another few years. We still have time. Besides, I think Bobby would want the baby to be born while we're still living in Sidney."

I didn't want to even think about moving. Bobby was all around me here, and I couldn't bear the thought of leaving his childhood home. Sandy was right though. I had to start thinking about our future instead of living in the past. I walked back to my bedroom, closed the door behind me. Staring at the dresser, I took a deep breath, opened the top drawer and pulled out the sealed letter John Baxter had given to me at Bobby's service, months earlier. I'd held the note in my hand innumerable times since then, but could never bring myself to open the envelope. It was time to face the world. Carrie Ann had shown me how destructive assumptions could be, and I had promised Bobby to never fall back into those habits again. My child deserved a full-time mother, not some sniveling adolescent clinging to the shadows of her past.

"Okay little one," I said, rubbing my belly. "I guess it's time to see what Daddy had up his sleeve."

Chapter 23

Lake Lanier, Georgia—June 2012

"Everything is set, Rob." Piper gushed with excitement. "The party is going to be fabulous." Slanting her head, she slipped the phone underneath her hair so she could hear better.

"I never doubted you. So, are you bringing a date?"

"No, I'd much rather mingle with my friends."

"Friends huh? I'm sure having the most eligible bachelors in the United States attending the party didn't influence your decision." Rob chuckled. "Did you invite your friend from Atlanta—what's her name?" Of course he knew much more than Lacey's name, but Piper didn't know that. She'd make sure her friend would attend, especially with the bait he'd used.

"Lacey? No, not yet. She hates parties. I don't want to give her time to think up an excuse to bail. But don't worry. She'll be at this event if I have to go to Atlanta and drag her here myself."

Tapping his fingers on the desk, Rob smiled at how ingenious his plan had been. "You're not worried she'll already have plans?"

"No, I have a backup strategy. I know it's a little devious to deceive my best friend, but Lace is gorgeous, funny, smart, and unfortunately dating a self-absorbed jerk. She deserves so much better. This will be the perfect opportunity for her to meet someone who'll appreciate her."

Rob knew that Nick was Piper's backup plan. And she had no idea that Rob was the one who'd strategically placed the man into Lacey's life. When he hung up the phone, Rob habitually rubbed the stubbles on his chin. Only three more days, the party would set in motion an irreversible domino effect. By midnight Saturday, Lacey would vanish.

****

Sidney, Georgia—August 1951

I slid my finger under the edge of the flap slowly tearing the seal and pulled out a single sheet of folded paper. Sitting down on the foot of the bed, I tried to imagine what my husband could have possibly asked John Baxter to get to him by Christmas. I took a deep breath, unfolded the document and read.

Dr. Henry James Madison, profession - medical - Birmingham Baptist Hospital

Wife: Kathleen, daughter: Christine

Address: 325 Mountain Brook Road, Birmingham, Alabama

William Butler Montgomery, profession - CPA - Atlanta - Arthur Andersen

Wife: Elizabeth, son: Warren

Address: 568 Willow Road, Decatur, Georgia

"My parents," I whispered. "Bobby, you persuaded John Baxter to find my parents, and you were going to give them to me for Christmas." A tear escaped the corner of my eye and trickled down my cheek as I thought of my wonderful husband. Even in his absence, he still looked out for me.

****

"I can't believe you talked me into this." Sandy pulled onto I-85. "You don't even have a plan, Maddie. Are you just going to knock on the door and ask Kathleen Montgomery to see her child?"

"For your information, I do have a plan, sort of." Slinking into the passenger seat, I shifted myself around, trying to get comfortable. "I won't know for sure until we get there."

"Something tells me taking off like this is a bad idea. You shouldn't be gallivanting around in your condition."

"Sandy, pregnancy isn't a condition. Well, I guess it is, but it's not like an illness. Before long, medical science will discover that exercise actually helps a woman through pregnancy. Besides, I'm going crazy waiting around the house these last few weeks." I twisted around again, tried to pull my knees up on the seat. That didn't work. Despite the roomy size of the cars in this era, being nine months pregnant made it difficult to be comfortable anywhere for very long.

"Doctor Meyerson said you've been working too hard. You're supposed to be resting. I just want to make sure you and the baby are healthy."

"I know and I love you for that. Hey, if I had my way, we'd be driving to Birmingham to see my mom, too. Decatur isn't that far from Sidney and seeing my Dad means a lot to me."

"Yeah, I understand, but there's no way we're going to Birmingham right now. We can take your road ride after the baby comes."

I laughed. "It's road trip, not road ride and if I were in my own time, I'd be going to Lamaze classes and working out every day."

"You've been working out all over north Georgia. And what's a Lama's class?"

I was convinced there were times she purposefully provoked me with our language barrier. "Lamaze." I poked her arm. "It's natural childbirth. They teach you how to breathe and prepare for labor."

"Everyone knows how to breathe, Maddie. It's already natural. And how do you prepare for labor? Oh never mind. Don't pull your famous change the subject act on me. My point is you've been working too much for this stage of your pregnancy."

"Maybe, but I want to make as much money as I can before the baby comes, so I can buy more property on the ridge." I knew that land would be worth a lot of money in a few years, and I wanted my baby to have the best life I could provide.

"You're forgetting one thing." She glanced over at me and smiled. "Daddy left the bottling plant to Bobby, which means it's yours now, at least until my brother comes home." Adjusting the rearview mirror, she glanced at the traffic and pulled around the car in front of us.

"Bobby wants to be an architect, Sandy. He wanted to give the plant to you, but he never got the chance. Besides, the property will be smack-dab in the middle of the lake in a few years."

"I've been thinking about that, and you just gave me a great idea."

"Of course I did, I'm brilliant." I laughed. "So what was my fabulous contribution?" Twisting my body sideways, I leaned against the passenger side door.

"Well, the Army Corps of Engineers has already

proposed a settlement for the property. It's not much, but Bobby was considering the contract. You could negotiate the price with them. And I know I can sell the equipment to the St. Petersburg plant. Then we could use all of the proceeds to buy property on the north shore."

I felt like I'd given Sandy a page from the future-pedia like Marty McFly's almanac. For a movie released when I was only one, I had far too much recollection of *Back To The Future*. Daddy's interest in time travel had more than rubbed off on me. All things considered, that had actually given me a huge advantage.

"I think you're the genius." Shifting again, I tried to rest my feet on the dashboard, but my right foot got caught, and I had to twist into Sandy's lap to release it.

She roared with laughter. "Are you okay?"

"I'm fine." After readjusting myself, I continued. "Seriously, Sandy. Your idea is brilliant. Together, we can purchase hundreds of acres up there." My knowledge of the future gave us an edge over the rest of the world, but I rationalized thinking we were supposed to buy that land.

"Okay, now it's your turn to be a genius." Sandy turned the corner. "Your daddy's house is right there, and it looks like he and your grandmother are walking down the front steps. If you don't have a plan yet, you better come up with one."

"Pull over here." I grabbed her leg and stared down the street. "Let me think for a minute."

Kathleen Montgomery took Warren's hand, walked across the street, then down the sidewalk in the opposite direction.

"Okay, follow them." I whispered in my best sl
voice. "But stay way back so they don't
suspicious."

"You don't have to whisper. They can't hear us,'
Sandy whispered back. "On second thought, this is kind
of exciting. I feel like a detective."

We crept at minimal speed, following them down
the street for two blocks, watching as they approached a
little park. Kathleen sat down on a bench while Warren
ran to the merry-go-round.

"Park the car here, Sandy."

We got out, walked to the playground and sat on
the bench next to my grandmother. She was striking,
with rich brown hair cut in a trendy bobbed style and
soft ivory skin. Her sleek figure accentuated by a
shirtwaist dress with its billowing skirt was so different
from the loosely clad, frumpy image of the grandma
whose lap I'd sat on as a child.

"How old is your little boy?" Sandy asked
Kathleen.

"He'll be four in a few weeks."

"He's so adorable," I said. "What's his name?" Of
course I knew his name and way more about him than
his mother knew. It was so odd looking at Daddy like
that, an innocent little boy unscathed by life. I wanted
to bend down and hug him. Of course, his mother
would've suspected I was some kind of lunatic if I'd
done that.

"Warren," she replied. "You look like you're due
any day now."

Then again, bending down to hug my dad would
have been difficult in my present state anyway. "I am,
in a week or two. I can't wait to be able to see my feet

again."

"I remember feeling that way." She chuckled. "I'm sorry, where are my manners? I'm Kathleen Montgomery."

"It's nice to meet you." I smiled and introduced myself. "Maddie Reynolds and this is Sandy, my sister-in-law."

"Are you new to the area?" She turned on her bench.

"No, we live up the road a bit in Sidney," Sandy said.

"But the Buford dam project is about to flood the town, so we have to relocate. I was thinking about Atlanta." That wasn't a lie. A misleading statement perhaps, but not an untruth and I didn't want to fib to Granny.

"That's awful. I've been reading about the dam project in the Journal. It will be a great asset to Atlanta, but I can't imagine having to lose my home like that."

Once the conversation started, we talked for about an hour. I watched Daddy play as much as possible without drawing Kathleen's attention to my interest in him. Even at three, he was a leader, organizing the games and taking control of every situation. The other children weren't jealous though. They seemed to look up to him, a pattern that would continue throughout his life.

When Warren ran up to his mother, another child followed right behind him. "Mama, can Billy come home with us and play at our house this afternoon. His mommy said it was okay. Pleeeeease?"

"Maybe tomorrow, sweetie. Remember I told you we have to go shopping this afternoon and pick up

Daddy's suits at the laundry. Run along and play now while you can."

"Yes, ma'am." He pouted a moment with his arms crossed then added, "But I'm not very sata...satificated." He nudged his friend. "Come on, Billy. Let's go swing." He reluctantly headed back to the playground, but stopped in front of me. "Hey, I know you."

"You do?" There's no way he could possibly have recognized me, but his acknowledgment was a little unsettling.

"Sure I do. You're the nice lady that gave me a red balloon."

"Oh?" I racked my brain. Surely he confused me with someone else.

He bent over, picked up a dandelion, and handed to me. "Sorry I didn't thank you before." Then he and his friend ran toward the swings. Halfway back he halted, turned around and called out, "Next time, bring your little boy. I like him." Warren smiled then scampered back to his friends.

I looked at Kathleen and shrugged my shoulders. "That was strange."

"My son has a vivid imagination. He seems to like you though."

"He's a sweet boy." I glanced at my watch. "Oh, look at the time, Sandy. We better get going. It was so nice to meet you Kathleen. I hope to see you again."

"We live just across the way on Willow. Number 568. You're welcome to drop by any time. I can introduce you around." She opened her bag, pulled out a pen and scrap of paper, and jotted something down. "Here's my number. Melrose 65937." She handed the paper to me.

Sandy stood, held out her hand to help me up. We waved goodbye and walked back toward the road. When we got in the car, I looked at Sandy and shook my head.

"That was flat out weird. My grandmother is so young, and Daddy, what in the world was he talking about?"

"I don't know." She turned the ignition. "But I have to hand it to you. You sure came up with a good plan on the spur of the moment. Do you think Warren was right? About you having a little boy?"

Trying to get comfortable, I shifted in every direction. "I think the whole thing was a little creepy, but it was great to see grandma again and Daddy was so adorable. I can't wait to drive to Birmingham to see my mother."

The whole drive home I thought about my childhood and that strong, sweet little boy who grew up to be my father. I had spent most of my life resenting him, blaming him for my mother's death, and competing with his sorrow for a place in his heart. It wasn't until I fell in love with Bobby that I understood the dynamics of a healthy relationship. I rubbed my bulging belly, soothing butterfly quivers of life shifting inside of me. My child may never even know his daddy. And I had written mine off, my teenage, cavalier attitude playing victim to his pain. Now, I missed him. A sudden flush of coolness flowed over me.

"You coming, Maddie?" Sandy asked heading up the front steps.

"I don't think so." I paused. "You were right about the trip to Birmingham."

"Aren't I always?" she teased then frowned at me. "Do I have to come open the car door for you, milady?"

"No." I grimaced. "I think you need to get back in the car."

"Why, what's up?" She cocked her head, eyed me with a puzzled glare.

"I'm pretty sure my water just broke."

Chapter 24

Lake Lanier, Georgia—June 2012

Rob approached Piper's terrace but paused when he overheard her talking on the phone.

"I can't wait to hear the latest chapter of Lacey Life...I know, and I promise your visit will be well worth your trip."

Pulling out his own cell, Rob tapped her number.

"Oh, I've got to take this, Lace. See you tomorrow." Piper switched calls.

"I take it Lacey is coming?" Rob smiled observing her reaction.

"Yes, but how did you—"

"Know?" He walked toward her. "Just a lucky guess."

Piper spun around. "Oh my gosh, how long have you been standing there?"

"Just a moment or two. I didn't mean to startle you." He offered a reserved grin. "It sounds like your plan worked."

"Of course." Piper pursed her lips with a confident pucker. "I told you I'd get her here. There's no way I'd let Lacey miss this party." She tucked her hair behind her ear and stuffed her phone in her back pocket.

"I'm glad your friends will join us, Piper. You've planned quite an event."

"I have, haven't I? Everything came together beautifully. I hope Lace meets some wonderful man who will sweep her off her feet."

Rob raised an eyebrow. "I have a feeling that Lacey's life will turn in a whole new direction before the night is over."

"I hope so." She shook her head. "Anyone would be better than that deadbeat she's dating."

It had taken an entire year for Rob to set all of the chess pieces in place. Only two more days and the queen would be captured. Check, but was it mate? Rob's final move would determine his future. And with unconscionable stakes at risk, the timing had to be perfect.

****

Sidney, Georgia—August 1951

"Maddie, you mean the baby is coming, now?" Sandy's voice exuded excitement. "Are you in labor?"

"Well, I've never done this before, but according to my extensive television training, when my water breaks the baby's coming." Sopping wet, I twisted around searching for something to soak up the mess. "I think there's a towel on the floor behind me."

"I'll get it." She reached over the seat. "I've got everything under control. Just relax." She handed the towel to me.

"That's easy for you to say." I stuffed the terrycloth under my derrière, looking up just in time to see Sandy dash inside the front door. "Where are you going?" Was she freaking out?

A few moments later, she flew back down the porch steps carrying my suitcase. "Doctor Meyerson will meet us at the hospital shortly." Jumping into the car, she threw my bag in the backseat, started the ignition, and answered the question I was about to ask. "I packed your suitcase a few weeks ago."

"I'm impressed." I laughed, but was met with an overwhelming surge of pain. "Holy crrrrrrrrraaaaap."

"Hold on Maddie." She backed out of the driveway. "I timed every possible route, and I know the fastest route. We'll be there soon, I promise." She peeled off down the road.

Sandy swerved around curves, over hills and down again with the expertise of a seasoned shiner. I steadied myself, gripping the dashboard in one hand and my belly in the other. The roller-coaster ride continued until a wave of nausea rumbled through my stomach into my throat.

"Sandy, please slow down. I feel like I'm riding with Al." I moaned and dug my fingers into her leg. "If you don't take these curves a little easier, we'll have a worse mess to clean up." *Dear Lord, please keep me from puking all over the windshield.* "Sorry. I have spent a lot of time with him lately. I'll slow down a little."

I started to pant using short breaths, which wasn't helping. Damn, TV made the process look so easy. What a misnomer.

"Take deep breaths, Maddie. Don't pant like a dog." Sandy laughed. "I guess maybe you needed to learn how to breathe after all."

"It's suppooooosed to—" Wracked with pain, I gave up on explanations. My abdomen hardened, contracting with a pressure I strained to control, but the need to push overpowered my best intentions.

Sandy reached over, squeezed my hand briefly then

picked up her pace, speeding toward the Northeast Georgia Medical Center. The contractions flowed in waves, each one more intense than the last. By the time we reached Gainesville, they were only minutes apart. Sweat oozed from every pore in my body, and my abdomen stiffened to a rock-hard mound. The excruciating pain squeezed and stretched at the same time with nauseating pressure ripping through my core. I bit my tongue to keep from screaming.

"This is all your fault, Bobby Reynolds," I shouted at the top of my lungs.

When we pulled up to the hospital, Doc Meyerson was waiting by the entrance with a wheelchair.

"You don't give a body much warning do you, Maddie?" Opening the car door, he chuckled.

Hardly the time for humor, I responded with a roll of my eyes. "Not my decision," was all I could squeak out before another contraction contorted my stomach.

"She's having those every few minutes," Sandy said.

"This baby's in a hurry." He helped me into the chair, wheeled me inside. "I'll give you something for the pain when we get you settled."

"No." Grabbing his arm, I gripped him tightly. "No drugs." I gasped for air, "Not good for the baby."

"But you need to be sedated." He pushed me through double doors and rushed down a long hallway.

"No drugs." Another contraction. "I don't care...how bad...contractions get..." A moment of relief ensued. There was no way I wanted to put those antiquated medications in my body. "If anyone tries to stick a needle in me, I'll—Ahhh." Pain took over again.

"Okay Maddie. I'll see that no one anesthetizes you

unless it's an emergency."

A nurse met us in the hallway and spoke to Doctor Meyerson as if I were some kind of mentally deficient invalid.

"I'll take her and get her ready, Doctor," she said. "We'll wash her down, shave her, and give her an enema. She'll be sedated in the stirrups and waiting on you in no time."

"Are you kidding me?" I shrieked. "Where's Sandy?" This was one time I had no patience for archaic methods.

"I'm right behind you, Maddie." She reached up, grabbed my hand.

"I'm sorry; she'll have to stay in the waiting room." The nurse scowled.

"But she's—ooohhhh—my coooooooach."

"This is no time to be thinking about sports," Dr. Meyerson said.

"Don't worry, Maddie." Sandy clutched my hand. "I won't leave you."

"That's not possible," the nurse interrupted. "We have rules, and there's specific protocol for deliveries." She turned to the doctor. "These women don't know what's best for them. We have to…"

Did she say *these women*—really? A moment of complete control washed over me. "If you know what's best for you, you'll shut your mouth and get out of our way." I clenched my hand around the doctor's arm again as the pains returned and felt his skin give way to my nails.

"Humph." She lifted her prim and proper little nose in the air.

"That's quite all right, nurse. This baby is coming

right now. There's no time to prep her." He handily dismissed the woman and wheeled me into the delivery room. "You'll have to wait here, Sandy." He pushed to close the door but my leg flew forward.

"No," I shrieked. "Sandy." Turning, I held Sandy's hand in a death grip. Another contraction. My fingernails dug in again.

"I'm not leaving her." Sandy stood in front of the wheelchair and stared at Meyerson. "Doc, she's been through enough with Bobby and everything. Please, I have to stay with her."

"Oh all right." He pushed forward, mumbling to himself. "I'm sure I'm going to regret this."

****

On Friday, August 3, 1951, at seven thirty-three in the evening, I gave birth to a six-pound two-ounce son, and though it was unheard of at the time, Sandy stood beside me through the entire birth.

"That was the most remarkable experience I've ever had," she said. "You've got to be exhausted. But look at him, Maddie. He's beautiful." She leaned over, touched his cheek with the back of her forefinger. "I can't wait to have a baby of my own."

"You will, someday." I gazed down at my sweet baby. "He is beautiful. I think Bobby would prefer handsome though." I kissed his forehead, put my little finger in the grip of his tiny hand.

Sandy sat on the foot of my bed, her eyes glued to my son. "Did you decide on a name yet?"

"How about Robert Andrew Reynolds." I looked at the baby searching for a glimmer of approval, and he made a little sucking motion with his mouth.

"I think he likes it." Sandy giggled. "Will you call

him Bobby?"

"No. There's only one Bobby Reynolds in my life." I smiled gazing upward as if Bobby's spirit was hovering above us then looked at Sandy. "His middle name is after your dad. What about calling him Andrew?"

"I love it." Reaching over, she rubbed the back of my son's little hand and grinned. "It's nice to meet you, Andrew Reynolds."

****

Sidney, Georgia—May 1952

I've heard that having a child changes everything. It's true. Andrew became the focus of my universe. Each day I watched him grow, learn and discover the wonders of his world. He was smart and all boy with his daddy's beautiful eyes and a thick head of dark brown hair.

Sandy treated him like she would her own child, constantly taking pictures of both of us and pasting them in albums with little notes describing every milestone: his first bath, when he started to crawl, his first words. She showed him pictures of Bobby and taught him to say Daddy.

Andrew's birth sparked a sense of motherhood from a totally different perspective, and thoughts of my own mother began to haunt me. After so many years, I had trouble visualizing her face in my mind. I hadn't seen her since my tenth birthday, the day she died, and despite knowing she was only a toddler here, my heart yearned to see her. By the time Andrew was nine months old, I could no longer ignore my curiosity. It was high time my son met his grandmother.

Sandy and I packed a small suitcase and a bag for

Andrew with everything we could possibly need. I secured his car bed in the back seat, covered the little mattress with crib sheets, and put a light cotton blanket over the side. With the handles up, we could throw the blanket over the top like a canopy to keep the sun from waking him.

We fed my son, changed his diaper, dressed him in a T-shirt and lightweight romper, then laid him on his tummy in the car bed and headed to Alabama. Sandy drove, and we brainstormed the entire trip, discussing various strategies of approaching my maternal grandparents without raising their suspicion as to why we were interested in their infant daughter.

"So, how did your parents meet, Maddie?" Sandy glanced in the rearview mirror.

"Daddy said he met Mom in high school after a big football game. He used to tell me stories about the Druid Hills Red Devils and his infamous quarterback years."

"Then your mom's family must have moved to Decatur."

"I guess, at some point." Frankly, I didn't remember much about my mother and I hated that.

The baby slept the entire trip while Sandy and I babbled. But I peeked under the canopy several times to check on him. During quiet times, I noticed how much he looked like Bobby.

As we approached Birmingham, Andrew began to stir. Sandy pulled into a Texaco station then ran to the bathroom while attendants filled the tank. I tended to my son. Picking him up, I noticed he felt unusually warm. I changed his diaper, took off his romper and moist shirt, then brought him up to the front seat to breastfeed, but he showed little interest. When I offered him a few cheerios, he whimpered, put his head on my shoulder, and sucked his thumb. By the time Sandy got back to the car, I was concerned.

"Andrew is burning up." I stroked his chubby pink cheeks, which usually caused him to giggle, but instead, he pouted. "He's lethargic and won't eat a thing."

Sandy wiped damp hair away from his brow, felt his head and grimaced. "I'll be right back." She dashed out of the car then came back a few minutes later with a damp cloth. Handing the rag to me, she started the ignition. "Cool him down with that."

"Where are you going?" I patted the cool cloth over Andrew's face and chest. "We have to get him to a doctor."

"I asked the attendant inside, and he said the hospital was just around the corner. We're almost there."

Five minutes later, we sat in the waiting room of Birmingham Baptist Hospital. I expected we'd be there for hours, typical of every emergency room I'd experienced, but a nurse immediately showed us to a small room and told us a doctor would examine my son directly.

Shortly afterward, a knock on the door preceded a tall attractive man who entered the room, closing the door behind him. He looked at my son, listened to his heart, and thumped his back a few times. After a brief examination, he put his stethoscope in his pocket and wrote a few notes on a pad.

"So what's wrong with him?" I rubbed my son's back, rocking him back and forth in my arms.

"It looks like you've got a very healthy baby."

Seeing my obvious confusion, he elaborated. "This must be your first child." He patted Andrew's arm and smiled. "Your son just got a little overheated. You'll need to keep him cool and offer milk or juice as often as he'll take it." He opened the door. "The next time you travel with him just make sure he stays cool. Don't nestle him in blankets. It can get awfully hot in the back seat of a car, and babies can't tell you when they're hot."

"Should we drive back to Georgia?" I looked at Sandy for her opinion.

"I don't think that's necessary," the doctor offered. "In fact, I'd advise against traveling tonight. I'd like to keep an eye on him. Were you planning to stay close by?"

"Can you suggest a nice hotel?" Sandy spoke up before I had a chance to reply.

"The Redmont, at the corner of 5th Avenue and 21st Street, is quite nice. As a matter of fact, my wife and daughter are meeting me there for dinner." He looked at his watch. "And I'd better get going. Elizabeth made reservations for six o'clock. If you get a room there, I can check on Andrew before we head home."

"Thank you doctor." Sandy quickly agreed. "It's so nice of you to offer. I'll go call the hotel right now." She promptly left the room.

Perplexed at her hasty decision, I thanked the doctor, stuffed his instructions into my purse, then walked out to the lobby in search of my sister-in-law. Why would she run out of the room that way?

"Sandy, what came over you in there?"

"I put two and two together." She grinned.

"Maddie, you must have been so upset about Andrew you didn't notice."

"Notice what?"

"His name tag. The doctor who just examined your son was Henry Madison, your grandfather. And he's meeting his wife and your mother at the Redmont in fifteen minutes."

"Oh my gosh. That was granddaddy? He's so young. I don't remember him looking like that at all." Turning to Andrew, I hugged him, kissed his cheek. "You're going to meet your grandma, sweetie."

By the time we registered and were shown to our room, it was already ten after six. We dropped our bags inside the door then went downstairs to the restaurant. We followed the maître-d' to our table, and Doctor Madison stood.

"Well, fancy meeting you here." He chuckled. "That was fast."

"Look Maddie, it's Dr. Madison." Sandy acted totally surprised.

I tried so hard not to stare at my Grandma and Grandpa. They were so vibrant and young. Then my eyes locked on Christine. My mother was this amazing, beautiful little girl. I wanted to run to her, hold tight and never let go. I wished I could protect her from the awful death she would face so early in her life. I had blamed her for abandoning me and taking Daddy's heart with her but now, I saw her from a whole new perspective.

Henry extended his hand to each of us and introduced his family. "This is my wife, Elizabeth. And this little one is Christine, our daughter." He touched the button nose of the toddler sitting in the highchair and she squealed with delight. "She's not much older

319

than Andrew."

I wanted to throw my arms around all of them, tell them who I was, but I knew better. "It's so nice to meet you, Elizabeth." I turned to my mother, stooped down to her level. "It's nice to meet you, too, Christine. That's a beautiful dress you're wearing."

Still holding my son, I introduced him to his grandmother. "Christine, this is my little boy, Andrew." She smiled, reached for his face. Andrew ignored her, grabbing a Cheerio instead from her highchair table.

"Beth, the Reynolds are from Atlanta," my grandfather said. "Maybe they can tell us about the area so we can make a more educated decision." He looked at me. "Say, why don't you join us?"

"Oh no, we don't want to impose." I spoke the words hoping he'd insist. *Please, grandpa, please insist.*

Sandy stepped on my toe. "If we can help, we'd be happy to join you. After all you did for us today, it's the least we could do."

He motioned for the maître-d' who pulled tables together.

"Henry has been offered a position at Emory Hospital in Atlanta," Elizabeth began, "and we've been going back and forth about whether we should uproot Christine or not."

"Oh, you'd love Atlanta." Sandy boasted the city's benefits. "It's beautiful and the people are so friendly." She nudged me under the table.

"Emory is one of the finest hospitals in the country practicing cutting edge medical advances," I added. "And Atlanta is the heart of the south. Actually, you'd really like Decatur. It's a wonderful place to raise a child."

As we talked over dinner, I totally sold my grandparents on the idea of moving to Decatur. It was so odd to talk with Henry and Beth as equals instead of viewing them as my old grandparents the way I'd remembered them. My mother and son entertained each other through the whole meal, taking turns feeding one another, each totally fascinated by the other. There was an odd connection between them. They communicated as if they understood something no one else knew. Perhaps they did.

By the end of the evening, we all had become friends, and my grandparents promised to have us over for dinner when they got settled into their new home. When we got up to leave, Christine reached out, fussing for me to pick her up.

"Goodness. How unusual," Beth commented. "She really likes you. Normally, Christine doesn't warm up to strangers."

I can't explain the energy that surged through me when I held my mother in my arms. I kissed her tiny cheek and tried desperately to hold back the emotion welling inside of me. "You come visit us, too, Christine." I reluctantly handed her back to her mother.

We thanked Henry again for taking care of Andrew, waved goodbye, then strolled toward the elevator.

As the door closed, I looked at Sandy. "Oh my gosh. That was mind-blowing."

"Do you realize what just happened?"

"You mean holding my mother in my arms?" I leaned back against the elevator wall, drained of energy. Was it fate, time or simply a little girl absorbing life in innocence? I wasn't sure, but somehow my mother had reached beyond the grave to give me a huge gift. At that moment I realized my mom would have never abandoned me. Somehow, through my grief and emptiness, I had rewritten history in my own mind. It was I who had created protective walls around my heart. I ran in fear. Not simply from love, but from my own dreams. I had abandoned myself. Bobby was right; my future would be what I made of it. Only I could discover the prize hidden in my Cracker Jacks.

Sandy spoke, breaking the flow of my revelation. "I'm sure that was bizarre, but not what I'm talking about. If we hadn't come to Birmingham, your grandparents may have never moved to Atlanta. You were meant to come back in time, Maddie, to set the space-time continuum straight. Everything you do here was meant to happen, meeting Bobby, having Andrew and helping Sidney. It was your destiny."

I hugged Andrew, gave him a big kiss. When the elevator door opened, we walked back to our room. Sandy put the key in the doorknob and I finally replied.

"If I was supposed to come back in time, then Bobby is still my destiny. He's not dead, Sandy. I feel it in the depths of my soul. And I'm going to find him."

Chapter 25

Lake Lanier, Georgia—June 2012

Rob stood on the corner of his porch, gazing across the cove. It was four thirty; the dominos had already begun to fall. Glancing over at Piper's deck, he caught a glimpse of Lacey. He stared, watching her every move, the lines of her beautiful body, how she softly sipped her wine appearing spellbound by the mystery of the lake. The sun, now low in the sky, had the same magenta glow as the night before, and the water shimmered, casting a stunning aura around her, like a dream. Hypnotized, Rob watched her swirl the wine in her glass. Swathed in the serenity and nature, he imagined himself standing beside her.

When Lacey turned and walked back into the house, Rob watched every step. Only a few more hours. Closing his eyes, he filled his lungs with rich mountain air then headed inside. It was time to get ready for the most important night of his life.

****

Sidney, Georgia—September 1953

I never gave up the search for my husband, but time marched forward. Sandy relinquished the empty skeleton that was once the family Co-Cola bottling factory to the Army Corps of Engineers. As planned, my negotiations brought in a lot more money than the original offer. Once we secured the land on the north shore of what would soon be Lake Sidney Lanier, it would appreciate enough over the years to assure our family's financial security. When the dam excavation began, my business thrived and still every cent we could spare went to purchasing more land on the ridge.

Sidney became a ghost town as more-and-more residents moved away. Some people literally transported existing houses to new property, but many simply took their belongings and surrendered the hollow shell of their past to wane beneath the rising lake.

By September 1953 the excavation was well underway. The Corps of Engineers began to carve the shoreline and soon the water would swallow abandoned homes, churches, and businesses as Sidney slipped into the bowels of Lake Lanier and faded into a forgotten world. I stayed in Bobby's house as long as I could, but finally conceded it was time to move into the home my husband had built on the ridge.

"Maddie, Al, and Sully just took another load to the house," Sandy yelled from the foyer.

Hearing her, I rushed from the kitchen into the dining room. "Shhh, Andrew is sleeping."

She cringed then whispered. "Sorry. The truck was full, and a storm is brewing. They wanted to take one last load and unpack the boxes before the weather breaks. Has Andrew been asleep long?

"No, I rocked him until he nodded off and put him down about fifteen minutes ago."

"Good. Most of the big cartons have already been moved, unpacked, and set up in the new house. The kitchen here is empty except for necessities we'll need for the next few days."

I draped the dishcloth I'd been using over the banister. "Sandy, relax. You're doing too much. We aren't in a race with time you know."

"Yeah, I'm just trying to make things easier for you and Andrew. Having the house set up instead of stacked in containers will at least give him a sense of the familiar. Besides, it'll be easier for me, too."

"Thanks." Sitting on the steps, I leaned back on my elbows. "I guess I'm still kind of dragging my feet. I'm so reluctant to leave this house."

She put her hand on my knee. "I'm glad you're finally admitting that."

"Sandy, this is the first place Bobby would come if—"

"It's been three years." She tucked her hair behind her ears.

"Two years, ten months and sixteen days, but who's counting? Look, I realize it's hard to keep hoping, but if Bobby were dead, I'd feel emptiness. I can't explain where he is, but deep down I know he's alive. And I *will* find him."

She sat down on the step below me. "I want to believe that he'll come back, too, but for now let's focus on moving into that beautiful house he built for you."

"That's another thing I wanted to talk to you about, Sandy. You don't need to live with me. Your house is ready, too. Just move in next door."

"Are you getting tired of having me around?" She glared at me.

"Of course not, but I'm not blind. I see what's going on between you and Al. He's in love with you,

Sandy. And I'm pretty sure the feeling is mutual." I leaned forward. "He wants to marry you, start a family, so please don't put your life on hold for me and Andrew."

"You and Andrew are my family." She stood, walked to the parlor window, and looked across the front yard. "If Al really loves me, he'll wait until—"

"Until Bobby comes home?" I interrupted.

Snapping around, she scowled at me. "I wasn't going to say that. I was going to say he'd wait until I'm ready."

"And when would that be." I pulled myself up from the steps. "When Andrew is in college?"

She didn't answer so I walked over and hugged her. "Sweetie, you're my sister, my closest friend. I couldn't love you more, but you're as hard-headed as that statue in the square."

"I love you, too, Maddie, and you know I love Andrew like he's my own child."

I shrugged, turned, and started up the stairs to pack my bedroom. Sandy followed me.

"We can go to Millie's for supper tonight," she said, walking into her room.

"That woman will be the last person to move away from Sidney. I'm so glad Al, Sully, and the rest of those guys are building a new diner for her in Oakwood. I don't know what we'd do without a Millie's." I tiptoed past my son's bedroom, peeked in on him, then walked toward my room. "If you need help come get me," I whispered. "I want Andrew to sleep as long as he can. The last thing we need the next few days is a fussy toddler."

A loud crack of thunder rumbled outside. "I hope

this storm doesn't wake him," Sandy said, closing the door behind her.

I looked around at the empty room Bobby and I had once shared. It would be hard to leave his home. He loved this old place. I could still feel him here, enmeshed between the walls. At times, I imagined him sprinting up the stairs, swinging on the porch swing, or swigging down his cup of coffee in the kitchen. I could still smell the soft scent of his English Leather; feel his presence next to me as I fell asleep at night. But I knew he wanted us to live on the ridge. Sidney would be completely underwater soon. We had to move. There really was no alternative. Still, I couldn't shake the feeling that when I left, I'd somehow lose another piece of him.

Grabbing an empty box from the corner, I opened the bottom drawer of my dresser and began to transfer the contents, folding each piece of clothing meticulously. By the time I reached the top drawer, I'd filled two and a half boxes. Placing my intimates in a third box, I pressed everything down to make room for incidentals.

I was about to close the last empty drawer when I noticed something pushed far to the back. I reached in, and pulled out Piper's little beaded purse. It seemed like a lifetime ago that I had gone to her new lake house and ended up at that fateful party. That night had changed my life. If it hadn't been for Piper, I would've never found Bobby, Sandy, or Sidney. Andrew wouldn't have been born, and honestly, I'd have never found myself. My life was empty in 2012. I'd simply gone through the motions never realizing what gifts life could hold.

I sat down on the edge of the bed, ran my fingers

over the tiny beads. I missed Piper, and Daddy, but despite what had happened to Bobby, I would never trade that life for this one, not in a million years. As I picked up the little purse to pack it in the box, I felt something hard inside. The purse had been empty when Bobby found me, hadn't it? Curious, I opened the top, peered inside, but saw nothing. Pinching the side of the bag, I still felt a hard object, so I ran my fingers along the lining, then saw a tiny zipper I'd never noticed.

Unzipping the pouch, a rush of adrenalin washed over me. I stuck two fingers deep into the pocket and pulled out a small brass ring with a tiny red ribbon tied around it. My heart raced as I remembered the last time I had seen the ring, the day Bobby disappeared. But it couldn't be Bobby's ring, could it? I glared at the brass ring, rolling it over and over in my fingers. No one else knew about the red ribbon legend. Bobby must have put the ring in Piper's purse, but how?

Feeling the inside of the pouch again, I searched for something, anything to confirm my deepest hope. There, stuffed into the lining, I felt a folded piece of paper, hard, almost like cardboard. I slid the object from its hiding place. I stared at the missive and my mouth dropped. Bobby's handwriting, scribbled on the back of an aged photograph. But not just a random photo, our wedding picture, the one Bobby had taken from Sandy the day we got back from our honeymoon. There was no way that photograph could have been in Piper's purse unless Bobby had put it there. I glared at the picture, inspecting it closely then flipped it over to read his words—words that sent chills into my soul. The note in my husband's handwriting said:

Maddie, Come to me in time, our place. I love you

forever.

"Sandy." I shrieked at the top of my lungs. "Come here quickly."

"What happened?" She flew into my room. "Are you okay? Is something wrong with Andrew?"

"No, we're fine. But look, Sandy." Trembling, I handed the picture to her.

"Where did you get this? It was in Bobby's billfold when he—"

"So was this." I held up the brass ring. "I gave the ring to him Thanksgiving morning, watched him put it in his front pocket right before he left to secure the windows. He's alive, Sandy. I knew it. I could feel it. But where is he? And why did he slip those things in my purse instead of just coming home? He must be in danger. Maybe he's trying to keep us safe."

Andrew whimpered down the hall. "Maaa maa," he cried.

"Do you want me to get him?" Sandy asked, moving toward the door.

"No. I probably scared him when I screamed. I'll be right back." Overwhelmed with emotion, I ran down the hall to tend to my son, leaving Sandy to inspect the photo. "Oh sweetie, Mommy's sorry. Come here darlin'. I didn't mean to wake you." As I picked up my son, he grabbed his blanket, laid his head on my shoulder, and sucked his thumb. Walking back to my bedroom, I comforted my little boy, clutching him to my chest, nuzzling him as he cuddled closer.

Sandy, still studying the picture she held in one hand, twiddled the brass ring between her thumb and forefinger in the other. She turned the photo over, read the inscription on the back.

"Oh my gosh, Maddie. Did you see this?" She glared at me.

"Yes. It's like some kind of riddle." Standing next to her, I rocked Andrew from side to side.

"No. Don't you see?" She looked at the ring, then back at the picture. "Bobby can't come home."

"That doesn't make sense. He had to have come home to put these things in my purse." I sat down beside her on the foot of my bed, Andrew still in my arms.

"Maddie, you of all people should get this. Think four dimensionally. It's true Bobby must have held your purse in his hands to place the picture and ring inside. But what if he couldn't come home? His note says: *Come to me in time.* I don't think Bobby meant come quickly, he meant come to him *through* time."

Cuddling my baby closer, I felt my heart skip a beat then pound harder, harder until I was sure it would burst through my chest. "Oh Sandy, that's it. Bobby disappeared because he fell through time. He found the portal."

"I've been thinking about this for years, how you got here I mean. I always believed you. Even though your story seemed completely whacky, it was the only explanation that fit the circumstances. The whole concept intrigues me."

"There were times when I doubted my own story. Sometimes I thought my memory twisted from my accident or that I'd simply created the future in a dream." I took the brass ring from her hand, held it tightly. "Bobby and I looked for the time crack for months and never found it."

She grabbed my leg. "The reason you and Bobby

couldn't find the portal is because it wasn't there."

"So you're saying I didn't come from the future?" I scrunched my brow.

"No, just the opposite. What if the portal wasn't there when you searched because it opens and closes, like a door?" She stood and started pacing in small little circles while she formulated her theory.

"So after I passed through, the door closed?"

"Exactly."

"Then how could Bobby have found it? And if he did, where is he?"

"One question at a time." She continued to pace. "Of course I'm not sure about any of this, but the theory makes sense. The police knew Bobby was on the scaffold, and there were indications that he fell off, right?" She ran her fingers through her hair exactly like I'd seen Bobby do so many times before.

"Yes. But they found no other clues." I rubbed my son's back.

"Right. If he slipped off the scaffold and fell through the portal there would be no trace of him." She paused. "But why was the time crack accessible then?"

"Something had to trigger the door to open."

"Right. So, what happened the night you arrived in Sidney? Was anything similar to the night Bobby disappeared?"

"Both time slips occurred at night, but that couldn't be a trigger. We searched the ridge at night plenty of times." I tried to recall every detail of both evenings. Then it hit me. "We combed the area at night, Sandy, but not during storms. Sandy, both times the portal opened, huge storms had blown through the entire area."

"And presto-change-o, the enchanted door materializes. Maddie, that's it. You were right all along. Bobby is alive, just not in 1949. Which begs the question, where is he?"

"No Sandy, not where, when? Bobby was thrust through time to the future, but to *when*?"

Chapter 26

Lake Lanier, Georgia—June 10, 2012

"Lacey, please wake up?"

I heard the voice calling me, muted, distant, as if I were listening underwater. I tried to answer her. "Piper? Is that you?" But my voice only drifted through the canyons of my mind.

"Lace, please, come back to me."

I felt her touch, her tears on the back of my hand. "I'm right here. Why are you crying?" Words screamed from my mind but couldn't reach her ears.

"You have to make it." She softly stroked my arm. "I'll never forgive myself if you don't."

"Piper, I'm okay." Why couldn't she hear me?

"It's all my fault. If only I hadn't begged you to come to that stupid party. Lacey, you just have to wake up."

"I'm here." Straining to see through a hazy fog, I peered at her through tiny slits too small for her to see.

****

Sidney, Georgia—September 1953

"*When*ever he is, Maddie, he held your purse in his hands."

"Then he must have been at the party. Either that or had access to Piper's house." My son began to stir. Stroking his hair, I rocked him back and forth.

"Possibly both." Sandy sat down on the bed beside me. "It doesn't matter though. At least we know he's in 2012. The question is how do we bring him back to our time?"

"Maybe we can't." I reached over, grabbed her arm. "Sandy, in 2012 the portal is at the bottom of the lake."

Thunder rolled forewarning the approaching storm. I stood, walked to the head of my bed and gently laid Andrew, now fast asleep, next to the pillows. Brushing a tiny strand of soft brown hair from his sleepy eyes, I smiled, leaned down, kissed his forehead then strolled to the window.

Sandy edged up behind me and put her hand on my shoulder. "So, now what?"

Outside I could see the storm looming dark and foreboding in the distance. The deepening blue-gray clouds blackened the mid-September afternoon sky to an eerie midnight glow. Trees swayed with the wind as it whipped through the yard, tossing leaves randomly through the humid air, a fitting ambiance for the torment in my soul. I turned toward Sandy, tears pooling in my eyes.

"This storm looks ominous." A wave of realization flooded my mind followed by a stabbing gnaw in my heart. I bit my lip.

"Yeah, Al said they're forecasting a doozy." Her gaze shifted to the sky.

"Sandy, do you understand what I'm saying, another violent storm?"

Turning, she stared back at me. "Oh, Maddie no. We can't just take off haphazardly in this kind of weather to hunt for a crack in time. It's too dangerous.

We need a plan first."

"Sandy, Bobby has been gone for three years. He doesn't even know he has a son. He's missing his life." I clenched my hands into fists, tightened my muscles then let go, attempting to release the tension and anxiety exploding inside of me. "I'm not saying we search the ridge. I have to do this, Sandy. Alone."

"No. I won't let you go alone."

"The key to the time portal has to be violent weather. The more torrential the storm, the better chance I have of finding the door."

She looked out the window again, stared at the darkening sky. "I want Bobby to come home more than anything. But"—she put her arm around me—"I don't know what I'd do if I lost you, too."

Picking up the brass ring, I flipped it between my fingers. "Bobby found a way to put this brass ring and our picture into Piper's purse. He wants me to come to him, Sandy. I have to try."

Overwhelmed with emotion, she began to cry. I took her hand, led her to the foot of the bed.

"Sit down." I patted the bed beside me. "I have a story to tell you." I recounted the Japanese legend I'd recited to Bobby the night he asked me to marry him, about the god of destiny who ties an invisible red string around the little finger of destined souls. And how I'd tied a small red ribbon around Bobby's little finger.

"The red thread connects those two people through eternity, Sandy. Regardless of time, place, or circumstances they're drawn together. The magical cord can stretch or tangle, but it will never break. Maybe it sounds silly. But Bobby found a way to reach across time to talk to me. I've got to go to him."

She looked at me with pleading eyes. "We know the portal is on the ridge somewhere. We'll have a much better chance of finding the crack if we look together."

"No, sweetie. Someone has to stay here with Andrew. Besides, I know exactly where the door is now."

"How?" Her hand trembled as she touched mine.

"Bobby told me in his note." I looked at the picture again, turned it over, and read the inscription on the back again. "He found the time crack. Look." Showing her the message, I read: *Come to me in time, our place.* The portal is where we always believed it was, at the foot of our bench where he first found me."

I gazed over at my sleeping child. I wanted to find Bobby with all my heart, but what if I shifted through time again? How could I leave my baby behind? Reality washed over me harsh and cold. I suddenly couldn't breathe.

"But what if I'm pulled back to the future? I can't leave Andrew behind."

"I'll watch him, Maddie. Go find his daddy. Bring him home to both of us."

"What if I can't get back? No. I have to take Andrew with me." Scooting around the bed, I bent over to pick up my child.

Sandy shot forward, grabbed my arm. "No, Maddie you can't. Think about it." She spun me around to face her. "You said yourself that the portal in the future is at the bottom of the lake. If you have Andrew when you go back through the crack, you both will drown."

"But I can't leave my son." Tears blurred my vision. I looked down at my sleeping child again. "This is impossible. I can't choose between my son and my husband!"

"Maybe you don't have to. Just find Bobby and bring him back. Only…"

"Only what?" I wiped my tears with the back of my hand.

"It's hard to say." She sat on the side of the bed again. "There are so many variables we don't know. We're not even sure the door will open again."

"Why wouldn't it?" I sat next to her.

"I don't know. We're talking about an anomaly, Maddie. It's possible that when Bobby went to the future the portal could have closed again, for good." She took my hand, looked deep into my eyes. "But you're right about one thing, Maddie. Bobby wants you to come to him."

I thought about what he'd said to me the night he spoke at the town meeting: *It defies all common sense. But sometimes if a leap of faith is all you have, you've got to take it.*

"Bobby doesn't even know about his son." I looked at Andrew again. "There has to be a way to bring them together." Turning, I pulled my sleeping baby to my breast and clung to him. "Mommy has to go away for a while, sweet baby," I whispered. "I love you with all my heart. And I'll bring your daddy to you somehow. If it takes me a lifetime, I swear to you that you and Bobby will be together." I kissed him gently, laid him back on my bed, stood and hugged Sandy. "I love you, too, sweetie. Please, please take care of him. I'll do everything I can to bring Bobby back. I promise, but if anything should happen to me—"

"Nothing's going to happen to you. But you know I

love Andrew like my own child. I'll take care of him. I promise. No matter what happens, Maddie, he'll know his parents. Now go before you miss the door. Find Bobby and bring him back to us."

Grabbing the picture and little brass ring from the bed, I drew in a deep breath then pushed them into my jeans pocket. I looked at Piper's purse, paused for a moment, picked the bag up, and handed it to Sandy. "Take care of this for me." Hugging her again, I sobbed. "I love you both so much. If there is any way possible, we'll all be together again. Soon."

I flew out of the bedroom down the stairs, into the Hudson. I could already feel the force of wind pushing against the car as I backed out of the driveway. Once on the open road, I could see sheets of rain in the distance connecting heaven with earth. As I drove closer to the ridge, a soft drizzle speckled the windshield. Fighting against time as well as the storm, I pressed my foot on the accelerator. The winding roads were slippery, difficult to navigate without automatic steering. My mind reeled through the past three years, bouncing back and forth between my son and the love of my life. I had to find a way to unite them.

When I approached the foot of the ridge, I pulled the car onto the side of the road. I could see Sully and Al huddling in the rain as they unloaded the final boxes from the back of the truck, but I didn't call out to them. Instead, I ran down the embankment slipping on soft, muddy soil, steadying myself by grabbing branches along the path. When I finally reached the clearing, I ran to the bench Bobby had built for us, our bench, our place. I jumped up and down on the ground all around it, but nothing happened. There was no portal. No crack in time. No Bobby.

"Why?" I screamed at the top of my lungs. Falling to my knees, I pounded on the bench, the pouring rain camouflaging my streaming tears. I collapsed to the ground, beating on the earth as if that would somehow force the portal open. Grabbing fists filled with mud I looked up to the sky through the deluge. I could see Al on the ridge above calling out to me.

"Maddie, we're coming. Just stay there," he yelled.

Completely drenched, I sat in the mud, my stringy hair stuck to my face and neck. "Bobby," I shouted into the driving torrent. The portal had to be here. Dragging myself upward, I stood on the bench seat, screaming at the sky while the rain pelted my face.

"Please God, help me find him."

Lightning streaked across the sky casting a burst of eerie light and thunder crashed, echoing all around me. A sudden surge of panic rolled through me. Dizzy and nauseous, I collapsed and fell, swirling into deep, black emptiness.

Chapter 27

Lake Lanier, Georgia—June 12, 2012

"The longer she stays in a coma—"

"Please, don't say it." Piper's voice echoed around me. "She has to wake up."

"Piper, I'm here." I called to her, and yet I couldn't have. I could feel tubes in my throat and my arms pinned to the bed, laden with wires. As hard as I tried, my body wouldn't move. Muted voices persisted, but I could do nothing to communicate. I strained to open my eyes, finally managing a tiny slit. Piper stood beside me while I rested in a bed surrounded by a cold, sterile room.

"Any change?" I heard the man's voice, but it wasn't familiar.

"Still in a coma," Piper replied. "I wish I had known that Cole was at the party. I'd have tossed him out on his butt. If it weren't for him, Lacey would have never torn off through that awful storm or had the accident. She has to come out of this."

"It's okay, Piper." He soothed. "She's gonna make it. Lacey is stronger than you know." He put his arm around her waist, hugged her. "You need a break though. Why don't you go eat something? I can stay with her."

"I'm not hungry." Piper pulled back from his

embrace.

"Maybe not, but you have to keep your strength up. Besides, Rob needs to talk to you. He feels terrible about what happened."

Their voices faded in and out of a vague fog.

"Terrible?" She sat on my bedside, took my hand. "If it weren't for Rob, Lacey would have drowned. He saved her life, Drew."

"Yes, I know, but he feels pretty badly. I think you could really help if you talked with him. He's waiting in the lobby. Why don't you take a break, talk to Rob, have some lunch. I'll call you if Lacey moves a muscle."

Piper softly placed my hand on the bed again. "Okay, but you promise you'll call."

"Yes. Rob will want to know the second she wakes up, too. Go on now."

"Thanks Drew." She scooted out the door. "I'll be back soon."

I yelled to her again. "Piper, please don't go." But nothing uttered from my lips. "Please don't leave me here surrounded by strangers." My body felt limp, useless, like an immobile shell trapping me. Imprisoned inside myself in a one-way observation room, I watched faded images through the hazy, soundproof glass of my eyes. I couldn't even blink, yet on the inside, I felt my heart race, my arms and legs move. I wanted out of this bed, this place. The stench reeked of alcohol and pine-scented disinfectant, that sterile odor that only hospitals and funeral homes have. I had to escape.

****

Lake Lanier, Georgia—June 9, 2012

Lacey's elegance caught Rob's attention the

moment she arrived at the clubhouse vestibule. He couldn't take his eyes off of her. The sleek, black Valentino gown she wore dipped low in front, accenting her breasts. When she turned toward the ballroom, he admired how the back of her dress fell to her waist in a sexy drape. Her long, chestnut hair glistened with golden highlights against her porcelain skin. She hesitated as if evaluating the guests then pulled her shawl from her shoulders and sashayed forward.

A satisfying smile washed over his face. For a solid year he had imagined this moment, calculated every event to insure the party would occur exactly as planned, and Lacey hadn't the slightest clue what she was walking into. He could have taken her right then, scooped her into his arms, carried her off, but he knew the consequences of aborting discipline. He'd have her soon enough. Patience would bring a far better reward. So he stood in the shadows and watched.

"Lacey," Piper squealed rushing down the staircase.

"You're here." She stood back to inspect her friend from head to foot before hugging her. "You look amazing."

"Luckily, I happened to stumble upon the perfect boutique." Lacey assessed her friend in response. "Piper, you look fabulous."

"Thanks Lace. Like I told you earlier, I have a feeling this is going to be a night to remember." She grabbed Lacey's arm, pulled her into the ballroom. "Rob and Travis are already here somewhere, and Drew is right over there."

Hearing Piper's comment about him, Rob slipped

up the spiral staircase, still tuning-in to their conversation in the foyer below.

"Wait, can I at least put my purse and shawl someplace?" Lacey asked.

"Oh, sorry. Here, give them to me." Piper turned to a valet. "James, would you please take these up to the parlor for me?" She handed them to the butler then looked back at Lacey. "There. Now, let's go. I think Drew just walked out to the terrace."

Lacey glanced at James as he disappeared up the stairs toward Rob. "Are you sure about handing over my purse to a complete stranger." She placed her hand on Piper's forearm.

"He's not a stranger, Lace. He's my pastor's son, and these are good people, remember?" Piper looped her arm over Lacey's and strutted into the ballroom.

Rob met the boy at the top of the stairs. "I'll take those in for you, James. I'm headed into the parlor anyway."

"Thank you, sir." He handed Lacey's belongings to Rob. "I'm supposed to be serving hors d'oeuvres now, but Piper asked me to—"

"I know. You go on to the kitchen. They need your help."

James turned and strode back down the stairs.

When they entered the ballroom, Lacey and Piper captivated the crowd, their striking beauty complementing each other, sunlight and moonlight strolling along.

"Piper." Travis Sullivan walked up behind the two women. "Where have you been hiding this vision of beauty?"

Stepping on her tiptoes, Piper hugged him. "Travis,

this is Lacey Montgomery, my best friend in the whole world." She placed her hand on Lacey's arm, slightly squeezing her fingers. "Lacey, this is Travis Sullivan. And don't let the sweet talk fool you. He's a great friend, but I'm sure he knew exactly who you were. I've talked about you enough."

"It's a pleasure, Lacey." Travis brushed a piece of lint from his lapel, then reached out and took her hand in his. "I've been looking forward to meeting you."

Rob nonchalantly strolled into the ballroom. Knowing he should keep his distance from Lacey, he could no longer resist. Her beauty and elegance bewitched him. Simply introducing himself to her couldn't hurt, could it? He walked up behind her, so close he could smell her soft scent.

"So this must be Lacey." Seduced by the fragrance, Rob reached for her shoulder then halted, put his hand on Piper's instead. There would be time to touch Lacey soon enough. For now, he had to keep temptation in check.

"Lacey, this is Rob, the neighbor I told you about last night." Piper's head slightly tilted and a flash of admiration gleamed in her eyes.

He leaned over to kiss her cheek, gazing past her to Lacey. "I'm glad you could make it to our little soirée, Miss Montgomery." Lacey stared at him with a puzzled glare as if she sensed his intentions.

"Rob is an architectural genius." Piper gushed. "I never could've pulled off the design of my deck without him."

"You flatter me, Piper. I'm sure you would've figured everything out on your own." He spoke to Piper with eyes fixed on Lacey.

"He does have a knack for getting things done," Travis broke in, patting Rob on the back. "This man is the most inspired person I've ever known. And speaking about inspired." Travis trolled after an attractive woman who happened to walk by.

"See, even Travis thinks you're invaluable, Rob." She tucked a strand of hair behind her ear.

"It's so nice to meet you." When Lacey extended her hand, again Rob impulsively reached out in response.

"Oh Lace, there's Riley," Piper said, pulling her friend toward the ballroom.

"I guess I'll see you later?" Lacey asked.

Rob grinned then replied with a solemn vow. "I'll catch up to you. You can count on that." Then he turned toward Travis and whispered, "I need a drink."

"My treat," Travis said.

Rob raised an eyebrow. "It's an open bar that I bankrolled."

"Exactly. The price is right." Travis laughed.

They had pulled the party off. And Lacey Montgomery was the guest of honor, unbeknownst to her. Everything was coming together exactly as Rob had planned. He and Travis strolled into the bar to meet his cohorts right on cue.

"Scotch, neat," Rob said to the bartender then sat next to Drew.

"Make that two," Travis added. "Everything set on your end?"

Drew threw back the tequila shot he had been staring at for the last five minutes. "I'm good. Where's Nick?"

"Right where he's supposed to be. His text came

through a few minutes ago. We're good to go." Rob glanced at his watch. "Now, we wait."

"That storm is moving in fast as hell. Blew open the front door of the clubhouse about ten minutes ago." Travis considered his whiskey, took a swig. "You don't think the rain will screw us?"

"Not a chance. I've invested way too much to let a lousy storm gum up the works." Rob polished off the rest of his scotch. "Come on fellas, it's time we joined the party." He smacked his empty glass on the table then made his way to the ballroom, his partners in crime following close behind.

Lacey appeared at the top of the staircase. "I understand perfectly," she snapped. "Too bad a flower vase full of water was the only thing handy." She called into the parlor, "He's all yours." Lacey glared at Cole. "Go back to your *client*, Cole." She spun on her heel and headed down the stairs.

The crowd below hushed. All eyes focused on Lacey's voice blaring over the silence. "Lawyers," she announced.

The soft background music noticeably louder now, echoed through the quiet. *Some enchanted evening...across a crowded room...once you've found her...never let her go...*

Rob's heart did cartwheels as he watched the scene unfold. He leaned toward Drew and whispered, "This is it."

"Are you ready?" Drew's hands shook. Tiny beads of sweat oozed from his brow.

"I have to be." Rob watched Lacey swoon and grab the banister to steady herself. His first impulse was to catch her, but he couldn't. This wasn't the time. The

346

scheme had to be carried out precisely as planned, or they would all lose. He felt compelled to do something, though. On impulse, he began to clap. One by one the guests followed suit, clapping gradually to what evolved into an energetic ovation. When Lacey's eyes met Rob's, she salvaged her composure and strutted down the rest of the stairs with her head held high. She rushed through the ornate foyer and flew out the front door.

Once out of sight, she pulled off her heels and dashed through the driving rain. Rob tore through the foyer after her. He couldn't lose sight of his mark. Everything depended on it.

Totally drenched by the time she reached her car, she fumbled with her keys, pressed the remote over-and-over before the lock released. Finally inside, she turned the ignition and peeled off down the road. Rob started his car, spun out of the parking lot with sheer adrenaline fueling his pursuit. This was it, the moment he'd waiting for, planned for. Every move he made now had to be perfectly timed. His heart pumped so hard, so fast, he thought his chest might explode.

When Lacey's car hydroplaned, she slid sideways. Water spewed everywhere. Rob slowed until he saw her pull off onto the narrow shoulder of the road. He flipped his lights off to keep from being seen, parked on the side of the road, then got out of his car. Throwing his tux jacket onto the passenger seat, he yanked off his tie, ripped through the buttons of his shirt. He pulled off his shoes, grabbed a T-shirt and hoody from the front seat, then put them on. Slipping into lightweight shoes, he slammed the car door and took off down the road on foot.

He could see Lacey grab her shawl, wipe the condensation from the windshield. When lightning flashed again, it lit the entire area. She might have caught a glimpse of his dark figure in the rear view mirror, but the image quickly dissolved into darkness. He darted forward. Thunder boomed and she peeled off spitting gravel behind her.

"Damn." Rob ran back to his car, flipped on his headlights, and tore after her. Pushing to perilous speeds, he closed in on her. As the gap between them lessened, Lacey picked up her speed. Suddenly aware of the peril his pursuit induced, Rob slowed. She had seen him and that threatened her safety. He'd come too far to lose her to an unexpected accident.

Lightning streaked across the night sky, casting a burst of eerie light while thunder boomed its own crescendo to the violent symphony of rain and wind. Lacey's car veered off the road briefly, but swerved back on the highway until her tire hit a pothole. A gush of water splashed over her hood. The car spun, slid off the highway and down the ridge into the base of an embankment.

Rob sped forward again. When he saw where Lacey's Lexus had run off the road, he pulled his car through the deadfall and brush, aimed his bright lights down the hill. He rushed toward her, skidding down the slippery slope. As he approached, he could see the airbag had exploded and trapped Lacey against her seat. She wrestled to push the bag out of the way, yanked at her seatbelt. The driver's side door was crumpled, but she crawled over the console into the passenger seat and escaped.

Rob watched intently as Lacey trudged back up the

steep hill toward the road. Darkness engulfed them both. He strained to keep his eyes fixed on her image while Lacey slogged through mud and brush, headed toward the dim flicker of Rob's headlights. He froze, held his breath and slowly edged behind a spruce. She passed so close he heard the heaving of her breath, so close he smelled the fragrance of her scent, so close he was sure she heard the pounding of his heart, so close. But she didn't notice him skulking behind the bushes.

She glanced back in the direction of her wrecked car and stumbled. Instinctively, he reached out, grabbed her arm. He couldn't let her plummet into the lake below. But she lunged forward, twisting, tugging against his grasp. He grappled with her clinging to whatever he could, caught her ankle, but she pulled away with the entire weight of her body, shrieking wildly.

A splintery branch ripped across Rob's hand and sliced Lacey's ankle. Their combined blood oozed between Rob's fingers, loosening his grasp. She hurled backward, tumbling and rolling endlessly, until she splashed into the icy, black water. Rob slid down after her, tripping over brush and muck. When he reached the shore of the lake, he peered into the depths where he'd seen Lacey's limp body plunge beneath the surface. Then, he looked high above the road to the top of the ridge.

Against the darkness and mist, he saw a spray of white Christmas lights sparkling around an old wooden bench. He reached in the pocket of his hoody, pulled out the small, waterproof flashlight he'd placed there earlier that morning then ripped off his sweatshirt, tossed it aside. He wrapped the strap around his arm, switched on the light. He'd left little to chance, but finding Lacey in the murky water was beyond his control. Turning back to the lake, he dropped his pants. Wearing only boxer shorts and T-shirt, he waded into the water, breathed in several times, and taking one final deep breath, dove into the murky depths.

Chapter 28

Lake Lanier, Georgia—June 12, 2012

I looked at the man beside me. Tall with deep blue eyes and graying hair, his kind face looked vaguely familiar, but I couldn't place where I'd seen him before. Perhaps I'd met him at Piper's party.

That's what everyone was talking about. I'd had an accident, been in a coma. But if that were true, then was everything I'd been through a dream? Dear Lord, please don't let my wonderful life in Sidney have been nothing more than a comatose fantasy. The town, Bobby, Sandy and Andrew, where was my baby? I screamed, but again my moans only echoed through the silent caverns of my own mind. With every ounce of strength I could conjure, I flew through the haze, took a deep breath, and gasped, gagging on the tube blocking my throat.

****

Lake Lanier, Georgia—June 9, 2012

Drew pulled his car over the edge of the ridge. Directing his headlights toward the lake below, he slammed on the emergency brake then tore out of the car calling out to them.

"Rob. Are you down there?" Hearing no reply, he skidded down the embankment. "Lacey, Rob, where are you?"

Finally seeing movement in the water, he pulled

out his cell phone and pressed 911.

Rob burst from the bowels of the lake gasping for air. He checked the proximity of the twinkling lights above, got his bearings, then dove down again into the depths of the inky water. Frantically, he repeated the same process over and over, searching the small area his flashlight's glow illuminated, grasping blindly through the water around him. He swam down to the lakebed, pushed off a rotting wooden bench back to the surface, combing the precise area Lacey had fallen into the black lake.

He couldn't lose her. Not after the lengths he had taken to bring her to him. Pushing off the bench again, he saw a reflection, a shimmer at first, just out of his reach. Lungs burning, he lunged toward the anomaly, stretching his reach forward, forward. A sudden surge of water thrust him toward the surface, spinning him round and round until he lost all sense of direction. Arms flailing with the force of the gush he felt a solid object bump against him. A burst of brilliant blue exploded beneath, illuminating the entire cove as if it were broad daylight. Through the blast of hazy, iridescent water, Rob saw her.

He grabbed Lacey's arm and pulled her limp body close, clinging to her as the force hurled them both through the chasm. Like the slamming of a door, the violent squall ceased. The dazzling light extinguished. Rob erupted through the surface, still clinging to Lacey.

Floodlights lit the shoreline of the cove and reflected off the silvery drizzle, casting a surreal glow as Rob emerged carrying Lacey's lifeless body. A handful of men waded into the shallow water along the beach, readying themselves for whatever task arose.

Rob held Lacey tightly, his grip still clenched like a vice. He shuffled his arms. Her head, which had hung backward, now lay against his shoulder.

Red and blue, flashing lights flickered as they approached on the road above. After parking their vehicles, the emergency crews unloaded equipment and forged their way down the precipice.

Drew stood anxiously at water's edge near the crest of the cove. When he saw Rob's torso burst through the surface with Lacey in his arms, he breathed a sigh of relief. He drifted waist-deep into the water until he was close enough to grab ahold of Rob's shoulder and help him to the shore.

"Thank God." He sighed. "I thought we'd lost both of you. Please, let me take her."

As Drew pulled Lacey into his arms, Rob collapsed into the shallow lapping surf. Two men rushed to his side, picked him up, and carried him up the steep hill to an ambulance waiting on the ridge above. Drew gently laid Lacey on the ground, listened for her breathing, but could hear no sound. He felt for a pulse. Nothing. He turned her head to the side to let the water drain from her mouth, tilted it back, and began CPR. He checked her airway, pinched her nose, and breathed four strong bursts of air into her mouth and lungs. Her pale face looked so fragile, so un-Lacey like. Her bluish lips turned cold and limp as he tried to breathe life back into her frail body.

"I need some help here," he yelled to the others.

Three men, who had been standing behind Drew helplessly watching, sprang to his side.

"Like this." He pressed down with the palm of his hands, one on top of the other, squeezing her chest and counting to himself. When he stopped, one of the men kneeled down beside him and took over with the chest compressions, while Drew gave her mouth-to-mouth resuscitation.

When the EMTs finally made their way to the water's edge, Drew stepped back and let them take over.

"Good job," one of them said, lifting her onto the stretcher. "You may have saved her life."

"No. Rob did that." Drew breathed in deeply. "But I hope I helped keep her alive."

The crew worked for some time to revive and stabilize Lacey. When she began to breathe on her own, albeit sporadically, they carried her up the slippery incline to the road where another ambulance waited. They pulled off and headed toward Gainesville, sirens blasting, echoing through the misty night sky.

As soon as he reached his car, Drew called Piper then sped off toward hospital. By the time he arrived at the emergency room, Lacey and Rob were already inside being treated. He pressed the staff for information, but their pat reply remained consistent.

"The doctors are doing all they can. As soon as we have any information, we'll let you know."

Piper flew through the emergency room entryway frantic with worry.

"Drew. Oh my Lord, what happened?"

"It's hard to explain." He greeted her with a hug. "Here, sit down. I'll tell you what I know."

"Is Lacey all right?" Piper asked, sitting on the edge of a waiting room chair. "And how did Rob end up here, too? Start at the beginning."

"What actually triggered the chain of events was

when Lacey walked in on Cole and Marissa Howard in the parlor."

Piper scowled. "I can't figure out how Cole even knew about the party. He wasn't on the guest list. And Marissa, well, I guess that isn't much of a stretch to figure out how she played into it."

"I don't know anything about that." Drew wrung his hands.

"I know. Sorry. Everyone saw that altercation though. I tried to go after Lace, but Nick stopped me."

"It's okay Piper. Don't blame yourself."

"I saw Rob take off after her, and then you. What happened next?"

"Lacey was so upset, and the storm, the roads were slick. We think she headed back to your house but got lost in the storm. Her car slid out of control and—"

"Dear God, please don't say her car crashed into the lake."

"No, an embankment. She apparently got out and was climbing up the ridge back to the road when she slipped and tumbled down the slope into the lake."

"Oh Drew, no."

"Rob was right behind her, Piper. He saw everything and dove in after her."

"Please tell me she'll be okay." She wrung her hands.

"He had a hard time finding her in that murky water. The storm stirred up a lot of mud in the lake. It was impossible to see much of anything." Drew stood, began pacing back and forth in little circles. "As soon as I saw what happened, I called 911 then slid down the hill to help. Rob found her, Piper. He pulled her out. But she was underwater for so long."

"If Rob pulled her out, why is he in triage instead of here with you? Did something happen to him?"

"I waded into the water to help him ashore, but when I took Lacey from his arms, he collapsed. Some of the guys carried him to an ambulance. I don't know what happened to him after that. I was too busy with Lacey."

Piper jumped up from her chair and walked to Drew. She grabbed a hold of his shoulders, looked dead into his eyes. "Drew, Lacey is my best friend. Please, tell me the truth. Will she be okay?"

"I don't know," he said in earnest. "I laid her down, checked to see if she was breathing. As far as I could tell, she had no pulse. She wasn't breathing, Piper. So, I did CPR until the EMTs arrived. I think they stabilized her, but I have to be honest, Piper, she looked awful. Her body was so cold, her face and lips were blue." Drew fell back into a chair, his clothes still soaking wet from the ordeal. He shivered, and the blood drained from his face. "Piper, I'm really scared she won't make it."

Chapter 29

Lake Lanier, Georgia—June 12, 2012

"I need help in here," Drew called out. "Hurry!"

A nurse ran into the room. "What happened?" She angled my head backward and removed the breathing tube.

"I don't know." Drew stepped back out of the nurse's way. "I was just standing here looking down at her, and she started to gag."

"She's finally coming around. Relax, Drew, that's a good sign."

The nurse held my face between her hands. "Lacey, can you hear me? You're okay, honey. You've been in an awful accident, but you're going to be fine."

"Damn, Rob's phone is off." Drew stuffed his cell in his pocket. "I promised him if Lacey woke up, I'd call him."

The breathing tube gone, I gasped for air, but reality felt worse than choking. I'd been in a coma since Piper's party. How long had I been hooked up to those tubes, confined to this bed. Long enough to create a dream world? This was the cruelest pain I could imagine. I'd finally found happiness. But it was all an illusion created in my mind. Dear God, I wish I'd never awakened.

Coiling into a fetal position, I stared blankly at the

wall. I didn't want this life, not without Bobby, Andrew, and Sandy. Everything I loved had vanished. I prayed my coma would return so I could go back to Sidney and the fantasy world I'd invented in my dreams.

****

Lake Lanier, Georgia—June 9, 2012

Sipping on Co-cola, Rob strolled into the waiting room to see Piper consoling Drew.

"Why the long faces?" He placed his cup on a side table then opened his arms to embrace Piper as she ran to him.

"Oh Rob," she squealed. "Thank God you're all right."

"You didn't think a little midnight dip would hurt me, did you? I just took in a little too much water. I'm okay now." He looked down and admired the scrubs he was wearing. "I think the look suits me, don't you? Maybe I'm in the wrong profession." He grinned to lighten the heavy mood.

"It's just like you to add levity to a serious situation." Piper released her hug, inspected him. "You're really okay?"

He laughed. "Heck, I woke up before they put me in the ambulance, but the EMTs insisted I go to the hospital." He rubbed the stubbles of his scruffy chin. "I figured it was the fastest way to get past the staff to keep an eye on Lacey, so I went along for the ride."

Drew stood, approached Rob, and gave him a half-hug-half-handshake, squeezing his shoulder. "One down," he said. "How's Lacey?"

"Well, she's finally out of emergency." He sat down, resting his elbows on his knees. They admitted her. We can see her shortly, as soon as they get her settled into a room."

Drew sat next to Rob. "Then she'll be okay?"

"From what I hear, Drew, you saved her life, resuscitating her on the spot like that. Thank God you were there." He patted Drew's back. "I sure couldn't have done that."

"But you found her and pulled her from the lake. Dear God, Rob. If you hadn't followed her—"

"It was a joint effort." Rob winked at Drew. "All the way."

A doctor strolled into the emergency room. "Montgomery family?" He looked around the waiting area.

Piper, Rob, and Drew all stood at the same time, rushed to the physician's side to get an update on Lacey.

"I'm Dr. Collins." He reached out and shook each of their hands. "Please, come with me."

They followed him into a small consultation room.

"Have a seat." He sat, thumbing through a file. "Lacey is in room 212. I assume you're her husband?" He looked at Rob.

"You assume?" Rob raised an eyebrow, glanced at Drew and Piper, then back to Dr. Collins. "Can I see her?"

The doctor sat back in his chair and crossed his legs. "When we're through here. But I need to warn you she's sedated. We put her into an induced coma."

Piper leaned forward while her hand flew to her chest. "Why?"

"Well, you two men definitely saved her life, but somewhere along the way, perhaps when she fell down that steep slope, she hit her head, hard. The impact must have knocked her out. It's really a miracle she survived the lake ordeal at all." Lowering his glasses to the tip of his nose, he glanced at her file again. "More than likely she was unconscious before she ever hit the water."

Rob drew in a deep breath then slowly let it out. "You mean if we hadn't been there, she would have died?"

"No doubt in my mind about that." Dr. Collins glanced at them over his spectacles. "She's a very lucky young woman."

"Will she be okay?" Piper asked.

Dr. Collins took off his glasses. "Well, she has some elevated intracranial pressure, cerebral edema." His explanation met with blank stares so he elaborated. "Basically, her brain is swollen from her injury. The swelling slowed down her blood flow, which deprived her brain of oxygen. But I've sedated her to keep her calm until the swelling subsides. Her prognosis is good though, thanks to you two men." Closing the file, he glanced at Rob. "She was treated very quickly. Still, we can't be sure until she wakes up. Just give her a few days." Standing, he shook Rob's hand again then walked toward the door. "You can go see her now," he said, leaving the room.

Piper stood, leaned over and hugged Rob then Drew. "I can't believe how lucky we were you two were there to save her. I'll never be able to thank you enough."

Drew eyed Rob then looked back at Piper. "No need to thank us. Let's go see her."

Pulling her cell phone from her purse, Piper motioned to the two men. "You two go ahead. I need to call Mr. Montgomery. He should know his daughter is in the hospital."

"You go with Drew," Rob said. "I'll take care of that, if you'll let me borrow your phone." He held his hand out, wiggled his fingers.

"Are you sure?" She offered a confused stare. "You don't even know him."

"I think the news will be easier for him coming from me."

"Okay, then." She handed her phone to Rob then turned to Drew. "Let's go."

She shot a glance over her shoulder, mouthed a sincere thank you to Rob, then she and Drew strode toward the elevator.

Rob pressed the bottom button on Piper's cell phone. "Call Warren Montgomery."

****

Three days after Lacey's accident, Warren Montgomery checked into the Holiday Inn-Lanier Center on Butler Street, four tenths of a mile from the hospital, to keep close tabs on his daughter. Piper, Rob, and Drew took turns standing vigil. What little sleep they afforded occurred in chairs by her bedside. Rob and Drew rented a room at the Gainesville Inn, a few steps from the Medical Center, but their beds remained untouched. Since that fateful Saturday night, Piper hadn't left Lacey's side. Having eaten little more than a few vending machine snacks and some fast food Rob supplied, Piper needed a break to reenergize. But shortly after she left the room, Lacey woke up.

"Miss Montgomery, can you hear me?" The doctor scanned her chart, checked vitals.

"She's been this way for the last twenty minutes,"

361

the nurse offered, disconnecting Lacey's IV. "She won't acknowledge or speak to anyone. She just stares blankly into space."

"Is she in shock?" Drew peered over the shoulders of the medical staff, unwilling to step any further away than they asserted.

"I don't think so." The doctor shinned a penlight into her eyes, flashing it back and forth several times. "She can hear us. By all indications, she's choosing not to respond."

"But why would she do that?" Drew shuffled side to side, repositioning himself to get a better view of the patient.

"It's hard to say." The doctor replied without looking up. "Head injuries are tricky. We still don't know why the mind responds in certain ways. I need to examine her, run a few tests." He turned to the nurse. "Bring Ms. Montgomery some crackers, soup, Jell-O. Maybe some light food will spark her interest."

"I should get Rob and Piper. They're just downstairs." Drew paused, clearly hesitant to leave Lacey's side. "You'll stay with her until I get back won't you, Doctor?"

He glanced at Drew. "Go ahead. The tests will take at least fifteen minutes. I'm sure I'll still be here."

"Good. I know they'll have questions for you."

Drew flew out of Lacey's hospital room and sprinted down the hall to the elevator, still trying to reach Rob on his cell phone. When the door opened to the lobby, he sped toward the cafeteria.

Rob sat across the table from Piper consoling her. "She's going to come out of this."

"But it's been three days, Rob." Tears streamed

from Piper's red, puffy eyes. What if she doesn't ever wake up?" Piper pushed the green beans around on her plate, shoving them under the roast chicken breast she still hadn't touched.

"That won't happen. Besides, the doctor only took her off the medication a few hours ago." He reached for her hand, squeezed it. "The swelling is down. That's a terrific sign. Just give her some time to get the drugs out of her system."

"I'm sorry, Rob." She sobbed. "I came downstairs to boost your spirits, and here I am sniveling like a baby."

"We're all tired, Piper." He clasped his other hand around hers. "This has been an incredible ordeal for all of us, more so than you even know."

"Oh my gosh. Your wife must be wondering about you." She looked into Rob's eyes. "Honestly, you really don't need to stay with us like this."

"I wouldn't be anywhere else." Releasing Piper's hand, he sat back in his chair. "And don't worry about my wife. She'll be here soon. I look forward to introducing her to you."

Sniffling, Piper leaned back. "Drew said you wanted to talk to me about something."

Rob rubbed his chin. "Yes. I have something to tell you. It's extremely important and you'll have to—"

Drew rushed into the cafeteria. "Rob," he called out across the room.

Both Piper and Rob looked up immediately.

"It's Lacey." He scurried toward the table. "She's awake."

"Thank God." Piper stood. "Just like her though, taking center stage right when things are getting interesting." She rushed from the room.

Rob stood then followed suit with Drew, leaving two barely-touched meals on the table. Piper paced in front of the elevator, pressing the up button with each pass. By the time they got to the 10th floor, Drew had filled them in on the few facts he knew, leaving out one major detail, that Lacey was despondent.

Piper sprinted into her friend's room. "Oh Lace, thank God you're awake. I was so scared." She bent down, hugged her friend, but Lacey remained curled in a fetal position. "What's wrong, Dr. Collins? Drew said she was awake."

"She is." He stood at her bedside scribbling something in the patient file.

"Then why won't she look at me? Lacey, it's me, Piper." She glared at the doctor. "You said she'd recover. Is there something wrong with her brain? She acts like she doesn't hear or see me."

"I assure you, Ms. Taylor, your friend is fully awake." Dr. Collins placed the file on a hook at the base of Lacey's bed. "Her brain activity is normal. She can hear and see everything. But Lacey has chosen to stay inside herself. Physically, she's fine, but emotionally she doesn't want to wake up."

"Why would she do that?" Tears welled in Piper's eyes as she took her friend's hand.

Lacey didn't move. She simply stared blankly out the hospital window.

Drew stepped through the doorway toward the patient, but Rob grabbed him by the arm, pulled him back. Then, without speaking a word, Rob slowly edged toward Lacey's bedside. He bent over, kissed her on the cheek, and whispered in her ear.

"Maddie, I'm here, princess. I love you."

Lacey's eyes widened. She spun around and stared at him in disbelief. Rob leaned in and scooped her into his arms. She clung to him, tears streaming down her cheeks.

"Oh Bobby. It wasn't a dream. You're real and alive. Your hair is shorter, darker—but oh Bobby, it's you." She kissed his face and neck. "I thought I'd never see you again. There's so much I have to tell you."

He whispered to her, his warm breath sending ripples of delight down her neck, all the way to her toes. "Apparently sun-bleached ducktails aren't in style anymore; imagine that." When she giggled, Bobby pressed his lips over hers in a long passionate kiss then finally let her slide down his body until her feet touched the floor.

"Can someone please tell me what's going on?" Piper watched the interaction between Rob and Lacey in complete dismay.

"I'll let Rob do that." For a long moment, Drew leaned against the wall, smiled, then reached for the doorknob. "I need to get cleaned up and make a few phone calls. You two fill Piper in. I'll be back in a bit."

Bobby looked at Drew, nodded his head and winked. Drew nodded back then slipped out the door.

"Looks like someone decided to wake up after all. I think Lacey will be just fine now." Dr. Collins walked toward the door. "I'll be back to check on you later, Ms. Montgomery."

"It's Mrs. Reynolds." Lacey beamed, staring at Bobby.

The doctor smiled. "I stand corrected." He left the room, closing the door behind him. The look on Piper's face displayed nothing short of sheer bewilderment. She plopped down in the chair beside the bed. "Okay, somebody better fill me in soon, or I'm calling the psychiatric ward."

"Piper," Bobby began. "I'd like to introduce you to my wife, Lacey Madison Montgomery Reynolds."

"My Lacey…is your wife? But—"

"Like I started to tell you downstairs at lunch, I've got something to tell you and it's a doozy."

Chapter 30

Lake Lanier, Georgia—June 12, 2012

Lacey stood on her tiptoes, her arms draped around Bobby's neck. "Oh Bobby, thank God you're alive." She nuzzled closer, tears flowing. "I was so afraid I'd never see you again. You won't believe what happened, and there's so much you don't know."

"And you, too, sweetheart." He tucked a strand of hair behind her ear. "Let's start from the party and fill in the gaps together along the way."

Bobby scooped Lacey up again, set her gently down on the bed, and snuggled beside her.

"Wait, this doesn't even make sense. What about you and Cole?" Piper asked. "And if you're married to Rob, how come you didn't tell me about that the night before the party, Lace, when I went on and on about him?"

"She hadn't met me yet," Bobby replied. "But she was already my wife." He looked at Lacey waiting for a reaction. And he got one.

"What? We didn't even meet until I—"

"I know sweetie, but think four-dimensionally. You were my wife. You just didn't know it yet."

"Now *I'm* confused. What are you talking about?"

"Remember when you saw Cole and stormed out?" She nodded. Bobby continued. "Remember the man in the crowd who looked up at you and began to clap?"

Lacey's jaw dropped as she put two and two together. "That was you? But how?"

"Time doesn't always move in a straight line, Maddie. The portal connects past to future. When I fell off the scaffold and suddenly found myself drowning, I knew I had slipped into the future, into the lake. I wanted to tell you, find you wherever you were to let you know what happened—but I couldn't. You hadn't met me yet. And if I were to tell you about your future, I would have altered the events as they occurred. I might never have met you. I can't even imagine the alternate time lines that might have resulted." Bobby shook his head in consternation. "I had to make sure the events of your life played out exactly as they had before, right up to the moment you slipped through time. So for us, time was more like a loop. You fell through the time warp and met me. If you hadn't, you would have drowned the night of the party."

"But—" Lacey stared at her husband with vacant eyes.

"If I never met you, princess, I wouldn't have been up on that scaffold or slipped forward in time to save your life."

"Oh my gosh." She leaned forward, threw her arms around Bobby's neck again, and hugged him. "Sandy was right. It was all supposed to happen."

"Okay you guys, I'm totally baffled. It's clear you two know each other really well, but what in the world is going on?" Piper settled back into the big chair, pulled her legs up, and wrapped her arms around them. "I have a feeling this will be a wild story."

"You've got to have an open mind, Piper, or you'll

never believe it." Lacey cuddled into her husband.

So, Rob/Bobby and Lacey/Maddie spent the next half hour telling Piper what had happened the night of the party, how Lacey had awakened from the accident to find herself in 1949 and how she and Bobby fell in love, married.

"A time crack?" Piper shook her head. "That's too weird. Sounds more like a science fiction movie. How could a worm hole just appear, scientifically I mean?"

"I know how you feel, Piper. I had a hard time believing it myself, but I assure you the portal is real." Rob ran his fingers through his hair. "From what I've been told by the world's top authority on the theory of time travel, Lanier's construction formed more than a lake. The excavation induced seismic waves that shifted faults, created an anomaly, a crack in time if you will, connecting the past to the future. Violent storm patterns produce electrical charges in the atmosphere that opened and closed the portal. When Maddie fell into the lake, she slipped through the crack into my time, 1949."

Rob and Lacey explained every detail that led up to the fateful Thanksgiving Day, 1950. But that's when their stories went in two different directions.

"So what happened after I disappeared?" Bobby crooked his finger and ran it over Lacey's cheek.

"Sandy and I were devastated. We never gave up hope though. I knew you were alive. You just had to be. I felt it with every fiber inside of me." Lacey continued the story from her point of view, telling both her husband and Piper the details of Bobby's disappearance. She explained how Baxter's men had combed the backwoods searching for Bobby, how they'd riled the bootleggers before befriending Al and the shiners.

"You must have been scared to death." Bobby squeezed Lacey's hand. "I should have been there to protect you."

"If you were with us, it never would have happened. But something good came out of the whole nightmare." Lacey snuggled into Bobby's shoulder. "Sandy and Al got really close. I think they're going to get married."

"You do?" Bobby chuckled. "Do you think I'd approve of this Al guy?" He tucked another strand of hair behind her ear.

"Oh yes. He's a wonderful man. He loves Sandy so much and Andrew, too."

Bobby raised an eyebrow. "Andrew? And just who is Andrew?"

She grabbed his hand, squeezed tightly. "Andrew is the love of my life. And I really need to tell you about him."

A suppressed smile slipped through his lips. He stroked her hair. "So, it sounds like you brushed me off and found yourself a new beau."

Lacey took her head off of Bobby's shoulder and looked deep into his eyes. "I'd never do that. You are part of me, Bobby Reynolds, but so is Andrew." She paused for a moment. "I was pregnant when you disappeared. Andrew is your son."

Lacey recounted the details of her pregnancy, Andrew's delivery and how wonderful Sandy had been. Her eyes once again overflowed with tears.

"We have to go through the portal again, Bobby, to get back to our son. He's so beautiful, and I promised him I'd bring his Daddy to him."

"I think maybe we should take a break for a while. We're all exhausted, and Piper looks down right dumbfounded." Bobby looked from Piper back to Lacey. "She's been shaking her head with a dropped jaw since we started talking."

"It's a lot to take in." Piper spoke matter-of-factly. "Completely off-the-wall bizarre, but no one could ever make up such an elaborate story. I've known Lace practically my whole life, and I'd know if she was lying."

"So you believe us?" Lacey peered over at her friend.

"I have to admit it's hard to wrap my head around the concept of time-travel." Piper scratched her chin. "But it's fascinating. And I'm absolutely convinced that you and Rob believe every word you've said. Plus, you two definitely know each other really well, and I can't see any other plausible explanation for that."

Bobby wiped the lingering tears from Lacey's cheeks and kissed her lips softly.

"Everything will work out, princess. I promise. Just sit back and rest for a while. I'll call Drew and ask him to bring us some food. You'll feel better after you've gotten something in your stomach."

"That's a good idea." Piper stood, stretched her arms above her head. "None of us have gotten a bit of rest or a decent meal in days."

Bobby stood, drifted toward the door then dimmed the lights. "You and Piper sit back and relax for a few minutes. I'll be back shortly."

"No Bobby, please don't leave me." Lacey sat up, ridged. "I couldn't bear to lose you again."

"You'll never lose me, Maddie. I'm here for good

this time. You're stuck with me, forever." He walked back to her, bent over and softly kissed her lips. "Now, close those beautiful green eyes. I'll be back in two shakes."

Bobby slipped out the door. He reached in his pocket for his smartphone and called Drew.

"Okay. It's time for stage two. You guys come on over and bring some food with you. Be sure to bring something Maddie can eat, too, like noodle soup and crackers...okay...see you soon." He hung up the phone and headed toward the elevator.

Lacey chronicled the last few years of her life in the dimly lit hospital room. Filled with questions, Piper begged to hear every detail especially when it came to Bobby. Why did he call her Maddie and princess, how did they get together, and the honeymoon? "Wow Lace." She sat forward, clearly enthralled. "You finally found it. You had to break the space-time continuum, but you found it.

"Found what?"

"Remember the night before the party when I told you Rob was madly in love with his wife? He's so over-the-top in love with you, Lace. Oh my gosh, you finally found the curl-your-toes-on-the-first-kiss love of your life."

Lacey turned onto her side, fluffed her pillow. "If you hadn't asked me to that party, Piper, I never would have met him."

Shifting in her chair, she looked at Lacey and shook her head. "As a matter of fact, Rob had a lot to do with that." She smiled an enigmatic grin. "We'll get to that later. I just can't believe you've lived four years in the past. And you never lost a moment of time here.

Your entire story is so freaky, but that's the hardest to imagine, that you fell through time, lived years there then came back an instant after you left." She laughed. "Hey, technically you're older than me now."

"I guess I am, technically." Lacey chuckled. "And I have a son, Piper. I have stretch marks to prove it." She pulled up her gown to reveal her stomach. "See? You saw me in my bikini the night before the party; when we sat in your hot tub, remember? My stomach was comparatively flat and smooth."

"Holy crap. That is so weird." Piper glared at Lacey's belly, got up, and touched her scars. "Those stretch marks totally weren't there a few nights ago. I mean, I believed you on some kind of weird cosmic level, but do you realize what those marks mean?" She answered her own question. "They're solid proof that time travel is possible."

"Ya think!" Lacey pulled her gown back over her belly and straightened the sheets. "Try living it. Oh Piper, I wish you could see Andrew. He's so smart and beautiful. I miss him so much. Bobby and I have to try to get back to him."

"Lace, no. It's too dangerous. You almost died and now you're considering going back through that black hole again." Piper's face grimaced as she considered the possibility of losing her friend.

"You'll understand when you have a child of your own." Lacey bit her bottom lip. "Sandy loves him, and I know she'll take care of him." She scrunched her forehead. "But I'm his mother. And Bobby's never even seen him."

A rap at the door broke the tension. Bobby peeked inside.

"Are you two awake?" He slipped through the doorway.

"Do you really think we'd really be able to sleep at this point?" Piper asked.

Lacey sat up in her bed. "Come in, sweetie."

"I hope you don't mind, I brought a few people with me." Bobby closed the door behind him. "They're waiting at the nurses' station. What do ya say? Are you up for some company?"

Lacey leaned forward and peered into the mirror on the wall. "Oh Bobby, I look just awful. You could have given me some warning. Can they come back later?"

He smiled. "They could. But they brought food, and I really think you'll want to see them."

"Who?" Lacey ran her fingers through her hair then pinched her cheeks for a quick flush of color.

Bobby walked over to her and sat on the corner of her bed. "It's a surprise."

"Don't you think we've had enough surprises lately?" She kicked him softly from beneath the sheets.

"So what's one more?" Piper chimed in. "Besides, you look fine. Especially considering everything you've been through."

"Okay, but wait a second." Lacey straightened her gown then pulled the sheet to her waist. "Go ahead. Let them in."

"Good. I'm really hungry," Piper said. "Not to mention curious."

Bobby walked to the door and leaned his head out. "Come on in. But maybe we should do this one-at-a-time."

Drew slipped inside the room hauling two big bags. He placed them on the counter by the sink. When the aroma of roast chicken and peach cobbler filled the air, Lacey perked up.

Bobby walked over, sat on the side of her bed, then took her hand in his. "Come on over here." He motioned to Drew. "I want to introduce you to my wife."

Lacey looked at the tall man. He stood about six feet, sixtyish but fit, dressed in jeans and a royal blue T-shirt. His deep blue eyes sparkled accenting his graying hair, and he had a familiar grin. As he walked closer to her, she felt an instant connection.

"You look familiar." Lacey eyed him. "You were here at the hospital earlier, weren't you?"

"I was." His grin beamed. "I was at the party, too. In fact, I've been waiting a very long time to meet you."

Lacey stared at the man then at her husband.

Bobby pulled her closer. "Maddie, I want you to meet Drew." He squeezed her. "Our son."

She glared at the man standing beside her. "Oh my God, Andrew." Tears flowed from her puffy eyes. She threw the sheets off to jump out of bed.

"Hold on now." Bobby held her back. "Slow down, Maddie, you're recovering from a brain injury. Please, be careful."

"I've got this, Dad." Drew held his hand up to his thirty-two-year-old father. "I've been waiting a lifetime for this moment." He easily scooped her into his arms and hugged her tightly.

"Oh Andrew, you're a grown man and so handsome." She pulled back, inspected him head to foot. "I'm so sorry I wasn't there for you. It was too dangerous to bring you with me. Oh my sweet boy, I held you in my arms only a few days ago and just look at you." She kissed his face over and over.

"This is flat out crazy." Piper leaned back in her chair. "It's hard enough to wrap my head around the idea Rob—excuse me, I mean Bobby—is your husband, but Drew is your son?" She looked over at the older man. "How does it feel to have a dad that's half your age?" She laughed.

"I have to say it took some getting used to, but I've been preparing for sixty years."

"What do you mean?" Tears streamed down Lacey's cheeks.

Andrew wiped the tears from his mother's face. "First, don't ever apologize for your decision, Mom. You made the only choice you could have made."

"I agree." The familiar voice murmured as an old woman walked through the door.

Lacey looked up, stared at her with an incongruous moment of confusion.

"Maddie. It's wonderful to see you." Her smile radiated.

Lacey beamed as she recognized the greeting. "Oh Sandy, I'd know that sweet voice anywhere." Lacey held her arms out to hug her sister-in-law.

Sandy walked over to Lacey and embraced her. "You're exactly the way I remember you."

"I just saw you a few days ago." Lacey stuttered through her tears. "You were so young."

"It's been sixty years for me, Maddie. And I'm not that old. They say the eighties are the new sixties." She laughed. "Besides, come hell or high water, I wanted to be around for this reunion. I've made every effort to take care of myself."

"I didn't mean it that way. You're as beautiful as ever." Lacey squeezed Sandy's hands.

Her hair was pure white, and while her skin showed faint wrinkles, she looked far younger than eighty-eight. Dressed in black pants and an azure-blue silk blouse, she was the picture of health.

"I'm so sorry I left you and Andrew behind."

Sandy bent over to kiss Lacey's cheek. "Now I won't hear any of that sorry business," she scolded. "Andrew and I were just fine."

"My sister's done all right for herself." Bobby draped his arm around Lacey's shoulder. "I'm really proud of her."

"Bobby Reynolds, you knew." Lacey elbowed him in the side. "Why didn't you tell me about Sandy and Andrew earlier?"

His face softened. "We thought it was best to tell you in stages."

"You've been through so much, Mom," Drew added. "We wanted to go slowly because of your head injury."

"I've spent the last year with Sandy and Drew, Maddie."

She scrunched her face, clearly puzzled.

"Okay," Piper spoke up. "So how did you end up here in 2011, Rob?"

"Yeah," Lacey added. "Why didn't you arrive the night of the party when I disappeared?"

"Beats me." He rubbed the stubbles on his chin. "All I know is I slipped off the scaffold, passed through a pretty spectacular light show, and damn near drowned in your lake. I knew immediately what had happened, thanks to Maddie. No clue why I arrived in 2011, though." He chuckled. "Time travel isn't an exact science."

"Yet." Sandy looked at her brother then to Lacey. "Personally, I think you were destined to arrive a year early to save Maddie's life. Scientifically though, the intensity of the storm and the strength of the seismic waves connected, and the loop dropped you accordingly.

"How did you know when, or even if I'd come back through the portal?" Lacey snuggled closer to her husband. "Especially since Bobby showed up a whole year earlier?

"That was *all* Sandy." Bobby pointed his chin toward his little sister. "We didn't know for sure, but her theory concluded that you'd show up close to the moment you left." He kissed Lacey's forehead. "When I dove in that lake, I had to be sure to let you slip through time into the past so we would meet, fall in love, and marry. That all had to happen, or I wouldn't be here to pull you out of the lake when the portal reopened, which was my only chance to save your life."

"That's incredible." Piper said. "It's amazing you pulled it off, especially that night, with all the rain. Lanier is murky on a normal day and dangerous with all the deadfall hovering beneath the surface. It's a miracle you both weren't trapped underwater forever."

Sandy shook her head. "It would've been my fault, too."

"That's not true, sis. You did everything humanly possible." He shot her his big brother scowl. "If it wasn't for you, Maddie would have died."

"How could you possibly think any of this was your fault, Sandy?" Lacey asked in earnest.

Sandy sat on the side of Lacey's bed, took her hand. "For the last ten years, I've been working on a method to induce the time chasm synthetically and control velocity, too. In layman's terms, I created a prototype that will allow us to shift through time to any day past or future, then return to our own time unscathed. I tried so hard to have the model activated before zero hour on the night of the party, but time ran out. Thank God Bobby was able to save you the old-fashioned way. I would've never forgiven myself if anything had happened to either of you."

"That was a risk I had to take. I was terrified I'd never find her." He stroked his wife's hair again. "I frantically dove over and over, searching through black water with nothing but a weak penlight. But when the portal opened, it cast the most brilliant light I'd ever seen. A split-second later, I saw Maddie drifting through the water."

"What if someone finds out about the portal?" Piper asked. "Imagine what could happen if that kind of power fell into the wrong hands."

"All the more reason to control the thing." Sandy added. "But before we dive into another subject, there's still someone sitting out in the hallway waiting to see Maddie." She turned toward the door. "Come on in, honey."

Ninety-year-old Al Rowland pranced through the door as light on his feet as ever. "Lacey Madison Montgomery Reynolds," he announced, "this is your life." He laughed and bopped over to her bedside. "It's nice to see you, Maddie." He leaned over and kissed her cheek. "We really missed you."

His aged face was still handsome, and Lacey

laughed when she saw him dance across the room.

"Not even time could slow you down, Al. I was so hoping Sandy would come to her senses and snag you." Lacey chortled. "I can't tell you how thankful I am that you were there for her and Andrew."

"Drew, see if you can grab a few chairs from the waiting area by the nurses station," Bobby said. "I think we have a lot of catching up to do."

Drew dashed out and came back moments later with three folding chairs. He set them up, walked over to the counter, and began disbursing *Lilly's Kitchen's* baked chicken dinner complete with mashed potatoes, fresh blue-lake green beans, and homemade peach cobbler, Bobby's favorite. Al sat and Sandy pulled up a chair next to him.

"It smells wonderful," Lacey said. "And I've always loved *Lilly's*." She paused. "Hey, is Lilly any relation to—"

"Yup. She's Millie's granddaughter," Bobby said. "Best grub in town." Everyone laughed, except Piper.

"I'll explain later, Piper. We'll get you in the loop yet." Lacey looked around at the cramped conditions. "I wish we had better accommodations."

"We'll cook a proper dinner for everyone when you get home from the hospital," Sandy said. "But right now, this will do just fine." She looked at Drew. "Thanks, honey."

Drew handed Lacey a bowel of *Lilly's* homemade chicken soup and some crackers. "If you want the whole meal, Mom, I bought enough, but the doctor suggested soup for you, and we thought that might be better for the time being."

"This is perfect." Lacey looked at Sandy and Al.

"You two look marvelous."

"Well, you know Al." Sandy winked at him. "He never slows down. We go dancing at the senior center on the weekends and walk a few miles every evening."

"We've had a good life, Maddie." Al said. "Thanks to you. Every day is a gift."

"Thanks to me? How did I have anything to do with your life?"

Setting his bottled water on the floor beside him he answered. "Where to start…if you hadn't come back to 1949 everything would have been different. Bobby wouldn't have built the house on the ridge or disappeared, the shiners wouldn't have gotten riled up, so Sandy and I would have never married."

"I probably would have married that cad, Richie Thompson," Sandy added. "He ended up marrying Becky Stewart and stepped out on her all the time."

"And then there's Drew." Bobby beamed. "He wouldn't have been born."

"Yes, and Drew was a Godsend to us." Sandy touched Al on the shoulder.

"As much as we wanted them, we never could have children of our own, Maddie." Al looked at his wife, put his hand on her knee. "If we hadn't had Andrew, our lives would have been pretty lonely."

"Oh Sandy, I'm so sorry." The light dimmed in Lacey's eyes.

"Don't be. Your son has been the light of our lives." Sandy looked over at Drew with adoring eyes. "Like I told you sixty years ago, Maddie. It was your destiny to go back in time. Everything you did was supposed to happen. You didn't change history, you made it right. And everyone you met had their lives changed for the better. It was kismet."

Al sat up in his chair, put his empty plate under it, then stretched his arm around Sandy. "My wife's a genius. You'd do well to listen to her. Do you have any idea how many lives you encouraged and improved by helping them transition during the whole lake ordeal?"

"Yeah, Mom. Your contribution to Georgia history is well documented. They even named a street after you when you disappeared. Madison Avenue, on the ridge," Drew said. "It's the main street running through Reynolds Plantation. I was so proud of that growing up."

"Reynolds Plantation?" Lacey's mouth drew into a deep smile.

"Yeah. How about that," Bobby said. "Somehow our family owns most of the land north of Lanier, Maddie. Imagine that. We've got quite a nest egg."

"To say the least," Piper chimed in. "The Reynolds family is right up there with Buffett."

"I wouldn't go that far, Piper," Sandy said. "But thanks to Maddie, between our property and investing on the ground floor of those two little companies, Apple and Google Maddie mentioned to me, I'd say we're quite comfortable."

"I'm happy you've had a good life but…" Her smile faded. "I missed seeing my son grow up." I held out my hand to Drew. "Did you get married? Do I have any grandchildren?" Lacey shook her head. "That's so weird to ask you that."

"I had a great childhood, Mom," Drew said. "I missed having you there of course, but Sandy and Al had pictures of you and Dad everywhere. They told me so much about you two. And they were wonderful parents." He walked over to them; put a hand on each of their shoulders. "Still are, too," he added.

"Sandy was the mastermind behind bringing you back, Maddie," Bobby said. I could never have accomplished our elaborate plan to bring you home without her."

"How so?" Lacey asked.

"That reminds me. I have something for you." Sandy set her plate on the table beside Lacey's bed then reached into her large pink pocketbook. Pulling out a small package wrapped in tissue paper she handed it to Lacey. "I believe this is yours, Maddie."

She stuck her finger under a piece of tape then slowly unwrapped the tissue to find a small time-worn bluish-black, beaded bag.

"Piper's purse," she said. "Oh Sandy."

"You asked me to take care of it for you, dear one. I've cherished your little purse for sixty years and swore that one day I'd put it in your hands again."

"Thank you so much." She held the bag to her chest in a loving embrace. "This little purse turned out to be the key to the time portal. What happened when I passed back through the rift, Sandy? How did you help bring me back to the future?" She ran her fingers over the small beaded purse and listened as they told her the story.

"When the time crack opened and sucked you back through, Al saw the whole thing from the ridge," Sandy said.

"Yup, most amazing thing I ever witnessed. It rained so hard that afternoon. I heard you yelling—saw you standing on that bench. When you slipped off, you hit your head really hard. You had to have been knocked out cold. I started down the hill staring right at you," Al said. "One second you were there, and the next you flat out evaporated into a brilliant blue light, right in front of my eyes."

"After that day, Sandy spent her entire life researching and studying everything she could get her hands on about time travel," Bobby added.

Al patted Sandy's leg and winked at her. "She's written several books and is quite an authority on the subject."

"Sandy and Al have been talking about this moment my whole life," Drew said. "Dad arrived a little earlier than we expected, but we knew he was coming." Drew walked back to his chair, sat down and crossed his legs. "And the brass ring and picture in Piper's purse—that was Sandy's idea."

"She saw them the day I found them, when we were packing," Lacey said. "That's when we figured out where the portal was and how it worked."

"And Sandy made sure Dad put them in your purse the night of the party," Drew said. "So which came first, Mom, the chicken or the egg?" He laughed.

"Okay, let me get this straight," Piper broke in. "My purse was at the core of this entire time travel ordeal?"

"Yes," everyone answered in unison. They all laughed.

"Geez, I have so many questions." Lacey looked at her husband. "Why did you call yourself Rob instead of Bobby?"

"That was my idea," Sandy spoke up. "Bobby obviously needed a new identity since he was declared dead in the early 1950s. No one would've believed he was the same man anyway. We had to reinvent him and paid a fortune to get a forged birth certificate into the system." She looked over at Rob. "My brother insisted on keeping his real name, but I thought Rob was much more professional. He had a lot of negotiations ahead of him to make our plan work, and he needed a strong, professional name."

Lacey lifted her head from Bobby's shoulder, looked at her husband. "It's nice, but I think I'll stick to Bobby if you don't mind." She smiled. "So, how did you discover Drew was your son? What is Sandy's theory about the portal? And how did you invent that prototype time machine?" She looked at her sister-in-law. "Do you think the portal will open again on its own—and suck someone else through?"

Bobby raised his eyebrows. "I guess we'll find out."

A knock on the door broke the merriment. "Sounds like I'm missing the party." Warren Montgomery entered the room. "Sorry I'm late."

"Daddy," Lacey squealed. "Oh Daddy, I've missed you so much."

"Yes well, your Robert has filled me in on all of that." He walked between the chairs making his way to Lacey's bedside then leaned down and kissed her forehead. "I've learned a lot from your husband. Have to admit I thought he was an escaped mental patient when he first approached me, but"—he turned and shook Bobby's hand—"you found yourself one helluva man, Lacey. I just wish you didn't have to travel so far to find him." Warren walked over to Drew, shook his hand then patted his back. "Son," Warren said. "You've done a remarkable job." He looked at Sandy and Al.

"All of you have. I can't thank you enough for bringing my daughter back to me."

"Daddy, you know everyone?"

"Quiet well," Warren replied. "But where's Nick? I'm surprised he's not here to welcome you home."

"You all know Nick, too?" Lacey glanced around the room.

Bobby raised an eyebrow. "I think my wife has underestimated my determination to bring her back to the future. I drew on every detail you had told me about your life—including flying to New York to find Nick and making sure that he'd move to Atlanta. I paid quiet a pretty penny for his scholarship at Emory."

"You gave him the scholarship, Bobby?" Lacey asked.

"How else was I going to convince him to move to Atlanta?" Bobby asked. "It was worth it though. He's a good man and will be an excellent lawyer. Now that you mention it though"—his smile faded—"I haven't seen Nick since this morning."

"Me either," Piper said. "I was so relieved to see Lacey awake, I hadn't noticed. You don't think—"

Drew stared at Piper, interrupting her mid-sentence. "I have an idea where Nick might be. And if I'm right, he could be in real danger. I better track him down." Pulling his phone from his pocket, he slipped out the door.

Lacey snuggled into Bobby, her contentment radiating. She had fulfilled her promise to unite her child with his father and was finally home, surrounded by everyone she loved.

Epilogue

After her release from the Gainesville hospital, Lacey Madison Montgomery Reynolds finally joined Bobby in the newly-renovated home he originally built on the ridge some sixty years earlier. During the year they waited for Lacey, Bobby helped his son build a beautiful new home right down the street, where Drew now resides. The Reynolds family owns Reynolds Plantation, which includes most of the property on the northern shores of Lake Lanier. The community, comprised primarily of original Sidney residents and their descendants, boasts hometown warmth rarely found in the United States today.

Warren Montgomery built a summer home in Reynolds Plantation as well; reconnecting with the daughter he'd lost after the devastating death of his wife, Christine. With Drew's house close by, Piper Taylor's beautiful new home built to the right of them, and Sandy and Al's home on their left, Lacey and Bobby finally live the blissful life they crossed space and time to attain.

Perhaps the existence of a crack in time might be difficult for some to believe, but there's a hidden cove on the northern shore of Lake Lanier where the spirit of Sidney blossoms—and two star-crossed lovers guard the portal that entwined their souls forever beneath the lake.

A word about the author...

Casi McLean's fascination with writing flourished even before she learned to read. At three, she beamed with anecdotes entertaining family and friends and, at eight years old, had published her first short story, "The Apron String Captain." But when her fourth grade teacher read aloud Madeleine L'Engle's *A Wrinkle In Time*, Casi's creativity spun into high gear, and she knew she was destined to pen novels of her own.

Casi grew up in McLean, Virginia, a suburb of Washington, DC. After graduating from the University of Georgia with a major in design and a minor in education, she returned to Virginia to teach English and creative writing. Now the mother of two adult sons, she lives in Atlanta, where she writes stories to stir the soul with mystery, fantasy, and romance.

Beneath The Lake, her debut novel, was a finalist in both The Chicago Fire and Ice and Atlanta Writer's Club 2014 Spring Contests. It is the first book of a time-travel trilogy and follows her five 2014 mystical novelettes, revealing the essence of Casi's imagination sparked by her childhood dreams.

http://www.casimclean.com